Dear Reader,

I often think thi... ...e calendar: the start of a new year with all the promise that holds, Valentine's Day, Spring brides and lots of beautiful flowers. Well, I hope I can make this particular season even more romantic for you with this month's selection of books for you to enjoy.

Last year we were able to announce popular author Margaret Pargeter's return to writing and this month we are thrilled to welcome much loved romance writer Mary Wibberley to the *Scarlet* family. Mary's heroine finds herself involved in *The Most Dangerous Game*, when she falls in love with her bodyguard. In *Craven's Bride*, by talented author Danielle Shaw, the last thing Max views Alison as is a potential wife! Award-winning Julia Wild tantalizes readers as they share a *Blue Silk Promise* with her amnesiac hero. And finally we are delighted to welcome yet another exiting new author, Lisa Andrews, to the *Scarlet* list with an intriguing and *Dangerous Deception*.

As always, I hope that you will enjoy all of these titles which I have chosen especially for you, but if there is a theme we haven't covered, or if you'd like, say, to see more exotic settings or more American authors on our list, why not write to me and I'll do my best to include *your* request over the coming months.

Till next month,

Sally Cooper

SALLY COOPER,
Editor-in-Chief – *Scarlet*

About the Author

Danielle Shaw was born in Watford, England. She studied fashion and design at the London College of Fashion and then joined the Royal Opera House, Covent Garden.

In 1967, Danielle moved to Geneva where she met her Swedish husband, and worked in various kindergartens. She returned to the UK and set up her own school.

Danielle is interested in reading, music, theatre, the local countryside and gardening. She also likes to exercise and swims three times a week. 'Above all, though,' says Danielle, 'I much prefer to write!'

We are delighted that Danielle is continuing to write and to bring you her latest book for *Scarlet*.

Other *Scarlet* titles available this month:
BLUE SILK PROMISE – Julia Wild
DANGEROUS DECEPTION – Lisa Andrews
THE MOST DANGEROUS GAME – Mary Wibberley

DANIELLE SHAW

CRAVEN'S BRIDE

SCARLET

Enquiries to:
Robinson Publishing Ltd
7 Kensington Church Court
London W8 4SP

First published in the UK by Scarlet, 1998

A copy of the British Library Cataloguing in
Publication data is available from the British Library

ISBN 1–85487–867–0

Printed and bound in the EC

10 9 8 7 6 5 4 3 2 1

CHAPTER 1

With an exasperated sigh Max Craven replaced the handset of the phone. Another hour? Damn it, he didn't want to wait another hour! He'd already had enough of the oppressive London heat. He wanted to leave now! Why on earth did Elizabeth whatsername have to be buried today of all days and, more to the point, why did his sister Constance have to help with the funeral arrangements?

Max banged his fist impatiently on the rosewood desk and watched tiny particles of dust rise in the air. There they appeared trapped in the narrow beam of sunlight, dancing on the heavy lead crystal inkwells. Dabbing absent-mindedly at the dust with the tip of his index finger, Max hadn't noticed his business partner standing in the doorway.

'What! Still here, Max? I thought you'd have packed up and left ages ago. Didn't you say you couldn't wait to leave the London smoke and dust – or are you having second thoughts, my friend?'

'Smoke and dust is right;' said Max, wiping the dust from his finger. 'Just look at it! It'a a wonder anyone can breathe in this heat.'

1

'Mmm,' replied Nigel, loosening his collar. 'I have to admit this present heatwave is beginning to take its toll on everyone in the office. Not that I'm complaining, mind you, especially when our new temp starts peeling off her layers. Have you seen what she's wearing today?'

Max shook his head and gave Nigel Painton one of his special looks – the dreaded 'Craven glare' – which meant he did not share his partner's obsession with the variety of temps who'd been gracing the office whilst the more permanent members of staff took their summer holidays.

'Well?' continued Nigel, changing the subject. 'Aren't you going to tell me why you're still here?'

'There's a funeral in the village and Constance says it's best to wait another hour until it's over . . .'

'Oh, I'm sorry. Anyone you know?'

'No. That is, I can't remember the woman, even though Constance insists that I should. Someone called Elizabeth . . . Benedict, I believe. Apparently she left the village years ago and moved to America with her husband. They later divorced and she returned to England. When she discovered she'd got cancer, she decided to come back to the village. There's a family plot or something.'

'In that case, what's this funeral got to do with you? I mean, if you can't even remember the woman?'

'Nothing, Nigel,' replied Max tetchily. 'But you've obviously forgotten how much my sister likes to get involved with village life. Not only has she offered to help with the funeral arrangements, she's even invited the mourners back to Haywood Grange for tea and consolation.'

'How jolly kind. Good old Connie.'

'That's not quite how I see it,' Max said, striding to the window. 'Constance is far too easygoing. She lets people walk all over her.'

'Not like you, eh, Max?' Nigel joined his friend by the window. 'No one could ever accuse Max Craven of letting people walk all over him!'

Forcing a rare smile, Max ran a hand through his thick, dark hair and turned his steely gaze in Nigel's direction. 'I expect everyone here at Craven and Painton thinks I'm a complete bastard and will be only too glad to see the back of me.'

'Nonsense,' replied Nigel unconvincingly, 'they'll all miss you terribly. Besides they haven't known you as long as I have, Max, and they haven't . . .'

'Go on,' urged Max, almost sensing what was coming next.

Placing his hand on his friend's shoulder, Nigel felt the muscles tighten beneath his grasp and saw the familiar dark shuttered look appear on Max's face. 'I was only going to say,' he murmered softly, 'they haven't had to cope with losing their only child and a devoted wife within the space of a few short weeks. Neither have they worked practically seven days a week to get this company on its feet, as you have.'

Releasing his grasp on Max's shoulder, Nigel turned to look at the almost empty desk and the boxes of files waiting to be transported to Haywood Grange. 'Give me a call when you're ready to leave and I'll help you load up your car.'

Some time later, loading the boxes into the jet-black Saab, Nigel wiped the beads of perspiration forming on his forehead. 'You know, Max, I'm almost jealous at the thought of you living in the countryside amongst all

3

those trees and fields. When I think of the birds singing their dawn chorus and fields of newly mown hay . . . How long will you be living with Connie, by the way? Perhaps I can come and pay you a visit?'

'You can come and stay whenever you like, Nigel. Constance and George have heaps of room. I shall be using the au pair's flat initially – and no sarcastic comments about au pairs, please! I'll look around for a place of my own later. Perhaps convert one of the barns or even buy a plot of land and start completely from scratch. Only remember, life in Church Haywood is far removed from London and the Wigmore Hall.'

Suddenly remembering his plans for the evening, Nigel clasped Max's hand warmly. 'Max, my friend, if you'll excuse me. Must dash, I'm off to the Wigmore tonight, in fact. Thank goodness you reminded me in time. Don't forget to leave me Connie's number, and if you ever get fed up with life in the sticks, you know you can always have my place for a weekend. At the moment Vanessa and I appear to be spending every other weekend with her family in Esher.'

'It will be wedding bells next, then,' Max teased.

'No way!' Nigel called, running back to the revolving doors of Craven and Painton. 'I've never been the marrying kind!'

He stopped himself just in time from adding, 'unlike you,' and paused only briefly to see Max's car pull away into the congested city street.

'Well, that was a rare occurrence,' the receptionist quipped acidly, flashing a vast expanse of thigh in Nigel's direction.

'What was?'

'Seeing Mr Craven smile. What with his black hair,

dark eyes and that jet-black car of his, my brother always says if Mr Craven dropped the "C" from his name he'd be just like one of those evil-looking birds who are supposed to guard the Tower of London.'

Aware that Nigel Painton did not approve of her criticism of his colleague, the receptionist shifted uneasily in her chair before adding, 'Well, I don't mean evil exactly. It's just that he always seems a bit sinister. He never says much and hardly ever smiles, although Katy in the mail room thinks he's dark and mysterious.'

'For your information, Mandy, I doubt if your brother would find much to smile about if his only child were killed in a road accident and his wife, trying to come to terms with her grief, lost her life in a fire which destroyed his hopes for the future!'

Annoyed with himself at having said far too much, Nigel slammed his own office door behind him and reached for his cigarettes. Thank goodness he and Vanessa were going to the Wigmore Hall. At least a Brahms symphony would have the required calming effect.

Inhaling deeply on his cigarette, Nigel considered the recent summer months. Heaven knew he needed something soothing, following one of Craven and Painton's busiest periods ever, and the shock announcement that after fifteen years of working in London Max Craven had suddenly decided to return to Church Haywood and work from what he called 'home'.

'You must be mad!' Nigel had pleaded at the time. 'You can't just give it all up.'

'No – not mad – just weary of it all.' Max had replied. 'And I certainly don't intend to give everything up, Nigel. I'd prefer to work out of town from now on.

Let's be honest, you've always been happier dealing with city contracts and I'm sure I'll find enough to keep me occupied with urban developments. Constance tells me they've released some land from green belt restrictions on the outskirts of Church Haywood. She feels it would be in everyone's interest if C and P could get the contract.'

'In what way?'

'My big sister,' Max explained, 'feels I would deal with any proposed building plans with an eye far more sympathetic to the surrounding communities. Besides . . .'

'Besides?'

'She also tells me I'm looking haggard and drawn and working too hard. Constance thinks I could benefit from a break with London life.'

Nigel studied his business partner of ten years with a critical eye.

'On the latter I'd be prepared to agree with Connie, but I wouldn't go so far as saying you look haggard . . . Tired maybe; perhaps you should have a check-up.'

'I already have!'

His face full of anxiety, Nigel had waited for what was coming next.

Sensing his colleague's concern, Max reassured him. 'Oh, it's okay, there's nothing to worry about. I'm perfectly fit and apparently in good shape for my age and not at all overweight . . . unlike someone else I could mention.'

Later, at his flat overlooking the Thames, Nigel struggled with the waistband of his trousers and recalled Max's remark.

'Perhaps Max was right after all: perhaps I should try

6

and lose a bit of weight . . . take up jogging? What do you think, Vanessa?'

Slipping into an ice-blue silk shift dress, Vanessa replied with a smile, 'I would think that's hardly your scene, Nigel.' Her gaze took in the newly crumpled sheets. 'I thought indoor pursuits were more your thing. I mean, just think how you would look after running round the streets, all red and hot and sweaty.' She tugged at one of Nigel's auburn curls. 'Of course, you could always join a gym – that's if you're really keen. But when would you find the time? We seem to be going to Esher every other weekend and now that Max has left . . . By the way, how did he seem?'

'Fine. Couldn't get away quick enough if you ask me. In fact he was positively seething because Connie said he ought to wait until after the funeral.'

'What funeral? Surely not another of Max's relations!'

'No, thank God! In fact it's of little consequence. I'll tell you about it on the way to the Wigmore.'

Reaching for his jacket, Nigel turned to admire Vanessa looking stunningly cool and elegant, despite the oppressive heat of the summer's evening. 'Tell me,' he murmured thoughtfully, 'would you describe Max as evil-looking and sinister?'

'Good gracious, no!' Vanessa's bright laughter echoed in the hallway as Nigel opened the door. 'No, most definitely not! In fact I would describe Max Craven as mildly moody, mysterious and . . .'

'And . . . ?'

'Very sexy.'

Watching Nigel's crestfallen face, Vanessa whispered in his ear, 'But not as sexy as you, Nigel darling. You

7

know I have a thing about red-headed males.'

'Thank goodness for that!' said Nigel, kissing her tenderly. 'For one awful moment you had me very worried. Although I think it would do Max a power of good to meet someone like you. It's been so long since Virginia died. I wonder if Church Haywood boasts any buxom rosy-cheeked maidens.'

Females of any description were the last thing on Max Craven's mind as his finger flicked the indicator switch, signalling his intention to leave the motorway. Emitting a deep sigh, he knew it would only be another twenty minutes before a row of tall larches heralded the first familiar sign of Church Haywood and, if he was lucky, the merest glimpse of St Faith's.

Although not a churchgoer himself, at least not since the deaths of Tara, his daughter, and Virginia, his wife, Max nevertheless found something strangely comforting about the golden sandstone tower with its ancient weather-vane. After the familiar dreary London skyline, St Faith's was a truly welcoming sight.

At the far corner of the churchyard, Alison Benedict choked back tears and stood by her mother's newly dug grave. So many flowers – there were so many flowers. Where had they all come from? She must come back again tomorrow and write down all the names. Everyone would have to be thanked and those whose names she didn't recognize would have to be located. No doubt Bunty and Constance would be able to enlighten her.

Wiping her eyes, Alison thought fondly of Bunty Lowther – her mother's old schoolfriend – and remem-

8

bered how on that last fateful day at the hospice Bunty had come to the rescue.

'Now don't you worry about a thing, Alison,' Bunty had insisted, taking her in her arms and placing a well-padded arm about her shoulders. 'I'll help you with all the funeral arrangements. Your mother . . . well, she knew just what she wanted. She wrote it all down, you see, and gave it to me for safekeeping.'

Initially, Alison was hurt and upset that Bunty knew all about Elizabeth Benedict's funeral wishes, when she, her only daughter, did not.

'Don't take it too badly, Alison. Your mother didn't want you worrying and upsetting yourself when you were right in the middle of exams.'

'But I should have been with her, Bunty!'

'You were, my dear. After all, you were . . . at the end.'

'No! I mean all the time. I should have been with her all the time! My exams could have waited. I could have taken those any time.'

Any time perhaps, thought Bunty to herself. But it was just as well Alison had passed her exams as an interior designer. Now that she was on her own – well, apart from her two stepbrothers in America – Alison Benedict would have to make her own way in the world.

Kneeling by her mother's grave, Alison fingered the cards on the wreaths and sprays of flowers, until she came to one she recognized. The simple black-edged card read, 'With Deepest Sympathy, George and Constance Henderson.' Constance Henderson, Alison mused. It was Constance who, along with Bunty, had kept her going through what had seemed like one of the longest weeks in her life.

9

In fact it had been Constance and Bunty together who, each day, while guiding her through the funeral arrangements, encouraged her to eat and offered so much kindness and support (both moral and financial) that she couldn't possibly hope to repay.

'Listen,' Bunty had proclaimed last night after supper, 'Connie and I were very old friends of your mother's and have only done what she would have done for us. As for repaying us, all I can say to that, Alison my dear, is don't insult us! We Church Haywood folk are a rum lot and take umbrage easily, or haven't you heard? I've merely dipped into the nest egg my mother left me, and Constance is having everyone back to Haywood Grange after the funeral for the simple reason that she's a far better cook than I am and her place is a damn sight bigger than this cottage!'

Of the latter there was no doubt. Haywood Grange was enormous compared to Bunty's cottage, and a great deal tidier. Eventually Alison, too distraught and overcome with kindness, had conceded defeat. This afternoon, wearing a simple mid-calf-length black linen dress and buoyed up by Bunty's well-rounded frame, she'd followed her mother's simple coffin into the still and welcome coolness of St Faith's church.

It was only now, as the rays of evening sunshine illuminated the stained glass windows, that a feeling of loneliness and panic began to surge in Alison's breast. Suddenly it was all over . . . there were dark shadows again. Where did she go from here?

For tonight at least it would be back to Bunty's cottage, but tomorrow she would have to return to Baker's Halt, the small terraced house where her mother had passed the final year of her life. The rent on Baker's Halt was paid until the end of July, which gave her another two and a half weeks. Chilled by the sun disappearing behind the church tower, Alison shivered. Two and a half weeks in which to organize her life!

Moving into the shadows and unaware she was being watched, Alison lowered herself into a kneeling position by the newly turned soil with its profusion of flowers, and wept uncontrollably.

Finding someone else in this particular corner of the churchyard took Max Craven completely by surprise. On hearing the clock strike he realized it was only eight o'clock. Why shouldn't there be other people like himself, wanting to experience the peace and tranquillity of St Faith's churchyard on a balmy summer's evening?

Peering into the shadows of a large beech tree, Max discerned that it wasn't 'people', it was a lone figure of a young woman, pale and slender and dressed all in black. It was small wonder he hadn't seen her when he'd first stepped from the gravel path on to soft turf.

Anxious not to alarm the solitary mourner, Max stood perfectly still, unsure whether to complete his mission or to slip away unseen. Moments later, deciding he could visit his daughter's grave in the morning, he decided to head back to his car and Haywood Grange.

As he stepped from the newly mown grass back on to the path, the sharp sound of leather on gravel in an otherwise still evening caused Alison to start with alarm. Hearing her gasp of surprise, Max turned to find her attempting to struggle vainly to her feet.

'I'm most dreadfully sorry for startling you like that.

I was trying to slip away without disturbing you. I didn't think anyone else would be here, you see.'

In embarrassed silence, Alison looked up to find dark, penetrating eyes staring straight into her own. Somehow they seemed vaguely familiar.

'Here let me help you,' Max continued, sensing the problem. 'I think you'll find you have the heel of your shoe caught in the hem of your dress.'

Assessing the situation, Alison reluctantly accepted Max's hand, noting as she did so the faint purple scar on his left wrist which disappeared beneath the crisply laundered cuff of his shirt.

'Thank you,' she murmured softly, brushing at the skirt of her dress to remove stray grass clippings. 'I'm not used to wearing dresses; I usually wear jeans.'

'I can't think of anything worse.' Sensing her bewilderment, Max added with a smile, 'Wearing denim in this heat. I would have thought shorts would be more in keeping at this time of year in Church Haywood.'

'Oh, no!' Alison protested without thinking. 'I never wear shorts!'

Presuming that this ashen-faced young woman, dressed from top to toe in black, had considered his remark vaguely suggestive, Max let go of her hand and stepped back firmly on to the middle of the path.

'Well, as you're back on terra firma, I can only apologize once again for startling you and bid you good evening.'

'Good evening, Mr Craven.'

It was Max's turn to register shock. How on earth did she know his name? He'd specifically asked Constance not to tell anyone he was returning to the village. They would all find out sooner or later, but he'd hoped for at least a few days' respite from prying eyes.

'I'm sorry, have we met before?' he enquired kindly. 'I've been away from the village for quite some time and only visit occasionally. You really must excuse me, I'm not terribly good at remembering faces . . . When I moved to London you were probably only a teenager.'

For a brief moment, staring down into Alison's pale, upturned face with its flaxen bob, Max registered not Alison but his own dear daughter Tara. Tara, whose mass of golden curls had tumbled to her shoulders, framing rosy-red cheeks and eyes the colour of cornflowers. Tara, who'd been such a picture of vitality, with so much to live for . . . Blinking and swallowing hard, Max once again registered Alison's tear-stained face and sombre appearance. Then he heard her murmur softly, 'I'm Alison Benedict, Mr Craven. I knew your daughter. Tara and I were both at St Katherine's. She was in the lower school when I was in the senior. I occasionally babysat for you and your wife. During the summer holidays your wife often asked me . . .'

Sensing Max's confusion, Alison continued, 'I used to keep an eye on Tara when your wife was playing tennis. We'd go for walks or I'd read to her. Of course I'd better explain. You probably won't know. I used to be Alison Webb . . . my mother remarried and we went to live in America.'

Alison! Alison Webb! Max could believe neither his eyes nor his ears. It was Alison who was with his daughter on the day she died . . . Alison Webb who had made Tara . . .

With his face now registering both contempt and

disgust, Max Craven turned on his heel and strode back to his car. In the hedgerow at the back of the church car park, a solitary blackbird serenading his mate flew up in alarm as the Saab roared into life and sped away.

CHAPTER 2

At Haywood Grange, Constance Henderson was stacking away the last of the tea things when she heard the resounding crunch of tyres on gravel. Quickly running to the front door, she found her brother still sitting at the wheel of his car. The bonnet she noticed, was only inches away from her precious wisteria.

'Max, dear, are you okay? You look as if you've seen a ghost.'

'I feel as if I have, Constance. Why the hell didn't you tell me Alison Webb was back in the neighbourhood? I stopped by at St Faith's, thinking I'd be alone . . .'

'But I did, Max! I told you I was helping with her mother's funeral. I distinctly recall last week and again this afternoon . . . That's why I suggested you delay your journey by an hour – until everyone had left – don't you remember?'

Max grunted as he swung open the boot of the car to retrieve his luggage. Yes, his sister had said something to that effect. But how was he supposed to know who Alison Benedict was?

'Well,' cooed Constance, attempting to pacify her obviously disgruntled brother, 'at least your timing is perfect; Bunty left about ten minutes ago. She sends her love, by the way, and other than George, no one else knows you're coming.'

Max wasn't listening; he was still concentrating on what his sister had said about perfect timing. Oh, that had been perfect all right, he thought to himself watching Constance fill the kettle. After ten years living away from Church Haywood, he'd chosen to visit St Faith's churchyard at precisely the same time as the young woman he held responsible for his daughter's death!

'I thought we could have some cold chicken, new potatoes and salad, if that's all right with you, Max . . . unless you'd prefer something a bit more substantial.'

'No . . . no, that's fine by me, Constance. As a matter of fact I don't feel particularly hungry. A sandwich would do perfectly well.'

'Max Craven!' Connie admonished. 'Sandwiches might be all right in London in that dreadfully austere flat of yours, but at Haywood Grange we go in for proper meals. You look as if you could do with some decent food inside you. All those business lunches and take-away meals.'

'Who's having a take-away?' echoed a voice from the utility room.

'No one,' announced Connie to her husband. 'I absolutely refuse to have them in the house!'

'Nagging you already, is she, Max?' enquired George Henderson, walking through to the kitchen in search of his slippers. He extended a large hand in greeting in his brother-in-law's direction. 'Good to see you again, old chap. About time too, if I might say so.'

16

'Let's say she's already criticized the way I look and made less than complimentary remarks about my flat,' said Max with a flicker of a smile. 'But anyway, as I've sold it, she can't complain any more.'

'Sold what?' enquired Constance.

'The flat.'

'Whew! Have you, by jove?' George gave a low whistle. 'Then it looks as if you really are serious about settling in Church Haywood after all.'

Placing the potatoes in a saucepan, Constance looked up in surprise. 'But what about your furniture? Surely you didn't sell that too?'

She was aware of Max nodding before he continued, 'By the sound of it it's just as well; you obviously didn't think much of my choice. The fellow who bought the flat said he'd be interested in the furniture too. Apart from a few pieces I put in store, I sold the lot.'

From where she was standing behind her brother, Constance shrugged her shoulders and cast a puzzled look in her husband's direction.

'Looks like you'll be going from the sublime to the ridiculous, then,' George announced, taking a bottle of Chardonnay from the fridge. 'The au pair's flat is pretty ghastly if you want my opinion. I told Connie we should do something with it before you arrived. She insisted it was probably best left for you to decide on colour schemes.'

'As long as the au pair isn't still living in it, I really don't mind.' Max grinned. 'All I want is to be left in peace.'

'Oh, she's long since gone,' Constance assured him. 'In fact I don't know why we still call it the au pair's

17

flat. Force of habit I suppose. No, we said goodbye to Heidi when the twins went off to university. How long ago is that?'

'Seven years.' George replied, handing Max a glass of wine. 'Gracious, doesn't time fly?'

It certainly does, thought Max walking through to the conservatory. Although he didn't really want to think about the Alison Webb that was, he had to acknowledge how she'd changed in the ten years since he'd last seen her. Ten years ago she'd been a skinny schoolgirl with long, fine hair in a ponytail, wearing the green and white uniform of St Katherine's. Now she was a slender, attractive young woman in her mid-twenties.

Max took a long deep gulp of wine. And what of Tara? What would his daughter look like now had she still been alive? Reaching out unconsciously, Max crushed the leaves of a scented geranium in a pot by the conservatory doors. In his present state of mind, he thought it should be Alison Benedict buried in the churchyard, not his daughter!

Aware of the lemon perfume wafting in the air from beneath Max's grasp, Connie announced, 'I see you've gone straight for the scented geraniums, just as you did when you were a boy. Mother always knew when you'd been hiding in the conservatory. By the way, what did you do with the cuttings I brought down for you the last time I came to London?'

Max's guilty silence was all Constance required to know her brother had obviously forgotten to water them. Even now, they were probably shrivelled in their pots, withering on some corporation tip.

'Definitely not the green-fingered member of the

18

family, are you, Max? I wonder if we'll ever make a country gentleman of you.'

'Looking round this conservatory and from what I can see of the garden, I would say you more than make up for my failings.'

'Why don't you just pop down and have a look at the rose arbour, then? Mr Jennings has been helping me restock it. Supper will only be about ten minutes. I'll get George to give you a call when it's ready.'

Leaving the conservatory with its brightly coloured pots of fuchsias, begonias and geraniums, Max stepped into the cool of the evening and watched the faintest slick of setting sun disappear behind an avenue of laburnums. He breathed in deeply, savouring each lung full of clear, fresh air. What a contrast from the choking heat of the past few weeks in London. It was, he decided – despite his shock confrontation with Alison Benedict – great to be home.

'Max bumped into Alison in the churchyard,' Constance whispered to her husband as she laid the table for supper. 'If you'd seen his face when he arrived. I thought for one minute he was going to turn right round and go back to London.'

'He didn't, though, did he?' replied George, carving the chicken.

'No . . . thank goodness. Nevertheless I'm convinced he still thinks it was Alison's fault Tara was, well . . . you know, even after all this time.'

'But that's preposterous, Connie! You know as well as I do that that can't be true. You really ought to tell Max one of these days.'

'I know, dear,' she said, putting her finger to her lips, 'but not now. I can see Max coming back up the garden.

Let's just wait a bit, shall we, and see what happens? Perhaps it might be an idea too to ring Bunty. I'll do it first thing in the morning.'

Unable to sleep due to a combination of birdsong, brilliant sunshine pouring through the faded chintz curtains and Jasper, Bunty's boisterous wire-haired terrier, whining and scratching outside her bedroom door, Alison got up to face Day One of her new life. From downstairs came the muted tones of 'Farming Today' and the sound of running water.

'Up already, Alison? I expect it was that damn dog of mine whining away outside your door. I was hoping you might have stayed in bed for an extra hour or two after the trauma of the past few weeks.'

Alison shook her head and patted Jasper warmly. 'Don't be too hard on him, Bunty. I was awake anyway. Besides, it's such a lovely day. Who wants to stay in bed when we've glorious weather like this?'

'Oh, there's plenty I could mention,' said Bunty, filling the kettle. 'Still, you'd best make the most of it. They're forecasting rain before too long.'

'In which case I shan't mind at all,' Alison replied. 'I've got to clear out Baker's Halt. The rent's only paid for another two weeks, remember. I'm sure I heard Mr Jessop say there are new tenants ready to move in in August.'

'You know I'll help at Baker's Halt if you want, and that you're welcome to stay on here as long as you like.'

'That's very kind of you, Bunty. I may well take you up on it. At least until I find a job and sort myself out.'

'It would appear you're not the only one sorting yourself out.'

Alison looked up with a puzzled frown.

'Connie told me a couple of days ago that her brother Max is coming back to Church Haywood. It would appear he's had enough of London or something. Of course it's supposed to be a secret – Max doesn't want to set tongues wagging just yet and wants to be left in peace. I'm sure Connie won't mind my telling you.'

'Oh, you needn't have worried about giving away Mr Craven's secrets. I've already seen him.'

'What! When? You didn't say, my dear.'

'I saw him in the churchyard yesterday evening. When I went back to Mother's grave to look at the floral tributes, Mr Craven was there.'

'You recognized him, then?' Bunty asked, pouring water into a large earthenware pot. 'How did he look? And did he recognize you?'

'In answer to your first question, Bunty, I suppose he didn't really look all that different from ten years ago. A little older and more careworn perhaps . . .'

'I'm not surprised,' Bunty interrupted, 'after all the tragedy he's had to endure. First Tara and then Virginia and the house . . . It's a wonder poor Max isn't grey all over.'

'Well, he's certainly not that! In fact, unless he's using that product they advertize on TV. I would say Mr Craven hasn't a grey hair on his head. I wouldn't say that about his face, though.'

'You mean he's got a beard and it's grey?' Bunty said in alarm. 'Well, that must make him look very peculiar indeed.'

Alison laughed for the first time in days. 'No, Bunty, you're jumping to conclusions. Mr Craven hasn't got a beard, grey or otherwise. It's his face that looked grey.'

21

'Hmph! That's hardly surprising, shutting himself away for ten years in that austere flat of his in London. Connie's been on at him for ages to come back home. She said it was like a bolt out of the blue when he rang. I don't suppose he told you why he's come back?'

'Hardly,' murmured Alison. 'In fact he didn't say much at all. He was coolly polite – as I remember from before. It was when I . . .'

'When you what?' Bunty asked, aware of the distinct change in Alison's voice.

'When I told him who I was. That I used to babysit for Tara. It was just like Mother used to say . . . "if looks could kill".'

Bunty patted Alison's shoulder. 'Surely not, my dear. I know Max Craven always had a certain way about him. Perhaps you were just imagining it. I expect he was just surprised to see you after all these years.'

Alison shrugged her shoulders and sipped at her tea. 'Perhaps. I suppose I probably was the last person he expected to see in that corner of the churchyard. Speaking of which, I'd better get a move on. I want to make a note of everyone who sent flowers. I also promised Oliver and Jasper I'd take some photos of the wreaths they sent. Jasper was convinced the girl who'd taken their order in New York wasn't concentrating.'

'That's hardly surprising,' Bunty remarked, sitting down at the table. 'I ask you, how can any female concentrate when confronted by that gorgeous step-brother of yours? I managed to drag Connie off to the cinema after Christmas to see his last film. Phew! What a body! You don't find many of those in Church Haywood! What a pity I have to make do with his

22

namesake!' Bunty poured tea into her saucer and placed it on the floor for her own Jasper, who licked greedily and noisily.

'I'd be prepared to bet your four-legged Jasper is far more faithful than the two-legged variety I know,' said Alison thoughtfully, stroking Jasper behind the ear.

'Meaning?'

'Meaning, lovable as he is, Jasper's left a trail of broken hearts all across America. I'm glad he's just my stepbrother.'

'And what about Oliver?'

'Oh, he's the complete opposite. Loyal and true to Brünnhilde, the one love of his life, even though she's a bit ungainly and was always getting in the way when I was last in New York.'

Bunty absent-mindedly stirred her tea. 'A big girl, is she?'

'You could say that,' Alison replied, with a wry smile. 'I was referring to Oliver's cello!'

Bunty chortled out loud, causing her own Jasper to stir from his soporific state at Alison's feet. 'Brünnhilde, of course! I knew it was something Wagnerian. How stupid of me. Somehow I was convinced it was Isolde. Mmm, when you think about it, Brünnhilde's quite an apt name for a cello. Mind you, it always amazes me how musicians manage to get their arms and legs around such instruments.'

'One thing's for sure,' anounced Alison, edging away from the table, 'with my leg, the cello would definitely be out of the question.'

Bunty studied the pained expression on Alison's face. 'Playing up a bit, is it, dear? You've probably been overdoing things.'

'I doubt it. Let's say I get good days and bad days. In fact there are days – weeks even – when it doesn't bother me at all. It's the scar tissue more than anything. Sometimes when it's damp . . . and didn't you say we're in for some rain? In which case I'd better get a move on. I'll have a quick shower and then get on my way.'

Slipping into her jeans, gingham blouse and sweat-shirt, Alison picked up a notepad and pen and headed for the back door. There she found Jasper looking up expectantly.

'Do you want to . . . ?' She got no further; Jasper's paws were already resting on the stool underneath the shelf where Bunty kept the washing powders and the dog's lead. 'Is it okay if I take Jasper with me, Bunty? I promise I'll make sure he doesn't do you know what in the churchyard.'

'That's fine by me,' a voice called. 'Just remember to take the spare key. I might pop over to the Grange later. I think I must have left my jacket there yesterday. I was so warm clearing up after the funeral, I quite forgot all about it.'

Mention of her mother's funeral brought a lump to Alison's throat. Hooking Jasper's lead on to his collar, she double-checked that she had notepad, pen and camera and headed down the garden path in silence.

'Poor girl,' murmured Bunty, shaking her head. 'Whatever will she do?'

Hearing the clock chime eight as she approached the main footpath of St Faith's, Alison was reminded of her last visit here only twelve hours earlier. This time she looked about her before walking to the freshly dug grave and, seeing no one in sight, ordered Jasper to sit whilst she wrote down the names and messages on each card of condolence.

'Such a profusion of flowers everywhere, Mother,' she sighed, 'and not a single violet. Still,' she told herself, 'who else apart from me remembers they were our favourite flowers?'

Having dealt with the last cellophane-wrapped sprays, still moist with morning dew, Alison's gaze drifted across the assorted headstones to another familiar grave. This however was not newly dug, nor was it covered in flowers. Tara! It belonged to Tara Craven, her dear companion of ten long summers ago.

Alison eased herself up from the grass and walked towards the grave, remembering as she did so long, hot, carefree summer days. Days listening to Tara's animated chatter, reminiscent of the brook that gurgled past the old mill or watching her play with the endless litters of kittens at Fenner's Farm. Sometimes they'd simply wandered aimlessly without a care in the world, through flower-laden fields and shady woodlands until . . .

'Oh, Tara,' she sighed, kneeling by the simple yet neatly tended grave. 'It shouldn't have happened. It just shouldn't have happened! Why didn't you stop when I called? If only . . .'

Without thinking, Alison ran her hand up and down her right thigh. Even through the thick denim she could still feel the raised scar tissue. She shivered; it was as if she was being watched. Jasper! Where was Jasper? In her anxiety to visit Tara's grave, she'd completely forgotten the dog!

Filled with panic, Alison turned to look for Jasper, only to see him bounding towards someone standing by

25

the beech thicket. Desperate to prevent the dog from extending his usual greeting of depositing muddy paws on every person he met, Alison struggled to her feet.

Cursing her leg, she was just in time to see Jasper's tail wagging furiously as he slewed to a halt at the feet of the only other occupant of St Faith's churchyard. But not in time, however, to stop him from leaving his muddied paw prints all over the beige-linen-clad legs of . . . Max Craven!

'Jasper, you bad dog!' she cried, reaching clumsily for the handle of the lead where it trailed in the damp grass. 'Mr Craven, I'm so terribly sorry. He must be pleased to see you. He never takes much notice of me when I call him, I'm afraid.'

'Then may I suggest, Miss . . . er . . . Benedict,' Max snapped angrily, rubbing at his trousers, 'that you get your dog booked in for some obedience lessons, and the sooner the better!'

'But Jasper's not my . . .'

Alison however got no further. Jasper's most recent acquaintance brushed past them without comment and strode angrily to his daughter's grave. There, plucking at the small spray of wild flowers newly picked by Alison, he flung them into the nearby bin.

With a stifled sob and clutching at Jasper's lead lest he should run away again, Alison hurried back to Keeper's Cottage as quickly as she could. She was surprised to find Bunty hanging out a selection of tea towels and tablecloths which she'd taken to the Grange for the funeral tea.

'Oh! I didn't expect to find you here, Bunty. I thought you said you were going to fetch your jacket.'

'There's no need, my dear. Connie rang just after you

26

left. She's given my jacket to Max. I think she wanted to get him out of the house for a bit. Apparently he's offered to call at the post office for her and said he'll drop it in on the way back.'

In that case, thought Alison to herself, I shall make sure I'm not around when Max Craven comes to call. Mention of the post office and the notepad in her pocket reminded her of the thank-you letters she needed to write. If she went upstairs to her room she could keep out of the way. Two hostile meetings with Max Craven in less than twenty-four hours, she decided, were more than enough!

Unfortunately for Alison, things didn't go quite according to plan. From down in the kitchen came an exasperated yell.

'Oh, Jasper! You naughty boy! Look what you've done!'

Hurrying downstairs, Alison found Bunty on bended knees picking up pieces of broken glass in the middle of a pool of milk.

'Careful!' she warned. 'There's broken glass everywhere. I was just going to put the bottle back in the fridge when he came bounding towards me. Put the little b . . . outside, will you? I don't want bloodied paws and vet's bills as well.'

Taking hold of Jasper's collar, Alison opened the back door and gently pushed the dog into the garden before reaching for a cloth to help with the mopping-up operation.

'Thank you, dear,' said Bunty, patting salt and pepper home-permed curls back into place. 'Now there's just one problem: we've no milk left and I was going to make baked custard tarts.'

'That's not a problem,' Alison replied without thinking. 'I'll pop along to the village and get some. I need more stamps and I really ought to get these photos developed for Jasper and Oliver. This time, if you don't mind, I won't take our four-legged friend.'

Bunty ignored the whining and scratching at the back door. 'No, he can stay in the dog house where he belongs – which isn't easy, is it,' she grinned, 'considering he lives indoors and then mostly on my bed!'

CHAPTER 3

Arriving in the village, Alison was on the point of going to the post office, it being easier to get her stamps before going to buy the milk, when she recognized a familiar figure. Max Craven!

'Damn!' she whispered under her breath. 'I'd completely forgotten he was going to the post office for Connie.'

Cautiously slipping into a shop doorway, she waited until Max closed the door of the post office behind him. Only then did she consider it safe to cross the road to the small supermarket. From there, she decided, she could pretend to shop and at the same time keep her eyes peeled for a certain person to reappear.

When the coast was clear and Max walked in the direction of the off licence, Alison – clutching the cartons of milk – zigzagged her way carefully behind the row of parked cars towards the post office. It being pension day, there was already quite a queue. A distinct hum of animated conversation filled the air.

'I'm telling you that was Max Craven,' an elderly voice insisted to her companion. 'Don't you remember? Mrs Henderson's brother – her from the Grange? He

29

visits her from time to time, always keeping himself to himself, mind you. It was his daughter who died after that dreadful accident and then his wife . . .'

Nodding in recognition, an equally elderly woman, wearing a dress of deep purple, continued, 'Why yes! Of course I do now. He was so handsome when he was a young man . . .'

'And still is, Rose,' a voice broke in. 'Still handsome and certainly still young if you compare him to the likes of you and me. Let's see . . . I suppose he must be almost forty. He won't be collecting his pension for a while!'

Rose smiled and pushed her pension book across the counter to be stamped.

'Well, Rose, what's the latest gossip?' a bespectacled young man enquired from behind the counter. 'Who's run off with whom? Who's having a baby and who's got their house on the market?'

'Don't you be so cheeky, young Alan! Can I help it if I know what's going on in Church Haywood? For your information, the only bit of news, apart from Mr Craven coming back to the village after all this time, is that Mr Jessop is thinking of selling that old stable block of his.'

'Is he?' came the interested response. 'I don't suppose you know what he's going to do with it?'

Rose shrugged her shoulders. 'I suppose it depends on planning permission and things like that. Ann Jessop said it would probably be too big for one dwelling, but if it was turned into units . . . you know, a bit like the art and craft centre at Little Harberry?'

'That's all right,' proclaimed Rose's companion, 'as long as they let it to locals. We don't want none of those outsiders coming in from town, pushing up property prices and trying to change Church Haywood customs.'

'I wasn't aware Church Haywood had that many old customs left,' commented Alan, passing Rose her pension money.

Listening in on their conversation, Alison's ears pricked up at the mention of Mr Jessop. It was Mr Jessop who owned Baker's Halt. He seemed a decent enough sort of man, but where were the stables Rose and her companion had been talking about? She knew the units at Little Harberry and had often gone there with her mother before the cancer took hold.

Placing the books of stamps carefully in her purse, Alison stepped back into the brilliant sunshine just as Max Craven was opening his car door. In his hand he carried a small posy of pink rosebuds.

'So that's what he drives,' she said to herself eyeing the sleek black Saab 9000. 'I'm not surprised. If they say owners can look like their dogs,' here she thought of the wiry-haired Bunty and Jasper, 'why can't drivers looks like their cars?'

Considering Rose's earlier comments about Max Craven, Alison concluded, despite his dark and abrupt manner, he really was an extremely good-looking man . . . if you liked that type, of course. The problem was, owing to circumstances beyond her control, Alison Benedict had as yet been denied the opportunity of discovering what her 'type' was.

Pushing thoughts of Max Craven to the back of her mind, Alison let her gaze once again alight on Rose's violet dress. 'Violets,' she sighed, 'I know Penny couldn't get violets in time for Mother's funeral, but perhaps if I were to call in and ask?'

Opening the door of the florist's, Alison breathed in the heavily scented air where long-stemmed red roses, delicate sprays of freesia and clusters of alstroemeria stood upright in buckets. Something about the myriad colours reminded her of Church Haywood's May Day festival. It was a time when the local children, grouped by age and each carrying a floral decorated garden cane, danced through the village to the maypole on the village green. 'That was one of the Church Haywood customs that Rose was referring to,' she murmured, bending down to savour the perfume from a deep, red rose.

'Pardon?' enquired Penny coming from the back of the shop.

'Oh, I'm sorry, Penny. I was talking to myself,' Alison explained. 'I overheard Rose and her friend discussing village customs when I was in the post office. The flowers . . . they reminded me of May Day.'

'And the next village festival – after the summer fête – will be the harvest supper,' Penny continued. 'You know, I think that must be one of my favourite times of year. All those wonderful chrysanthemums of russet, gold and ochre. They seem to last so much longer than these summer flowers and are perfect for wedding and funeral disp . . .' Penny put a hand to her mouth in embarrassment. 'I'm sorry, Alison! Me and my big mouth! I was quite forgetting. It was yesterday, wasn't it? How did it go? I hope the flowers were all right.'

'Yes, they were beautiful. In fact that's one of the reasons I'm here . . . to thank you . . . and to ask if there's any chance of getting any violets for Mother. They were her favourite flowers.'

Penny shook her head sadly. 'I'm sorry, I did try ringing round. It's not really the time of year for violets.

Even if I'd managed to locate some, chances are they would have been flown in from abroad. I'd have to buy a whole box and they'd be . . .'

'Very expensive?' Alison finished Penny's sentence for her.

'Now if you wanted baby rosebuds,' Penny added brightly, pointing to a multi-coloured display in the far corner of the shop. 'At the moment I can get all colours of those. They're not as delicate as violets, I know, but they're very pretty and seem to last an awful long time. In fact a man came in just before you and asked me to arrange a posy. I'm sure he said it was for a grave. I wondered if it was for your mother's. He mentioned something about not arriving back in Church Haywood until after the funeral and I . . .'

'No!' Alison broke in, remembering Max Craven getting into his car. 'They won't be for my mother's grave, I expect they'll be for T . . . someone else's.'

Yes, thought Alison, dejectedly leaving the shop, I expect they're to replace the flowers I placed on Tara's grave this morning. The wild flowers Tara and I used to weave into our hair when we were young are obviously far too common and ordinary for Max Craven!

At Keeper's Cottage, Bunty was doing battle with an unwieldly ball of pastry, whilst keeping an eye on Jasper from the open kitchen window.

'You can whine and bark all you like, Jasper. You are not coming back inside this kitchen until everything is safely in the oven.'

Sensing defeat, the young dog gave up and, his attention distracted by a small tortoiseshell butterfly hovering above pale pink blackberry blossom, he bounded towards the bottom of the garden. Bunty smiled at his antics and plunged her hands deep into the stone flour jar, ready to sprinkle both pastry board and rolling pin with flour.

As if on cue, the doorbell rang and the startled Bunty, who was mid-flour dispersal, sent a cloud of white all over the table and floor.

'Blast!' she cried. 'Who on earth? It can't be Alison, I told her to take the spare key . . .' Grabbing a red and white check tea-towel, Bunty rubbed the surplus flour from her hands and hurried to the front door.

Though it was ages since she'd last seen her visitor, Bunty would have recognized the dark hair and finely chiselled jaw anywhere.

'Max! Max Craven, you rogue! Why have you left it so long?'

If Max appeared to mind being engulfed by Bunty's generous frame, whilst his chest was crushed against her ample bosom, it certainly didn't show. Instead he kissed her warmly on the cheek before holding her at arm's length and handing over her jacket.

'Hello, Bunty. How nice to see you again. You haven't changed a bit, and before you start nagging me for staying away too long, let me tell you Constance has already done it for you.'

Bunty smiled. 'Has she indeed? Well, that's what big sisters are for. Now come along in and tell me what you've been doing with yourself. I've some scones in the oven and I'll put the kettle on for a coffee. You have got time, I take it?'

'Coffee would be wonderful. I've all the time in the world,' Max replied, following her through to the chaotic kitchen. 'That is, according to my sister. She thinks I should have a long rest, but quite how she expects me to make my living is another matter.'

'I'm sure a couple of weeks doing nothing won't do you any harm.' Bunty motioned Max to a Windsor chair and reached for the kettle. 'Oh, no! Wait a minute!' But it was too late, Max had already sat down and the seat of his beige linen trousers was covered in a fine layer of flour.

'I'm sorry, Max.' Bunty apologized, rubbing vigorously at the trousers with the tea-towel. I shook flour everywhere when the doorbell rang. I hope the trousers won't be ruined. Such lovely linen too.'

'I shouldn't worry about them too much, Bunty. I've already had some young woman's uncontrollable dog plastering me with muddy footprints today. I'm sure the addition of a bit of flour won't make much difference.'

Thoughtfully eyeing the faded paw marks on Max's trousers, Bunty went in search of a clothes brush. 'This will do the trick, at least for the moment. If they need to be dry-cleaned . . . we've a dry-cleaners in the village now. Did you know?'

Max shook his head and took the clothes brush from Bunty's hand. He was anxious to brush his trousers himself. His seat was still smarting from the vigorous rubbing with the tea towel.

'I didn't see the dry-cleaners when I went to the village for Constance, but I did notice the new mini-supermarket, florist's and wine merchant's.'

Bunty gave a broad grin. 'Oh, yes, the wine merchant's! As you can imagine, Max, they do a roaring trade. Why, only last week . . .' From the back of her mind, a small warning bell sounded and, deciding against further discussion on the drinking habits of

35

Church Haywood locals, Bunty turned her attention to the florist's instead. 'As for the florist's, Penny is a gem. She's only been open since Christmas but already has a wonderful reputation. If you'd seen the flowers she did for poor Elizabeth's funeral . . . I expect Connie told you all about that, didn't she?'

At this point Max merely nodded. He wasn't particularly keen to discuss Elizabeth Benedict's funeral. Nevertheless, he had to admit to himself, from what he remembered of the scene in the churchyard yesterday evening, the flowers were certainly beautiful and tastefully arranged.

'Of course,' Bunty continued, placing the lid on the coffee pot, 'your sister and I felt it was the least we could do for Alison. She's such a sweet girl and life hasn't been easy for her, you know . . .'

Max was in the process of thinking that at least Alison Benedict had had a life – unlike his daughter – when the kitchen door flew open and in bounded a wire-haired terrier, followed by Alison clutching two cartons of milk.

'Oh! I'm sorry, Bunty. He just sort of flew past me when I opened the door and . . .!' Alison stared in horror at Bunty's guest, sitting at the kitchen table still clutching a clothes brush.

'Alison! Why, we were just talking about you. You're just in time for coffee. Isn't that right, Max?'

At the mention of his name, Max rose abruptly and walked towards the back door. 'If you don't mind, Bunty, I think I'd better get a move on. Constance said something about an early lunch and there's something I need to do.'

'But I thought you said . . . Anyway, you mustn't go

36

out of the back door, especially as you came in by the front . . .'

With his hand resting on the brass door handle, Max turned back with a totally bewildered look upon his face.

'If you come in by the front door then you must leave by the front door. It's unlucky, my dear,' Bunty remarked, matter-of-factly.

Ignoring Alison, Max gave Bunty a sardonic smile. 'In that case I shouldn't worry about it, Bunty. I've already had more than my fair share of bad luck in the past ten years. I'm sure I didn't get that by exiting from the wrong door!'

'Goodness me! Who's upset him?' Bunty asked, watching Max walk away.

'I have.'

'You have . . . but how?'

'As I told you earlier, "if looks could kill". I'm still convinced Mr Craven blames me for Tara's accident.'

'But that's ridiculous! How could he possibly . . . when you were in hospital yourself for weeks after the accident? Why, for a while your poor mother and I thought you were going to die!'

'Well,' Alison replied acidly, 'perhaps Mr Craven hoped and wished that I had.'

'Alison!' Bunty shook her head in disbelief and silently reached for the coffee pot. One minute Max Craven was charm personified and eager to stop for coffee, and the next he was like a changed man and couldn't get out of the cottage quick enough.

'You're sure he wasn't upset by Jasper? Perhaps he doesn't like dogs.' she added brightly, passing Alison a cobalt-blue mug.

'Oh, he probably views Jasper and me with the same disdain, considering this morning's episode at St Faith's.'

'Why, what happened at St Faith's?'

'Let's just say our four-legged friend – or at least *your* four-legged friend – was a great deal happier to see Mr Craven than the other way round. In fact Jasper left his calling card all over those immaculately pressed trousers.'

'You don't mean Jasper . . .!' Bunty said in alarm.

Reading her mind, Alison replied, 'No, not in the way you're thinking, Bunty. But do you remember when Tara was small, and I showed her how to make potato prints on large sheets of white paper, sitting at your kitchen table?'

Bunty nodded thoughtfully but failed to see the connection.

'Well,' explained Alison with a twinkle in her eye, 'substitute expensive beige linen for white paper and muddy paw-prints for potato prints.'

It took Bunty some time to realize the significance of Alison's statement before she emitted a loud, 'Oh, no! In that case,' she ventured, 'did he – Max I mean – think Jasper was your dog?'

'Yes, very much so, and even suggested I take him to training classes!'

'Oh, Alison, my dear, I'm so sorry. I know Jasper's a bit of a handful, but you shouldn't get the blame for his unruly behaviour. Perhaps I should ring Connie and get her to explain to Max.'

Alison shrugged her shoulders and took her empty mug to the sink.

'I really don't think it's worth bothering about. Mr

Craven has obviously got some extremely fixed ideas in that stubborn head of his. Besides, didn't he say something about an early lunch? Heavens! If you ring and he's in the middle of eating . . . I don't want the blame for giving him indigestion as well!'

Watching Alison go upstairs to deal with her correspondence, Bunty turned back to the now over-warm pastry still spreadeagled across the pine kitchen table. With a hefty sweep she brought the rolling pin down on top of it. 'Damn! This pastry will probably taste like paving slabs now.'

Looking up to the ceiling, where she heard the overhead creak of floorboards in Alison's bedroom, she whispered with a sigh, 'Well, I certainly do intend to bother about it. So there!'

Contrary to the impression he'd given, Max had not returned to Haywood Grange for an early lunch. Instead he drove back to St Faith's for his third visit in less than twenty-four hours. On this occasion, he was relieved to find no dogs and no Alison Benedict, only the song of skylarks from on high and the gentle, low buzzing of bees from the ivy-clad stone walls.

Carefully lifting the rosebud spray from the floor of his car, Max walked to his daughter's grave and placed the flowers on the grassy mound. Swallowing hard, his eyes moved along the inscription on the simple headstone.

IN MEMORY OF TARA LOUISE CRAVEN
ONLY DAUGHTER OF MAX AND VIRGINIA CRAVEN
BORN . . . DIED . . .

To Max, the months, years and dates were just a blur which ended abruptly in, 'AGED TEN YEARS'.

He gave a low groan. 'Aged ten years and dead ten years, Tara, but at least here at St Faith's you have a perfect resting place, which is more than can be said for your poor mother.'

Reaching out to remove a stray rose petal, Max thought of his wife. Virginia had been cremated according to her wishes and her ashes scattered off the coast of Cornwall, a favourite holiday haunt when Tara was small. Max had never been back to the West Country since. Holidays – who needed holidays? Ten years ago Max Craven had had no need of holidays. The only thing he had craved then was work, work and more work.

In that respect Craven and Painton had proved to be Max's *raison d'être* and his perpetual excuse for remaining in London. Even there however, he found he wasn't to be left alone. Constance had visited him frequently, hoping her dogged persistence would eventually persuade him back, even if it was only for family birthdays and anniversaries.

'At least now Max is home I won't be going to London quite so often.' Constance was whispering down the phone to Bunty.

'And I dare say you'll feel a great deal better having him home again, Connie. I know how worried you've been about him. Ten years is a long time for a man like Max to cut himself off from the world.'

'Yes,' Connie replied, thoughtfully. 'I think he needs cheering up a bit. Which reminds me . . .'

Returning from posting the bulk of her thank-you letters, Alison heard Bunty's voice say quite clearly, before she replaced the handset of the telephone, 'Yes,

'I'm sure Alison will look forward to it; I know I shall.'

'What will I look forward to?' Alison enquired, bending down to stroke the now sleepy Jasper, curled up in his basket.

'Dinner at Haywood Grange on Saturday week – a sort of welcome home for Max. Connie's invited us both.'

Alison groaned. 'You're joking, of course! You saw how Mr Craven reacted to me when I came back with Jasper! Oh, Bunty! Surely you could have made some excuse for me. Can't you go on your own?'

'Nonsense, Alison. It will do you good to get out. I'm sure you're exaggerating this Max business.'

'Well, I'm not,' Alison snapped tetchily. 'Oh, I'm sorry, Bunty, I didn't mean to snap, I just wish you'd asked me first, that's all.'

Placing a comforting arm on Alison's shoulders, Bunty said softly, 'I'm sure it won't be that bad, my dear; after all, we'll be a party of fourteen.'

'Fourteen!'

'Well, you know the size of the dining room at Haywood Grange and how Connie likes to surround that magnificent dining table of hers. Besides, you could do with putting on some weight. Look at you. You're so thin I can hardly see you. You're like a . . .'

'In that case,' Alison interrupted. 'If I'm so thin, I'm sure you and Connie won't miss me. There'll be plenty of other people to . . .'

Bunty shook her head. 'Oh, no. That wouldn't do, Alison. That wouldn't do at all. That would make thirteen, and you can't have thirteen people sitting at a table.'

'Why ever not?'

'Because it's unlucky.'

At the mention of the word 'unlucky', Alison was reminded of Bunty's earlier superstitious proclamation when Max had chosen to leave by the back door.

'In that case,' she said, walking into the garden, desperate for some fresh air and the chance to end the conversation, 'tell Connie to do what they do in that restaurant I once went to with Oliver and Jasper – and put a teddy bear on the fourteenth chair!'

CHAPTER 4

Stepping reluctantly from the shower, Alison slipped into a knee-length cotton kimono and tied a towel around her hair. Bunty heard her sigh as she crossed the landing to her bedroom.

'Now come along, Alison! No more sighing. Try looking at it from the point of view that we're doing Connie a big favour. And just think of the wonderful food she'll have waiting for us. I must admit I'm starving!'

'Well, I'm not,' replied Alison wearily. 'In fact I'm not hungry at all.'

Absent-mindedly running a hand across her stomach, Alison longed for Bunty to excuse her from this evening's dinner party. It was true that she wasn't hungry. In fact she'd hardly eaten a thing during the past forty-eight hours through fear of coming face to face once more with Max Craven. Now the uncomfortable knots she felt twisting at her insides only served to remind her of the abject fear and panic still to come.

Sensing Alison's reluctance, Bunty tried to make light of the matter.

'Take it from me,' she announced with a grin, 'if I

turn up without you, Connie will send Max over to collect you himself! And then what will you do?'

Bunty's statement had the required effect, Alison's kimono fell rapidly to the floor and she hurried to her wardrobe.

'Are you sure my black linen will be okay?' She held the dress against herself. 'Apart from my old Laura Ashley print, the contents of my wardrobe appears to be jeans, jeans and more jeans.'

Filled with a sudden pang of remorse, Bunty patted her on the shoulder.

'I'm sorry, my dear, I realize it's still early days since your mother's funeral. The black linen will be perfect and if you don't feel very chatty, I'm sure the others will understand.'

Outside Haywood Grange, Bunty gave Alison's hand a squeeze. 'Chin up. Think of us as a couple of spare females brought in for the evening. In little more than a few hours, your ordeal will be over.'

A few hours, thought Alison to herself, wishing she were anywhere else other than this manicured expanse of lawn and gravel. Fixing her attention on the twisted and gnarled trunk of Connie's prize wisteria, Alison became aware of Bunty grabbing her hand once more and found herself standing in a flower-filled hallway.

'Hello, you two,' said George Henderson, with a broad grin. 'We thought you weren't coming. Connie was just about to send Max over with a search party. Trouble with the car?'

'No,' Bunty replied, with a knowing glance in Alison's direction. 'We thought we'd walk over. It's such a lovely evening.'

'Come along, then,' George called. 'Let's go and join the others.'

Bunty watched him lead the way and motioned to Alison to follow.

Relieved to find the rest of the guests in animated conversation, Alison sipped at the kir she was handed and looked carefully about the room. She noticed Max Craven almost immediately. He was standing by the open drawing room windows talking to Tom and Evangeline Carstairs. Tom Carstairs, grey-haired, grey-suited and with skin of similar pallor, was the local solicitor who'd dealt with her mother's will, such that it was; and Evangeline . . . Evangeline Carstairs was quite another matter.

From the top of her expensively hennaed head to the toes of her green, purple and gold stilettoes, Evangeline was a garish blend of fabric and colour. As vibrant shades of green and purple fought against a background of burnt orange, finest silk chiffon wound itself intricately around exposed sun-tanned flesh, before being forced into the tight waistband of a silk shantung skirt. The skirt, George Henderson couldn't help but notice as he passed Evangeline another kir, was slashed almost to the thigh.

'Evangeline, how colourful you look,' George announced. 'You remind me of something exotic from the hot-house at Kew.'

Evangeline gave a throaty laugh. 'Oh, I'm exotic all right, George. Quite the little passion-flower in fact, or hadn't you noticed after all these years?'

'Course I have, my dear,' George teased, 'But then I know you're already spoken for and Connie keeps me on such a tight rein.'

45

As Evangeline took a deep gulp of her drink, George raised an eyebrow in Max's direction. Too busy thinking of Evangeline Carstairs' earlier pronouncement – she was, after all, anything but 'little' – Max was in the process of trying to interpret George's gesture when he felt his sister's hand on his arm.

'Max, do come and say hello to Bunty and Alison, then as everyone's here we can go and eat. If we don't sit down soon,' Connie urged softly, 'Evangeline will be under the table!'

'Then why don't we sit down right away?' Max suggested, anxious to avoid this meeting as much as Alison. 'Don't forget I saw Bunty and . . . er . . . Miss Benedict only the other day.'

Grabbing Max's arm and steering him across the room to where Bunty and Alison were talking to Penny from the florist's, Connie was heard to remark something about her brother's manners and 'the other day indeed!'

Max bent and kissed Bunty warmly on the cheek and acknowledged Alison with a curt, 'Miss Benedict.'

She in turn replied with a polite tight-lipped, 'Mr Craven.'

'Good gracious, you two!' Connie exclaimed. 'What is this, *Pride and Prejudice*? Just in case you hadn't noticed, we're in the twentieth century now. Tonight you're in the Grange at Church Haywood and not Netherfield Hall and we're all on first-name terms. Now, Max, as tonight's dinner is supposed to be in your honour, you'd better lead the way.'

Connie was on the point of suggesting Max show Alison to her place at the dining table when George intervened.

'Alison, my dear,' he said, recognizing the panic in her eyes. 'Would you be so kind as to allow the oldest person here to escort the youngest in to dinner? And you, Max, can perhaps . . .'

'Push a way through for the fattest!' Bunty broke in jovially, anxious to relieve the tension, and she hooked her arm in Max's elbow.

Seated at the table, Alison breathed a sigh of relief when she saw Connie take her place at the far end of the table and gesture to her brother to sit by her side. With his sister on one side and Evangeline Carstairs on the other, Max, Alison concluded, was no longer a threat.

As the meal progressed with talk of set-aside and milk quotas, tennis tournaments, the forthcoming summer fête and even the rumours that Jessop's Stables were to be sold at long last, Alison found herself relaxing and avoided, as far as possible, looking in Max's direction. Only once did their eyes meet, leaving her feeling distinctly uncomfortable.

Leaning lasciviously in Max's direction, where she revealed an ample expanse of crêpey, tanned bosom, Evangeline placed a heavily beringed hand on his arm and demanded loudly, 'Fascinated as I am hearing about our delightful farming community in Church Haywood with all its quaint little ways, what I really want to know, Max Craven – and I'm sure everyone else does too – is what you intend to do now you're back?'

'Do? I'm not quite sure what you mean, Evangeline.'

'Of course you do, you crafty thing! You've obviously got something up your sleeve. What are you planning? Come on, now, spill the beans.'

From where she sat further down on the opposite side of the table, Bunty considered Evangeline's choice of

47

words. In some ways they seemed strangely appropriate. Max was occupied pulling at his shirt cuff to hide the scar on his left hand, whilst Evangeline did the spilling, by way of her drink.

Spotting imminent disaster, Max made a grab at Evangeline's glass before the remaining burgundy wine seeped from the table on to burnt-orange shantung silk.

'Oh, dear, how clumsy of me,' Evangeline said, dabbing at the wine with one of Connie's best white Irish linen napkins. 'Not to worry, though. You're quite safe, Tom, it hasn't gone on my skirt. You won't have to take me back to Hong Kong for a replacement.'

'I'm so glad,' came the cool reply from Alison's side as the embarrassed Tom Carstairs looked in his wife's direction.

Sensing acute discomfort all round, Connie looked anxiously towards her husband for support and made for the door. 'George, perhaps if you'd care to pour the dessert wine and I'll see to the puds.'

'I'll give you a hand if you like,' Bunty said, rising from her chair and hurrying after her friend.

In the kitchen Connie gave an exasperated sigh. 'I told George to watch Evangeline with the wine; you know what she's like once she gets going.'

'Don't let it worry you, Connie. Besides, knowing Evangeline, she'd probably had a few before she even arrived. We're all used to her by now.'

'Perhaps,' said Connie with a frown, as she eased a summer pudding from its mould on to a glass serving plate. 'But if you want my opinion, I think she's getting worse. Poor Tom, how on earth does he cope with her?'

'By ignoring her as best he can,' Bunty replied. 'In

their own way, you know, I think they're perfectly happy. I mean, as long as Evangeline has her new car every year plus her Harrod's charge card . . .'

Connie straightened a crystallized violet on an individual chocolate mousse. 'Yes, but what about Tom? What do you think he wants?'

'Continued success with his practice, a quiet life and the chance to go fishing whenever he can.'

'Well, the practice is certainly doing well and Evangeline never seems to mind him going fishing, so two out of three can't be bad. Now can I suggest you stop worrying about Tom and Evangeline before that raspberry bombe you're holding melts away to a gooey puddle?'

Suddenly reminded of the twelve people waiting for her in the dining room, Connie braced herself and moved towards the door.

In the hallway she turned to Bunty with a whisper. 'You know, I only thought it would be a good idea to invite Evangeline and Tom as they were such good friends with Max and Virginia all those years ago. Poor Max . . .'

'Connie!' Bunty said with a good-natured grin. 'Do shut up! Max is a big boy now and these dishes are heavy, so will you please get a move on!'

Duly admonished and back in the dining room, Connie was both surprised and relieved to find the conversation had settled back to normal. George was doing the rounds with the dessert wine and Max was describing in great detail the state of the décor in the au pair's flat.

'You know,' he said with a wry grin in his brother in law's direction, 'when I wake up in the morning I'm never quite sure if I'm in the Swiss Alps or Church Haywood. With all those posters of Lake Geneva, the Jet d'Eau and snow-covered mountains, I'm almost persuaded Connie expects me to yodel for my breakfast.'

'Just be thankful I don't make you sing for your supper, Max,' Connie teased, placing plates and dishes on the table. 'Anyway, as I told you, you're perfectly at liberty to decorate the place . . . that's as long as you don't use those same dreary greys and sombre colours you had in your London flat.'

Talk of greys and sombre colours prompted Evangeline to turn her attention to her husband. Tom was busily occupied talking to Alison.

Evangeline traced an orange-painted fingernail on the tip of Max's scar. 'Oh, you can't have gloomy colours, Max. You must go for bright, cheerful colours, and the person you need to help you is right here in this room.'

'Really, Evangeline?' Max replied quizzically, looking at the various guests gathered around the table. 'Who exactly do you mean?'

'Why, Alison, of course! She's totally transformed our spare room.'

At the mention of her name, Alison looked up. What on earth was Evangeline saying about her?

Evangeline's husky and somewhat slurred voice drifted down the table in Alison's direction. Unfortunately, owing to George's generous servings of wine and the copious amounts consumed by the majority of guests at Haywood Grange, she could only discern odd snatches of Evangeline's conversation. When she caught the words, 'She's simply wonderful! You must get Alison to advise you; I would never have dreamed . . .' Alison felt two spots of colour rise in her cheeks and tried to pretend she hadn't heard. It was already too late. Evangeline was waving a pudgy hand to attract her husband's attention.

'Tom! Tom! Do tell Max how pleased we are with the spare room since Alison's worked her magic. I mean who would have thought you could do so much with such a dreary old room. It's quite a transformation and I had such fun going to town with her to choose the fabrics.'

Much to Alison's embarrassment, Tom Carstairs continued to sing her praise with such a string of glowing accolades, and Max was at last forced to take note and pass comment. He would have to, he acknowledged silently to himself, if only to shut Tom up and more importantly Evangeline, who was beginning to get on his nerves. If she put her hand on his wrist or his knee one more time he would . . . Well, what *would* you do, Max? an inner voice enquired. Get up and leave the table? Hardly. This dinner party is supposed to be in your honour, you know.

It was the lesser of two evils, Max decided: leave the table and offend his sister and their fellow guests or begrudgingly acknowledge Alison's presence for the first time since they'd sat down to dinner. Slowly and deliberately looking in Alison's direction, yet avoiding eye-contact, Max said softly. 'In that case, if Miss Ben . . . er . . . Alison is as talented as you would have me believe, Evangeline, I hardly think she would be interested in the interior design of a very ordinary au pair's flat here at Haywood Grange.'

'Oh, I'm sure she would, wouldn't you, Alison? It

would be a wonderful project to work on.'

Fortunately for both Max and Alison, Connie chose that particular moment to usher everyone back into the drawing room for coffee. Having been sitting for so long, Alison found it difficult to extricate herself from her chair and the nearby table leg. Bunty came to her rescue.

'Having problems, Alison?' she enquired kindly. 'Here, grab hold and I'll give you a tug.'

Smiling at her own predicament, Alison offered Bunty her hand and, while Bunty heaved her free, watched Evangeline make a bee-line for Max and entwine her arm in his as they left the room. Suppressing a giggle, she whispered to Bunty, 'By the looks of it it's not only me who's having problems. Did you see the look of utter disdain on Mr Craven's face?'

'Poor Max!' said Bunty. 'Evangeline's been pestering him all evening. He won't get any peace until he agrees to go and admire your handiwork in their spare room at The Firs.'

Still clutching Bunty's arm as they walked back to the drawing room, Alison kept her thoughts to herself. Certainly Evangeline had been most insistent that Max should visit The Firs. Yet, innocent as she was, Alison was convinced it wasn't really the spare room Evangeline had had in mind when she'd issued her invitation.

Grateful for the diversion when Bunty and Alison eventually joined the others, Max left a bewildered and disappointed Evangeline mid-sentence and went in search of his sister.

Connie, having served everyone coffee, turned her attention to her brother's grim face with its ashen pallor. 'Sorry,' she whispered. 'I didn't realize Evangeline would come on quite so strong.'

Max sipped thoughtfully at his coffee and turned his back on the guests. 'You could at least have warned me beforehand,' he hissed. 'My God! It was like sitting next to a praying mantis all through dinner.'

'Then your best bet,' Connie replied, 'is to go and sit with Tom if you want to avoid her in future. Evangeline always steers clear of her husband at social gatherings.'

Muttering something about hoping there wouldn't be any 'in future' as far as Evangeline Carstairs was concerned, Max finished his coffee and walked deliberately in Tom's direction. There he found George and Tom deep in conversation over the recent release of green belt land for development and the proposed sale of Jessop's Stables.

'Who do you think would be interested in buying them?' Max enquired.

George shrugged his shoulders. 'Someone with plenty of money, certainly no sense and a good imagination.'

'You can say that again,' Tom quipped. 'A very good imagination, I would say! Oh, I don't doubt the place has huge potential, but if it's not dealt with aesthetically . . .'

'As I'm so out of touch with the area, just remind me, where exactly are these stables? Somehow I don't remember them.'

George turned to Max with a grin. 'Quite possibly because you never did your courting in Church Haywood, Max. The stables were part of the old Manor House and were the local lusting ground in the fifties and sixties.'

Max considered his brother-in-law's remark. No, he hadn't done much courting in Church Haywood and certainly when he'd met Virginia most of their courtship had taken place in London, initially because he'd been studying in London, and later because he'd worked there.

When he had taken up his first position working for a team of highly respected and established London architects, it had been better to live in the city. It was only later, after his marriage to Virginia and the birth of his daughter, that Max had decided country life would be better for his wife and child. Now, years later, he recalled Virginia's initial reaction to his suggestion.

'You can't be serious, Max! Leave London and move to Church Haywood. But it will be like living in the back of beyond! What on earth shall I do all day?'

'For a start, look after Tara,' Max had responded, somewhat taken aback.

'But I won't know anyone . . . !'

'Of course you will. There's Mother and there's Constance and George and the twins. Constance knows everyone and she'll soon introduce you. Don't forget too, there'll be a wonderful village school for Tara – plus the swimming pool and tennis courts at Haywood Grange.'

Suitably mollified by the latter, Virginia had agreed on condition that Max keep the London flat. So began the early years of Tara Craven's childhood, and her mother had been introduced to Evangeline Carstairs.

Hearing Evangeline's raucous laughter from the far end of the room, Max shuddered. All those years ago, Virginia and Evangeline had been the best of friends. Only now did he begin to question what on earth the two women could possibly have had in common.

Max felt George's hand on his shoulder. 'Looks as if our guests are going home, Max. Let's bid them all goodnight as quickly as possible, shall we? Then we can all relax and hopefully Connie will leave you in peace for a bit. You look as if you could do with it.'

'Does it show that much?'

'Only if you look closely. Don't forget, I'm used to Connie's little soirées. Even I have to admit sometimes they can be a bit of an ordeal.'

Max watched Tom help Evangeline into a purple and orange shot-silk jacket and breathed a sigh of relief. 'Let's just say I could have done without you-know-who in such close proximity. How was it you described her earlier: looking like some exotic hot-house flower? Good lord, George! Either you're mad or you need glasses!'

'Neither,' said George with a wicked glint in his eye. 'But next time you go to London, Max, try and visit Kew. You have my word, some of those exotic plants are perfectly revolting and quite hideous to look at!'

Max emitted a rare smile and walked to where Constance was beckoning. For his sister's sake, he decided, he would be the perfect gentleman when it came to bidding their guests goodnight.

Having applied yet another coat of Pagan Glow to her overlarge mouth, Evangeline left a large orange splodge on Max's cheek. 'Promise me,' she gushed, clinging unsteadily to his chest, 'you will come and see the spare room.'

Desperate to be rid of her, Max replied convincingly, 'Of course; I'll get Constance to bring me over some time soon.'

'Oh, don't bother about Connie! She's already seen it; come on . . .'

Evangeline got no further as Tom unhooked his wife's arms from Max's jacket and led her away to the open doorway. 'Come along, dear, Connie and George are waiting to go to bed and Alison and Bunty are waiting to say goodbye. Alison looks exhausted, poor girl. Don't forget, it's been a very harrowing time for her just lately.'

Although Tom had lowered his voice, to avoid being overheard, being in such close proximity to Max meant his words had found an audience.

Smoothing his crumpled jacket, Max considered Alison where she stood by Bunty's side. A harrowing time was right, he concluded, if all the snippets of information he'd heard about Alison Benedict since his arrival were correct, yet he still felt ill-disposed towards her.

Pale and drawn in her simple black linen dress, she'd seemed strangely out of place during the evening's fiasco. Hearing her whispered, 'Goodbye,' Max responded with a polite, 'Goodnight,' and stopped himself from adding, Quite possibly, Alison, you've hated tonight as much as I have.

CHAPTER 5

Hearing movement from the au pair's flat next day, Connie ran quickly up the back staircase and tapped gently on the door.

'Max, as you're awake, I was wondering if you'd like to come to church with me? George is convinced you won't want to, but I'll ask anyway . . .'

One look at Max's face told Connie that George's assumption had been perfectly correct. 'Oh, well,' she sighed, shrugging her shoulders, 'it was just a thought. Another day, perhaps? George said to tell you the Sunday papers have arrived and he's got some nice home-cured bacon on the go.'

Sensing his sister's disappointment at his complete lack of interest in ecclesiastical matters, Max gave her a reassuring hug. 'Constance, like Evangeline wanting me to look at her spare room, I promise I will come to church with you one day soon. For the moment, however, I'd appreciate it if you . . .'

'Would just leave you alone?'

'No,' continued Max, 'I'm not asking you to do that. I need a bit of breathing space, that's all. You forget I've been living on my own and looking after myself for a long while now. It's not easy being the centre of attention – as I was last night.'

'George told me it would be a big mistake and I shouldn't have subjected you to such an ordeal . . .'

'Constance,' Max broke in kindly, 'it wasn't exactly an ordeal. In fact it was extremely thoughtful of you. Let's say perhaps I wasn't ready for it just yet – and neither will you be . . .'

Connie threw him a puzzled look. 'Ready for morning service,' Max enlightened her. 'If you still intend to go, that is?'

'Crikey!' gasped Connie, looking at her watch. 'Is that the time? I'd better fly.'

'Well, you've already got the halo,' Max insisted, kissing a confused Connie on the forehead. 'You know, I've always thought of you as not only my big sister but my guardian angel as well.'

Swallowing hard, Connie patted Max's arm and turned towards the staircase. 'Don't forget George and the bacon. It's almost ready.'

'By the way,' Max called as she headed back down the stairs, 'is it my imagination, or does Alison Benedict walk with a limp? Well, not exactly a limp. I noticed sometimes she appears to have difficulty walking.'

From where she was standing, halfway down the stairs, Connie stopped and reached pensively for the banister rail. 'Surely,' she replied softly, studying Max's bewildered face, 'you haven't forgotten? The accident . . . Alison's leg? I thought you remembered. She was in hospital for weeks. In fact at one time they thought she might never walk again.'

Seeing the shuttered look on Max's face, Connie chose not to continue and carried on downstairs.

'George!' she urged on reaching the kitchen, 'look, I must dash, but Max has just asked about the accident. Not the accident exactly, but Alison and her leg. I thought he remembered but obviously not. So be careful when you see him, will you? I'll be back as soon as I can.'

Struggling with the handle of the grill pan, George gaped open-mouthed as his wife made for the door. 'But Connie! You can't go and leave me to explain to Max!' But his plea fell numbly against the closing split-level stripped pine back door.

'Talk about closing the stable door after the horse has bolted,' muttered George, reaching for the tongs to turn the bacon.

'Pardon?'

George looked up startled as Max entered the kitchen. 'Oh, morning, Max. Sorry, you caught me talking to myself. Now, can I tempt you to some breakfast? Proper home-cured bacon, this. None of your foreign muck here at Haywood Grange.'

Choosing not to offend George by declaring he hardly ever ate breakfast, let alone grilled bacon, mushrooms and tomatoes, Max accepted the plate he was offered and sat down at the kitchen table.

'I was right, then,' George said, giving the bottle of tomato ketchup a hefty thump. 'I told Connie I didn't think you'd be up to St Faith's after last night's episode. Can't say I blame you. I restrict myself to Christmas, Easter and Harvest Festival.'

'And leave Connie to pray for you in between,' Max joked.

'What? Oh, yes,' George replied, glad to divert Max's attention away from more sensitive issues.

Buttering a slice of toast, Max looked pensive. 'George . . . I've been wondering about . . .'

With bated breath, George Henderson braced himself and silently cursed his wife for leaving him like this to deal with the problem of Alison. Only to his surprise it wasn't Alison and the accident Max had in mind.

'Jessop's Stables,' Max continued thoughtfully. 'I don't suppose you could take me over there this morning?'

Reaching for his cup of tea, George swallowed hastily until he almost choked. He stood up. 'Why, of course, Max. No trouble. Let's go right away, shall we?'

Surprised by his brother-in-law's eagerness to leave the table, Max continued, 'Hang on a minute! It's not that important that you can't finish your breakfast.'

George however thought otherwise, and, picking up his car keys from the kitchen dresser, turned and was already walking towards the kitchen door.

'What about the dishes and the table?' Max called after him. 'We can't go and leave them. Won't Connie . . . ?'

There was no response, however. Max heard George switch on the ignition of the Range Rover.

Approaching the footpath to St Faith's, Alison left Bunty's side.

'I'll just go and pop these on Mother's grave. I won't be a moment.'

'These' were the African violets Penny had given to Alison the previous evening with the words, 'I know it's not proper violets, Alison, but it suddenly occurred to me they might make a nice display during the warm summer months. Try them and see what you think.'

Placing the terracotta pots with their deep violet-coloured flowers on the grave, Alison half-expected to find Max Craven lurking in the shadows. To her relief she found herself alone.

'I haven't thanked you yet for last night,' she remarked, returning to where Bunty stood waiting by the church door.

'What for?'

'Declining Mr Craven's offer of a lift home.'

'Alison!' Bunty chided. 'You heard what Connie said last night. Good gracious, my dear, the way you speak Max's name, you make him sound like that villainous Mr Rochester from Jane Eyre!'

'Was Mr Rochester a villain?'

'He was in my book,' Bunty replied. 'Why, didn't you think he was?'

'No, not exactly. I've always thought him dark and mysterious. I suppose I always felt sorry for him really. It couldn't have been easy for him, having a wife who deceived him like that.'

'In that case, how about feeling just the teeniest bit sorry for Max? It was very hard for him, you know, losing Tara and then Virginia . . . in such tragic circumstances too.'

'You think I don't know that, Bunty?' Alison asked incredulously. 'Don't forget, I was there too, at least when Tara . . .' She stopped mid-sentence when she saw Connie running up the path.

Watching Alison walk briskly in through the heavy oak door of St Faith's, Bunty turned to face her friend. 'Trust me to put my foot in it, Connie. It's my own fault really. I suppose Alison's going to take quite some time coming to terms with her grief.'

'Let's hope it doesn't take Alison as long as it's taken Max, that's all I can say.' Connie reflected on her conversation with her brother before her hasty departure. 'Correct me if I'm wrong, Bunty, but do you get the distinct impression there's a conflict developing between Max and Alison?'

'I don't know about developing,' Bunty whispered, opening the church door for her friend. 'In fact I think it's well and truly established, though Lord knows why.'

'Then, as we're in His house,' Connie continued, nodding towards the altar, 'perhaps He'll have the grace to enlighten us during the next hour . . . or at least show us the way to remedy the situation.'

'Amen to that,' came the hushed reply.

George Henderson negotiated the uneven and overgrown track to Jessop's Stables. 'This is why I insisted on using my wheels and not yours. I don't think you'd be any too pleased having all that gleaming black paintwork scratched by brambles and blackthorn.'

'Probably not,' Max acknowledged. 'It's certainly overgrown up here. I never would have found the place on my own.'

Stepping down from the Range Rover, Max stopped and surveyed the view. Every so often through the twisted maze of bramble, briar rose and blackthorn, he discerned odd patches of mellow sandstone masonry and was reminded of one of Tara's favourite bedtime stories – *The Sleeping Beauty*. If Tara were with him now he was sure she would be thinking . . .

'Well, what do you think of it?' George picked up a gnarled stick and hacked at the unwielding, tangled undergrowth. 'If you want my opinion, I think it's bit of a nightmare.'

Max rubbed thoughtfully at his forehead. 'I don't know about that. I was thinking the exact opposite. In fact more of a fairy-tale.'

'Aren't fairy-tales supposed to have happy endings? Then mark my words, Max, anyone taking this little lot on can expect quite a pantomime before they walk into the sunset to find their crock of gold.' George laughed cynically. 'In fact, in this case they will have said goodbye to their crock of gold long before they get to the other side of the rainbow.'

'I take it you don't believe in magic or fairy god-mothers?'

With a suspicious look in his eye, George studied Max carefully. Oblivious to the thorns snagging his sweater and trousers, he was forcing his way through a gap in the hedge. 'Of course,' he said, following in pursuit, 'I was forgetting, I suppose you and your partner have dealt with some equally horrendous dere-lict properties in your time.'

Leaving George to disentangle his own sweater from a stubborn blackthorn spike, Max wandered through the central archway of the stables. With a stable block on either side, he was surprised to dis-cover an identical feature, complete with archway, on the other. Turning back to look at George, he announced, 'It's pretty amazing, isn't it? To think after all these years . . . It's definitely Regency and the stonework is in surprisingly good condition. I don't suppose it would be too difficult to connect up the electricity.'

'Yes, but don't forget there's no gas on this side of the

village, so what about heating? The place is far too big for night storage.'

'Open fires, log burners, oil-fired central heating.'

'Whew! You'd need to be a sheikh or have shares in an oil company to fuel a place this size.' George waved his arm to encompass the entire area of stonework. 'Crikey, can you just imagine what size tank you'd need?'

Max turned to George with a cryptic smile. 'Not just one tank, George, possibly four.'

'Four! Bloody hell! In that case, Max, the best thing old Jessop can do is demolish the place and sell the land instead or . . .'

Luckily for George, Max was too engrossed in the roof structure to notice the pregnant pause in the conversation. He had intended to say 'set fire to the place', but in the circumstances thought better of it.

'I doubt it,' Max replied, wandering through to the opposite archway. 'This is bound to be a listed building. When I said four tanks, I meant four small ones, not something that looks like a BP refinery.'

George studied his left forefinger, in an effort to remove a stubborn rose thorn. 'Then you mean you'd turn it into four units, a bit like the craft centre at Little Harberry?'

'Perhaps,' Max replied thoughtfully, walking from the cool shade of the covered archway back into brilliant daylight. There he closed his dark eyes, lifted his face to catch the warmth of the morning sun and breathed in the heavy, flower-scented air of the summer hedgerow.

If Mandy, the receptionist from Craven and Painton, had been passing at that moment, seeing the late July sunlight shimmering on Max's thick hair, she would most certainly have repeated her brother's earlier observation. Silhouetted against the stone archway, eyes closed and deep in thought, Max Craven could easily have been guarding the Tower of London. Only in this case he was guarding his innermost thoughts and desires.

With the church bells heralding the end of morning service and coffee being served near the font, Alison walked shamefacedly to Bunty's side.

'Bunty, I'm sorry about my outburst in the churchyard. It was most uncalled for.'

'Don't mention it, dear. I realize it's been a difficult time for you. Connie said the same about Max too. I suppose seeing you again was bound to open up old wounds. When he sees you, it's inevitable that he should think of Tara. You spent so much time with her, after all.'

'Think of her, Bunty? Yes, as I think of Mother almost all the time, but it's not fair Mr Craven should hold me responsible for Tara's death.'

For a brief moment Alison's attention was caught by the sunlight radiating on to the head of an angel in a stained glass window. An angel who by some trick of the light looked just like Tara. Alison shuddered and turned to face Bunty with tears glistening in her eyes. 'It's not fair,' she repeated in a barely audible voice. 'Not fair at all. I was the only one there. Only I know what happened and why Tara . . .'

'Why Tara did what?' Bunty urged gently, taking hold of Alison's arm. But the moment was lost when an elderly parishioner, missing her footing, stumbled against Alison's side.

'You were saying . . .' Bunty reiterated, anxious for Alison to continue.

'What was I saying?' Alison asked in alarm.

'Something about being the only one who knew exactly what hap . . .'

'Stop! Don't say any more, Bunty! I don't want to talk about it, not now and not ever! So if you'll please excuse me, I'd like to go back to Keeper's Cottage. I have the most awful headache.'

'What was all that about?' Connie asked in surprise, coming up with the last of the hymn books left behind in the pews. 'Alison looks quite dreadful. If I didn't know otherwise, I'd say the poor girl looked as if she'd seen a ghost.'

'And I'd say you were probably right!'

'What on earth do you mean? Seen a ghost! Not here in St Faith's in broad daylight, surely?'

'Not exactly seen,' said Bunty, taking Connie to one side, 'but perhaps been reminded of one. Anyway I don't think we should discuss it now. I don't want Alison to know I've said anything. Look, when we get outside, just behave as if nothing has happened and I'll give you a ring tomorrow. Alison normally takes Jasper for a walk in the morning . . .'

Curious to know more, Connie reached for Bunty's arm. 'But Bunty! You can't just walk off without telling me what you know!'

'I'm afraid I can, for the simple reason I don't really know anything. Let's say it's gut reaction, shall we?'

'But you said . . .'

'I said I'd ring you tomorrow, Connie, so please . . .'

Catching up with the sombre-faced Alison, who was waiting by the lych gate, Bunty called out chirpily, 'I was saying to Connie, I think you should give those stepbrothers of yours a ring. It will probably cheer you up. Isn't it cheaper to ring the States on a Sunday?'

'Yes,' continued Connie, going with the flow, 'after all my dreary guests last night, it will probably do you good to speak to some younger people.'

'They weren't dreary,' Alison replied politely, 'and the food was simply wonderful.'

'Then you must come again soon,' Connie replied. Seeing Bunty shake her head, she added, 'but we won't make arrangements for that now, you've got your phone call to make. Remember me to Oliver and Jasper and send them our best wishes.'

Watching Connie walk away, Alison gave a deep sigh of relief. Yes, it probably would do her good to have a chat with her two stepbrothers. But that would only be possible if Oliver wasn't in the middle of rehearsals and Jasper wasn't dating some *Baywatch* lookalike. Besides, what was the time? It was now almost half-past eleven and she never could remember the time difference between the UK and the States. Looking to where Bunty was pulling a stray piece of bindweed from an otherwise well-tended grave, Alison walked on, oblivious to the mystery she'd provoked.

Later, attempting to remove the red wine stain caused the previous evening by Evangeline's clumsiness, Connie turned to her husband. 'What have you and Max been up to? He certainly appears a great deal happier than he did last night.'

'I took him over to have a look at Jessop's Stables. He seemed full of ideas for the old place, but then I suppose these architect chappies are all the same. Show them a barn and they see a palace.'

'Unlike you, George,' Connie teased. 'Show you a barn and you automatically think of pigs and cattle.'

George smiled and watched Connie squeeze lemon juice on the burgundy stain before rubbing it with salt.

'Of course,' she said, reaching for the kettle, 'I should have dealt with this last night; it might be too late to remove the mark completely. Still, it's worth a go. Can you just hold the fabric taut while I pour on the hot water?'

Watching the stain miraculously disappear, George said softly, 'You'll be pleased to know Max didn't mention Alison or the accident, so with luck the topic won't crop up again for a bit.'

'I wouldn't be so sure about that,' replied Connie thoughtfully.

'Why ever not?'

'Just something Bunty said after church that's got me thinking. Anyway, with luck she'll be able to throw some light on it tomorrow.'

At Keeper's Cottage, Bunty delighted in hearing Alison's voice in animated conversation with Oliver.

'Yes, I'm fine, so's Bunty and we went over to the Grange last night for a dinner party. What? No, nothing in particular. It was a sort of welcome home dinner for Connie's brother.'

Alison purposely avoided further mention of Max and asked Oliver if he'd received the photos she'd sent of her Mother's funeral.

'Yes, they were beautiful flowers, weren't they . . . and don't worry I've already written and thanked everyone. Anyway, look, I'd better go, Bunty's phone bill and all that. Give my love to Jasper and tell him to behave himself. Bye.'

At the mention of his namesake, the four-legged Jasper went bounding into the hallway and sat at Alison's feet in anticipation of what was to come. 'Oh, all right,' she sighed bending down to pat his head. 'I'll take you for a walk. Come along.'

In brighter spirits Alison reached for the dog's lead.

'Everything okay in the States?' Bunty enquired.

'Mmm, fine, thanks. Needless to say I couldn't get hold of Jasper, but that's nothing unusual and anyway, Oliver said he spoke to him only last week. Apparently he's got a pretty tight filming schedule ahead of him, so this week he's relaxing in sunny California.'

'It's all right for some,' Bunty quipped, pouring a sherry.

'Well, we certainly can't complain; our summer's been pretty good so far. Wouldn't it be lovely if it stayed that way for the summer fête?'

'It's not the summer I was thinking about,' Bunty said rubbing her thigh. 'My hip has been giving me real gyp just lately, Alison. It's the winter I'm dreading.'

'Then perhaps I should send you out to stay with Jasper for the winter.'

Bunty roared with laughter. 'Oh, yes, I can just see Jasper's face if I was to arrive on his doorstep. Mind you, it's a thought . . .'

Hearing his name mentioned three more times, Jasper tugged impatiently at his lead and dragged Alison towards the back door, leaving her to ponder on Bunty's last remark . . . and Bunty to make a telephone call of her own.

On Alison's return, she found Bunty looking particularly pleased with herself. 'Well, that's my winter sunshine sorted out,' she said smugly. 'I rang my brother in Australia, and Bob and Freda have invited me to stay for Christmas and New Year.'

'Bunty, that's wonderful! Oh, dear! What about Jasper, have you . . . ?'

'Oh, I'll put him in kennels for a fortnight.'

'A fortnight! But you can't go halfway round the world for a fortnight. How long is it since you've seen Bob and Freda?'

'Twenty-five years,' Bunty replied with a nostalgic sigh.

CHAPTER 6

By the end of what proved to be an eventful week, Alison had persuaded Bunty to consider going to Australia for at least two months.

'Are you really sure, Alison?' Bunty asked for the umpteenth time. 'Two months is a long while for you to take on my dog and the cottage. That's quite a favour you'll be doing me.'

'And what about the favour you'll be doing me?' Alison enquired. 'Don't forget you'll be giving me a roof over my head while I get this project of mine off the ground.'

'Oh, yes, I meant to ask. How's it going? Did you manage to see Mr Jessop, and what did Tom Carstairs advise?'

Moving to the kitchen table with her mug of coffee, Alison took a bulky envelope from her bag and placed it in front of Bunty. 'You can see for yourself, it's all there in black and white. Oliver's already contacted Tom Carstairs about my legacy from my stepfather. With luck there should be enough to rent one of the units from Mr Jessop.'

'It's definite that he's no longer going to sell, then?'

'Not exactly definite,' Alison continued brightly. 'But if Mr Jessop lets the Stables as four craft units – a bit like Little Harberry – we shall only really need the basic four walls and a loo. It shouldn't be too difficult to put in the electricity and . . .'

Thinking of her rheumatism, Bunty broke in, 'Yes, but what about heating? It will be jolly cold stuck out there in the winter.'

'Calor gas,' Alison explained undeterred, 'and quite possibly lots of sweaters! Don't forget I shall only be using the Stables – or at least my quarter of them – as an office. I'll be out most of the time visiting clients. Oh, Bunty! Isn't it exciting? Just think, thanks to my stepfather, I can start up my own little business.'

Bunty placed her own careworn, reddened hand on Alison's smooth and delicately boned white one, and patted it gently. 'Yes, and I'm very pleased for you, my dear. You deserve it. I only hope . . .'

'You hope what?' Alison queried, sensing Bunty's tone of concern.

'That Bill Jessop doesn't change his mind. He has been known to in the past, you know.'

'Perhaps,' sighed Alison, taking her empty mug to the sink, 'but this way Mr Jessop doesn't have to wait for the right buyer to come along with the money. He can start getting rent almost immediately. Even Mr Carstairs said, prospective buyers are thin on the ground at the moment; a) because Mr Jessop is asking such an inflated price, and b) because the Stables are in such a bad state of repair, if you're talking about using them for offices or private dwellings.'

'In that case, as you're going to be out for the rest of the day and appear to have everything in control, I might pop over and see Connie.'

Pausing at the door, Bunty turned back. 'If I could offer a word of advice, Alison: can I suggest you get a proper letter sent off to Bill Jessop as soon as possible? Request a definite letter of acceptance on his part – just in case.'

'Oh, Bunty,' Alison sighed, giving her a hug. 'What is this, another of your superstitions? Don't worry, I'll write to Mr Jessop this very minute and deliver it in person, before I catch my train.'

At Haywood Grange, Bunty sat in the conservatory and gazed admiringly at Connie's displays of tubs and hanging baskets.

'You know, Connie, I don't know how you do it. Every year you surpass yourself with your geraniums and fuchsias. I was only saying to Alison the other day . . .'

'Yes, and how is Alison? Come along, Bunty, you know I didn't invite you here to talk about my plants! I've been waiting with bated breath all week for what you've got to say.'

'In that case, I'm afraid you might be disappointed. You see, I don't really know any more than I did last Sunday. Hard as I might try, I couldn't get a peep out of Alison.'

Connie folded her hands dejectedly in her lap. 'Oh, dear, what a pity. Still I suppose you could at least tell me what prompted your curiosity last Sunday morning. And in case you're wondering, it's quite safe, Max isn't here. He's gone to London.'

'So Evangeline's pesterings have eventually driven Max away,' Bunty said, with a cynical smile.

'Not exactly. Max has gone to see his bank manager.

Mind you, I told him only this morning before he left, as far as Evangeline is concerned, it would be better to get it over and done with. The sooner he goes to see her spare room, the sooner she'll leave him in peace.'

'And pigs might fly!'

'Oh, I'm sure Max can take care of himself as far as Evangeline is concerned. She's all talk and no action.'

'I wouldn't be so sure of that,' Bunty retorted. 'Anyway, about Alison.'

'Yes,' whispered Connie, 'about Alison. Do tell. I'm all ears.'

Bunty shook her head ruefully. 'Of course I could be wrong, but it was the way Alison said it. She seemed so desperate . . .'

'Said what? Why was she desperate? Oh, for God's sake, Bunty! If this has anything to do with Tara's accident, then it concerns Max, and me too come to that.'

'We . . . ell, I can only tell you how the conversation began and how it ended. Alison thanked me for not accepting Max's offer of a lift home and somehow we ended up talking about Mr Rochester.'

'But we don't know a Mr Rochester! At least, I don't.'

'Course we do! School . . . *Jane Eyre*, remember?'

Connie gave an exasperated sigh and waited for Bunty to continue.

'Apparently Alison felt sorry for Mr Rochester because his wife deceived him, and I said I felt sorry for Max . . . so couldn't Alison do the same . . .'

'Why? Because you think Virginia deceived Max?'

'I'm not sure,' Bunty replied lamely. 'I've not thought about that for a long while. However, you know how Alison's got this bee in her bonnet about

Max blaming her – well, not exactly blaming her, but perhaps holding her partly responsible for Tara's death.'

'But it was an accident! Everyone knows it was an accident! Weren't they playing chase or something . . . and didn't they say at the inquest, Alison was chasing Tara and when Tara ran in front of the car . . . ?'

For a long while Bunty remained silent, juggling thoughts around in her head, trying desperately to remember back to ten long years ago.

'Yes, I know that,' she murmured thoughtfully, 'but you see, Alison said – and here I remember her every word, 'It's not fair Mr Craven should hold me responsible for Tara's death . . . I was the only one there. Only I know what happened and why Tara . . .'

'Yes, go on!' Connie urged impatiently. 'Why Tara did what?'

Bunty hung her head and gave a low moan. 'That's just it, Connie, I don't know. Alison never said any more. When I tried to find out, she shut up like a clam.'

'But we can't leave it at that! We've got to find out what Alison was implying. It could be important.'

'I don't doubt it. Have you any suggestions how we can find out? Because I certainly haven't!'

Connie hesitated for a moment. 'If she wouldn't tell you, perhaps she might tell me. Tara was my niece, after all.'

'And if she doesn't, what then?'

'We could always get Max to ask her.'

'For goodness' sake, Connie! Don't you think the situation is bad enough between Alison and Max as it is? I for one don't want Alison to suffer any more than she has already. And no doubt, as Max is your brother, you must feel likewise about him.'

Connie rose from the cane armchair and walked into the garden with an air of despair. 'If only Max hadn't gone to London. If only he were here. Perhaps we could have approached him about it together?'

'But as he isn't, there's not a great deal we can do about it, is there? For the moment I suggest we just keep mum and hopefully . . .'

'Yes?'

'I was going to say, hopefully one day we can persuade Alison to change her mind. In which case I'd be prepared to hazard a guess that all of us – Max included – won't much like what she's been keeping to herself all these years.'

With Connie worrying about Max, he meanwhile was almost enjoying the prospect of a day in London. Particularly because he knew at the end of the day he would be able to turn his back on the hustle and bustle of city life and head back to the peace and relative tranquillity of Church Haywood. Peace, that was, if you discounted the likes of Evangeline Carstairs.

Now away from Evangeline's clutches, Max began to see the funny side of the situation. Yet he still found it puzzling to think that, years ago, Virginia and Evangeline had been the best of friends, with what had appeared to be so much in common. For the two women it had been a round of tennis tournaments, weekly sessions at the gym, charity lunches and, when Max was working away in London, trips to the local cinema and theatre.

At the time, Max had been glad Virginia had Evangeline to take her mind off his long absences. He'd certainly been busy, taking over the business from old Mr Butler and establishing Craven and Painton in its own right. Though latterly he'd begun to wonder if he'd spent too much time away from his family. Virginia, he reminded himself, had never complained, had she?

With a new-found spring in his step, Max hurried to the familiar revolving doors.

'Why, Mr Craven! What a surprise! Does Mr Painton know you're coming?'

'No, Hayley, I thought I'd . . .'

'Max! You old rogue! What the devil are you doing here? Why didn't you let me know you were coming to town?' Stepping from the lift, Nigel Painton shook Max's hand warmly. 'Gosh, it is good to see you. The place isn't the same without you, you know. How long are you staying?'

'Not long, Nigel. In fact I'm only here for the day. I've got an appointment with my bank manager at two-thirty.'

'My word! That sounds ominous; nothing serious, I hope.'

Max shook his head. 'Shall we say I think I handle my bank manager better than you do yours, Nigel?'

'Quite possibly. But that's not surprising, as I spend my money as fast as I make it. Correction – Vanessa spends my money as fast as I make it.'

Max raised a quizzical eyebrow. 'Still going strong, is it, between you and Vanessa?'

'Yes, and she's going to be damned sorry she's missed you. Are you sure you can't stay over? There's plenty of room at the flat, you know.'

'I know, and it's very kind of you, Nigel, but I really must get back to Church Haywood this evening.'

'At least you won't say no to a spot of lunch. There's a super new restaurant just opened in St James's.'

Hailing a cab, Nigel ushered Max into a taxi and proceeded to bring him up to date with happenings in the London office, though something told him Max's mind was really elsewhere.

'How's life in the sticks, then, and how's Connie? I must say, although you're not exactly rosy-cheeked, you're already looking so much better.'

'Really? I wasn't aware that I'd been looking that bad. But "life in the sticks", as you call it, is a far cry from the fume-filled streets of London, and as for Connie and the natives . . . I think we're gradually adapting to one another's little ways.'

'And if I may make so bold, who's the special someone who's causing you to forgo an evening spent with Vanessa and myself and return to Church Haywood in such a hurry?'

Reaching for his glass of wine, Nigel knew immediately he'd said the wrong thing. Max fixed him with the familiar 'Craven glare'.

'For your information, Nigel,' Max replied coolly, 'the only thing special about Church Haywood – apart from my sister and her extremely genial husband – is a certain property that's taken my interest!'

Used to dealing with Max, Nigel ignored his friend's brusque manner and changed the subject. It was safer, he decided, to discuss the forthcoming programme at the Wigmore Hall and the Barbican and enjoy the tempting meal now arriving at their table.

Back in a taxi, Nigel insisted Max return to the office with him, if only to say hello to the members of staff, all recently returned from their summer holidays. 'You know, they still can't believe you're serious about giving up the London office.'

'Then it's up to you to convince them,' said Max, as he stood at the foot of the pink granite office façade, then jumped back into the taxi and waved Nigel good-bye.

'But Max – !'

But Max had already gone, lost in the endless stream of snaking traffic. There he was just another solitary passenger looking out on to a seething row of black cabs with their brake lights flickering in the oppressive London heat. 'You know, you don't miss it at all, do you?' Max heard himself whisper under his breath as he bought an evening paper and boarded the train at King's Cross for Church Haywood.

Having first studied the financial pages, Max turned his attention to his fellow passengers. It was quite a novelty travelling by mainline train for the first time in ages. After a while he was reminded of the game he used to play with Tara. What was it called – 'Misfits'? Yes! That was it, and Max decided to try and fit the tired, grey faces, devoid of all emotion, to the most likely of occupations.

Civil servants, bankers and lawyers were the most easily recognized, followed by the upwardly mobile, complete with their mobile phones. These, Max noticed, appeared to spend more time switched on than off. Suppressing a smile and to pass the time, he began visualizing his fellow travellers in a scene from an old black and white movie. Only in this instance it wasn't black and white but more navy and grey pinstripe.

Lulled by the rhythmic rocking of the train, Max fought the temptation to close his eyes and concluded wryly that the weapons being drawn on the 5.36 from King's Cross were a far cry from those seen on *The 3.10 to Yuma* all those years ago. This evening's 'guns' had been substituted by the latest in slimline communications technology, and the sixty-four-thousand-dollar question was, who was going to be next 'on the draw'?

'Mr Craven . . . Max . . . I think you should wake up. That's if you intend to get off here. We've arrived in Church Haywood.'

Startled, Max looked up to find an almost empty compartment and Alison Benedict, shaking him gently by the shoulder.

'Gracious! I must have fallen asleep. Thanks, Alison. I suppose we'd better get off before the train takes us on to goodness knows where.'

'Scotland, quite possibly,' she said with a faint smile, as he helped her down on to the platform.

'In that case I'm jolly glad you were on the train. Where were you sitting? I didn't see you when I got on.'

'Oh, I was standing at the back of the compartment.'

'Standing! Why . . . ? I mean . . .'

'I only managed to catch the train at the last minute. Someone bumped into me on the main concourse and I dropped my folder. It took ages to gather up all my sketches. When I got on the train – just as the whistle blew – all the seats were taken.'

Forgetting his earlier animosity towards her, Max seemed puzzled.

'But why didn't you come over? You could have had my seat.'

A flush of colour appeared on Alison's cheeks as she avoided his gaze.

'Simply because like everyone else you paid for your

ticket . . . and you got there first.'

Max studied Alison's heavy portfolio, stuffed with fabric and designs.

'Yes, but I would have offered you my . . . You mean to say no one offered you their seat?'

'Mr Cra – I mean Max. I don't wish to sound impertinent, but are you a frequent rail traveller?'

'No. Which is possibly why I fell asleep. Why do you ask?'

'Only because it's been quite some time since I've been offered a seat on a train.'

'Then in that case,' Max said deliberately, remembering the look on Alison's face when he'd last offered her a lift, the night of Constance's dinner party, when she'd been with Bunty, 'perhaps you'd allow me to drive you home? I take it you are still living with Bunty?'

'Yes.'

'Is that yes to the lift or yes to the reference to Bunty?'

Feeling decidedly ill at ease, yet knowing how much her right leg was beginning to ache, Alison whispered softly, 'Yes to both, if you really don't mind . . . Max.'

Aware of her struggling with his name for the second time that evening, Max looked Alison directly in the eye. 'Then can I suggest you wait here outside the station, while I walk to the car park and fetch my car? Heaven knows why they built the station car park so far from the station.'

'Perhaps to encourage some form of daily exercise?'

Max grinned as he walked away. Something told him Alison Benedict had quite an acerbic sense of humour.

Alone and waiting on the newly laid paving slabs, dappled by the evening sunshine, Alison studied the discarded remnants of stale chewing gum. 'Filthy habit!' she whispered under her breath. 'Those slabs have only been down a few weeks. Why can't . . . ?' But she got no further as her attention was drawn by a sleek black car pulling up at the kerb.

Within seconds Max was standing by her side, relieving her of her portfolio and helping her into the front passenger seat.

'That's quite a weighty folder you've got there,' he remarked, stirring the engine into life once more. 'What were you doing in London?'

'First I went to an exhibition on Aboriginal art and then I went to look for some colour swatches.'

'Aboriginal art. That sounds interesting.'

'Oh, it was!' Alison replied, quite forgetting who was driving her home. 'Their colours and techniques are simply amazing, I thought I . . .'

'Go on,' Max encouraged, sensing her sudden attack of nerves. 'What did you think?'

Alison hesitated for a moment before continuing, 'I thought I could use some of their ideas in my work. I'm hoping to set up my own business, you see.'

'Ah, yes! Interior designing, isn't it? I remember Evangeline and Tom Carstairs singing your praises only last week. I must go and have a look for myself one of these days.'

At the mere mention of Evangeline and Tom, Alison found herself blushing. 'It was only their spare bedroom.'

'Yes, but even spare bedrooms have to look good, I would imagine, especially if it's anything to do with The Firs.'

Alison didn't reply. She could only remember further

embarrassing incidents on the day she'd gone to London to look for wallpaper samples and curtain fabric for The Firs. One thing had been certain that day: no one dared sit while Evangeline Carstairs was standing on a train!

Looking out of the window at Keeper's Cottage, Bunty was surprised to see Max helping Alison from the Saab.

'Well, I never! Fancy that, I wonder . . .'

Alison turned and waved to Bunty, who hurried to the front door.

'We bumped into each other at the station,' Max called. Then, fixing Alison with a grin, he said, 'Well, sort of. I suppose I should really say – '

'He fell asleep and I woke him up when we pulled into Church Haywood, otherwise he would have gone on to Scotland,' Alison interrupted with new-found confidence, now that she was back on familiar territory.

Max passed Alison her folder. 'And very grateful I was too. In future I'd better be more aware when I'm travelling by train. Although today was more than enough for a while. I think I'll stay in Church Haywood from now on, or else use my car.'

And what a car it is too, thought Alison to herself after Max had driven away. All that wonderful leather upholstery, and Max was so . . .

'Alison, cooee! Did you hear what I said? Would you like a glass of lemonade? I made some especially for you. I thought you'd be thirsty.'

At Haywood Grange, George was pouring drinks of a different kind.

'So you saw Alison on the train? What a coincidence.

83

Any idea what she'd been doing in London?'

'Yes. Seeking inspiration from an Aboriginal art exhibition at the Barbican. She said the colours and textures were truly amazing and that she would like to use them for one of her projects.'

'Then I expect she'll make a very good job of it. She's a damn clever girl, is Alison, and extremely talented when it comes to interior design.'

'So everyone keeps telling me,' Max said thoughtfully, sipping at his glass. 'Perhaps I should call in on Evangeline after all?'

CHAPTER 7

'You're what?' Connie asked in amazement, pausing in her dead-heading of the geraniums.

'Thinking of going to have a look at Evangeline and Tom's spare room. Isn't that what you advised, Constance? Everyone keeps talking about Alison Benedict's talents, so I thought I should find out for myself. Perhaps I might be able to use them.'

'What on earth do you mean, Max?'

Max tapped the side of his nose. 'For the moment, I'm saying nothing. All in good time, as they say. Do you think Evangeline and Tom will be up by now?'

Connie looked at her watch; it was just after nine o'clock. 'Tom yes, Evangeline no. Besides, this weekend wouldn't be a very good time. If I remember correctly, they're expecting Tom's brother and his family.'

Max looked put out, and crushed a scented geranium leaf between his fingers. It quite ruined his plans for the day.

'Stop looking like a spoilt child, Max! Tom's relations are only here for the weekend; I'm sure another couple of days won't make any difference for whatever you have in mind. If you're bored and want something to do, you can go and post Cousin Henry's birthday card.'

Conceding defeat, Max picked up the cream envelope and headed for the village.

With the card posted, Max called first at the florist's for his usual order of flowers for Tara's grave and then at the off-licence. From there it was only a short drive to find Bill Jessop.

'Max Craven! What a surprise! I was going to ring you later. Tom Carstairs said you wanted a word.'

'I hope I'm not interrupting anything,' Max asked, following Bill through to his oak-panelled study.

'No, not at all. At least nothing that can't wait. I was in the process of replying to a letter from Alison Benedict. She was enquiring about the old stables.'

'As a matter of fact, that's one of the reasons I'm here,' Max explained, reaching in his pocket for his diary and the letter from his bank manager.

Some time later, when Ann Jessop took away the empty coffee tray, Max stood up and held out his hand. 'It's been nice doing business with you, Bill. I'm glad we managed to resolve the financial aspect so quickly.'

'I certainly don't believe in wasting time as far as money and property are concerned,' Bill Jessop replied shrewdly. 'I'll contact my solicitor a.s.a.p., if that's all right with you?'

'Perfect. It will give me something to get my teeth into for the next few months. I'm beginning to get bored after weeks of doing nothing. My sister's already got me running errands for her.'

Bill grinned and shook his head. 'I think this proposed project of yours is going to take longer than a few months, Max . . . but then you're much younger than I am. Anyway, all the best with it. I shall look forward to seeing it take shape.'

Watching Max switch on the ignition and engage first gear, Bill suddenly raised his arm in the air and ran back inside to his study. When he returned, Max saw he was holding a letter.

'Here,' he said, passing the letter through the open window, 'this doesn't really relate to me any more. Perhaps you could write to Alison instead?' Stuffing the letter in his jacket pocket, Max glimpsed the flowers and bottle of champagne on the back seat of the car.

At the churchyard, discarding the old flowers and positioning the newly arranged, delicate pink posy, Max whispered softly, 'Tara, my dear, it looks as if your father is going to be staying in Church Haywood for quite some time. At least your Auntie Connie and Uncle George will be pleased. I'd better go back and tell them my good news.'

'What's this – champagne! Goodness, what are we celebrating?' George asked, unloading bales of hay from the Range Rover. 'You can't have won the lottery, Max. They don't announce the numbers until eight o'clock tonight.'

'No, George, but you could say this is a gamble of a different kind, and one for the moment I don't want anyone else to know about.'

Accepting her glass of Moët, Constance asked excitedly, 'Well, what is it? What is this wonderful news you and George have been keeping from me?'

'Correction, Connie,' George broke in. 'I've only just found out myself that Max is . . . well, I suppose I'd better let Max tell you himself.'

'I've just agreed to buy Jessop's Stables,' Max said nonchalently.

'What! But how . . . I mean why?'

'For the simple reason, Constance, that I like a challenge. I also think they'll prove to be a good business proposition.'

'So that's why you went to London, to see your business partner. Craven and Painton are going to . . .'

'No, Constance.' Max topped up her glass. 'This has nothing to do with Craven and Painton. I'm buying Jessop's Stables with my own capital.'

George raised an eybrow and gulped at his champagne, whilst his wife tried to comprehend the significance of her brother's pronouncement. 'But what do you intend to do with it? Surely not live there?'

Max laughed heartily. 'No, I don't think so, though I must admit with careful and sensitive planning it would make a superb residence. I was thinking more along the lines of turning it into four separate units.'

'Like Little Harberry?' Connie ventured.

'No. Not like Little Harberry. In fact the complete opposite.'

Constance drained her glass and placed it on the glass-topped conservatory table. She sat down with an anxious look upon her face.

'Don't look so worried, Constance. I have no intention of ruining the place. In fact I want to improve it. Recreate that wonderful Regency style and make sure I only let to local people and not outsiders.'

Connie breathed a deep sigh of relief and reached for her glass. 'In that case, brother dear, you can refill this and I suggest we all drink a toast to Jessop's Stables.'

'Correction number two.' George said jovially. 'I suggest we change that to "Craven's Stables!" '

'Craven's Stables!' came the unanimous reply.

On the Monday afternoon, Evangeline Carstairs waved her husband goodbye, looked hurriedly at her watch and ran upstairs.

'Two o'clock already,' she gasped to her reflection in the dressing table mirror. 'I thought Tom was never going to finish his lunch and go back to the office. Of all the days to suggest . . .'

Suggest? Suggest what, Evangeline? An inner voice enquired.

'Suggest going to bed,' she replied, addressing her reflection with a voice of sheer disbelief. Pushing her hair away from her face, Evangeline turned her attention to the bed where, only a few moments ago, Tom had made his suggestion.

Having spilt coffee on his shirt that morning in the office, and living so near, Tom Carstairs had decided to return home for a change of shirt and a spot of lunch. Heaven knew there should be plenty of food left after the weekend. Evangeline, as per usual, had practically killed the fatted calf in honour of his brother and his family.

Sitting on the bed, unbuttoning the stained shirt, Tom had watched his wife carefully reapply the familiar coat of Pagan Glow. In the heat of the August afternoon, savouring Evangeline's perfume and perhaps a little light-headed from the two glasses of wine he knew he shouldn't have had with his lunch, Tom reached out for Evangeline's hand.

'Evangeline . . . why don't we . . . ? I mean, I don't

have to go back to the office this afternoon. It was, after all, quite a hectic weekend entertaining Paul and his family.'

Recognizing the familiar (yet rarely used) tone in Tom's voice, Evangeline was filled with alarm. It had been weeks – no, months – since they'd made love. Somehow Tom never seemed interested. In fact Evangeline got to thinking about the earlier days when they'd first moved to Church Haywood. He hadn't been that interested in making love then either, but in those days there were so many things to distract her attention away from the loveless (or should that be sexless?) nights spent in Tom's bed. In those days there was tennis, gym, swimming at Haywood Grange, a wonderful assortment of builders working at The Firs and of course there was . . .

'Virginia Craven,' she'd whispered.

'Virginia Craven?' Tom had asked in surprise, when he'd been expecting different words to spring from Evangeline's lips. 'What made you suddenly think of Virginia Craven?'

'Oh, I don't know, train of thought perhaps. I was thinking it was hot and sunny like this when she died. I suppose it must be coming up to the anniversary. Ten whole years, who'd have thought it?' Evangeline forced a mournful sigh and hoped that she'd lied convincingly. Fortunately Tom had interpreted her current mood as a 'no' and decided to return to the office.

Overcome with a rare sense of guilt, Evangeline had followed her husband downstairs. 'Tom,' she called as he opened the front door. 'Tonight, perhaps we can tonight . . . ? Have an early night, I mean. It will probably be a lot cooler.'

Tom bent down and kissed her affectionately on the cheek. 'Yes, why not? You're right, it probably will.'

For the moment however, Evangeline felt anything but cool as she brushed her hair and sprayed yet more perfume on her throat and breasts. In fact she was burning. Burning with desire for Max Craven, and he would be here in less than an hour! Filled with a sudden flash of inspiration, Evangeline changed her clothes and hurried to the spare bedroom.

'Max! How lovely to see you, and punctual to the minute. Do come in.'

'I don't believe in being late for appointments, Evangeline,' said Max coolly, following her into the hallway of The Firs, with its mock marble pillars and recesses, housing an array of bone china ornaments and glass.

'Glass of wine?' Evangeline called, walking through to the designer kitchen. 'Tom opened a nice bottle of Chardonnay this lunchtime.'

'No, thanks, I prefer not to drink in the afternoons, particularly if I'm driving.'

Evangeline looked disappointed but saw no reason why she shouldn't have another glass herself. 'Come and sit in the lounge, then,' she urged, following her pre-arranged plan. 'Come and see our latest acquisition. Tom's bought me one of those new wide-screen televisions. It's simply wonderful and just like having your own cinema.'

And it quite easily could be! Max thought to himself, coming face to face with the hideous monstrosity that appeared to take up a third of the room. Along with Evangeline's disastrous purchases of every colour imaginable. Trimmed with lace, braid and tassels – Max thought the room resembled one of the old-fashioned cinemas he'd visited as a child. Only the usherette with her tray of choc-ices and drinks was missing! Out of the corner of his eye, Max spied Evangeline's collection of videos and supply of chocolates. There was even a bag of popcorn! Seeing him smile, Evangeline took it as approval.

'It's good, isn't it?' she said. 'You must tell me what sort of films you like and come over one evening.'

'I haven't been to the cinema for years; I don't have time. Actually I'm more into music.' Max replied, moving back towards the door.

'Oh, well, never mind. In that case, perhaps we can find you a nice musical. Do come and sit down.' Evangeline patted the cushion of the heavily fringed settee.

'If you don't mind,' continued Max, looking at his watch, 'I'd rather see Alison's handiwork now, if that's all right with you, Evangeline. I promised Constance I would take her to the wholesalers to get some things for the fête.'

Disappointed, Evangeline wandered back into the kitchen with her empty glass. 'You're sure about the wine?' she asked, studying the almost empty bottle.

Max shook his head and watched Evangeline drain the remains of the Chardonnay into her glass with an, 'Oh-well-might-as-well-finish-it-it's-pointless-putting-that-little-drop-back.' He then proceeded to follow her as she led the way upstairs.

Grasping the gold and white china door-handle, Evangeline's spirits rose. She'd been waiting for this moment since the night of Connie's dinner party. Okay, so she hadn't been able to get Max into the right frame of mind downstairs and it was a pity he'd refused a drink, but . . .

'Right, here we are, then, the Carstairs' spare bedroom *à la* Alison Benedict. Shut your eyes, Max, while I open the door. That way you'll get more of the impact.'

'I don't think that will be necessary, Evangeline. I'm hardly a child waiting for Father Christmas.'

No, you're not. You're most definitely not! thought Evangeline to herself, eyeing Max appreciatively from top to toe. But has this Mother Christmas got something special lined up for you!

Despite his protestations, Max was forced to close his eyes while Evangeline opened the door of the spare bedroom with one hand and undid the top buttons of her blouse (to expose yet more cleavage) with the other.

'Right, you can look now!'

Nothing could have prepared Max for the shock when he opened his eyes, particularly taking into consideration the interior decor of the downstairs rooms, which were reminiscent of a bordello, ornate Victorian parlour and film set from a *Carry On* film all rolled into one. 'Nile' or 'Khyber', Max couldn't remember; he'd been at school when he'd seen them.

'Well, what do you think?' Evangeline asked eagerly. 'I know it's plain and perhaps not quite what I would have chosen myself initially but I'm getting used to it now. I was even thinking of asking Alison to do my bedroom next. Tom adores it of course, mind you he always did say he preferred simple things.'

In response to this last statement, Max refrained from repeating what was going through his mind. Instead he turned his attention to the tastefully simple and uncluttered design of the room.

'Primroses,' Evangeline declared.

'Primroses?'

'Yes, primroses. Alison asked me what flowers I liked. I gave her a list of all the exotic ones first. Orchids and lilies and those big amar-wotsit-things. You know, the ones you get as Christmas presents. But she asked me to suggest something simpler and I thought of the banks of primroses we get along the lane in the spring.'

'Mmm, I see,' Max said thoughtfully, looking about the room at the delicate shades of primrose yellow and green, complete with hand-painted border, toning upholstery and unobtrusive furniture.

Evangeline waited expectantly. 'What do you think of the furniture? I bet you're beginning to wonder where the bed is.'

'I hadn't,' Max replied – he'd been too busy studying all the minor details – 'but now you come to mention it . . . ?'

Max's dark eyes flashed quickly about the room until they alighted on a range of pale ash, fitted furniture. 'Let me guess,' he said. 'One of those is a wardrobe and the other a bed?'

Trying not to show her disappointment, Evangeline walked over to the wall, released a lever and planned her next move.

With the bed secured in position, she motioned Max to sit down.

'Go on,' she insisted, 'try it. You know, I always thought these fold-away beds would be uncomfortable, but they're not. Tom's brother and his wife said they hadn't slept so well for weeks and during the day, when the bed was folded back, it made an ideal playroom for their two kiddies. I didn't really want them leaving their toys all over the house, you know.'

Ignoring Evangeline's chatter, Max sat down on the edge of the bed, deciding that from this level he was able to take a far better look at the primroses Alison had painted so beautifully.

'I'm right, aren't I?'

'Pardon?'

'Right about the bed. It is comfortable?'

'Oh, yes,' Max answered, in reply as Evangeline sat down by his side.

'But you haven't tried it properly yet, Max. You know what they say when you go to buy a bed. You have to lie down on it and put your feet up for a bit. Here, let me take your shoes off for you. I can't have you putting your shoes, lovely as they are, on my nice clean covers – can I?'

'Evangeline!' Max remonstrated. 'I came here merely to look at the interior design. Not because I wanted to buy or even try a bed!'

Refusing to take any notice, Evangeline ignored his remarks and, slipping off Max's shoes, lifted his legs on to the bed. Whereby she quickly kicked off her high-heeled mules and joined him.

'There,' she cooed, running her hands down his shirt-front towards the waistband of his trousers, 'isn't that better? You can really get the feel of things now, can't you?'

Pushing her arm away, Max said angrily, 'I don't want to get the feel of things, thank you, Evangeline!'

'But why? There's no harm in it, is there? I was a good friend to Virginia; why can't I be your friend too? I expect you miss her, it's been ten long years . . . and you must get very lonely. When you come to think of it, although I was older than Virginia, we had so much in common. We were very close, you know, a bit like your daughter Tara and Alison in a way. You know, that's funny, I've never even thought of that before.'

At the mention of his wife and daughter, Max rose abruptly from the bed. Evangeline immediately made a grab for his left hand and began stroking his scar. 'Poor Max,' she whispered. 'Won't you even let me make it better? Virginia wouldn't have minded. She was a great one for sharing things, you know.'

'What on earth are you implying?' Max snapped. 'Virginia and I never went in for wife-swapping if that's what you're getting at!'

With Evangeline realizing her well laid plans hadn't gone as smoothly as she'd hoped, and the lunchtime wine beginning to take effect, she let go of Max's hand and rolled on to her stomach. Gazing at him through heavily mascaraed lashes, she watched him move to the door.

'Who said I was talking about wife-swapping? I never mentioned wife-swapping.'

'Well, I certainly didn't do the rounds with my neighbours' wives, if that's what you're suggesting!'

'Of course not,' she purred sarcastically, 'you were the ever-faithful Max, working away in London for your beautiful wife and your pretty little daughter, so you could give them everything they wanted.'

Max was beginning to lose his temper. 'Of course I worked hard to give them everything they wanted! Damned hard, in fact! Virginia understood that and I certainly never heard her complain!'

'Not to you, perhaps,' came the sardonic reply.

It was Max's turn to grab hold of Evangeline's hand. 'What the hell do you mean by that!'

Seeing the anger well up in Max's dark countenance, Evangeline began to panic. Maybe she'd gone too far, and her wrist was hurting.

'You're hurting my wrist, Max. Let go or I'll scream!'

Oblivious to the fact it could be pretty embarrassing if someone were to come in and find Max and Evangeline together in the bedroom, he ignored her plea. 'You can scream all you damn well like, Evangeline, but I'm not letting you go until you finish what it was you were going to say!'

'All right,' she spat bitterly, 'I'll tell you! It's about time you knew anyway.'

Still holding on to her wrist, Max sat back down on the bed. Instinct told him it was best to be sitting for what was coming next.

'I'm waiting,' he said icily. 'It's about time I knew what?'

'That Virginia had . . . a lover.'

'A lover! I don't believe you! You bitch . . . you're lying!'

'I wish I was, Max, believe me, I wish I was. I'm afraid it's true.'

'But she always swore she loved me,' Max said in a daze. 'Every time I came home and we . . .' He stopped short; he had no intention of discussing shared intimacies with his wife. Not here, and most definitely not with Evangeline.

'Oh, yes, Virginia loved you all right, but you were never there, Max, and she needed someone to well . . . you know?'

'No, I don't! Good God! Lots of women have husbands who work away from home for long periods at a time. You surely don't expect me to believe they all . . .' Max found he couldn't continue.

'Most women, no . . . Virginia was different, you see.'

Max didn't see. He was blinded by anger and hurt. Turning on Evangeline, he demanded. 'In that case, who the hell was he? Perhaps you'd care to enlighten me; that's obviously what you intended.'

'I can't . . . because I don't know,' Evangeline lied, suddenly frightened by the ominous look in Max's eyes. Anxious to change the subject, she added quickly, 'Anyway she never saw him again after Tara's accident.'

CHAPTER 8

With Evangeline's words still ringing in his ears, Max slewed the Saab to an abrupt halt. The car's front bumper nudged the twisted, gnarled trunk of the wisteria.

'Max!' Connie called out in alarm. 'What on earth? This is Heywood Grange, not the Silverstone Circuit! That wisteria has been there for the best part of sixty years and I'd like it to remain there if you don't mind! Max . . . Is there anything wrong?'

Connie studied Max's sombre appearance. His furrowed brow and eyes almost black with anger. 'Max? Everything's all right, isn't it? Oh! Don't tell me, Bill Jessop hasn't changed his mind about selling the Stables when you've had such wonderful ideas for . . .'

'No, Constance, it's not Bill Jessop. It's that damned woman Evangeline! Do you know what she . . . ?' Max stopped himself. How should he continue? With what Evangeline did, or what she said? Either way he felt sickened by the events of the past half-hour. God knew it was bad enough being pinioned to the bed by her, yet it was even worse hearing her accuse his wife of being a whore. Okay, so Evangeline hadn't exactly used the word, but in Max's eyes she might as well have done.

Having witnessed Evangeline's little display and knowing she and Virginia had been the best of friends . . . didn't that make them two of a kind?

Checking to see she had her shopping list for the wholesaler's, Connie watched in silence as Max removed his jacket and threw it across the back seat of the car. 'I take it Evangeline was on form, then,' she added brightly, getting into the front passenger seat.

'Meaning?' Max snapped, icily.

Connie sighed. 'Meaning, my dear Max, she probably made a pass at you. Poor Evangeline. The trouble with her is that she's never been able to resist a good-looking male. And even though you're my brother and some would argue that makes my opinion somewhat biased, I would go as far as saying, you are an extremely good-looking specimen of homo sapiens.'

If Connie was expecting a flicker of a smile to surface on Max's face, she was very much mistaken. He remained tight-lipped and stony-faced and uttered not a word. Digging Max playfully in the ribs, she continued, 'Come along, don't take any notice of Evangeline. Tom knows all about her little peccadillos . . . he also knows she's extremely harmless.'

Harmless. Harmless! Max wanted to shout. Telling someone about their wife's infidelity hardly fell into the category of *harmless*. Yet, close as he was to his sister, it was not a topic he felt inclined to discuss.

Driving to the wholesaler's in silence, Max allowed his mind to concentrate on finding the new out-of-town industrial development. Connie meanwhile found herself going over her recent conversation with Bunty. Somehow or other she must broach the subject of Alison and the accident.

Pushing the cavernous blue trolley through the automatic doors of the warehouse, Max followed Connie to the desk. There she signed in and was given a clipboard which she hooked on to the rim of the handle Max was holding.

'I'm afraid this is all going to be a bit boring for you, Max. I'll be as quick as I can. I need to find some suitable things for the tombola and kiddies' toys for the bran tub.'

Connie studied her list and with Max in gentle pursuit, set off for kitchenware. 'Glasses and fruit dishes,' she said, lifting a set of both from the shelf. 'They're normally quite a good draw for ticket sales.'

Max said nothing and studied the inner depths of the trolley. Something about it seemed strangely familiar, which for the moment escaped him.

Sidetracked by an array of garden furniture, Connie stopped thoughtfully. 'You know we really could do with some new garden furniture but it's far too late in the season now. Perhaps next year. To be honest I'm surprised it's still on display. They normally start putting the Christmas decorations out now.'

'Christmas!' gasped Max, 'but it's only August!'

'Exactly, brother dear, and if you're in business, time to plan for the festive season. You know, after this weekend's fête, we start planning the harvest supper. And next on the agenda will be Christmas.'

Max groaned and turned into the next aisle, where, horror of horrors, he saw a young assistant with her arms draped with tinsel. Hurrying away, he moved towards the toys. Wasn't that the next thing on Connie's list?

Watching her fill the trolley with inexpensive novel-

101

ties for both sexes, Max pondered the question of the bran tub.

'Constance, if the toys are all wrapped up, what happens if a girl picks out a boy's toy or vice versa?'

'We have two tubs,' Connie replied. 'One for the boys and one for the girls. That way there's no mistakes and no tears. Which reminds me, I'd better buy some wrapping paper, blue for the boys and pink for the girls.'

'How conventional,' Max quipped.

'Well, what would you have me do, then, Max, pink for the boys and blue for the girls? If you were a small boy, would you go for a pink-wrapped present? No, of course you wouldn't! It's traditional, that's all. Girls like girlie things and boys . . . well, you know.' Anxious to finish the shopping, Connie left Max standing by the toys.

Studying the array of hard-faced dolls, with blonde hair, curvaceous bosoms and scarlet-painted mouths, Max shuddered. What ever happened to innocence and the days of baby dolls when little girls wanted to emulate their mothers, nursing their own 'babies' in their arms? Did today's children really want this assortment of garish playthings?

'They really are quite revolting, aren't they?' a voice murmured softly, by Max's side. 'I take it from the look on your face we share the same opinion?'

Max studied the middle-aged woman who was holding a boxed doll in her arms.

'I'm here to buy my granddaughter's birthday present.' She tilted the box so Max could see its contents. 'It's very realistic, isn't it, and just like a baby?'

Max appeared relieved to discover that at least there

was one little girl somewhere who wanted to have a baby doll to play with until – he saw the writing on the box.

'Do you know,' he said to Connie, when he caught up with her by the gift-wrapping, 'according to the box that doll even vomits!'

'Really, Max? How nice,' said Connie, oblivious to his last remark. She was too busy pondering the wrapping paper.

'There!' she said. 'Does that make you any happier? As a result of your earlier comment, I've made one concession. The girls can have the floral paper and the boys can have the one with cars on.'

Studying the floral paper decorated with spring flowers, Max's eyes rested on clumps of primroses. Through thought-transference, he found his mind wandering back to the ghastly scene with Evangeline and the delicate primroses Alison had painted on the bedroom wall.

Stuck at the back of a long queue, thoughts of Alison naturally turned to thoughts of his daughter. It was then Max remembered what the thick plastic lining of the trolley reminded him of . . . Tara's cot. Well, not her proper cot; that had been a wonderful confection purchased from the baby room at Harrod's. No, the trolley Max was now pushing towards the till was just like Tara's travel cot. A deep blue contraption on wheels that collapsed in on itself (not, of course, when Tara was in it) and fitted quite easily into the boot of the car.

Max shuddered at the memory of the hours spent watching his daughter sleep contentedly and remembered his late father's words. 'You see, my boy, little

Tara doesn't give a fig where she sleeps. Babies don't care where they sleep as long as they're comfortable and warm. All those frills and lace, quite unnecessary! Why, I remember when Constance was a baby and we went to stay with friends, she even slept in a drawer!'

Looking at Connie now, where she was paying her bill, Max found it hard to believe his sister was ever small enough to sleep in a drawer. Ghosts from the past and Evangeline's stinging words caused Max to shudder a second time.

'Oh, dear, I do hope you're not catching a chill, Max. We can't have you going down with something just before the fête. We're going to need as many hands as possible on Friday night and Saturday morning. There's an awful lot to do.'

'Don't worry, Constance, I'm sure I'm not catching anything. It must have been standing under that air-conditioning unit,' Max lied. 'I shall be okay once we're back out in the warm.'

Unloading the shopping into the hallway, Max sighed. Much as he didn't mind helping set up the stalls for Saturday's fête, he would far rather be elsewhere whilst it was taking place. Perhaps if he was to give Nigel a ring he could go and spend the weekend at Nigel's flat. Hadn't his partner said he could have it any time? Especially as Nigel seemed to be spending more and more weekends in Esher with Vanesa and her parents.

Leaving Connie to oversee the stowing away of her purchases, Max ran upstairs to the flat to make his phone call.

'Max! I was just going to ring you, what a coincidence! The decorators are moving into the flat this weekend – I'm having the whole place revamped – and as Vanessa's off to see her sister in Paris, I thought it was about time I popped down to see my old chum in Church Haywood.'

Max's heart sank. He made some excuse about the fête.

'Why, that's even better!' announced Nigel. 'I'll be able to see all the locals at once!'

The local uppermost in Max's mind at that moment was Evangeline Carstairs. She was the last person Max wanted Nigel to meet. As if on cue, Constance tapped on Max's door.

'Max, Tom Carstairs has just been on the phone; he tried ringing the flat but the line was engaged. He'd like to see you tomorrow at ten o'clock if that's all right?'

'It isn't really, I was supposed to be meeting someone in the planning office to discuss the Stables. Perhaps I'd better ring him back.'

'Oh, don't bother now, I gather Tom was ringing from home. He left work early. It would appear Evangeline was upset about something.'

A myriad thoughts flashed through Max's mind. Tom Carstairs had been summoned home by Evangeline because she was upset? Upset by what? What on earth would she tell Tom? That Max had called to see the spare room? That he'd made a pass at her and forced her on to the bed? Perhaps knowing Evangeline – and sadly Max realized he did only too well – she would even tell her husband that Max had tried to rape her!

Some women had been known to, hadn't they? At least if some of the tabloids were to be believed. It was only after some poor devil's reputation had been sullied and his career ruined that the truth came to light.

Watching Connie disappear down the stairs, Max drummed his fingers against the door frame. There was nothing for it but to face Tom with the truth at ten o'clock the following morning.

'By the way,' Connie's voice echoed from the hallway, 'thanks for taking me to the wholesaler's. I shan't expect you to help me wrap the parcels for the bran tub. Alison's offered to help me; she's . . .'

Connie's last words echoed in the stair-well and remained there.

'Damn!' Max whispered softly. 'I forget to tell her Nigel's coming for the weekend.'

At ten o'clock the next morning, a slightly wary and apprehensive Max found himself ushered into Tom Carstairs' office. Tom, who had been on the phone, replaced the handset thoughtfully and jotted down a few scribbled notes.

From where he stood, Max felt unable to discern the solicitor's frame of mind but was highly relieved when Tom's sombre, grey face broke into a welcoming smile.

'Max. Pleased you could make it at such short notice. I did try ringing you yesterday afternoon but I gather you were out.'

Out, yes, an inner voice whispered in Max's head, but out where, Tom? Have you any idea, I wonder?

Tom studied a letter on his desk. 'I've heard from Bill Jessop's solicitor about the proposed sale of the Stables. I take it he's keen to complete the transaction as soon as possible and I just wanted to check that you still intend to go ahead with it.'

'I see no reason why not. Though no doubt there'll be plenty of people in Church Haywood who'll be thinking I must be mad.'

'I doubt it,' Tom replied.

'You surprise me, Tom. How can you be so sure?'

'For the simple reason that most of the locals will be only too pleased someone with Church Haywood connections is undertaking the rebuilding, not some unknown property developer from outside the area.'

Warmed by Tom's comments, Max proceded to outline his proposed plans for the Stables and was reassured by the positive response. It was only when Tom's secretary brought in the coffee that the general benevolent atmosphere in the office altered.

'Mr Carstairs,' she said, placing the tray on the solid mahogany desk, 'your wife's on the phone. I told her Mr Craven was with you, but that only made her more insistent.'

Max froze in his chair, watching Tom pick up the receiver.

'Evangeline . . . Yes, dear, he's with me now. No, I haven't discussed it with him yet . . . but I will, I promise.'

Even from where he was sitting on the other side of the desk, Max discerned Evangeline's hysterical voice, shouting instructions to her husband. Tom hung up the phone with an audible sigh and looked Max straight in the eye.

'Max, this is all rather embarrassing, but I take it you went to The Firs yesterday afternoon.'

'Yes. If you remember, you and Evangeline both suggested I take a look at your spare room and Alison Bendict's . . .'

'Evangeline said you made a pass at her,' Tom broke in.

'That's a lie! I never even . . .'

'Oh, don't look so worried, Max. I certainly don't believe her. I know Evangeline only too well. I've had years of experience.'

Max was aghast. 'But why . . . ?'

'Why put up with it, or go along with that little charade on the phone a few moments ago? I'll tell you why, Max. Because in the circumstances I feel it's the least I can do.'

Max was puzzled. Tom Carstairs knew his wife had behaved like a common whore, yet in the circumstances felt it was the least he could do! The mind boggled.

'Don't look so shocked, Max. You see, I blame myself really.'

'I'm afraid I don't understand.'

'No, I don't expect you do. In fact I don't suppose a lot of people do, yet they must know about Evangeline and, well . . . you know.'

Tom shrugged his shoulders and continued. 'I suppose it all stems from the fact that I couldn't give Evangeline children. She desperately wanted a family, you know. I expect that surprises you, doesn't it? She adored your little girl and . . .' Recognizing the familiar pained expression on Max's face, Tom changed the subject slightly. 'Not only could I not provide Evangeline with the child she wanted, but I also failed her miserably in bed. Let's just say her needs were different from my own.'

Not knowing how to respond, Max sat in silence and absent-mindedly stirred his coffee.

Tom rose from his chair and walked slowly to the window where the sun's rays brushed his grey complexion with a healthy glow. 'You know, years ago I offered Evangeline a divorce, to give her the chance to have children with another man, but do you know what she said?'

Max shook his head.

'To love and to cherish . . . in sickness and in health, until death us do part. Odd, isn't it?'

Max refrained from advising Tom he had the order of service the wrong way round, nor did he query the unspoken words 'forsaking all other'. Instead he watched Tom return to his desk and sit down.

'In her own way, I believe Evangeline loves me, Max, and strange though it may seem I love her too. Always have and always will, which is why years ago I decided to turn a blind eye to her many men-friends.'

'Many! You mean . . . but how long ago? Oh! I'm sorry Tom, I have no absolutely no business to pry.'

Tom gave a wistful sigh. 'That's okay, Max. In fact, in a way, it's a great relief to be able to talk about it. I've never been able to before. It's not the sort of thing . . . is it?'

Nodding in agreement, Max considered their conversation. If Tom had known all along about Evangeline's infidelity, then had he also known . . . ?

He swallowed hard and felt a lump rise in his throat. It was now or never; he had to ask Tom about Virginia. 'Tom, yesterday Evangeline mentioned Virginia and I was wondering, did . . . ?'

'Virginia know about Evangeline's little affairs? Yes, of course she did. They were the best of friends, weren't they? In fact when you came back to Church Haywood with your wife and daughter, no one could have been more delighted than myself. It took Evangeline's mind off not having children and . . . well, let's just say she behaved herself for a bit.'

'That wasn't exactly what I was going to ask,' Max said softly. 'What I really wanted to know was . . . did Virginia . . . did my wife have men-friends too?'

There was an embarrassed silence as Tom shifted papers uneasily about his desk. He was no longer able to look Max in the eye.

'I want an honest answer, Tom,' Max pleaded. 'Please don't lie to me! I intend to find out one way or another.'

'No Max, Virginia didn't have men-friends plural . . . but I think there was one man, and I can only apologize if it was Evangeline who told you. She had no right!'

Max watched in stunned silence as Tom uncharacteristically slammed his fist on the desk top, sending the remains of the coffee-cup flying. Mopping up the coffee dregs with a spotless white handkerchief, Tom studied the soggy papers relating to the Stables.

'Will you . . . I mean, do you still intend to go ahead with this project?'

'I've given Bill Jessop my word.'

'That's not legally binding.'

'It is in my book,' Max replied curtly. 'Besides, I think I shall need something to take my mind off things.'

Tom held out his hand as Max made to leave. 'Max, I'm sorry, truly sorry. I can forgive Evangeline many things but not this. Do you think you could try and forget it?'

Confronted by the 'Craven glare', Tom knew what he'd just asked was virtually impossible.

Ignoring the unanswered question, Max turned to face Tom with a determined set of jaw. 'I want to know who he was . . . will you tell me his name?'

Tom shook his head sorrowfully and reached in his drawer for a black leather-bound bible. Placing his hand upon it, he replied simply, 'I honestly don't know'.

Storming in through the front door of Haywood Grange, Max was surprised to find Alison standing in the hallway. Acknowledging her with a brief nod, he strode past both Alison and his sister and made his way to the back staircase and the au pair's flat. It was then that he remembered Alison's letter given to him by Bill Jessop.

Some time later, when Connie knocked on the door, Max knew what was coming.

'I know,' he said opening the door, 'I was bloody rude to Alison and I apologize.'

Surprisingly, Connie didn't reprimand him. 'I know, dear, you've a great deal on your mind. I'm sure Alison understands.' Connie stood uneasily, fingering the single rope of pearls at her throat. 'Max, concerning Alison . . . there was something Bunty said the other day . . . Something about Tara's accident and what really happened. Only it would appear, perhaps we don't really know what happened that day after all.'

'Constance,' Max said, deliberately, 'you're my sister and I love you dearly, but as I wish to refrain from a full-blown argument, I really would appreciate it if you'd leave me alone.'

Watching Connie close the door behind her, Max re-read Alison's letter and wondered if he could take any more. First the revelation from Tom and Evangeline about his wife's infidelity and then Alison Benedict trying to make some excuse about Tara's accident.

111

Snatching a sheet of writing paper from the drawer, Max picked up his pen and wrote hurriedly with long sweeping strokes.

'Dear Miss Benedict, Mr Jessop has passed on your letter concerning the Stables. Much as I would like to help your business venture, I am unable to do so. I intend to live at the Stables myself.'

CHAPTER 9

At the breakfast table, Bunty watched Alison's eyes brim with tears as she read the newly delivered letter.

'I don't believe it!' Alison cried, 'I just don't believe it! How could he do such a thing?'

'Alison, my dear. Why, whatever's wrong?'

'It's the Stables, Bunty. I won't be able to have one of the units after all.'

'But that's not fair. I thought you said Mr Jessop agreed and you'd already written to him for confirmation.'

'I did,' sniffed Alison. 'Don't you remember? I wrote straight away when you advised me to . . . and even delivered the letter in person.'

'In that case, it isn't right! If Bill Jessop replied to your letter, then he's broken his word. We must do something about it, Alison.'

'Oh, it's nothing to do with Mr Jessop. He no longer owns the Stables. It would appear he agreed to sell them the day he received my letter.'

'Then what about the new owner? Surely he'll be interested in renting out the units? Perhaps you could write to him instead? Have you any idea who he is?'

'Oh, yes. Very much so. In fact you can see for yourself who the new owner is.' Alison pushed the sheet of fine quality cotton writing paper across the table and reached for her handkerchief.

In silence Bunty read and re-read the brief letter, recognizing from the card he sent each Christmas the familiar, bold, black scrawl of the signature belonging to Max Craven!

'Max . . . I don't believe it!'

'I've already said that . . . twice in fact, I think.' Alison added weakly.

'But what on earth does Max want with a place the size of the Stables? He surely can't mean to live there all alone.'

'Perhaps he's got a new girlfriend.'

'Nonsense! If Max had a new girlfriend, Connie would be the first to know about it. You forget she's Max's sister.'

'And you forget Max Craven also happens to be extremely remote and aloof. Even verging on the rude, if you want my opinion.'

Alison was thinking back to the earlier meeting in the churchyard and the more recent, abrupt acknowledgement at Haywood Grange.

'I admit he can give the appearance of being a bit stand-offish,' Bunty said, folding the letter and replacing it in its envelope, 'but I've known Max since he was a small boy. Mark my words, there's something deeper going on in that stubborn head of his that's prompted all this.'

When Friday came, Max viewed Nigel's imminent arrival with mixed feelings. On the one hand it would be good to see his business partner again. On the other, there was the prospect of introducing Nigel to the locals. The only consolation being, there were bound to be hundreds of people attending the Church Haywood summer fête. With luck, at some opportune moment, Max and Nigel could slip away unnoticed.

There was precious little chance of Max going unnoticed however, at least by Bunty and Alison, when they arrived to help set up the stalls for the tombola and bran tub. Connie looked up and waved.

'Hello, you two, glad you could spare the time. Thank goodness the weather forecast is good for tomorrow. Max and George are already inside the marquee, setting up tables for the produce show.'

Bunty popped her head round the corner of the canvas flap and called in George's direction. Max she simply ignored.

'You don't have to ignore him on my account,' Alison hissed under her breath. 'It's me he's upset, not you.'

'Don't you believe it, Alison. I might look tough and thick-skinned but believe me, beneath all this excess of cellulite, I can feel hurt and betrayal just as much as you.'

'Oh, Bunty,' Alison sighed, 'what would I do without you?'

'Don't forget you're going to have to manage without me when I go to Australia.'

'That's not until December.'

'I know, my dear, and in the meantime we're jolly well going to have to rack our brains about finding you somewhere else to set up shop. Did you manage to get in contact with the "glass lady" who was also hoping to rent one of the Stables' units.'

'Who's talking about the units?' George enquired,

115

walking through to collect another trestle table.

'I was,' replied Bunty acidly, 'and I don't mind saying I think it's pretty despicable of Max to let Alison down, particularly when she'd built her hopes up so much.'

'I'm sorry, Bunty, I'm afraid you've lost me.' George rested the table against the side of the marquee. 'How has Max let Alison down?'

Too embarrassed to remain in the vicinity with Bunty explaining the delicate situation, Alison wandered off back to the car park. There she was in the process of removing the large cardboard box, containing sheets to cover the produce tables when her attention was taken by a flash of red shiny metal.

'Excuse me,' said the driver of the gleaming, red sports car, 'I wonder, have I arrived in the right place to find Max Craven? The gardener at Haywood Grange – did he say his name was Jennings? – said I would probably find him here and would I give him these?'

Alison noticed the stranger was carrying a vicious-looking pair of wire cutters in one hand and a roll of heavy-duty wire in the other. Oh, yes, he's here all right, she wanted to say. Instead she merely nodded and closing the boot of the car replied. 'Mr Craven's in the large marquee. Perhaps if you'd care to follow me.'

'Only if you'll let me carry that box. It looks pretty heavy.' Nigel peered into the box at the layers of sheets, then at the wire-cutters he was holding. 'I say, what is this? Shrouds and instruments for the sacrificial slaughter?'

Alison smiled weakly and found herself thinking of someone she would like to slaughter at that very moment. Only, knowing her luck of late, it would probably end up with Max performing the sacrificial ritual and herself on the receiving end. She was after all what was required, if all the Dennis Wheatley books she'd read as a teenager were correct, by way of being the pure and innocent, unsullied local virgin.

'You'll find Mr Craven in there.' Alison motioned towards the marquee.

'And where do you want the box?'

'Oh, that's to go in the marquee too, but don't worry, I can manage.'

'No way!' remonstrated Nigel, placing the cutters on the sheets and looping the wire on his arm. 'If I can't be a knight in shining armour here in this picturesque setting of Church Haywood, then where can I be? Certainly not in London,' he continued. 'The last time I offered to help a young lady in London, she thought I was going to mug her!'

Studying his Burberry tweeds and expensive leather brogues, Alison thought Nigel, with his beaming smiling face, looked anything but a mugger.

Recognizing the familiar voice, Max looked up as Alison lifted the canvas flap for Nigel to enter.

'Nigel! What the . . . ? How on earth did you know I was here?'

'Sent on a mission by Merlin the wizard, or in this case Jennings the gardener, he of the long white beard. I was then helped on my way by a charming sea-sprite and I come bearing gifts.'

To Alison's surprise, Max roared with laughter when he saw the contents of the box Nigel was carrying and he made the connection with Alison's newly cropped urchin cut and her sweatshirt, decorated with appliquéd sea-horses.

'Nigel, have you been drinking?'

'Haven't touched a drop, my friend. That isn't to say I don't intend to, once you've finished here for the evening. I trust we can walk to the local hostelry?'

Patting his friend warmly on the back, Max relieved Nigel of the box and directed him to the far end of the marquee where George was erecting the last of the tables. Alison meanwhile, still smarting from the shock of Max's letter, returned to Bunty's side.

There she overheard Bunty whisper to Connie, '. . . Well, I for one think it's pretty underhand, Connie. Perhaps you could persuade Max to reconsider. Lord knows, he doesn't want all of that vast place to himself, does he?'

Connie shook her head sadly. 'I'll try, but he's been so . . .' Seeing Alison approach, Connie continued, 'Bunty's been telling me all about it, Alison. I can't promise, of course, but I'll see if I can persuade Max to change his mind.'

'Oh no! I'd rather you didn't. I . . .'

'But Alison,' Bunty interrupted, 'you're going to need somewhere to work.'

'I know, but in the interim, Evangeline rang me only this evening, just as we were leaving, and said she'd like me to redesign her bedroom. For the moment at least I've something to do.'

'Of course, Evangeline!' Connie continued. 'Max was only saying yesterday what a wonderful job you'd made of their spare room. He was very impressed, you know. He thinks you're very talented and should do very well as an interior designer.'

'Hmph!' muttered Alison miserably, walking back to the car. 'If that's the sort of encouragement he gives to people whose work he admires, I'm better off without it, thank you very much!'

Bunty said nothing in reply; her thoughts were elsewhere.

On the Saturday morning, the villagers of Church Haywood woke to clear blue skies and brilliant sunshine. Placing the last slices of bread in the toaster, Connie gave a deep sigh. 'Thank heavens for that; at least we should get a good turn out. With all the restoration work needed on St Faith's, we have to make as much money as possible.'

Nigel buttered a slice of wholemeal toast and reached for the marmalade. 'That was a wonderful breakfast, Connie. I can't remember the last time I breakfasted so well. With Vanessa it's just yoghurt and muesli. And you know, if I eat any more of the latter, I swear I shall end up with buck teeth. I'm convinced it's really rabbit food in fancy packaging.'

Connie smiled and filled Nigel's cup with freshly brewed tea. 'It's nice to see someone eat breakfast. Most of the time I can only tempt Max with tea and toast.'

'What! You mean to say you're still waiting on him, the lazy so-and-so? No wonder he's looking much better.'

'Not for much longer,' Max broke in. 'Waiting on me, I mean. I shall soon be moving out.'

Connie looked up in alarm. 'But that's preposterous! You can't even consider moving into the Stables just yet. They're not even fit for horses at the moment, let alone humans!'

'Stables?' queried Nigel. 'What have you been keeping from me, Max?'

Later, walking to the fête, Max explained his proposed new venture.

'At first I thought I might let the place. Then one thing led to another and I ended up thinking, why not live there?'

'From what you say, it sounds pretty impressive, so when shall I get to see what Connie refers to as "Craven's Stables?" '

'I'll take you this afternoon,' Max replied, 'once the fête's in full swing and I'm no longer needed.'

Nigel's face lit up on hearing the sound of the Boys' Brigade Band fill the air. On high hung red, white and blue bunting and somewhere across the field a wayward balloon shot skyward, whisked away by a sudden gust of wind. Hearing a child's plaintive cry, Nigel's eyes scanned the crowd for the unhappy youngster.

'I know just how he feels; exactly the same thing happened to me once. I pestered my mother all afternoon for a balloon and the minute I got one I let it go. I remember I bawled my eyes out for the rest of the day.'

Knowing his partner as he did, Max thought it unlikely Nigel could ever be miserable. It must be wonderful to be so positive, in fact. Which was why, at that precise moment, Max decided, as far as his new venture was concerned, he would only let positive thoughts occupy his mind from now on. He'd had more than enough negative moments this past week. First with Evangeline, and then Connie chattering on persistently about Alison. Now it was time, he concluded, to concentrate on Craven's Stables.

Unfortunately, as the afternoon wore on, Max discovered things weren't going to be quite so easygoing and straightforward as he'd hoped.

Breathing in the air filled with the aroma of frying onions for hot dogs and the sweet smell of candy floss, Nigel's face shone like a child's. 'You know, Max, this is all truly amazing. I haven't been to anything like this for years. To be honest, I didn't think village fêtes like this still existed. Come on, how about a hot dog?'

Declining Nigel's offer, Max watched in bemused silence as Nigel painstakingly squeezed first a layer of mustard along the entire length of his hot dog, before topping it with another of tomato sauce.

'I don't know how you can,' Max teased. 'Just wait until I tell Vanessa.'

'You wouldn't dare,' came the muffled reply. Nigel savoured his first bite and a surplus blob of ketchup dropped on to his shirt.

Walking across the field, Nigel caught sight of Alison, who was again wearing blue. 'I say isn't that my sea-sprite? What a wonderful colour that is. It always reminds me of Vanessa in her blue silk.'

Max followed Nigel's gaze to where Alison, dressed in blue chambray, was talking to the vicar. 'Oh, you mean the girl talking to Reverend Mr Hope?'

'Young woman, more like!' Nigel replied. 'Well, as he's the Reverend Mr Hope, who would that be, Faith or Charity? You know you never did introduce us last night. Damned rude of you I thought at the time, too, Max.'

Finishing his hotdog and wiping his mouth with a handkerchief, Nigel continued, 'Mind you I can quite understand why you'd want to keep the little sea-sprite a secret. And I thought you said there weren't any decent women in Church Haywood.'

Pondering Nigel's reference to Hope, Faith and Charity, Max explained. 'Oh, you mean Alison Benedict. She was a friend of Tara's. Her mother died recently and . . .'

'Was that the funeral you mentioned, the day you left Craven and Painton?'

'Good heavens, Nigel! You've got a good memory. I'd better watch what I say in future.'

'And that child had better watch where she's going or else . . .'

It was too late. Having just made her lucky dip from the bran tub, Rosie Jennings was running to catch up with her grandfather when she tripped over a tent peg and went crashing to the ground. Momentarily stunned, she studied the gash on her leg with delight. It was only when she examined her newly acquired bran tub toy that she burst into floods of tears.

'But it's broken,' she sobbed. 'It's all broken.'

'I don't think so,' said Nigel, rushing to her side and examining the injured leg. 'What do you think, Max? Not broken, but certainly a very nasty cut.'

Max knelt down on the grass to examine Rosie's knee. 'No, no broken bones, but it's bleeding quite badly. I think we'd better use a handkerchief to . . .'

'But it is broken!' Rosie remonstrated, holding up the model aeroplane. 'Look the wing's all smashed and the nose is all bent.'

Max looked at Nigel in amusement. So it wasn't the injured leg that was upsetting the child, it was the broken toy. Nigel produced his ketchup-stained handkerchief and shook his head. 'I don't think we'd better use this. Covered in all that sauce and mustard, it's not very hygienic, is it?'

'And mine's not white, it's Paisley,' said Max, producing a patterned handkerchief from his trouser pocket.

Rosie's face lit up. 'Gosh, is that a real cowboy's handkerchief you got there, mister?'

'Happen it is,' drawled Nigel in true John Wayne fashion. 'Would you like my pardner to tie it round your leg, to make it better?'

'Wow! Yeah,' came the delighted reply. 'Will you, mister?'

'Why sure thing, missie,' Max continued, influenced by Nigel's attempt at a western accent. 'And if you want us to help you find your folks, well, just hop on to my shoulders.'

Revelling in this new-found attention, Rosie studied both men carefully and then burst into tears once more.

'Oh, dear, what's the matter? Look if you're upset about your plane I'm sure we can find you another.'

Through her tears, Rosie gazed up at Max and sniffed. 'S'not the plane. It's me dad, he said I was never to go wiv strangers and I was to stay wiv me grandad . . . only I don't know where he is now . . .'

'I swear you'll be quite safe with us,' Nigel interrupted. 'Scout's honour.'

'Scouts is stupid! Me brother was a Scout,' echoed a voice.

Tying the folded hankerchief on Rosie's leg, Max looked in Nigel's direction and whispered. 'She's got a point, you know. We can't be too careful, can we? Don't want to be accused of child-molesting.'

'But we can't leave her here, Max. That cut looks

pretty deep and needs attention. Also, no one else around here seems to be taking too much notice of her.'

Lifting Rosie high into the air, Max said cautiously. 'Look, why don't you sit on my shoulders? That way you might be able to see your dad or your grandad. Perhaps you could also tell us your name.'

'Rosie . . . Rosie Jenn' gs.'

'Rosie, that's a nice name.' Nigel announced.

'No, it's not. It's stupid! I want to be called Clint or Tom, but me mum won't let me. And at that stupid chris'nin' the other week, the vicar splashed water all over me face and called me Rosemary. Ugh!'

With Rosie unable to see Max's face from where she was sitting, he allowed his face to break into a broad grin. Nigel meanwhile suppressed his smile with a ketchup-stained handkerchief and pretended to sneeze.

'Where were you last?' Max enquired, attempting to solve the mystery of the lost child. 'Perhaps someone there will recognize you.'

'At the bran tub. That silly woman wouldn't let me pick from the boys' barrel. I didn't want no stupid girls' toys. Then Al'son came along and said if I wanted a boy's toy, I could have a boy's toy! I like Al'son, she's nice. I told me mum Al'son never wears skirts and dresses so I . . .'

Listening to this garbled conversation, Max could only assume the 'silly woman' Rosie was referring to was his sister Constance. He also assumed correctly that Alison had probably taken over from her at the bran tub. 'Right, then,' Max called triumphantly. 'I think we're on the right track, Rosie, so hold tight.'

Alison looked up in surprise to see Max, followed by

Nigel, trotting along with a small child on his shoulders. She stood open-mouthed.

'It's broken, Al'son,' Rosie called down tearfully.

'Oh, dear!' gasped Alison in alarm. 'Then we must get you to the first aid tent.'

'No, not her leg,' whispered Max, as Alison's gaze rested on the injured limb. 'Her aeroplane. It looks as if it's been in the Battle of Britain.'

'Don't be daft, mister. They didn't have Concordes at the Battle of Britain, they had Spitfires and . . .'

Max raised a quizzical eyebrow and looked towards Alison for help.

'She said she was here only recently. Apparently her name's Rosie Jennings or something . . . Would you happen to know who she belongs to?'

Suppressing a giggle, Alison turned to Max and Nigel. 'Of course I do. You should too, Max. It's Mr Jennings' granddaughter – Connie's gardener, remember?'

'But I thought she said. Oh, I see now! Rosie – Rosie Jennings!'

'That's what I said, mister!' came the retort from the direction of Max's shoulders.

'Otherwise known as Clint . . . after Clint Eastwood, I suspect,' broke in Nigel '. . . or Tom after . . . ?'

'Tom Cruise,' explained Alison, in *Top Gun*.'

Talk of *Top Gun* reminded Rosie about her plane. She held it out for Alison's examination. 'Al'son, can I have another Concorde please?'

Alison studied the plastic dustbin filled with sawdust. 'Oh, Rosie. I'm afraid we can't open every parcel just to find another Concorde. It wouldn't be fair on the other boys . . . or girls . . . would it?'

'S'pose not,' sighed Rosie, tugging at the knot on Max's handkerchief.

'I know, what we can do,' Nigel announced cheerfully, and three pairs of eyes turned expectantly in his direction.

CHAPTER 10

'Look, trust me . . . er . . . Alison. That's if I can call you Alison. I'm Nigel, by the way . . . Nigel Painton. We'll ignore my friend Max here as he was so rude as not to introduce us yesterday evening.'

Nigel held out his hand and Alison responded. Concerned about Rosie's welfare, she'd forgotten how upset she'd been to receive Max's letter, until Nigel mentioned the word 'rude'. So, she wasn't the only person to think ill of Max Craven. Yet somehow, seeing him trotting along with Rosie shouting, 'Giddy up, mister,' astride his shoulders made her wonder if this was the same Max Craven she'd first encountered in the churchyard.

He must be a Gemini, Alison thought to herself: split personality and all that – two people. One nice and the other . . .

'Alison?' queried Nigel. 'As I was saying – trust me, or at least agree to my suggestion? What do you think?'

'I don't know. I've only just come on duty, to take over from Connie at the bran tub. I can't leave it unattended.'

'No one is asking you to. I'll take over . . .'

127

'What!' exclaimed Max. 'You'll take over? But you don't know . . .'

'Of course I know what to do. I merely take the money, direct the boys to the boys' tub and the girls to the girls'. Isn't that right, Alison?'

'Not exactly,' replied Alison, looking knowingly in Rosie's direction, where she was peering with delight at the trail of congealed blood oozing down her leg.

Nigel nodded in understanding and turned to face Max. 'Right, that's sorted, then. You and Alison take Rosie to the first-aid tent to get her leg seen to and then go and look for her father or grandfather. It will be more respectable if you go together. Rosie's far too heavy for Alison to carry and, as you say, you can't take her on your own.'

Unaware of the conflict between the pair, Nigel nudged Alison towards Max with a, 'Don't worry about me, I'll get along just fine,' and a jovial, 'So long, pardner,' to Rosie.

'Bye, mister, see ya.'

Watching the St John Ambulance volunteer clean Rosie's leg, Max whispered to Alison, 'Do you think it's going to need stitching?'

'I doubt it. It doesn't look half so bad now most of the blood's been cleaned away.'

'She won't like that.'

'Won't she? Why?'

'Because when Nigel and I picked her up, she seemed positively delighted with her injury. She probably thinks of it as a war wound or something. By the way, did she really have a battle with my sister over the bran tub? She told me she thought Constance was a silly woman!'

Alison nodded thoughtfully and smiled. 'So I gather. Rosie's such a tomboy but as I said to Connie, if she wanted to pick from the boys' bran tub, what harm would it do?'

A few moments later, Rosie came running over, waving Max's handkerchief in the air.

'Hey! Take it easy,' Max called. 'We don't want you falling over again, do we?' He winked in Alison's direction. 'Especially as we've got to go and round up your folks, er – Clint.'

Rosie giggled and reached out for Max's hand. 'Do you want to ride on my shoulders again?' he enquired.

'No thanks, mister. 'Cos like this I can hold your hand and Al'son's too. Al'son,' came the inquisitive voice, 'why have you got legs today?'

'Oh, you mean why am I wearing a dress? That's because it's a special day, Rosie. I thought it would be nice to wear something pretty.'

'But you never wear anythin' pretty, Al'son, you always wear jeans and sweatshirts, 'cept when you're at chris'nins. Anyway, what do you think, mister? Don't you think Al'son looks better in jeans?'

Rosie fingered the soft blue chambray fabric encircling Alison's legs. It didn't look right somehow, seeing Alison's calves and ankles. She waited expectantly for Max's reply.

'I think Alison looks very pretty . . . in both jeans and dresses.'

Oblivious to Alison's blushes, Rosie sighed and kicked at a soft drinks can lying in the grass. 'Goal!' she shouted triumphantly, watching it land between the wheels of a pram.

'Rosie! Where the hell have you been? I've been

129

looking all over the place for you and your grandad's been worried sick. We thought we'd lost you!'

'Sorry, Dad, I . . .'

'Just you wait till I get you home . . .'

Max coughed politely. 'Rosie had a bad fall. My colleague and I found her and decided we should take her to the first-aid tent.'

Suddenly aware of Rosie's companions, Darren Jennings looked up in a state of confusion.

'Oh! I'm sorry. It's just that you hear such terrible things about kids these days and we thought . . . Rosie, your leg – what have you done?'

'It's okay, Darren,' Alison explained. 'It's not as deep as we first thought, though I expect it will leave quite a scar.'

'A scar! Yippee! Just wait till I show 'em at school.' Rosie went bouncing around the pram that carried her baby brother. She was already thinking of the wonderful scab she would have to show her friends. And, if she picked it when Mum wasn't looking, then she would have an even better scar to show them. How simply great! All she had to do now was find her grandad, so they could compare war wounds.

'Grandad! Grandad! I fell over an' cut me leg and . . .'

'Why, if it isn't my little cowboy! I've been looking everywhere for you. I thought you'd been captured by Red Indians!'

Darren Jennings sighed and turned to Alison and Max. 'No wonder she's as bad as she is. He's forever encouraging her. The wife worries like mad about her . . .'

'Don't worry, it won't last,' Alison broke in kindly. 'I

130

remember I was always . . .' but she stopped herself. Max was watching and listening. Somehow it seemed suddenly inappropriate to mention what she used to get up to when she was small.

Smoothing down his long white beard, Harry Jennings walked over to Max and held out his hand. 'Mr Craven, thank you. Rosie's been telling me all about her adventures . . .'

With Max's and Rosie's attention elsewhere, Alison peeped into the pram at the sleeping baby. All rosy and pink, newly changed and fed, he looked the picture of contentment. Gazing down at him, she felt an unfamiliar stirring in her stomach. Babies. Would she ever have babies? Years ago she'd vowed she would *never* have babies. Especially if you had to let a man . . . and especially after what she and Tara had seen.

A grubby hand reached for Alison's and she heard a voice ask softly, 'Al'son, what about my plane?'

'Your plane! Of course I'd quite forgotten, how silly of me.'

'What's this about a plane?' Darren Jennings enquired.

'Al'son and the man said I could have a new one. Isn't that right, mister?'

'Mr Craven to you, young lady!' old Mr Jennings corrected. 'And anyway, you musn't go round asking people for toys . . .'

'But I din't!'

'No, she din't – I mean didn't,' Max protested. 'Rosie broke her plane when she fell over. She was very brave when the St John Ambulance lady dressed her leg and we thought she deserved a new one.'

Suitably mollified, Harry and Darren Jennings al-

131

lowed Rosie to head in the direction of the village toy shop for a replacement Concorde.

'I only hope we can find one,' Max murmured in a low voice to Alison as he hoisted Rosie once more on to his shoulders.

Twenty minutes later, lovingly clutching her new plane, Rosie called down to Max and Alison.

'If God's on his cloud, do you think he can see my new plane?'

Alison cast Max a furtive glance and replied, 'I expect so.'

Rosie extended her plane high into the air with a contented sigh.

'That's good then, 'cos God loves Concorde too.' Sensing the grown-ups' air of bewilderment, Rosie explained. 'In church, at the chris'nin', the vicar said God loves Concorde. He did, honest. I heard him!'

'Actually, she's right,' Alison whispered, with a bemused smile.

'You're joking!' hissed Max. 'Surely you don't expect me to . . .'

'During the service for morning prayer, it does say "God, who art the author of peace and lover of concord". Of course that's not quite how Rosie's interpreted it, but it's true nonetheless. Perhaps you should go to church some time and hear for yourself.'

'I stopped going to church when my wife died,' Max said through tight lips, 'and vowed never to go again.'

The rest of the journey back to Rosie's house was spent in silence.

Relieved of his duties at the now depleted bran tubs, Nigel hurried towards Max's car.

'So our young friend "Clint Cruise" has been returned safely to her folks at the ranch, then.'

Max nodded and switched on the ignition. 'That's right, and she's now the owner of a brand new Concorde aeroplane. By the way, here's your change.'

'I hope there wasn't any trouble with her parents over that.'

'No, not once Alison and I explained. You know you really didn't have to pay for it, Nigel; I would willingly have . . .'

'I know, Max, but the kid deserved it for pure entertainment value alone. I'm only sorry Vanessa wasn't here to witness it, that's all.'

'Do I detect a note of broodiness in your voice, my friend? A sudden desire to settle down and raise a family perhaps?'

'Quite possibly,' said Nigel in reply. 'I must admit, seeing you and Alison with little Rosie between you, I got to thinking . . . You know, you certainly made a charming picture.'

Recognizing the shuttered look on Max's face, Nigel changed the subject immediately. 'Right, then, let's go and take a look at the famous Craven's Stables I've been hearing so much about!'

Returning to Haywood Grange, Max was surprised to find Connie on the front door step talking to Harry Jennings.

'Why, if it isn't my friend Merlin!' Nigel exclaimed. 'What's he doing here at this time on a Saturday evening?'

'Your friend Merlin just happens to be our friend Clint's grandad. Surely you hadn't forgotten? Oh, dear, I hope this doesn't mean she's gone missing again.'

With a worried frown, Max hurried from the car towards Connie.

'Max, Mr Jennings has just called over to thank you again for looking after Rosie this afternoon.'

'That's right, Mr Craven.' Harry held out his hand. In it was a child's drawing. 'Rosie did this for you after she had her bath. She wanted to bring it over herself but Michelle said no, it was far too late. Anyway she insisted I brought it over and wouldn't go to bed until I promised. Besides,' he grinned, 'I knew I wouldn't get any peace until I did. I'm sorry to disturb your Saturday evening.'

Max took the picture graciously and smiled at the subject matter. There was Rosie sitting on Max's shoulders, proudly holding her new plane. Complete with fixed Cheshire-cat grin and gashed knee (with the blood so painstakingly detailed) there was no mistaking the tousle-haired youngster who'd caused Max to smile more than once that afternoon.

'I've another in my pocket for Alison,' Harry announced. 'I think it's supposed to be of the three of you. You can judge for yourself.'

Harry reached into his pocket and pulled out the second picture. Sure enough there were the Max, Alison and Rosie look-a-likes. Rosie with extraordinary long arms reaching up for Max and Alison's hands, and Alison with equally extraordinary long legs, wearing a blue dress and blue shoes.

'Our Rosie's certainly a character,' Harry announced with a grin. 'She fair wears us all out, yet surprisingly she adores her great-grannie and sits with her for hours chattering away and drawing her pictures.'

'You mean to say your mother's still alive!' Max asked in amazement.

'Oh, yes, and still going strong. She's ninety-five now, you know. Of course she's been house-bound for years – apart from when we take her out in her wheelchair. And her memory. Why, that's simply amazing. Only this afternoon, when Rosie was describing her adventures, mother remembered back to when you were a small boy, Mr Craven. She also told Rosie how Alison used to make your little girl daisy-chain necklaces.'

For the first time in ages, Max didn't shy away from the mention of Tara. Instead, leaving Nigel to give Connie his opinion of Craven's Stables, something prompted him to walk with Harry to the main gates.

'Of course,' Harry continued thoughtfully, pushing his bike along the gravelled drive, 'there was a time years ago when we all wondered if Alison would ever walk again. She was a brave lass, you know, Mr Craven. Mother said at the time she'd never seen Alison run so fast. She even caught up with your daughter at one point and tried to stop her running in front of that car. Mother said it was like watching those animals, what are they called . . . lemmings or something? Anyway, even though your Tara saw the car she still ran straight out in front of it, while poor Alison tried to drag her back. Apparently your lass never stood a chance and Alison's leg was trapped between the car and the wall.'

Max stood in stunned silence. Alison had tried to stop Tara from running in front of the car? Surely not! That wasn't what had been stated at the inquest. There must be some mistake. Desperate to ask Harry to repeat what

135

he'd just said, Max heard Connie's voice calling from the house.

Max hesitated. 'Harry, about your mother . . . ?'

'Yes, Mr Craven?'

'Oh, it doesn't matter. Another time; my sister's calling. Thank Rosie for her delightful picture, will you, and remember me to your mother?

'Will do, Mr Craven. Why don't you pop over and see her some time? I'm sure she'd be tickled pink to see you again. Well, I'd better get on my way and deliver Alison's drawing. No doubt Rosie will be peering anxiously from her bedroom window, waiting for my return.'

With Harry's revelations ringing in his ears, Max walked to the front door where Connie and Nigel were waiting. His feet felt like lead weights and his mind struggled to recall Harry's every word.

'Your lass never stood a chance and Alison's leg was trapped . . .'

Alison's leg! Max puzzled. He never did get the explanation from George and Connie about Alison's leg. In the distant past he had a vague recollection that Alison used to be an asthmatic. And what was it Connie had said the other day, when she and Bunty had been talking about the accident?

'Max, dear, you look exhausted. I'm not surprised, if what Mr Jennings says is true and you've been carrying Rosie about for the best part of the afternoon. Supper won't be for at least another hour. That's if you and Nigel haven't changed your minds about joining us. Why don't you go and have a shower? I see you've both got blood on your shirts. Presumably from Rosie's knee?'

Nigel grinned. 'Max's is the genuine article all right, Connie, but I have to confess mine is tomato ketchup. I had a hot dog and sort of overdid it with the sauce. Serves me right for being so greedy.'

'In that case you'd both better go and change,' Connie insisted. Smelling the air as she walked indoors, she added, 'You know, I think we've been exceptionally lucky with the weather today. If my nose serves me correctly, I'd be prepared to bet we're in for some rain.'

At Keeper's Cottage, Alison woke with a start. The bedroom window, having worked loose from its catch, was banging rhythmically with the wind. Quickly running to the window to close it, she caught sight of the sheets Bunty had decided to peg out before they went to bed.

They were from the box Nigel had carried into the marquee yesterday evening. The same sheets he'd described as shrouds. In the eerie moonlight, with the sheets casting ghostly shadows about the garden, Alison found herself thinking of Max and the odd way he'd looked at her when they were taking Rosie to buy a replacement Concorde.

Returning to bed, with a strange stirring in the pit of her stomach, Alison pulled the sheet and patchwork quilt closely about her, and prayed desperately for sleep to calm her troubled thoughts. Every time she closed her eyes however, she 'saw' Max Craven smiling down at her, with Rosie sitting merrily astride his shoulders.

'Go away, Max!' Alison murmured softly. 'Please go away and leave me alone. I mustn't feel even remotely attracted to you. You blame me for Tara's death and I have to go along with that . . . letting you believe it at least for as long as we're both living here.'

But Max wouldn't go away, not even as Alison slept. In her dreams he appeared before her looking as dark as night. Dressed in a magician's robe, covered in gold crescent moons and blue chambray stars, his steely gaze chilled her very soul. Even Nigel was there too. Dressed in white, with a red stain on the fabric at his chest and carrying . . . What was he carrying? A pair of wire cutters and a roll of garden wire!

Tossing and turning in her sleep, Alison then saw herself. Wearing only a filmy white shroud, she was being dragged in by a midget. Only it wasn't a midget. It was Rosie!

'Come along, Al'son,' Rosie was saying, 'Mister wants you. He wants you 'cos you're pretty. He wants to see your legs. I told you, you should have worn jeans.'

Propped between Rosie and Nigel, Alison was aware of Max walking towards her and with her heart beating wildly in her breast, she was swept into his arms and carried to the sacrificial altar. Struggling, she fought hard against him, feeling the heaviness of his body and his warm breath against her throat.

'No!' she cried, forcing him away, her hands entwining themselves in his thick hair as she did so. 'No!'

'Jasper! You bad dog! Stop slobbering at Alison's throat and get off her bed this minute!' Bunty's voice echoed from the bedroom door. 'I'm so sorry, my dear, did he startle you?'

Rubbing her eyes and trying to acclimatize herself to the semi-gloom, Alison peered to where Bunty stood framed in the doorawy.

138

'I think there's a storm brewing,' Bunty explained, 'so I thought I'd better get those sheets in – before they get blown away. That wretched animal must have shot past without me realizing. When I heard you call out and I saw he wasn't in his basket, I put two and two together. I bet you thought you were being attacked by some evil hairy monster.'

'Something like that,' Alison said shakily, reaching for the glass of water on the bedside table.

'I knew we shouldn't have had that cheese for supper,' Bunty called behind her as, grabbing Jasper by the collar, she marched him back downstairs to the kitchen and his basket.

At Haywood Grange, Max was also experiencing a troubled night. Unlike Alison, however, he hadn't even attempted sleep. His mind was too active, too preoccupied with a jumble of thoughts racing in his head. Too preoccupied in fact with an unsolved puzzle.

In some ways Max's current puzzle reminded him of one he'd bought at a church fête years ago. Then, as a small boy, he'd set about completing the newly purchased jigsaw, only to find to his bitter disappointment that there was a piece missing. In Max's eyes the puzzle was no good! Incomplete, it was useless! Even as a young boy, Max Craven had always required perfection.

'Perfection.' He sighed wearily, rubbing at tired eyes. 'Has that been my problem? Wanting things to be too perfect?' Virginia had been perfect, hadn't she? The perfect wife and mother, or at least so he'd thought until his recent encounter with Evangeline.

Tara too – hadn't she been the perfect daughter? Always so beautifully behaved. A joy to encounter,

139

enjoying life to the full and never one to cause trouble. Yet, according to Harry Jennings, Tara had not only deliberately run out in front of the car, she'd nearly been the cause of Alison's death too. And what about the driver of the car? Until now Max had never even considered him. 'Poor bastard,' Max whispered, 'I bet he never got over it.'

Walking into the galley kitchen of the flat, Max was secretly glad Nigel was staying in Connie's guest room. Seeing Max drink whisky at two o'clock in the morning would doubtless arouse suspicion. Filling his glass yet again, Max fetched a fresh sheet of writing paper and began jotting down everything and anything that suddenly seemed relevant.

At the top he put '1. Alison's leg. Why is this a mystery?' And underneath continued in numerical order, until he had the following,

2. Why did Tara run in front of the car?
3. Virginia. Who was her lover?
4. Why did her lover leave her and when?
5. Was the fire really an accident?

CHAPTER 11

On Sunday morning, Max woke with a heavy head to discover equally heavy skies laden with rain. Hearing a frantic knocking at the door, he quickly hid the whisky bottle. Then, hurriedly folding the piece of paper with the last word 'accident', underlined in broad black strokes, he placed it in the drawer alongside Alison's letter.

'Oh, good, you are up.' Nigel said, brightly. 'In that case you can take me to church. I want to see the famous Reverend Mr Hope in action. Connie tells me St Faith's is a wonderful church to worship in.'

So that was it, Max thought angrily. This was his sister's doing. Ever since he'd returned to Church Haywood, Constance had been trying to get him to go to church with her. Now she'd even put Nigel up to it.

'I don't . . .' Max began.

'Whatever you were going to say, Max, I refuse to listen,' Nigel interrupted. 'We must go and give thanks for yesterday's wonderful weather and the success of that amazing fête. Don't forget, I have to leave for London before lunch, so you'll soon be rid of me.'

Locking the flat, Max followed Nigel in silence to the front door where they were met by a beaming Connie. Though it was not in her nature to gloat, she nevertheless patted Nigel on the back and mouthed a silent 'well done' when Max wasn't looking.

'Who knows,' said Nigel, walking through the churchyard, 'I might even see my friend Merlin and the sea-sprite again. I don't suppose our little "Clint" will be in church, will she?'

'I very much doubt it,' replied Max with a wry smile. 'Our little Clint probably has better things to do, like playing with her aeroplanes. I expect she only comes to church for "chris'nin's".'

Listening to the Reverend read the order of morning service, Max let his gaze drift around the church. Constance was right. St Faith's was a wonderful church. All those beautiful stained glass windows set in mellow sandstone and . . .

'Author of peace and lover of concord,' Reverend Mr Hope intoned, causing Max to start and look across to the pew Alison was sharing with Bunty. Willing her to look in his direction, he was not disappointed when she met his questioning gaze with a brief but knowing smile.

'I stand corrected,' Max whispered softly, after the service and followed her to the back of the church where the congregation hovered, waiting for coffee and biscuits.

'I shan't say I told you so,' teased Alison good-naturedly, 'but I'm quite sure you didn't believe me yesterday, did you?'

For a moment Max hesitated and looked into her eyes. Yesterday, against the blue chambray, Alison's eyes had appeared a clear blue; today however against the blackness of her raincoat they looked different . . . like . . .

'Stormy seas,' he murmured to himself.

Alison looked up with a puzzled frown.

'Oh! I . . . was thinking, if this weather gets any worse we could be in for a storm.'

'Perhaps the Reverend knows something we don't.'

This time it was Max's turn to look bewildered.

'His choice of closing hymn, or didn't you notice?'

Max raised a quizzical eyebrow.

' "For Those in Peril on the Sea",' she enlightened him.

'Of course,' came the none too convincing reply. 'I trust you received your picture from our budding Picasso.' Max passed Alison a coffee from the tray Bunty was holding.

'Yes.' She grinned. 'And did you notice the emphasis she placed on my legs? Poor Rosie, I think she was quite disgusted, seeing me in a dress. It must have been quite a shock for her.'

Mention of Alison's long legs caused Max to look in their direction. Today, however, they were barely visible beneath the mid-calf-length raincoat, and her slender feet were hidden in black-buttoned ankle boots.

Aware of his penetrating gaze sweeping over her from top to toe, Alison felt her cheeks flush with colour. Nervously, she sipped at her coffee, anxious for a diversion.

'Well, that looks promising,' Bunty hissed to Connie, returning the empty tray to the table behind the screen. 'At least today they're speaking.'

Connie raised her eyes towards the altar with a

murmured, 'Thanks be to God. He must have heard my prayers.'

'They do say the Lord moves in mysterious ways, Connie. But in this case I think we have young Rosie Jennings to thank for the current thaw in the Max/ Alison affair. Sorry! Bad choice of word, that.'

'You don't mean you think Max and Alison . . .' Connie asked incredulously.

'Gracious no! Why, those two have been at each other's throats ever since Max came back to the village. Although . . .'

'Although what . . . Bunty?'

'Although I have to admit they made quite a charming picture yesterday, setting off for the village together in search of a replacement Concorde for Rosie.'

Watching Bunty pick up the tray to gather the empty cups, Connie saw her friend turn and give her a knowing wink. 'Surely she can't mean . . . can she?' Connie whispered under her breath. 'I mean, Alison and Max – but that's preposter . . .' Connie's sentence remained unfinished, however. Watching Max and Alison once more in animated conversation, it didn't seem quite so preposterous after all.

Hearing the sound of water in the washing-up bowl, Alison excused herself and, taking Max's empty cup, helped Bunty and Connie with the drying up.

'Quite a turn-out today,' Connie remarked, stacking away the last of the saucers. 'You know, it never ceases to amaze me. We get a better turn-out on a wet day than we do when the weather is bright and sunny.'

'Possibly because they can't think of anything better to do,' Bunty replied caustically.

'Bunty!' Connie and Alison echoed together.

Bunty looked surprised at their outburst. 'Well,' she continued, 'I mean St Faith's isn't exactly the most warm and welcoming of places on a dreary and depressing day like today.'

Placing the used, damp tea-towels in a plastic bag, Connie remonstrated. 'There I beg to disagree. I know St Faith's isn't exactly warm, temperature-wise, thanks to the awful heating system – or should I say lack of it – but it's certainly welcoming. Why, only moments ago, Max's friend Nigel was saying he couldn't remember the last time he'd been in such a friendly church. Which reminds me, I'd better get a move on, Nigel will soon be leaving to go back to London.'

'You mean he's not staying for lunch?'

'No, Bunty, he's not. He's going to Heathrow, to meet his fiancée.'

'In that case I hope she's nice,' murmured Bunty.

'Meaning?' queried Alison.

'Meaning simply that. I hope she is nice, because Nigel seems such a pleasant young man and therefore deserves someone nice.'

Sensing three pairs of eyes in his direction, Nigel joined the three women as they approached the church door. Even before they stepped into the porch, they heard the persistent sound of raindrops cascading into ancient guttering.

'I trust St Faith's roof is in a state of good repair,' Nigel remarked jovially in Bunty's direction.

'Oh, the roof's okay. It's the tower that's in need of restoration now. That's why we're glad yesterday's fête was so successful. Church funds, you know.'

Nigel watched Connie and Bunty reach for their

umbrellas in readiness for the deluge. To his surprise Alison didn't have one.

'What's next on the fundraising agenda?' he asked.

'The harvest supper at the end of September,' Alison replied.

Breathing in deeply and closing her eyes, she turned her face upwards to feel warm raindrops caress her skin and hair.

Nigel was transfixed; most women hated getting their hair wet. Bunty and Connie, presumably because of having their curls and waves turned into wire wool, and his lovely Vanessa (who always shied at the first raindrop) at having her long blonde tresses turned into what she called rat's tails.

'Alison's the lucky one,' Bunty explained, putting up her umbrella. 'Wet or dry, long or short, her hair always looks lovely.'

Exiting from the solid oak doorway, Max caught the tail end of the conversation. Casting his mind back to that first fateful meeting with Alison, he remembered her flaxen bob hairstyle, bathed in late evening sunlight. Today, however – darkened by the rain – her newly acquired urchin cut framed her delicate face to perfection.

'You see,' exclaimed Nigel, acknowledging Max's presence, 'she really is a sea-sprite.'

For the second time that morning, Alison felt herself colour and, bidding Nigel a sincere but brief farewell, hurried to Bunty's side. Max meanwhile, watched by an astute Connie and Nigel, could only gaze after her with a puzzled look on his brow.

Watching Nigel's car disappear from view, Max returned to the kitchen where Connie was basting the roast potatoes. Now fully recovered from the previous night's over-indulgence with the whisky bottle, he savoured the smell of crisply roasting potatoes, pale golden Yorkshire pudding and a wonderful sirloin of beef. For the first time in weeks he felt hungry and was secretly glad Connie had insisted he join them for Sunday lunch.

'Lunch won't be long now,' she said, placing the basting spoon on its rest. 'I only need to make the mustard and get some of George's . . .'

'Here, let me,' Max insisted, reaching for the familiar yellow tin, 'and if you'll remind me where George keeps his lethal concoction of horseradish.'

With a bemused smile, Connie motioned to the far corner cupboard and whispered, 'Welcome back, Max,' under her breath.

At Keeper's Cottage, preparations for lunch were on a much simpler scale. bunty opened the oven door and examined the four chicken breasts, (two for today's lunch and two to have cold tomorrow.)

'Almost done,' she said. 'Gracious, I didn't realize how hungry I was. It must have been that walk home. Though why I let you persuade me to do that, I don't know.' Patting her frizz of curls, she turned to Alison with a grin. 'Your mother always used to like being out in the rain, too.'

Talk of her mother reminded Alison she'd not seen to the African violets as she'd intended that morning on leaving St Faith's. Owing to the wonderful weather they'd been having – until now – they were still blooming beautifully. Looking at Bunty, who was suppressing a yawn, she decided she would go after lunch. Once the dishes were cleared away, Bunty no doubt would be having an afternoon rest by a blazing log fire.

An hour later, changing into her usual attire of jeans and sweatshirt, Alison fetched her Barbour and wellingtons. At the door, Jasper looked up with a deep longing in his eyes. He'd already given up on the idea of his mistress taking him for a walk. Bunty was breathing deeply and noisily, her mouth slightly ajar and the Sunday papers spreadeagled across her wide girth.

For a brief moment Alison was reminded of the down and outs, with their 'blankets' of newspapers, huddled in the inner city streets on her last visit to London. Shuddering at the total despair of their sad existence, she swallowed hard. When had the majority of them last eaten a decent meal as she'd just done? And how many of them would be spending this particular Sunday afternoon like Bunty, warm and sheltered from the relentless wind and rain.

Succumbing to Jasper's soulful, brown-eyed appeal, Alison quickly grabbed his lead and the customary plastic bag with its poop scoop and headed for the door. There, young woman and young dog breathed in the earthy dampness of the unusually cold late August Sunday afternoon.

Downwind a faint smell of woodsmoke met Alison's nostrils. No doubt someone else enjoying the warmth and comfort of a post-lunch log fire.

'Autumn in August,' Alison murmured softly to herself. Jasper looked up quizzically. He was confused because she'd stopped by the gate. They were still going for their walk, weren't they? Knowing the gate opened on to the woodland path beyond, Jasper darted forward on his lead before Alison had a chance to change her mind.

Deciding to exhaust the dog completely before visiting the grave, Alison headed in the direction of the woods. There, as a result of the overnight deluge, trees and undergrowth, previously parched and sun-shrivelled, appeared to revel in the welcoming gift of long-overdue rain. In the dismal greyness of afternoon, everywhere was bathed in a refreshing curtain of green.

Kicking at the yielding leaf mould beneath her feet, Alison's gaze swept ahead to what in May had been an expansive carpet of bluebells. Sadly, the once drooping racemes of flowers were now just a spent mass of green, spiked stalks and rain-spattered leaves.

Doubtless excited by the scent of a rabbit or some other small, furry creature, Jasper lunged towards a maze of bulbous seed-heads, yapping excitedly as he did so.

'Jasper, leave!' Alison commanded. 'Rabbits and squirrels are also entitled to rest on a Sunday.'

Rest, Alison pondered, looking at her watch. How long had Bunty been resting? It was now almost three o'clock and she had asked to be woken at four. There was a particular film she wanted to watch on television.

Quickening her pace, Alison clipped Jasper's lead back on to his collar and ran swiftly in the direction of the churchyard. Once there, she deadheaded the African violets, pinching away their limp and soggy, brown wilted flowers and took them to the waste bin in the far corner.

At the the lych gate, with her usual cursory glance in the direction of Tara's grave in case Max should be there she noticed his ever-present floral display for his beloved daughter. Pausing only briefly, Alison cast her mind back to the morning's church service and remembered Max's knowing smile in her direction when the Reverend spoke of 'concord'.

Smiling to herself and bending down to remove a stray seed head caught in Jasper's collar, she found herself making a connection between the dog's thick, wiry coat and Nigel Painton's wiry auburn curls. It was inevitable, therefore, that her mind should wander from auburn curls to the sleek black head of Max Craven.

How appropriate then to step from the footpath and discover Max's sleek black Saab moving swiftly in her direction. Startled, she nodded in acknowledgement as the car sped past, unaware that she'd released the catch on Jasper's extendable lead. What was the saying: give him an inch and he'll take a yard? In Jasper's case his 'yard' meant lumbering ahead towards a densely filled verge of cow parsley.

Moments later, hearing a screech of brakes and aware of a car heading back towards her, Alison waited with bated breath.

'Jasper!' she called desperately, but there was no response from the far end of the lead. 'Oh, never mind,' she sighed. 'Perhaps that's just as well.' The last thing she wanted was Jasper leaping all over Max Craven.

Without turning to look, Alison heard the car come to an abrupt halt, followed by the sound of a door slamming and anxious footsteps running to catch up with her. When she felt a hand – Max's hand – on her shoulder, a tremor ran through her entire body.

'Alison. Can I offer you a lift? You look positively drenched. What on earth are you doing out in this awful weather?'

Oblivious to the continuing rain, Alison held up

white-knuckled fingers, tenaciously gripping the handle of Jasper's lead.

'Oh!' Max said warily, looking first at the distant movement in the tangle of weed and cow parsley and then at the immaculate leather interior of his car. 'I take it you've Bunty's dog on the end of that lead?'

'Right first time,' Alison announced with a cheeky grin, regaining her composure. 'And don't worry, Max, I wouldn't dream of embarrassing you by accepting your offer of a lift. As you can see, I'm perfectly dressed for the rain, whereas you yourself are not.'

Taking in her Barbour, sturdy jeans and wellingtons, Max felt the unwelcome presence of rain, dripping from the leaves of an overhead beech on to the back of his neck. Lifting his jacket collar, he studied her carefully.

'Well, if you're really sure? I suppose I had better get back. Constance won't thank me for dripping water all over her magnificent carpet.'

For what seemed like an eternity, Alison looked up into his dark, penetrating eyes. Was he waiting for a response to his question?

When none came, Max stepped from the kerb and opened the driver's door. He was still looking at her expectantly.

'Th . . . thanks for the offer anyway,' she mumbled, feeling less composed than she had only moments ago. 'Another time perhaps?'

This time, the sound of the car's pulsing engine caused Jasper to give up on his investigations in the undergrowth. He bounded back in Alison's direction just as Max disappeared from view. Flushed and with her own pulse racing, Alison lifted the latch at Keeper's Cottage.

With the vision of Max's lingering farewell still fresh in her memory, Alison announced softly, 'I wish you didn't make me feel like this, Max Craven. I should hate you for the decision you took over the Stables and yet . . .' Shrugging her shoulders, she continued, 'Oh! This is ridiculous; I really must stop . . .'

'What's ridiculous and what must you stop?' enquired a bleary-eyed Bunty, emerging from the sitting room. Rubbing her eyes, she peered first at the clock and then into the small kitchen mirror. 'Gracious! Is that the time? And just look at the state of me. I look like the wreck of the Hesperus!'

Alison grinned and, anxious to draw Bunty's attention away from her earlier question, began quoting from Longfellow's poem.

'Mind you, you two don't look much better yourself.' Bunty quipped when Alison's recitation came to an end, looking first at Alison's dripping wet hair and muddy boots and then the bedraggled dog. Jasper, she noticed, was trying to nose his way through to the sitting room and the fire.

'Oh, no, you don't!' Bunty cried, grabbing him by the scruff of the neck. 'It's a bath for you, young man!'

At the mere mention of the word, Jasper scuttled between Alison's legs. Although only a recent resident at Keeper's Cottage, the word 'bath' – not one of his favourites – was one he instantly recognized.

Having hung up his damp jacket and dried his hair, Max joined Connie and George in the drawing room. There, Connie poured tea into blue and white Royal Doulton cups and gestured to a freshly made fruit cake and scones placed on the dumb waiter.

Max took his tea and declined the offer of cake.

'I thought you'd be hungry after your walk, Max,' Connie said, passing George his cup.

'Constance, I'm still recovering from that enormous lunch. Besides, I never said I was going for a walk. I merely went to have a look at the Stables. You're forgetting, with no proper access road as yet, it's like a quagmire up there after all this rain. Why, I barely stepped out of the car.'

Connie stopped pouring her own tea in bewilderment. 'If you didn't go for a walk, how did you manage to get so wet?'

'Oh, that,' Max replied, without thinking. 'That was when I stopped for Alison.'

'You mean you took Alison with you? How nice! Then I take it you've changed your mind about renting part of the Stables for her interior design business? I am pleased! I wonder why Bunty never said anything this morning.' Connie looked across at her husband with a satisfied glow. 'Did you hear that, George? Isn't it wonderful? Max is going to let part of Craven's Stables to Alison after all.'

'No, Constance,' Max announced flatly. 'I'm not doing anything of the kind.'

'But you said . . .'

'I didn't say anything of the sort. I merely said I stopped for Alison and the reason I stopped was to offer her a lift *after* I'd been to the Stables.'

Unable to cope with the hurt and obvious disappointment registering on his sister's face, Max strode uneasily to the window. Gazing into the storm-soaked garden he stood transfixed. The rain was lashing against a climbing lace-cap hydrangea, bouncing from leaf to leaf and flower to flower, before finally landing against the window pane in an explosion of droplets.

Tracing a single raindrop with his finger as it meandered down the window pane, Max emitted a barely audible sigh. There had been raindrops on Alison's face where they'd dripped from the urchin-cut spikes of hair clinging to her forehead. Raindrops he'd wanted to reach out and brush away from her cheeks . . . raindrops like silent tears.

Had Alison looked like that when she'd shed her tears? The morning she'd received his brutal letter announcing his intention with regard to the Stables? Goodness knew, Constance had reminded him about it often enough. And Bunty too, of course. In fact Bunty had been positively seething with anger when she'd bumped into him quite by chance in the village. It had almost been a case of 'pistols at dawn'!

'Pistols at dawn,' Max whispered to himself, oblivious to George and Connie who, deciding to ignore him, were now engrossed in the Sunday papers. The last time his thoughts had turned to duels had been on the train from London. All those commuters armed with their mobile phones and . . . Alison's dear, sweet face, gently rousing him from sleep.

With arousals of a different nature stirring within him, Max reached out to crush the customary scented geranium leaf between his fingers.

'Max! What on earth do you think you're doing?' Connie shrieked in alarm. 'Just look what you've done to that poor hibiscus!'

Still clutching the crushed flower head, Max left the room in silence.

'Well! What do you make of that?' Connie asked, rising from her chair.

She walked to the door, only to be stopped in her tracks by George.

'No, Connie! Leave him!'

'But you've only got to look at him to see there's something wrong,' Connie remonstrated.

'I know.'

'You know? Then why didn't you say? Why didn't you do something to stop him?' Connie hesitated with her fingers on the door handle. 'Look, I need to go and talk to him . . .'

'*You* might need to . . . but I don't think it's what Max needs,' came the dignified but firm response. 'I think he needs to be left alone for a while. Don't forget, there's ten years of mixed emotions churning away in that proud, stubborn head of his. Let's be honest, Connie, we both know there are unanswered questions relating to both Tara's accident and Virginia's death. Max's coming home has finally set the cogs in motion for those questions to be answered. Something tells me it's not going to be easy for Max and . . . it's certainly not going to be easy for Alison.'

'What are you implying?'

'To be honest, I don't rightly know. But I have a horrible feeling we're not going to like what comes crawling out of the woodwork.'

George studied his wife's ashen face and her white knuckles gripping the door handle. Then, releasing her fingers, he held her hand in his, saying. 'Don't look so worried, I'm sure it will be all right in the end.'

CHAPTER 12

The next morning, replacing the phone on its hook, Connie walked into the hallway to find Max examining his post.

'I don't know,' she said with a smile. 'We've never seen so much of the postman as we have since you came back. You must need a sack all to yourself. Perhaps you should get yourself a secretary.'

'Nonsense, Constance, I'm perfectly capable of dealing with a few letters.'

Connie raise a bemused eyebrow; in her opinion Max's pile of envelopes was more than just a few.

'Anyway, most of these are merely courtesy letters from Nigel, keeping me informed of what's going on in the office, and the others . . .'

'The others . . . ?' Connie queried.

'. . . relate to Craven's Stables. Preliminary letters with regard to the planning application, etc.'

Connie hesitated and drew a deep breath. 'Max . . . about Craven's Stables . . . Bunty's been on the phone. She said Alison is still very upset about your decision and she was wondering . . . in fact we were both wondering . . . couldn't you perhaps change your mind and let Alison . . . ?'

Connie got no further. Max, fixing his sister with a look as ominous and dark as the skies outside, strode in silence towards the front door.

Moments later there was the resounding revving of an engine and the Saab shot down the gravelled driveway, narrowly missing George who was returning in the Land Rover.

'Crikey! What's got into Max?' George asked in alarm. 'Has there been an accident.'

'No . . . I was just, er . . .'

'You were just what, Connie?'

'Asking Max about Craven's Stables and letting Alison . . .'

'Oh, Connie!' George gave an exasperated sigh. 'Why didn't you take heed of what I said yesterday and simply leave things alone?'

'But Bunty said . . .'

'In that case, you and Bunty had better learn to step back for a bit. Alison and Max aren't the church fête or the WI jumble sale, you know. They have feelings and need to . . .'

'But I only wanted to help.'

George placed a reassuring arm on his wife's shoulders. 'Take it from me, old thing, the best way you can help is by leaving them both alone.'

'You're sure?'

'Positive,' George said with a grin, 'and I'm gasping for a cup of coffee, so how about it?'

'All right,' sighed Connie, 'but first I'd better ring Bunty.'

'You did what!' Alison asked in alarm, looking up from where she was studying colour charts for Evangeline's bedroom.

'I asked Connie to have another word with Max about Craven's Stables.'

'Oh, Bunty! I do wish you hadn't. I honestly think we should forget all about my original idea of renting a unit at the Stables. Besides,' she said, indicating the colour charts and fabric samples laid out on the table in front of her, 'I have Evangeline's bedroom to design and after that quite possibly a project for Penny. She was saying, Tony's business commitments mean he never has time for jobs in the house and as the florist's is doing so well . . .'

Bunty nodded approvingly and, in view of the conversation she'd just had with Connie, decided it was probably best to change the subject.

'Perhaps you can do something for this place too, whilst I'm out of the way in Australia. I'll pay you, of course.'

'You'll do no such thing!' Alison said indignantly. 'In fact, come to think of it, that's a wonderful idea. It will be my way of saying thank you for all you've done for me.'

'I wouldn't hear of . . .'

'Quiet Bunty!' Alison teased. 'It's my turn to be bossy now. You just carry on doing whatever it is you planned to do today. Wasn't it the jumble sale and preliminary preparations for the harvest supper?'

Leaving Alison to concentrate on Evangeline's bedroom and the even more exciting project of Keeper's Cottage, Bunty picked up her car keys and left to deliver leaflets for the forthcoming jumble sale.

Watching her go, Alison turned to the dozing Jasper with a deep sigh. With one ear cocked, the dog opened one eyelid in the hope that Alison would mention the magic word 'walk'. When it wasn't forthcoming, he turned his back on her, leaving her to ponder on colour charts, fabric swatches and, last but by no means least, Max Craven!

What on earth had Bunty said to Connie and what had she in turn said to Max? More to the point, what had Max been going to say to her yesterday afternoon, just before he got back in his car? She was convinced he'd been about to say something. With a wry smile, Alison murmured softly, 'I'm making it all appear like a game of consequences, just like Tara and I used to play when I was looking after her.'

The name 'Tara' echoed in her head. Was she just imagining it, or had Max whispered 'Tara' as he stepped from the kerb to his car?

Three weeks later Evangeline poured the remains of a bottle of gin into a heavy lead crystal tumbler, dropped in two ice cubes, a slice of lemon and the merest splash of tonic and climbed the stairs to her bedroom. Leaning against the doorframe, she studied Alison, who was at work stripping a multi-patterned wallpaper from the walls.

'Are you sure you don't mind doing that, Alison? You know, I can still get that young fellow in from the village to give you a hand.'

Alison shook her head. 'No, thanks, Evangeline. I'd much rather do it myself, that's if you don't mind it taking a little longer. I prefer to see for myself what's under all these layers of paper. It's important to make sure the walls are thoroughly prepared.'

Trying to hide her disgust at Alison's short un-painted nails, Evangeline compared them with her own artificial ones, painted with Pagan Glow to match her lipstick.

'Don't worry,' Alison pulled away at yet another strip of wallpaper. 'Handcream and cotton gloves at night work wonders. I really do prefer the hands-on approach, you know.'

'So do I, dear, so do I,' muttered Evangeline, walking unsteadily back downstairs, 'but not in the way you're thinking, I'm sure!' Taking a video from her extensive collection, Evangeline slipped it in the machine, slumped back on the settee and took a large gulp of her drink.

'Wearing cotton gloves in bed. My God! What a dreadful thought! I can't think of any man wanting to go to bed with a woman wearing cotton gloves. How can you run your hands over a man's . . . ? Still,' she mumbled drunkenly, 'from what I've seen of Alison Benedict since she's been living in the village – and clever as she is, I must admit – I doubt if her talents extend to knowing how to please a man in bed.' As the credits began to roll, Evangeline thought of the man she'd so hoped to please.

'Max Craven,' she hissed under her breath, 'you don't know what you were missing when you rejected me.' Ignoring the opening sequence of the film, Evangeline thought angrily about her further attempts at getting Max Craven alone. All to no avail; they had only left her feeling bitter and resentful.

Even last night (with Tom away at a seminar) when Max had called at her request to collect the bags of clothes for the coming jumble sale, Evangeline had been thwarted. The ever-conscientious Alison had decided to work late in the bedroom and Max, on learning she was still in the house, had offered to give her a lift home.

'Damn you, Max Craven! I'll get my own back, just you wait and see!' Gulping back the remains of her drink, Evangeline pressed the pause button on the video and went in search of another bottle.

Later that evening, moments after she'd left The Firs, Alison recognized the familiar sound of Max's car.

'Hop in,' he called, running round to open the passenger door.

'I'm quite capable of walking.'

'I know you are, Alison, but I wanted to ask you something.'

Alison froze with the clasp of the seatbelt in her hand. Ask her something? What on earth could he mean? Recently she'd overheard Bunty and Connie in conversation, whispering about Tara, Virginia and the accident. Surely Max wasn't going to ask her about that! Reluctantly she got into the car.

'Here, let me,' Max said, reaching across, taking the seatbelt from her grasp. When their hands touched and Alison smelt his now familiar aftershave, panic rose in her breast. She wished he wasn't quite so close. And what was it he wanted to ask her?

'Don't look so worried, I'm not going to ask you to rebuild and redecorate the Stables.' Max stopped suddenly. 'I'm sorry, that was a bit insensitive of me, I suppose. I understand from Connie it's still a bit of a sore point with you.'

'I'm not going to lie to you and tell you it doesn't matter.' She replied tartly. 'Because it does, or at least it did. Anyway, I'm getting used to the idea now. I'm working on this project for Evangeline and Penny's asked me to do something for her and after that . . .'

161

It was Alison's turn to stop suddenly. She was talking far too quickly and Max was still holding her hand. Looking down, she became aware of the contrast between her own workworn reddened fingers and Max's long, smooth, tanned ones.

Sensing her embarrassment, Max released his grasp on her hand and clicked the seatbelt buckle into place. Before moving away, he pulled surreptitiously at the cuff of his shirt, beneath the sleeve of his navy wool blazer, and covered up his scar. They then drove the rest of the way to Keeper's Cottage in silence, and only when they arrived did Max return to his original reason for meeting Alison from work.

Reaching on to the rear passenger seat, Max pulled at a Harvey Nichols carrier bag and dropped it on Alison's lap.

'What is it?' she asked, peering inside.

Max grinned, 'I'm not exactly sure what the correct name is. I called it a shawl but my sister tut-tutted and told me it's a syrup or something.'

Unable to contain her laughter, Alison announced with a giggle, 'I think you mean a serape. But what's it for?'

'Oh, sorry! I forgot to explain. It's for Clint.'

'Clint?'

'Perhaps I should have said Rosie. Remember how she wants everyone to call her Clint?'

Alison nodded in understanding. At least she thought she was beginning to understand, and she let Max continue.

'It came from a pile of things Evangeline was clearing out. For the jumble sale? Remember? That's what I called to collect yesterday. Only when I saw it on top of the bag, it reminded me of that blanket affair Clint Eastwood wears over his shoulders in all those westerns. So . . . I gave Constance a donation for church funds and I was wondering . . .' Here Max fixed Alison with a look of pure earnestness. 'I was wondering, as you're very clever with your hands, if I could persuade you to cut it down to size for Rosie.'

'What a wonderful idea, Max, of course I will. It will be a pleasure.'

Something in the way Alison spoke his name and looked deep into his eyes caused a desperate longing in Max's breast. A longing he hadn't known for years, not since . . .

'When would you like me to do it?'

Max stirred himself. Alison was speaking. What had she said?

'I was wondering if you wanted it in a hurry. Is it for any particular occasion?'

'Oh, yes. Sorry, I was miles away . . . Would it be too much to ask if you can finish it in time for next week's barn dance and harvest supper? From what I understand, the entire Jennings clan are going to be there in force. Constance tells me they even intend to take Great-grannie along in her wheelchair! It sounds as if we could be in for quite a pantomime.'

'In which case,' replied Alison continuing the theme of their conversation, 'your wish is my command.'

'Mmm.' Max hesitated. 'In that case – as a friend of Tara's, would you consider coming with me to the harvest supper, that's if you're not already promised elsewhere?'

'No, but I did promise Bunty I would help in the kitchen . . .'

163

Trying to conceal his disappointment, Max remonstrated, 'But you can't spend all night in the kitchen! Surely Bunty will release you from her apron strings for a couple of dances?'

'I can't dance,' Alison replied weakly.

'Of course you can! Why, I thought all women loved to dance. Or are you only saying that because you're frightened of me treading on *your* toes.' Max continued brightly. 'Besides, don't forget it's a barn dance. Surely it doesn't matter how you dance, and I promise . . .'

Sensing her unease as she struggled nervously with the seatbelt clasp, Max said softly, 'I'm sorry, I've not been particularly tactful today, have I, Alison? Do I take it by saying you can't dance you mean . . . because of your leg? Constance did tell me . . .'

Anxious to lessen his embarrassment, Alison tried to make light of the situation. 'Actually, I do quite enjoy dancing. However, I don't think it's very amusing for my partners when I have to leave the dance floor, hobbling like Long John Silver. It doesn't always happen, of course, but if it does, people invariably think I've left my partner because he's just crippled me, which isn't the case at all.'

Max was now standing by the passenger door, offering his hand. 'In that case,' he grinned, helping her from the car, 'I'm prepared to risk it, so expect me to come and drag you from the kitchen stove.'

At the door of Keeper's Cottage, Alison called back. 'What about the serape? Shall I bring it over when I've finished it?'

'No, don't worry,' came the reply. 'I'll come and collect it; perhaps we can take it to Rosie together?'

Peering out from her vantage point behind net

curtains, Bunty glowed with contentment. 'Perhaps we can what together?' she murmured. How annoying that Jasper, on hearing Alison's voice, had bolted to the door, sending the kitchen stool flying, thus denying Bunty the end of the conversation.

'Mmm, a lift home two nights in a row, that's . . .'

'Bunty! Stop it!' Alison commanded good-naturedly. 'And stop looking at the Harvey Nichols bag like that. For your information, it's not a present from Max, it's something he's asked me to do for Rosie Jennings.' Alison took the serape from the bag and laid it across the hall table.

'It's a bit big for her, isn't it?' Bunty enquired suspiciously, still unsure if Alison was telling the truth.

'Exactly,' came the reply. 'Which is why Max has asked me to alter it for her. Now are you satisfied?'

With a nonchalant shrug Bunty walked into the kitchen, straightened the kitchen stool and proceeded to take the beef casserole from the oven. She wouldn't say another word to Alison, she decided, for fear of upsetting her. After all, 'things', as she and Connie referred to them, seemed to be taking their own course after all. However, if Alison should by chance take Jasper for a walk after dinner, she could always ring Connie and tell her the latest news.

Whilst Alison picked up her scissors to trim the serape down to size, Evangeline struggled with a different implement.

'Bloody lemon!' she cried, grasping the sharp-bladed knife. 'Why can't you bloody well keep still?'

Arriving home, Tom Carstairs called from the hallway, 'Having problems, dear?'

'It's this bloody lemon, it keeps moving. Damn! I've

cut my finger now. Get me a plaster, will you, Tom?'

Tom Carstairs paused briefly in the kitchen doorway and studied his dishevelled wife. She was holding her finger under the running tap.

Stepping forward, he turned off the tap, reached in his pocket for a clean white handkerchief and led Evangeline to a chair. There he told her her to keep the handkerchief on the wound, whilst he fetched the first aid box from the top shelf.

With Evangeline studying her newly plastered finger, Tom eyed the chaos in the kitchen. The slices of discarded lemon, the tray of melting ice cubes and the none too brilliantly hidden gin bottle only served to confirm his recent suspicions.

Evangeline had always liked the odd drink or two, but lately he'd begun to realize the situation was becoming more serious. The problem, however, was how to approach it. When Evangeline made to leave her chair, Tom put a firm but kindly hand on her arm.

'I'll get whatever it is you want, my dear. Don't worry about my dinner. I'm sure I can do myself an omelette or something.'

At the mention of the word 'dinner', Evangeline stared about the kitchen. Where was the chicken she'd intended to cook for their dinner? She had remembered to get it out of the freezer, hadn't she? And hadn't she already peeled and prepared the potatoes and onions for Tom's favourite – Lyonnaise?

'I thought perhaps we could have a little drink before dinner,' she said, casting glazed eyes in Tom's direction.

'I think perhaps you've already had your little drink, Evangeline. Now why don't you go and watch a video or something, while I get us something to eat? It won't hurt to have trays on our laps for once.'

Like a child, Evangeline allowed Tom to lead her gently from the kitchen to the sitting room. Watching him switch on the video of the film she'd tried to watch that afternoon, she gazed first at her finger and then at her husband.

'Tom,' she drawled drunkenly, 'I bet you think I'm jusht like my finger.'

'Your finger? I don't understand.'

'Yesh. I think you think I'm like my finger . . . plashtered!' Emitting her familiar deep throaty laugh and waving her wounded finger in the air, Evangeline watched the troubled Tom head towards the kitchen door.

With the supper things cleared away and the kitchen back to its usual neat and orderly state, Tom made a large jug of strong black coffee. Placing it on the oval onyx coffee table, he poured his wife a cup and passed it to her with a worried frown.

'Evangeline, I . . . er . . . think we ought to talk.'

'Ooh!' giggled Evangeline like an admonished schoolgirl, still much the worse for drink. 'That sounds ominoush, Tom.'

'I'm being serious, Evangeline, we really do need to talk. You see, I think you've got a problem – a drink problem.'

'A drink problem! Of courshe I haven't got a drink problem. I jusht had a couple of drinks before dinner and you shay I've got a . . . Why thatsh pre . . . preposh . . .'

'I think you mean preposterous,' Tom interrupted.

'Yesh, thatsh jusht what I mean, pre . . . Anyway

you've already said it and I haven't . . . a drink problem that is.'

Tom shook his head sadly. Now wasn't the time to discuss his wife's increased drinking of late. Perhaps it would be better to get a decent night's sleep and maybe discuss it again in the morning. At least in the mornings she was usually sober and a great deal more coherent than she was at present.

To Evangeline's delight Tom dropped the subject, leaving her to ponder on something that had been buzzing through her head all day.

Listening to Tom locking the house for the night, Evangeline climbed the stairs to the recently decorated guest room. She and Tom were using this room while Alison worked on the master bedroom. Alison? Evangeline puzzled. She was sure what she'd been trying to think of had something to do with Alison.

Slumped on the bed, studying Alison's exquisitely hand-painted primroses, Evangeline hazily recalled how yesterday Max had given Alison a lift home. Today – yes, even today – she'd been sure it was Max's car she'd seen drive past not long after Alison left The Firs. Did that mean, therefore, Max had deliberately planned to collect her?

'You bastard!' Evangeline muttered under her breath. 'You couldn't face coming here to meet her, so you waited until you saw her leave.'

Desperate for both a drink and a cigarette, Evangeline drummed her fingers on her knees. Tom had forbidden her to smoke in the bedroom and to her horror she found the spare gin bottle (which she usually kept hidden in the linen drawer) empty. 'Damn!' she groaned. 'When Alison left, I forgot to take the empty one down and bring the new one up.'

Mention again of Alison caused her thoughts to wander back to Max. Photos! That was it – photos! Hadn't Connie rung and asked her for some photos for the harvest supper? It had been Alison's idea. They were trying to organize a few quizzes and games. Alison had suggested people take along interesting old photos and mementoes of Church Haywood.

'Well, Alison, my dear, my photos might not be all that old, but they'll certainly prove interesting, particularly if your name is Max Craven!'

When Tom Carstairs opened the bedroom door, he was deeply touched to find his wife studying their wedding photo in its antique silver frame. With a rare show of affection he sat down and drew Evangeline into his arms.

'It will be all right, my dear,' he said stroking her thick hennaed hair where it fell against her shoulders. 'We'll solve the problem somehow. Downstairs in the kitchen, I was thinking. I'm convinced I know exactly what to do.'

'So do I, Tom.' Evangeline replied with a cruel smile, glancing secretly at the silver frame. 'So do I!'

Back at Keeper's Cottage, Alison switched off the sewing machine and replaced its cover. Pleased with her night's efforts, she sighed contentedly.

'Finished, have you?' Bunty enquired, looking up from her armchair.

'Not exactly, but that's the machining out of the way. Because Rosie's quite small, I've been able to make two serapes from the one. I only need to finish the fringing and knot it, and that will be that, as they say. I'm sure Max will be pleased.'

'I'm sure he will,' Bunty replied, with a mischievous grin.

CHAPTER 13

Unclipping the maroon silk backing from the photo frame, Evangeline bit her lip pensively. In the cold light of day, she wasn't as confident as she had been the previous evening. Ringing Tom on some pretext – to make sure he was still at the office – she laid the sealed pink envelope on the bed beside her.

Lighting another cigarette, she inhaled deeply. Could she really do it, or should she just let sleeping dogs lie? In the long run, what would she gain? It certainly wouldn't send Max rushing into her arms, would it?

'In fact, quite the opposite,' she whispered with a sigh. And, running her finger along the V-shaped seal of the envelope, she decided to conceal the unopened envelope back inside the frame. Stubbing out her cigarette, Evangeline opened the bedroom window to disperse the tell-tale smell of tobacco smoke and spied Alison walking up the drive.

Yes, she told herself, placing the frame back in its original position. It would be far better not to upset Max or Alison at the moment, particularly as the bedroom was only halfway completed. Pausing on the landing she peeped in to survey Alison's efforts to date.

The dove-grey effect Tom had chosen was certainly pleasing and once the amethyst and grey silk drapes and borders were in place . . .

'Good morning, Evangeline,' Alison called cheerfully, hanging up her jacket in the cloakroom. 'I've made the stencil for the border and brought it with me. You can let me know what you think.'

'I'll make us some coffee,' Evangeline replied. 'Sitting room or kitchen?'

'Definitely kitchen! As you can see, I've my working gear on again. I'm hoping to finish the walls today.'

With a tinge of envy, Evangeline studied Alison's appearance. The tall, slim figure was dressed in denim dungarees, white short-sleeved T-shirt and tennis shoes. Unlike Evangeline, Alison possessed no designer labels, yet she still looked perfectly lovely.

Evangeline filled the kettle and watched the carefully cut-out stencils being laid across the table. Alison's eyes, she noticed, today reflecting the denim, were a clear bright blue. Rubbing subconsciously at her own puffy red-rimmed eyes, Evangeline ran her hands through her thick hennaed hair with a sigh. It had been getting exceedingly difficult to manage of late.

Alison's urchin cut, she pondered to herself, I wonder . . . But Alison was asking her something and the kettle was boiling.

'You see,' Alison repeated. 'Amethyst clematis, interwined with a grey-green foliage. What do you think, or would you prefer something stronger? If we go and hold this against the walls, you can decide for yourself.'

'No. No, I'm sure that will be perfect,' Evangeline called, following Alison upstairs. 'Yes, there you are you see, simply perfect. Now, let's have our coffee, shall we?'

Returning hurriedly to the kitchen, there was only one thought uppermost in Evangeline's mind. Alison had spoken of something stronger in relation to paint shade. In Evangeline's mind 'stronger' meant only one thing. Brandy in her coffee! Nothing could have made her happier than when Alison announced she would take her own coffee upstairs and Evangeline was able to reach for the flat, slim, handbag-sized bottle.

'I'd better get on,' Alison called from the landing. 'I promised to help Bunty with some table decorations for the harvest supper and then I must finish off your serape for Max.'

With her hand poised on the brandy bottle, Evangeline froze. What had Alison said? Something about her serape for Max? What on earth did she mean? Taking a large gulp from the bottle, Evangeline poured a generous measure into her cup and walked through to the hallway.

'Did you say something about my serape for Max? Whatever do you mean, Alison?'

Leaning over the banister rail, Alison enlightened her. 'Oh, only that Max gave Connie a donation for your old serape and he asked me to cut it down to size for Rosie Jennings. You know how much she's into Clint Eastwood and those spaghetti westerns.'

When Tom Carstairs returned from work, he was both angered and disappointed to find his wife in exactly the same drunken state as she had been the previous evening.

'My bloody serape!' Evangeline screamed at him, the moment he walked throught the door. 'My bloody

173

serape! Do you hear that, Tom?'

'Yes, I hear you,' Tom sighed, 'but I'm afraid I don't understand. To be perfectly honest, I'm not at all sure what you're talking about.'

'My serape!' Evangeline screamed again. 'The one I bought from Harvey Nichols. Cashmere and silk, it was, and it cost me a bloody fortune!'

Me, more like, Tom thought perversely. 'What's happened to this serape, then? Have you lost it?'

'Of course I bloody haven't!'

'Evangeline, my dear, I do wish you wouldn't swear, it isn't . . .'

'I'm not bl . . . Oh!'

'Perhaps if you explain from the beginning,' Tom suggested kindly. 'And if you haven't lost the serape, what exactly happened to it?'

'Alison's got it and she's cut it up!'

'What! You mean Alison stole it and . . .'

'No, of course I don't! Don't be stupid, Tom! Alison's not a thief.'

'Then why has Alison got it and why has she cut it up? Really, Evangeline, I'm afraid I still don't understand.'

'I gave it to Connie for the jumble sale.'

'Then where's the problem?' Tom asked, with an exasperated sigh. 'I mean, if you didn't want it any more and you gave it to Connie for the jumble sale? Are you angry because Connie gave it away?'

'Oh, she didn't give it away,' Evangeline snapped bitterly. 'Max gave her ten pounds for it and asked Alison to . . .'

Tom didn't bother to listen to the rest of the explanation. Suddenly the problem of the discarded serape was all fitting into place like a puzzle. It wasn't the fact that the serape had been cut up, it was the fact that Max had bought it and then given it to Alison to cut up for . . . Rosie Jennings . . . if Tom had heard correctly?

Placing a calming hand on her shoulder, Tom chose his words carefully. 'Really, my dear, if you didn't want it any more – and by all accounts Max gave Connie far more for it than it was ever likely to fetch at the jumble sale – then surely . . .'

'That's not the point!' snapped Evangeline. 'Can't you see . . . ?'

'Probably not,' broke in Tom, 'but what I do see is, you threw it out, Max bought it, Alison is cutting it up – or more appropriately in this case – cutting it down in size, and little Rosie Jennings is going to be delighted. Heaven knows it can't be easy for the child, what with her brothers and sisters, parents, grandparents and even great-grannie, all crammed together in those two cottages.'

'Then they shouldn't breed like rabbits!' Evangeline retorted.

'I know, I know,' Bunty acknowledged with a deep sigh in Alison's direction. 'Jumble sale one week and harvest supper the next. You don't have to tell me. I already know it was bad planning.'

'I wouldn't exactly say bad planning, just a bit exhausting for the committee. Look on the bright side, Bunty. The takings from the jumble sale will pay for the food for the harvest supper; ticket sales from the harvest supper will help with the autumn bazaar and, at the end of the year there should be a

175

more than generous contribution to St Faith's restoration fund. Also don't forget the Christmas Fayre . . .'

'That's one thing I do intend to forget,' Bunty said, ironing the last of the red and white check tablecloths, 'simply because I shan't be here!'

'Of course, I'd quite forgotten. You won't be here for the Christmas Fayre. You'll be in Australia.'

'Exactly,' came the smug reply, 'and for once someone else can worry about finding a Father Christmas. I wonder who . . . ?'

'Oh, please don't let's talk about finding a Father Christmas now. Gracious, it's only September. We haven't even had autumn yet.'

Knotting the final strands of fringing on the serape, Alison cast her mind back to earlier autumns. Autumns of her childhood, in fact. What her mother had always referred to as Indian summers. Happier times when they'd all been together. Tranquil autumn days lost in perfect innocence and the idyllic, rural charm of Church Haywood.

'Autumn,' she whispered longingly. 'How I love the autumn.'

'Well, autumn's not for me. Give me long, hot summers any day; that's why I'm going to be greedy this year and have two.'

Bunty studied Alison's puzzled expression with a wry smile. 'By going to Australia for Christmas, I shall be having two summers, you see.'

Alison merely nodded and shivered. Two summers! She couldn't imagine anything worse. Especially if they were like the summer Tara had died.

'Are you all right, my dear? Perhaps I should light the fire. There's a definite chill in the air this evening.'

'No, I'm fine, thanks, Bunty, though I'll probably go and fetch a sweater. Don't forget, Max is calling for me. We're going to take the serapes over to Rosie. Hopefully we should just about catch her before bedtime. Max is convinced she'll want to wear one of them to the harvest supper.'

'And what do you intend to wear?'

Alison shrugged her shoulders. 'You know me and my amazing wardrobe. I had thought about jeans but then Penny told me about that shop in town. You know, the one next to the art and craft shop at the back of the market square? Apparently they're having a sale.'

Bunty nodded and Alison continued with a wicked glint in her eye. 'Who knows,' she said, 'I might even wear a skirt and surprise Rosie for a third time this year . . . by displaying my legs!'

Crossing the market square, with thoughts of Rosie's delighted face still fresh in her mind from the previous evening, Alison was surprised to bump into Evangeline.

'Fancy seeing you in town, Alison. I thought you'd be busy helping Bunty and Connie, moiling and toiling away, as they say, for this evening's bun fight.'

'They can manage quite well without me,' Alison replied tartly, trying to ignore the underlying tone of Evangeline's voice. 'Besides I've only popped in for half an hour. I'm on my way back to the village hall now.'

Evangeline studied the plastic carrier bag Alison was holding. 'Good lord! Is that place still open? I thought it closed down years ago. You don't mean to tell me people still go in for all that tie-dye stuff and batik?'

Feeling herself go hot with anger, Alison studied Evangeline's own array of carrier bags.

'Hmph!' she later remarked to Bunty. 'It wouldn't surprise me if it cost more to produce those designer-emblazoned carrier bags of hers, than it did to produce my one wrap-around skirt!'

'Don't let Evangeline bother you, Alison,' Bunty said kindly.

'I don't. But sometimes she really annoys me. She can be so unpredictable and so bitchy.'

'In that case it's probably the drink.'

'The drink? What on earth do you mean?'

'Oh, come on, Alison. Surely you must have realized by now that Evangeline has a little . . . well, you know . . . problem?' Bunty raised an imaginary glass to her mouth.

'You're joking! I know at Connie's dinner party she drank a lot. You can't mean she's an al . . . ?'

Alison stopped abruptly when a committee member came in carrying a tray of food. For the rest of the afternoon she found herself thinking of Evangeline's erratic behaviour of late. If what Bunty said was true, then it certainly explained a great deal.

At The Firs, Evangeline threw the last of the empty carrier bags on to the floor, raked her scarlet fingernails through her hair and went to find her husband.

'Well,' she demanded, 'what do you think?'

Without thinking at all, Tom remarked incredulously, 'My God! What have you done to yourself?'

Eyeing her sombrely dressed husband, Evangeline retorted, 'Just in case you'd forgotten, Tom, it's a harvest supper and barn dance we're going to, not a meeting of the local parish council.'

'I know, but that doesn't mean . . .'

'Doesn't mean what . . . ?' Casting a withered look in Tom's direction, Evangeline strode purposefully towards the drinks cabinet. Something told her Tom didn't approve of her new purchases. Though to be honest she didn't give a damn.

At that moment she didn't need his approval of the clothes she was wearing, or her new hairstyle either. But she desperately needed a drink! The problem was, would Tom let her have one? These past few days when he'd been at home, he'd been watching her like a hawk. To her dismay he'd even found some of the secret bottles she kept hidden away.

To her surprise, on this occasion Tom made no attempt to stop her when she took the cut crystal stopper from the whisky decanter. 'Want one?' she asked, half expecting him to say no, and was completely taken aback when he answered with,

'Why not? There's only going to be wine and beer at the village hall. As we shall be walking . . .'

Evangeline froze. It wasn't the thought of walking to the harvest supper that bothered her, it was more the prospect of the cardboard-tasting boxed wine they always served on these occasions.

Aware of Tom eyeing her suspiciously and knowing he wouldn't agree to a little top-up, Evangeline placed her glass on the coffee table and walked through to the hall. 'I'll go and fetch my bag and we can be off. That's if you're ready?'

'That's fine by me. It should be a good evening by all accounts.'

'Who says so?' Evangeline called out, crossing from the landing to the bedroom.

'I bumped into George and Max this afternoon. They

179

were collecting bales of hay to put on the stage to make it look more authentic. George was telling me Connie's delighted with ticket sales. Oh, yes, and by the way, Max asked me to tell you Rosie Jennings is delighted with your serape. He and Alison took it over last night.'

Poised with her hand on the dressing table drawer, Evangeline felt a venomous surge of jealousy flood her entire body. It wasn't that she didn't like Alison. She did, and she was much in awe of her many talents. What irked her most, however, was that Alison was young and pretty and recently fortunate enough to command Max Craven's undivided attention. Why, she'd even been allowed to sit in the confines of that wonderful black Saab.

Being the only black Saab in Church Haywood, it hadn't escaped Evangeline's notice that whenever she saw Max with a passenger, more often than not it was Alison Benedict.

'Although you're not quite old enough to be her father,' Evangeline whispered to an imaginary Max, 'your daughter often wished Alison were her big sister. I wonder what Virginia would have thought.'

Memories of Max's dead wife came winging back as Evangeline rummaged through her bedroom drawer. 'Damn! Where is that bloody bottle?'

All too soon realization dawned. Tom had been there before her!

With a cynical smile, Evangeline walked to her wardrobe and reached for a Gucci shoebox. Success at last! This was one place Tom hadn't thought of looking.

'Evangeline!' Tom called. 'Are you coming? If you don't hurry up we shall be late and miss all the food.'

'You're quite welcome to it, my darling,' Evangeline hissed sarcastically. 'It's hardly likely to be Fortnum and Mason.' Then, concealing the brandy bottle in her handbag, she strode defiantly back to her dressing table and reached for the silver photo frame.

Congratulating themselves on their efforts, Bunty and Connie emitted deep sighs of satisfaction as they surveyed the village hall. Red and white checked cloths adorned the tables. Garlands of hops, wild flowers and berries hung suspended from the walls.

'Alison's table decorations are a novel idea. You know, I kept wondering what on earth she was going to do with all those old flower pots.' Connie's gaze encompassed the terracotta pots placed in the middle of every table. In each pot stood a creamy white candle (like those used on St Faith's altar) and from every pot cascaded more autumn flowers, seed heads and foliage.

'I have to confess I was a bit concerned at first when she started talking about surrounding the pots with moss to cover the oasis . . .'

'Me too,' Bunty interrupted, 'that was until I saw her raking all the old moss from my back lawns.'

Connie laughed. 'Yes. She even got George and Mr Jennings doing it. It was amazing how much they raked up. I thought I might use what's left for my winter flowering baskets.'

'Speaking of Mr Jennings, I see he's managed to bring his mother here tonight after all.' Bunty nodded to the far corner where the Jennings family were positioning old Mrs Jennings' wheelchair.

Duly installed, Maude Jennings flashed her sons, daughters, grandchildren and great-grandchildren a

181

toothy smile, despatched her eldest son to get her a drink from the bar and settled back to enjoy the evening.

'Well, we are honoured,' Bunty acknowledged with a gentle smile in Maude's direction. 'She's actually put her teeth in for once!'

'A little bird tells me that's for Max's benefit,' Connie added with a grin. 'Apparently Maude wants to tell him all about the old days in Church Haywood . . . and what he used to get up to as a boy!'

'Poor Max, I do hope she doesn't monopolize him for the entire evening. I was hoping he and Alison . . .'

Bunty got no further. An embarrassed hush fell upon the hall.

'What the . . . ?' a lone male voice echoed from the far corner, when into the room walked Tom and Evangeline Carstairs. 'Nice clothes, shame about the face!' he quipped.

'And the hair!' his female companion replied.

All eyes were on Evangeline as they swept from the top of her newly cropped head, Armani T-shirt and CK jeans, before finally resting on her Nike trainers.

'Bloody hell!' came a third voice, who refrained from continuing as his mother rapped at his knuckles.

Anxious to divert everyone's attention, Connie motioned to the country and western group, busily tuning up on the stage. When the first strains of 'You Are My Sunshine' reverberated from behind the bales of hay, Connie greeted Evangeline with a welcoming smile.

'Evangeline . . . and Tom!' How lovely to see you both. For a while we thought you weren't coming. Let me show you to our table. George and I thought you

182

might like to join our party for the evening. However
. . . if you'd rather . . . ?'

'No. That would be fine, Connie,' Tom broke in.
'I'm sure Evangeline would far rather sit with you than
. . .' Tom's gaze drifted towards the Jennings family
gathering where Maude Jennings was already joining in
the chorus of the song.

Looking away in disgust, Evangeline followed Connie to the opposite end of the hall. If she was expecting
to see Max sitting with the guests then she was very
much mistaken. Summoned to the kitchen, Max was
helping George with a barrel of beer.

'Good lord! Have you seen what Evangeline is
wearing?' George whispered loudly. 'You know, I
never thought I'd ever see her wearing jeans. Dressed
like that, she's certainly entered into the spirit of
things!'

'Spirit of things is right,' Bunty acknowledged sarcastically, entering the kitchen. 'You know, when she
bent and kissed me, I could have sworn I smelt brandy
on her breath.'

'Shh, Bunty,' Alison chided. 'Someone might hear
you.'

Bunty looked about her, first at Max and George, and
then at Connie and Alison. 'Well, all of us here know
what Evangeline's like for a little tipple.'

'Nevertheless, I don't think you should discuss it
now.'

'Okay. Point taken, Alison. So let's discuss instead
when we're going to have the quiz and take a look at all
those wonderful old photos you've gathered together.'

'I still think we should stick to the original plan and
have the quiz after the harvest supper. That way the

food will have time to settle, the band can have a break before the country dancing and those wishing to study the photos can do so without fear of being sent flying by an eightsome reel.' And I, thought Alison to herself, can sneak away to the sanctuary of the kitchen and thus avoid the dancing all together. She hadn't forgotten Max had threatened to come and drag her away.

'Speaking of things original,' Max teased, 'I have to say the first question on the village quiz is hardly original. Why, I remember that one from when I was a boy. I mean anyone who doesn't know "ecclesiastical bales amongst the trees" is Church Haywood should be . . .'

'Don't be such a spoilsport, Max,' Connie replied. 'You forget we have newcomers in the village, who've never been to one of our harvest suppers before.'

Duly admonished, Max smiled and winked at Alison.

'. . . and, speaking of when you were a boy, Max Craven,' Connie continued, 'you're in for a big surprise. By all accounts Maude Jennings wants to have a word with you about all the naughty tricks you used to play when you were still in short trousers! So brace yourself; you could be in for an embarrassing evening.'

While Alison was trying to imagine what the tall and immaculate yet casually dressed Max Craven would have looked like as a little boy, in short trousers with grubby knees, and Max himself was busy thinking back to his youth, Evangeline was planning a surprise of her own. Unbeknown to everyone on that balmy late September night, Connie had never spoken a truer word. They were all in for an embarrassing evening.

CHAPTER 14

'You always were such a mischievous little boy,' Maude Jennings chortled in Max's direction. 'Why, I remember when . . .'

'Now, Gran,' broke in a voice, 'I'm sure Mr Craven doesn't want to hear any more. He's been sitting with you for at least twenty minutes. You must let him go back to his family.'

Maude Jennings looked puzzled. From what she could remember, Max hadn't got a family any more. His wife – an outsider – to whom Maude had taken an instant dislike, had been killed in that fire and his dear, sweet daughter . . . Maude began to tremble.

'Maude? Are you feeling unwell?' Max enquired, deep concern reflecting in his dark eyes. Someone's opened a window. Shall I see if I can find you a rug . . . or maybe we can borrow Rosie's serape?

Maude shook her head and reached for Max's hand with her bony, twisted fingers. 'No,' she said, forcing a weak smile. 'You leave our Rosie with her stirrup or whatever it is you call it. You know she even wears it to bed!' Maude bent in Max's direction, still clinging on to his hand. 'No,' she whispered hoarsely, 'I'm not ill. I was just thinking about the day your little girl was killed. I still have nightmares about it and I'm sure poor Alison Webb – only she isn't Alison Webb any more, is she – must have nightmares about it too.'

'I didn't know you were there when it happened,' Max remarked incredulously. 'They told me there weren't any other witnesses; they said only the driver of the car . . .'

'Oh, I wasn't there, but I saw it all the same.'

'Then why didn't you say? Why weren't you at the inquest?'

'The family thought it would do no good. I'd broke my hip, you see, so I was in bed . . .'

'But if you were in bed, how could you see? I don't under . . .'

Sensing Max's air of frustration, Maude gave his hand a gentle squeeze. 'They'd put my bed by the window, you see. I was all propped up on pillows and the like – I got bored not being able to see anything – so there I was looking out of the window, when I saw the two girls running across the field.'

'Go on,' Max urged kindly.

'At first I thought they were playing tag, but when they got nearer I heard Alison calling to your Tara. Alison was telling her to stop.' Maude's eyes filled with tears. 'No, not telling her to stop, pleading with her to stop. Begging her, in fact. It's funny, you know, I remember it all so clearly but the family said it was probably my tablets . . .'

'What did you remember so clearly, Maude?' Max cast a furtive glance in the direction of the Jennings family. Please God they didn't come over now and interrupt this conversation. He *must* find out what happened.

186

With a puzzled look, Maude cocked her head to one side in bewilderment. 'Now where was I?' she sighed.

'You were saying . . . Alison was begging Tara to stop.'

'Oh, yes. So I was. Well, there they were running across the field, Alison calling out stop and Tara taking not a bit of notice. It was only when Alison – you know she suffered something terrible with her asthma – nearly caught up with your little girl that she stumbled and fell . . .'

A feeling of panic rose in Max's breast. 'What happened when Alison fell? Can you remember, Maude, did you see?'

For a moment it was as if Maude wasn't in the village hall at all. It was ten years ago and she was back in her old bedroom propped up in bed. Outside skylarks were singing on the wing, the sun was shining in glorious blue skies, and Tara and Alison were running across a meadow full of daisies. They even had daisy chains in their hair.

'Y . . . ee . . . es, I saw it all. Alison fell over and for a minute, Tara stopped too. You know, I even thought she was going to go back and help Alison up – but she didn't. Instead she looked back to where they'd just run from. It was almost as if she was frightened of something or someone. Then, leaving Alison in a crumpled heap, she just turned and ran towards the road. When the car came round the bend and down the hill, she ran straight out in front of it.'

Maude reached into the sleeve of her cardigan for a handkerchief and blew her nose. 'You know, Max, Tara saw that car coming, she must have known she didn't stand a chance, and by the time Alison struggled to her

187

feet . . .' Maude shook her head and wiped again at her eyes. 'When I remember how that poor girl limped after your Tara, begging her to stop, only to have her poor, poor leg all mangled up like that.'

Turning round to check on his mother, Bob Jennings caught sight of Max's ashen face completely drained of colour. He decided it was time to intervene.

'Now, Mum,' he commanded, moving her wheel-chair to one side. I think it's about time we let Mr Craven get back to his sister and family.

Feeling suddenly weary, Maude Jennings conceded and allowed herself to be wheeled away.

Watching her go, Max heard her remark caustically, 'Having a sister and brother-in-law's not what I call family. Family is like what we've got!' Suddenly fed up with her dentures, Maude removed them, wrapped them in the recently used handkerchief and surveyed her sons, daughters, grandchildren and great-grand-children with a beaming, toothless grin.

Delighted to see Max free at last, Rosie threw her serape across her shoulders and in a blur of camel and beige stripes and fringing flung herself against his knees. 'Now that that silly band has stopped play-ing,' she begged, 'are you goin' to dance with Al'son?'

Stunned by Maude's disclosure, Max gazed with unseeing eyes at Rosie's freckled face radiating pure innocence. Alison! He must find Alison. To think how he'd blamed Alison for Tara's death and all the time . . .

'But if the band's stopped playing, there won't be any dancing,' he replied weakly.

'Course there will, 'cos me brother's doin' the disco,' came the chirpy reply. 'What shall I get him to play . . . Blur, Oasis, Spice Girls?'

'Spice what?' Max replied numbly. 'I'm afraid you've lost me, Rosie.'

Rosie studied Max's face. Usually it was what she called a 'smiley face,' at least it was when she was in Max's company. But tonight, thinking it looked sad, she determined to do something about it.

'Look,' she said, grabbing Max's hand, 'you go and find Al'son and I'll get me brother to play you something nice. Yeah!' she added brightly remembering seeing her older brothers with their girlfriends at family discos. 'Something slo . . .' Rosie stopped herself from saying 'sloppy' and added 'slow' instead. 'Mmm, yes, that's it! Something slow 'cos of Al'son's leg.'

The last two words rang in Max's head, with pictures of Constance, Bunty, Harry and Maude, each voicing their concern. Even Rosie was worried about Alison's leg! Yet only months ago, finding her at St Faith's, he'd felt not concern and sympathy for Alison but hatred and contempt. Leaving Rosie to find her brother, Max set off desperately to find Alison.

She was alone in the kitchen when he entered. And for a while he watched in silence as she emptied the remains of the harvest supper into shiny black bin bags. Sensing his presence eventually, Alison turned warily.

'I'm sorry,' Max said softly, 'I didn't mean to startle you.'

'I think you said something like that once before. In the churchyard, the day of my mother's funeral. Remember?'

Max faltered. 'About that day, Alison, I'm afraid I was very rude to you. You see, I thought . . .'

'I know what you thought, Max, and . . .'

189

'And I was wrong,' Max interrupted as he moved cautiously towards her. 'You see, I've been told what really happened on the day of the accident.'

'You've been what! But no one else was there except me and Tara . . . and the driver of the car of course. How? I don't understand.'

'Maude Jennings told me.'

Before Alison had chance to say anything, Max continued, 'Maude saw it all from her bedroom window. She saw you running after Tara. Heard you begging her to stop. She also said she thought you and Tara were running away from someone or something and that Tara . . . deliberately ran out in front of that car.'

Alison gasped and dropped the bag she was holding, scattering paper plates and the remains of rice salad across the floor. Grabbing a handful of kitchen roll, she knelt down to scoop up the rice and stray plates.

'Alison!' Max was on his knees beside her. 'Please, you must tell me! Is that what happened? Was Maude telling the truth?'

Alison said nothing and only stared down at her lap. Then, having discarded the kitchen roll, she nervously fingered the sash of her wraparound skirt. One end, she noticed, was in her hand; the other was beneath Max's knee. She was quite unable to move.

Max sighed deeply. 'You don't have to say anything. In fact, by saying nothing at all, you've only convinced me Maude was telling the truth.'

'I . . .' Alison began. She got no further. The door burst open and a miniature Clint Eastwood called out. 'Come on, Max, if you're goin' to dance with Al'son. Me brother's found a sloppy record.'

Ignoring her slip of the tongue, a delighted Rosie watched Max help Alison to her feet and lead her towards the door. 'I think it's called "United",' she said with a puzzled frown, 'and he said it's by Peaches and Herb . . . though we always have custard with peaches. And why they're singing about a football team, Gawd only knows, as Great-Gran would say!'

For a brief moment, forgetting the seriousness of their earlier conversation, Max and Alison burst out laughing and to Rosie's satisfaction, Max reached for Alison's hand, put his arm round her waist and led her gently to the dance floor. There the strains of 'Re-united' were just beginning to play.

'There's something I need to know,' Max urged, softly in Alison's ear. 'What was it you and Tara were running away from that day?'

Sensing her every muscle go taut within his grasp, Max almost feared she was going to try and run away. 'No!' he pleaded. 'Please stay. Later perhaps . . . Perhaps you will tell me later, Alison? We mustn't let it spoil this part of the evening.'

It was meant more as a request than a question. Alison knew he would ask her the same thing over and over again, until he finally got his answer. For the moment, however, she allowed herself to relax, delighting in every minute spent in Max's arms.

Oblivious to onlookers and holding her close, Max breathed in the delicate sweet fragrance of Alison's perfume and felt her newly shampooed hair brush against his cheeks. After a while he chuckled softly. Alison looked up, startled. 'Sorry, did I tread on your foot?'

'No, I was just laughing at Rosie thinking the song

was about a football team. 'Reunited' – that's quite ironic,' Max murmured, drawing her close once more. 'I suppose we are in a way, because of Tara.'

It was at this point that Evangeline chose to re-enter the hall. She'd been making numerous visits to the ladies ever since she'd arrived. Only now did Tom suspect what was in the handbag Evangeline clutched so desperately to her bosom, every time she left the room. A bottle. It could only be a bottle!

Evangeline froze. In the dimly lit hall, Max Craven was holding Alison in his arms. He was also whispering in her ear and appeared totally unaware of anyone else in the room. Registering anger and jealousy, Evangeline felt her fingers tightened on her handbag. This time there was no point in hurrying back to the ladies' cloakroom. The half-bottle of brandy was finished, the evidence discarded behind the incinerator.

Tom reached out for Evangeline's arm and, finding her curiously unresisting, drew her into the chair by his side. His wife's flushed appearance proved what he already suspected. If Evangeline wasn't yet drunk, she was certainly well on the way.

Drumming her nails on the table, Evangeline looked anxiously for her glass. 'Oh, dear, I must have finished my drink. Can you get me another glass of that disgusting wine, Tom?

'I think you'd better have orange juice from now on,' Tom hissed, his voice brittle. 'I think you've had more than enough for one evening as it is.'

'But I've only . . .'

'Oh, don't come the innocent with me, Evangeline! You think I don't know about all the little trips you've been making to the cloakroom this evening. I wonder what's so precious that you've had to take your bag with you on every occasion. Perhaps if I were to look inside?'

'Please your bloody self!' Evangeline announced triumphantly. Snatching at her bag, she threw it at Tom, who on opening it remained tight-lipped and silent.

'Well?' Evangeline snapped. 'Found what you're looking for?'

'On this occasion no,' Tom sighed wearily, passing the bag back. 'But I've certainly found plenty of evidence relating to your drinking these past few days. I have to say, I'm really disappointed in you, Evangeline. I thought we . . .'

Ignoring Tom's hurt expression, Evangeline rummaged in her handbag for a packet of peppermints, popped a snow-white disc between her scarlet lips, tugged at her newly cropped hair with her fingers and announced, 'How long is this dreary music going on? I thought Bunty mentioned something about old village photos. I can't wait to be reminded of Church Haywood in the dark ages and all those long forgotten, quaint old customs. Why,' she added a bit too brightly for Tom's liking, 'we might even see some ghosts from the past.'

Max was still holding Alison's hand when the disco finished and Rosie's brother put the last of his records and tapes away. Without warning someone turned on the light switches, flooding the hall with light. While the assembled gathering became accustomed to the harsh neon glare, George pointed to the newly erected boards at the far end of the hall.

'Ladies and gentlemen,' he called. 'For those of you

who want to wallow in nostalgia, if you'd care to form an orderly queue . . .'

'Gracious, you make it sound just like the war, George,' someone quipped jovially.

'As I was saying, before I was so rudely interrupted,' George grinned. 'Perhaps you'd care to form an orderly queue and walk round in a clockwise direction. Is that right, Alison?'

Releasing her hand from Max's grasp, Alison nodded. 'Yes. The older photos are at the beginning and progress through to the Silver Jubilee celebrations and beyond to the present day, right at the end of the hall.'

Mention of the Queen's Silver Jubilee reminded Max of Tara's birth. She was only a baby when he and Virginia had pushed her in her pram through the high street towards the village green, to join in the local festivities.

Then Church Haywood had been a sea of red, white and blue bunting. The older children had joined the fancy dress procession; there had been an attempt at an 'It's a Knockout' contest between local village groups; a celebrity cricket match on the village green and later that night a Jubilee Ball. No wonder everyone had gone home exhausted.

Through a sea of faces, Max found his attention drawn to Alison's red, white and blue cotton skirt and white broderie anglaise blouse. Tara had been wearing a white broderie anglaise dress and mobcap (to protect her from the sun) all those years ago. Max reached for Alison's hand once more. When she turned to face him, she heard him whisper, 'Tara'.

'I'm not sure,' Alison replied, unaware of what

thoughts were rushing through his head. 'Perhaps we can look together to see if we can find her on some of the photos.'

Masking his bewilderment, Max rubbed his eyes and joined the group anxious to study the photos. Evangeline, he noticed, remained seated, clutching at a bright pink envelope.

Listening to the interminable, 'Ooh-look-there's-wots-is-name-gosh-I-remember-that-and-hasn't-it-altered?' Evangeline became bored. Turning to Connie, she asked impatiently, 'How long are they going to stand drooling over those photos? I thought we were here for a barn dance. Can't we have some lively music after that dreary disco?'

'The band are just tuning up again, Evangeline, so you'll be able to dance to your heart's content.'

'Dance or stumble?' Bunty whispered in Connie's ear. 'You realize she's half-cut? You've only got to look at her eyes.'

'Oh, dear,' sighed Connie. 'In that case I only hope Tom will be able to cope with her. There's no knowing what she'll do now.'

'Then, if you'll excuse me,' Bunty continued, 'I'll leave the dancing to you and George. I'll go and finish off in the kitchen. I noticed Alison's already gone back to clear up. You know she's not into leaping about the floor.'

'By the looks of it, neither is Evangeline,' Connie said drily.

Cajoling everyone on to the dance floor, the caller announced. 'The Dashing White Sergeant', followed by an Eightsome Reel. 'And there'll be no sitting down until I say so,' he grinned, picking up his fiddle.

'Sounds like they're having fun,' Alison remarked some time later.

'Mmm, most of them,' Bunty mused. 'That is until they come face to face with Evangeline. I'm surprised she's still standing.' Bunty moved to the doorway and peeped into the hall. 'Oh, lord! Poor Max. It looks as if Evangeline is trying to drag him on to the floor for a Gay Gordons.'

At the mention of Max's name, Alison hurried to Bunty's side, only to hear Max apologize, and politely but firmly refuse the proposal.

'I'm sorry, Evangeline. I'm not really in the mood for any more dancing, and I'm absolutely useless at the Gay Gordons. If you'll excuse me, only I promised to help Alison take the rubbish . . .'

At the mention of Alison's name, something in Evangeline's head snapped and in a simpering, sarcastic tone of voice she repeated Max's earlier words. 'I'm sorry . . . I'm not really in the mood . . . and I'm absolutely useless . . . Now where in the dim, distant past have I heard those words mentioned before?'

'I beg your pardon?' Max asked in surprise. 'I don't exactly follow you. What precisely are you getting at, Evangeline? Surely you're not implying I've said that to you in the past?'

By this time, those on the dance floor were merrily dancing, oblivious to the confrontation taking place by the kitchen door.

'Oh, no,' Evangeline simpered. 'It wasn't you who said it, Max, it was your darling wife.'

'Virginia? But Virginia's been dead for ten years! Besides, I really don't see what my aversion to the Gay Gordons has to do with Virginia. Quite frankly,

Evangeline, I think this is all a bit unnecessary.'

'Oh, do you? Oh, do you indeed?' Evangeline reiterated, reaching into the pocket of her jeans. 'Well, I don't! I don't think it's at all unnecessary. Why, I remember Virginia sitting in my kitchen at The Firs. Poured her heart out to me, she did, Max. And do you know what she said?'

Alison watched Max shake his head and had the distinct impression that even if Max didn't want to know what Virginia had said all those years ago, Evangeline was just about to tell him.

Attempting to emulate Virginia's clear, clipped tone, Evangeline repeated what she'd heard. 'You've got to help me, Evangeline, I'm absolutely desperate. Just how do I tell Max I'm sorry . . . that I'm not in the mood. I'm absolutely useless at lying. Besides, the whole situation is beginning to get out of hand and "you know who" wants me to go away with him. He keeps begging me to leave Max and . . .'

'How dare you?' Max broke in. 'You're lying, you bitch! Why, you don't honestly expect me to believe what you're saying is true?'

Inserting a scarlet fingernail into the pink envelope, Evangeline tore it open and studied its contents. 'Oh, you don't have to believe me, Max, darling,' she said, with cruel smile as jagged as the tear on the ripped envelope. 'But don't they say the camera never lies? Perhaps you'd better look at these and judge for youself. Who knows, you might even see someone you recognize.'

As Max reached out for the photos, Evangeline drew them back quickly, then changed her mind. 'No,' she said with a sardonic smile, 'they're no good to me any more. Here, you can have them, Max, but I'll tell you one thing, it's certainly not you sitting half-naked by Virginia's side . . .'

Unable to listen to any more, Alison turned and snatched the photos from a startled Evangeline with a resounding 'No!' which echoed into the September night as she ran from the hall. While a disgusted and furious Bunty grabbed hold of Evangeline's arm and frogmarched her back to face her husband, Max set off in pursuit of Alison.

CHAPTER 15

Out of breath and slumped against the stone wall behind the rows of parked cars, Alison clasped the photos to her breast. She didn't need to look at them. She'd already guessed their subject matter.

'You bitch, Evangeline! You cruel, heartless bitch! How could you? Wasn't it bad enough that he lost . . . ?'

'Alison!' Max gasped, rushing to her side 'Why didn't you stop when I called you? Why did you take the photos? Please, let me see . . .'

Knowing it was impossible to run any further, Alison nevertheless hoped to delay the inevitable . . . The time when Max would discover for himself evidence of his wife's infidelity.

'Alison, please!' Max begged.

Numbed and helpless, Alison felt Max prise the warm, curled photographs from her grasp. Leaving her still resting against the wall, he walked back towards the hall's kitchen door. In the bright beam of the security lighting, he held the photos up for examination.

Even from where she was standing, Alison saw the determined set of Max's jaw harden when he realized the cruel truth. The truth she'd so desperately wanted to hide from him. The reason behind Tara's death and quite possibly, although she'd not realized at the time, the circumstances that had invariably led to Virginia's untimely demise.

In stunned silence Max put the photos in his jacket pocket, walked back to Alison and took her roughly in his arms. 'Who was he, Alison? Who the hell was he? What was his name?'

'I don't know,' she cried lamely, 'I honestly don't know.'

'You surely don't expect me to believe that!'

With Max's fingers digging deep into her bare arms, Alison replied weakly, 'You've got to believe me, Max, it's the truth . . . Please, you're hurting me.'

Conscious of his vice-like grip on her bare flesh, Max was full of remorse and, releasing her from his grasp, murmured profuse apologies.

'It doesn't matter,' she replied, rubbing at the red marks on her arms. 'You have every right to be angry.'

'But not with you. Not with you, Alison. Tell me, please. If you don't know the man on the photos, why didn't you want me to see them?' Max waited and watched Alison's eyes slowly fill with tears. She turned her head away, unable to face him.

'Because,' he heard her whisper through a choked sob, 'I didn't want you to get hurt. I didn't want you to get hurt like . . . Tara.'

'Tara . . . but I don't understand! Do you mean to tell me Tara knew about this . . . ?' Max stopped, shook his head in disbelief and forced himself to continue '. . . Tara knew about these photos, she knew about my wife's lover?'

Against the din of the band and loud voices rising to a crescendo, it was Max's turn to shout '*No!*' Only, unlike Alison's cry, it was so plaintive and desperate and full of anguish that she found herself drawing Max into her arms, desperate to hold him close, desperate to lessen the pain.

With her tears on his face and the warmth of her body pressed against him, Max felt a surge of emotions well up inside. Anger and hurt fought against desire to return to the hall and drag the name of Virginia's lover from Evangeline's taunting, scarlet lips. Alison's lips however prevented him from doing so, plus the overwhelming desire to hold her close.

A tremor of unexpected pleasure surged through Alison's body as Max's lips sought hers. A tremor which was met halfway by panic and dark shadows. Sheer panic and fear, in fact. The fear of where this was all going to end.

Sensing her panic and once again in control of his own emotions, Max released her from his embrace, saying only, 'I'm sorry . . . Tara was . . .'

Dazed and confused, with her heart beating wildly in her breast, Alison could only reply weakly, 'Oh, yes – Tara.'

Taking her hand like a child's, Max led Alison back to the warmth of the hall. There they were met by an anxious-looking Connie, standing at the open doorway.

'Max . . . Alison . . . I've been looking everywhere. Are you okay? Only Bunty told me about Evangeline and the photos and . . .'

Max's face filled with renewed anger. Connie put a restraining hand on her brother's arm. 'She's gone, Max. Evangeline's gone. Tom's taken her home. He's asked me to apologize to you for . . .'

'Apologize? Apologize! Do you realize what that woman did, Constance?'

'Max – we think Evangeline's an alcoholic. Please try to understand . . . she probably didn't realize what she was doing, she . . .'

'No! Don't go on. I don't want to know. I don't want to hear any more. I've had enough for one night, thank you. I'm leaving!'

'You don't mean you're leaving Church Haywood? But what about Craven's Stables?'

Ignoring her questions, Max reached into his jacket pocket for the photographs. 'However, before I do go,' he said icily, 'and as you're my sister and you always appear to know everyone and everything, perhaps *you* can tell me who this man is with his hands all over my wife's breasts?'

With trepidation, Connie took the photos Max extended in her direction.

'And don't tell me you don't know him,' Max snapped impatiently. 'Because it's painfully obvious from the look on your face that you do!'

'I wouldn't lie to you, Max,' Connie replied softly. 'I don't think it would help, that's all.'

'Let me be the judge of that, Constance. You see, I think it would help. It would help me, and as Tara's friend it would also help Alison.'

'Alison!' Connie's face filled with alarm. 'How would it help Alison? Tara was a child and Alison only a teenager when this was . . . They couldn't possibly have known.'

'When this was what? And what couldn't they possibly have known?' Angrily Max snatched the photos from Connie's grasp and flung them on the table where they scattered like a collapsed house of cards. At that point he felt his entire world was beginning to collapse about him too.

Turning in Alison's direction, he drew her towards the table in full view of his sister. 'Look at her, Constance! Just look at Alison's face! Yes, of course she was a great deal younger when . . . when "all this", as you so charmingly put it, was going on. Tara was a child and Alison . . . In fact they were like two innocents together. And somehow,' here Max picked up the worst of the photos, 'they were both subjected to this! Though God alone knows how! Alison, it would appear, won't tell me – but one way and another I intend to find out!'

Connie stared open-mouthed at Max and Alison. Surely it wasn't true? Alison and Tara couldn't possibly have known about Virginia's affair, could they? At the time even Connie hadn't known for sure. She'd been suspicious; it had been pure speculation on her side initially. Then of course there'd been that dreadful day of Tara's accident and Virginia, so full of grief and melancholy, had taken solace in drinking until she'd appeared quite simply to give up the will to live.

'I'm waiting,' Max continued, bitterly.

'Waiting?' Connie asked, dazed.

'For his name. I want to know the bastard's name.'

'Miles . . . Miles Norton, or was it Horton? I really can't remember.'

Connie studied Max's ashen, questioning face. 'That's the truth, Max. As you can imagine, Virginia never introduced us.'

'So you're not denying you saw the two of them together!'

'Not exactly. We met quite by chance at one of Evangeline's tennis parties. He was a very good player,' Connie added without thinking.

'Hmph! That's obviously not all he was good at,' Max replied sarcastically, casting a sidelong glance at the photos. 'What puzzles me is why I never met him. I certainly don't remember him.'

'Quite possibly because he only appeared when you were away. You were, if you recall, away for long periods at a time, Max.'

'You're surely not implying this was my fault? That I'm to blame for all this! For Tara and Virginia and the fire?'

There was a deathly silence in the kitchen. 'The fire,' Max repeated, huskily. 'You don't think Virginia set fire to the house deliberately? She wouldn't have . . .'

'No, Max.' Connie placed a reassuring arm on his shoulder. 'No, Virginia wouldn't have done that. We all know she began drinking after Tara's accident. She also became a virtual chain-smoker.'

Max rubbed at the purple scar on his wrist. The scar from the injury he'd sustained when he'd rushed back from London and driven to the burnt-out shell of what had once been his home. The officer on duty had begged him not to go into the cottage. Virginia – or at least all that remained of her – had already been taken away in the ambulance.

Disregarding the warnings, Max had pushed past the remaining firemen in search of anything, anything that would give him hope. Anything that would bring his daughter and wife closer. Spying the charred remains of a small teddy bear on what had once been the hall table, Max had reached for it in desperation. It was then that the main banister rail collapsed and he had thrown up his arm to protect his face; only the actions of a quick-thinking fire officer had saved Max Craven from serious injury.

'Your wife was probably so emotionally exhausted following the death of your little girl, sir, that she fell asleep with a lighted cigarette in her hand,' the kindly WPC had suggested at the time, before George and Connie had taken him away to the hospital.

Now, thinking back to that long, painful night, Max sighed ruefully.

'No, Virginia wasn't emotionally exhausted. She was drunk! Drunk through attempting to drown her sorrows and appease her guilty secret.'

With a shudder, Max dislodged Connie's arm from his shoulder, slumped at one of the stools and buried his head in his hands. It was there George found him when he pushed his way back into the kitchen.

Oblivious to the tense situation, George called out chirpily, 'Come along, you three, they're about to play the last waltz or whatever it is they play at barn dances. I've come in search of my dear wife and as Max and Alison are here too, what could be more perfect? Max can dance with Al . . .'

George got no further. He saw Connie shake her head and turn her gaze in the direction of the photos on the table. A resounding 'Oh, dear!' escaped from his lips and he watched Max rise from the stool and walk numbly to the kitchen door.

'Thanks all the same, George, but I'm no longer in the mood for dancing. However, I'm sure Constance will oblige.'

When the door opened, Alison felt a cool and wel-

205

come burst of air on her face. Reminded of her presence, Max turned in her direction.

'Alison. I can only apologize on behalf of myself and my family, for ruining your life. For subjecting you to all this . . .'

'Oh! But you haven't,' she cried. 'You . . .' But Max had already turned on his heels and walked away into the late September night.

It was an extremely subdued quartet who met in the porch of St Faith's the following morning. Bunty and Connie distributed the prayer and hymn books in silence, whilst George carried the sheaf of corn to the altar with Alison in pursuit to pick up the stray pieces of chaff.

'Harvest Festival,' she sighed. 'This should be a time of celebration.'

With the organist playing a resounding opening to 'We Plough the Fields and Scatter', Alison looked anxiously about her. Sensing who she was looking for, Bunty leaned sideways and whispered in her ear, 'He's gone. Max has gone. Connie told me just before we sat down.'

Not wanting to believe her, Alison looked across to the neighbouring pew, the pew that had been used by the Craven family for generations. Looking up from her hymn book, Connie's eyes made contact with Alison's. She smiled sympathetically.

'Gone!' An inner voice echoed in Alison's head. Gone – but gone where? Max couldn't have gone to London, could he? Surely not, she told herself. He'd only recently sold his flat and most of his furniture and he wouldn't just walk away from Craven's Stables. Not when he had such plans for it and . . .

Alison felt Bunty tug at her arm. The hymn had finished and the rest of the congregation were sitting down, waiting for the Reverend Mr Hope to climb the pulpit steps and deliver his harvest sermon.

'All is safely gathered in,' he began. Deep in her heart Alison could think of only one thing. How she'd felt last night when she'd 'gathered' Max into her arms. At the time it had seemed the most natural thing to do. It was only when he'd kissed her that she'd felt the beginnings of panic. Then, when he'd whispered 'Tara', she wasn't even sure if Max was referring to his daughter or, if in the uncertainty of the moment, he'd thought she herself was Tara.

'And you're sure Max has gone?' Alison found herself struggling to ask Connie, as they left the church.

'Afraid so. He was adamant. Packed his bag and left, first thing this morning.'

'But what about Craven's Stables? Surely he won't just turn his back on the project? I mean, he's only recently had news of the planning permission. He had such plans . . .'

Connie shook her head sadly, remembering the tall, remote figure of her brother as he tossed a weekend bag into the boot of the Saab. It had been no use remonstrating and pleading with Max to stay. He was a Craven through and through. Strong-willed, determined and proud.

'Oh, I dare say he'll continue with the stables. Perhaps he'll just get the basic shell renovated and then put the place back on the market. Who knows? What I do know, however, Alison, is that Max was very concerned for your welfare.'

'My welfare? But why? I don't understand.'

'Following last night's shocking revelations about Virginia and – well, you know what – it would appear Max holds himself personally responsible for the pain and anguish you must have experienced these past ten years.'

'But that's ludicrous!' Alison protested. 'It has absolutely nothing to do with Max. Surely you don't believe it was his fault Virginia was having an affair with that man?'

'Then . . . you did know about it,' Connie enquired, gently. 'You and Tara both knew?'

Alison nodded and plucked at an imaginary piece of fluff on her jacket.

Connie hesitated, trying to choose the right words. 'Can I ask how you knew . . . how you found out about it? I mean, did Tara tell you or did you perhaps see them together?'

A look of sheer panic filled Alison's face. 'I'm sorry, Connie, I'd really rather not talk about it! If you'll excuse me, I promised I'd take Jasper for a walk. He didn't get much exercise yesterday. I spent most of the day decorating the village hall.'

'And it looked quite delightful,' Connie called, watching Alison rush away. 'Everyone said what a splendid job you made of . . .'

Connie jumped when she felt a hand on her shoulder.

'Oh, sorry, my dear. I didn't realize you were miles away.'

'George! For one minute I thought – I hoped – it was Max.'

'Sorry to disappoint you, old thing, I'm afraid it's only me.'

208

'Not so much of the old,' Connie scolded, forcing a grin.

'Well, at least I've made you smile.'

'Oh, you can always do that, George,' Connie said affectionately, slipping her arm through his. 'Thank God our lives have never been as complicated as Max and Alison's.'

'What makes you think Alison's life has been complicated?'

'Something she said, or, more to the point, something she didn't say when I was asking her about Virginia and that . . . that man! Oh, George, you know I blame myself for not telling Max. When I first suspected Virginia . . . I should have told him. For Tara's sake if nothing else.'

'Connie, my dear, I'm a great believer in letting life take its natural course.'

'But . . .'

'No, let me finish. My great-grandmother insisted our lives were mapped out for us. We follow a series of paths and are occasionally given the choice which one to follow. You and I have been lucky. Our paths crossed and we're still on the same one.' George bent and kissed his wife. 'And for that I say Alleluia! However, I've always believed your dear brother to be less fortunate.'

'What do you mean?'

'Only that I think he's got a few more paths to cross before he finds what he's been searching for all these years.'

'And do you . . .' Connie began with a faltering voice. 'Do you think Alison is what Max has been searching for?'

'Connie! What is this with Max and Alison?'

209

Connie shrugged her shoulders. 'I think she's right for him, that's all.'

'That's all!' George teased. 'In my book that's quite a lot. There's the age difference for a start, and . . .'

'And?'

'Well, I suppose at the moment I can't think of anything else. Though I have to confess they always look sort of right together. Almost as if they belong.'

'Exactly!' Connie replied, with a satisfied smile. 'As for the age difference, I don't think it either matters or shows. Because of the life she's led, travelling all over the place with her stepfather and stepbrothers – before Elizabeth came back to England – Alison has shown herself to be a very independent and mature young woman.'

George held up his hands in mock defence. 'All right! All right! You don't have to convince me any more. I'm sold on the idea. That is . . .'

'That is what?' Connie enquired, with a puzzled frown.

'That is as long as it's what both Alison and Max want.'

'You make it sound as if there could be problems.'

'As I see it,' George explained, 'I genuinely believe they're deeply attracted to each other, but I don't think Alison could cope with the situation if after last night's revelations Max now starts thinking of her as a daughter substitute.'

'But surely that's not possible!'

'My dear Connie, anything is possible. You said yourself how Max apologized for ruining Alison's life. Okay, so I know he's gone away, but mark my words, he'll be back. And when he does return, let's hope and pray he'll be looking for a soulmate and not a daughter.'

Connie was pleased George had used the word 'soulmate' and not lover. Despite wishing for Max and Alison's paths to cross once more, there was still a certain something niggling away in her head. Whatever it was, she couldn't remember it now. Besides George was speaking again.

'As I was saying, Connie, anything is possible, so we must wait and see. In the meantime however, do you think we could possibly make a move? Do you realize, for the first time in weeks, it's going to be just the two of us for Sunday lunch. After all the excitement and commotion of last night's pantomime, I thought you and I – er – could perhaps have a little rest after lunch.'

Looking knowingly in her husband's direction, Connie smiled and reached for his hand. Who said there was no pleasure in life once you got older?

Listening to the bells of St Faith's as she lay in her husband's arms, Evangeline sighed. 'You really should have gone to church, you know. You are a warden, don't forget, and it was Harvest Festival.'

'I'm sure they can manage without me for once,' Tom whispered as he stroked Evangeline's hair.

'Does my hair look that dreadful?' she asked wistfully, running her fingers through a mass of short hennaed spikes.

'Let's just say I preferred it long.'

'It's going to take an awfully long time for it to grow.'

'You could always buy a wig,' Tom said, trying to be helpful.

'What, here in Church Haywood!'

'No, I meant in London. I thought we could go to London for a few days.'

Evangeline studied the concern in Tom's grey eyes. 'I've been an absolute bitch, haven't I? I mean, I know I behaved badly last night, Tom, but I just couldn't stop myself. I felt as if I'd been programmed to go out and destroy their lives. Do you think they'll ever forgive me?'

'They say time always heals,' Tom replied, matter-of-factly.

'But I told Max all about . . .' Evangeline's eyes filled with tears at what little she could remember of the previous evening and she felt her mouth go quite dry. Perhaps if she were to have a drink? But Tom had insisted they spend a lazy morning in bed. He'd even forgone his parochial duties as church warden for her sake.

'You . . . you really think I have a problem, then . . . concerning my drinking?' Evangeline enquired nervously, grateful to feel Tom's reassuring arms around her shoulders.

'No, my darling, I don't think *you* have a problem. *We* have a problem, Evangeline, and I'm positive it's something we can resolve together.'

CHAPTER 16

The mere thought of going to The Firs on Monday morning filled Alison's heart with dread. How was she going to react when confronted by Evangeline? More to the point, how would Evangeline react when confronted by Alison? As she'd remarked to Bunty over breakfast, there was no getting away from it: Evangeline's bedroom had to be finished and the sooner the better.

'Best behave as if nothing has happened,' Bunty said, trying to be helpful.

'Easier said than done,' Alison replied. Watching Bunty spread honey on freshly toasted bread, she secretly wished the paint she'd been using in Evangeline's bedroom had gone on quite as smoothly. That was the trouble with rag-rolling, if you were going to do it properly; it took so much longer.

Still, she brightened, after today she could hopefully begin the stencilling. With luck she could say goodbye to The Firs by the end of the week and turn her thoughts to her next project. The prospect of working for Penny from the florists was far less daunting.

As it was, Alison's fear and dread of coming face to face with Evangeline was swept almost literally under the carpet when, having rung the bell to The Firs, she was greeted by the cleaner Madge Hastings.

With the vacuum cleaner drowning out the sound of the bell, Madge opened the door wide, swooped down and flung the doormat into the front porch, where it landed at Alison's feet.

'Oh, my Gawd!' Madge yelled, switching off the Hoover. 'You fair gave me a fright, Alison! I completely forgot you was coming today. Now what 'ave I done with your letter.'

'Letter? What letter?'

Madge delved into the pockets of her blue and white check overall.

'The one the missus give me for you.'

Hearing Madge refer to Evangeline as 'the missus' could only mean one thing. Evangeline was not at home. When she was, she expected Madge Hastings to address her as Mrs Carstairs.

Alison breathed a sigh of relief. 'I take it she's not here.'

'No ducks, gawn to London, she has, with Mr C. Won't be back till the end of the week. 'S'all in the letter, I 'spose.'

At this point Madge found the aforementioned letter and handed it to Alison with a smile. 'Good, tho', innit, 'cos it means I shan't be having her breathin' down my neck about "this smudge on the furniture" or "that bit of fluff on the carpet". Sometimes she's so bleedin' particular.'

Seeing Alison would not be drawn into conversation on Evangeline, Madge picked up the front doormat, thrashed it against the porch brickwork with a vengeance, and placed it back on the floor.

With Alison standing in the hallway reading the letter, Madge sighed and closed the door, casting an eye in the direction of the carrier bag propped against the hallstand.

'Still,' she said, thoughtfully, 'I s'pose I shouldn't go on about her really, not after wot she give me this morning for my Shirley.'

Disregarding the letter for a moment, Alison's curiosity was aroused.

'Oh, and what was that, Madge?'

'You can see for yourself,' Madge explained, lifting up the carrier bag for Alison's inspection.

Peering inside, Alison was amazed to see an Armani T-shirt, a pair of CK jeans and Nike trainers. 'But they're brand new! She only bought those last . . . She wore them to the barn dance. Why on earth does she want to give them away?'

'Beats me,' Madge replied, clutching the bag to her ample bosom. 'All I know is that she says to me this morning, "Oh, by the way, Madge, there's a few things in the bag by the door for your daughter."' Peering into the bag, Madge continued, 'And I shall be takin' them home with me right quick, in case she comes back and changes her mind!'

'I don't think there's any danger of that,' Alison reassured her. 'In her letter, Evangeline states quite clearly that she won't be coming back until Friday night at the earliest.'

With a sigh of relief, Madge put the bag down by the front door.

'I'll make us a cup of coffee in a tick,' she called, watching Alison climb the stairs.

'Thanks all the same, Madge, but don't bother. I can

215

make one for myself later on. I'd prefer to get on with the decorating if you don't mind. Once I start this last wall of rag-rolling, I'd prefer not to be interrupted.'

'Suit yourself,' came the reply. Switching on the vacuum cleaner once more, Madge retorted, 'Rag-rolling, indeed! Wot on earth's wrong with woodchip and emulsion?'

In London, at the offices of Craven and Painton, Nigel was also turning his thoughts to paint colour charts and fabric swatches. Thoughtfully, he turned to Max. 'I don't suppose the sea-sprite would be interested in redesigning the offices.'

'I very much doubt it. It's far too big a project for Alison to take on single-handed.'

'Pity. It would be a real pleasure to see her again. Wouldn't it be nice for Vanessa to meet her too? I thought perhaps we could all . . .'

'No, Nigel! We could not! I've already told you, I don't want anyone to know I'm in London. I don't intend to stay here for long anyway. If you so much as breathe a word . . .'

'Okay, okay. Point taken. You have my word.'

With an anguished sigh, Max strode to the window. Why on earth had he come to London when he hated it so much? After Church Haywood the air seemed so full of pollution. And the noise . . . well, the noise was unbearable.

'You know you're more than welcome to stay at the flat with us. Vanessa really wouldn't mind.'

'I know,' Max broke in kindly. 'I appreciate your offer . . . and your concern, Nigel. It's just . . .'

'Just what?'

216

'Just that I need to sort a few things out, that's all.'

'And I take it you still don't want to talk about it?' Nigel asked, already knowing what the answer would be.

Max shook his head and walked towards the office door. 'Not at the moment, but rest assured, as I value your friendship, Nigel, *if* I do ever want to talk about it, you will be the one to whom I unburden my soul.'

'Crikey! How profound,' whispered Nigel under his breath, watching the door close. 'This has got to be serious!'

Buzzing through to reception, Nigel gave instructions that no one was to say Max had been at the office. 'And don't forget,' he reiterated, 'if you're in any doubt what to do, just direct any difficult calls through to me and I'll deal with them.'

For Tom Carstairs, his phone call had been anything but difficult. He'd had no trouble finding the number he sought. Now, driving through one of the quieter London suburbs, with his wife studying the *A – Z*, he had no trouble finding the way either.

'Right, this must be it,' Tom announced, pulling up outside a neat but nondescript double-fronted house. To anyone else it looked pretty ordinary. Net curtains at the windows, making it impossible to see into the clear glass windows. A blue-painted front door with brass door-knocker and letterbox, polished to Madge Hastings' high standard, Evangeline noticed, and a well-scrubbed front step.

Tom helped his wife from the car and placed his hand on the wrought-iron gate. Evangeline hesitated, taking in her unfamiliar surroundings. The avenue of trees, whose leaves were just turning to their autumn colours, the neatly clipped privet hedge and the newly trimmed postage stamp of front lawn.

'Evangeline?' Tom questioned, desperate not to show any anxiety in his voice. They'd come this far. Surely she wouldn't change her mind now? Although, to be honest, he wouldn't have blamed her if she had. It was going to be an enormous step to take. Placing a reassuring hand beneath her elbow, he said softly, 'Well, my dear, shall we go in?' For a fleeting moment Tom watched as her face filled with new-found fear and panic.

'Don't worry, Evangeline. This is going to be our new beginning. Remember what I said? *Our* problem and we face it together.'

Giving her hand a comforting squeeze, Tom led his wife towards the blue front door.

Max Craven was less fortunate, inasmuch as at that moment he had no one to lead him by the arm. Leaving Nigel and the office, he'd telephoned Connie, purely to reassure her he was okay and to tell her that in no way was she to try and contact him.

'But, Max!' Connie had protested.

'I mean it, Constance. I want to be left in peace, and whatever you do you are not to keep pestering Nigel.'

'I was only going to ask about the Stables,' Connie added weakly.

'What about the Stables?'

'You will be coming back to check on their progress, won't you?'

'My builders are perfectly capable of managing on their own. They know what I want.'

'But do you know what *you* want, Max?' Connie

whispered softly into the mouthpiece of the phone.

Connie's question remained unanswered. Max had already hung up the phone and was heading back to his cheerless hotel room. Mention of the Stables had only served to accentuate his complete and utter despair.

Evangeline gazed about her at the sea of unfamiliar faces. Thank heavens, she thought to herself, reaching for her handbag, not one familiar Church Haywood face anywhere . . . apart from Tom, of course. Tom heard her audible sigh.

'Okay?' he whispered. 'At least they all look normal.'

Evangeline smiled wryly. Trust Tom. What on earth was he expecting? Self-confessed alcoholics weren't freaks with one eye and horns sticking out of the tops of their heads. Nor did they walk around wearing placards that proclaimed their obsession for booze! No, if all the people in this room had alcohol-related problems, then they appeared – as Tom had so correctly described them – quite a normal-looking bunch on the whole.

Sensing Evangeline's unease, the young girl with peroxide-blonde hair sitting by her side announced confidently, 'You can smoke, you know. It's only the drink that's a no-no.'

Mention of the word 'drink' only served to remind Evangeline of her last drink – the remains of the half-bottle of brandy, consumed in the grimly decorated interior of the ladies' cloakroom at the village hall. Since then Tom had hardly let her out of his sight, not to mention the fact that he'd locked all remaining bottles away and pocketed the key.

'I always knew that redundant gun cabinet would

come in useful one day,' he'd announced, trying to make her feel better. The problem was, it hadn't helped than and it didn't help now.

Sitting on a chair covered with a dust sheet, Alison sat back and admired the finished rag-rolled walls.

'At least that's finished,' she said with a contented sigh. 'I can begin the stencilling tomorrow.' Picking at a blob of grey on her paint-stained hands, she studied her fingernails. 'Alison Benedict, your hands are a disgrace. Why, they're not fit to be seen!' Unlike Max Craven's, a voice echoed in her head.

Stretching her hands out across the knees of her denim dungarees, Alison remembered Max's slender, long-fingered hands as they'd reached for her on so many occasions. That first meeting in the churchyard after her mother's funeral; the evening he'd fallen asleep on the train and given her a lift home; and then of course last Saturday.

Last Saturday, when he'd led her on to the dance floor, his touch had been both firm and confident, yet at the same time full of tenderness and concern lest she should stumble. Later, however, following the harrowing incident with Evangeline and the incriminating photographs, Max's grip had been vice-like.

Rubbing at her arm, where his fingers had grasped her bare flesh, she remembered how his anger had been followed by profuse apologies and concern. Then, with the realization of what she'd silently and knowingly endured all these years, Max's manner had altered yet again.

It was the almost brutal physical contact with him that she remembered so vividly. Yet at the same time, it was the scene that hurt and haunted her the most. She'd been unable to shake it from her mind.

Desperate to relive the moment when Max's lips sought hers, Alison could only recall the panic and inner turmoil she'd struggled against. The fear and sheer panic in her breast, which Max had interpreted so incorrectly. Assuming his own unexpected surge of emotions had upset her, he'd held her away from him, taken her hand in his, and returned her to the comforting warmth and safety of the hall like a child.

'And what did you say, Max?' Alison murmered softly, before clasping her hands to her face.

Emitting a desperate sigh, she knew she had to recall his last words. She had to, if only to try and dispel the ghosts and shadows from the past and put her life and her future into some sort of perspective.

'The future! Why, you fool, Alison Benedict! You honestly didn't expect there was a future for you and Max Craven? What a preposterous idea! How could there be? Oh, yes, of course he held you in his arms and even kissed you. But at that moment he was desperate for consolation and you just happened to be there!'

Rising from the chair, Alison walked quickly to the bedroom window. There she stopped abruptly and turned to scrutinize the newly decorated walls with a critical eye.

'What was it you were thinking only moments ago?' she reproached herself. 'Something about the future and perspective? Well,' she continued with a brittle smile, 'there's certainly no future for you with Max Craven, especially after Saturday night. Why, when he led you back to the hall it was Tara he mentioned. He even held your hand like a child. He probably even thought you were his daughter!'

Alison felt a cold shiver run through her body. For one brief idyllic moment, Max had held her in his arms like a lover, and the next she was little more than a child!

'Future and perspective,' she repeated over and over again, sealing the lids on the paint tins and gathering her tools together. 'Forget about the future and concentrate on the perspective, in particular the perspective of this room!'

In her mind's eye, Alison saw the finished bedroom with its stencilled border of trailing clematis and pale amethyst silk drapes. Yes, it would look lovely, she would make sure of that. Irrespective of her personal feelings towards Evangeline at that particular moment, she would not let them cloud her professional judgement when finishing the room.

Locking the house and dropping the key through the letterbox (Mrs Hastings had her own key and always went in by the back door), Alison retraced her steps to the main gates, pondering as she did so how Shirley Hastings would react to Evangeline's latest donation to her wardrobe.

'It really was amazing,' Alison announced, while setting the table for dinner. 'At first I couldn't believe it. It was all there in the carrier bag. Jeans, T-shirt and trainers.'

'But they must have cost a fortune!' Bunty called from the kitchen, where she was peering into a pan of steaming vegetables.

'Precisely. If you'd seen Mrs Hastings this morning, with that bag in her arms. She was positively possessive and . . .'

Bunty gave a puzzled frown as she placed a tureen on the table.

'. . . I'd be prepared to bet she thought I might take them from her, thus depriving her Shirley,' Alison explained.

'But that's daft! I mean, any comparison between Madge Hastings' Shirley and yourself, Alison.' Bunty roared with laughter.

'I don't know. If you carry on serving me meals like this, Bunty. I may very well end up like Shirley!'

'Never in a million years.' Bunty said, passing Alison her plate. 'Besides, I thought we deserved a special meal this evening after – well you know – the events of the past few days.'

For a moment, forgetting the roast sirloin of beef with its onion gravy and Yorkshire pudding, Alison's thoughts turned to Max. What would he be dining on this evening? It was common knowledge that, while he'd lived with Connie and George, despite his repeated request for independence, Connie had always insisted he eat his main meal of the day with them.

'Penny for them, Alison?' Bunty called softly, passing the dish of roast potatoes.

'Oh, I was just wondering what Max would be eating this evening. I don't suppose Connie has heard . . .'

Bunty shook her head. 'No, he's given strict instructions that he wants to be left in peace. Come to think of it, it's probably what he could do with right now. You know he probably hasn't had much of it at all during the past ten years. It can't have been easy for him, mourning first Tara and then Virginia, especially as he thought she was so perfect. It must have been a dreadful shock when he saw those photos . . .'

'Bunty, please! I'd rather not talk about the photos if you don't mind.'

'No, of course not. How insensitive of me. Let's get on and eat, shall we? I've made us a nice blackberry and apple pie for pudding.'

Bunty studied Alison's anxious face and, reaching out across the table, patted her hand reassuringly. 'Max will be fine, you'll see. In fact I think we'll all be okay from now on.'

It was Alison's turn to look puzzled.

'I think,' Bunty announced with a grin, 'Evangeline has been a genie in disguise and not the wicked witch we think her to be after all.'

'I can tell you've been discussing Church Haywood's winter pantomime, but quite what it's got to do with us I fail to . . .'

'Showing Max those photos was like rubbing Aladdin's lamp, and instead of a genie, out popped not only Max and Virginia's past, but events that have affected us all in one way or another over the past ten years.'

Finding it hard to see it in such a simple and light-hearted way, Alison couldn't resist the urge to say, 'And you think if we're all granted three wishes, we can make everything perfect!'

'No, Alison, I don't,' Bunty replied matter-of-factly. 'But it doesn't hurt to dream, does it?'

Later that night, getting ready for bed, Alison was consumed with guilt and wished she hadn't been quite so abrupt with Bunty.

'Oh, well,' she sighed. 'At least I'll be able to make it up to her when she's in Australia. Heaven knows the kitchen here could do with a complete facelift. It will certainly take my mind off the Christmas I could have had if I'd gone to the States.'

Re-reading the letter she'd received from America that morning, Alison felt tears prick her eyelids. The letter was from Oliver, inviting her to join Jasper and himself for Thanksgiving, and if not Thanksgiving, then why not Christmas and New Year?

At any other time she would have jumped at the chance of seeing her stepbrothers again. They were, after all, such good company, and it would have given her the opportunity to get away from the inner turmoil, confusion and despair that was tearing at her very soul.

Yet she knew perfectly well she couldn't go. She'd already committed herself to doing work for Penny, had volunteered to help with the costumes for the village pantomime, and as for Christmas . . . She couldn't let Bunty down at this late stage. Bunty, who'd been like a second mother to her, was looking forward to Christmas Day on Bondi Beach.

'Well, Christmas here at Keeper's Cottage will certainly be a far cry from Christmas in Australia or New York,' she mused.

Folding the wafer-thin sheet of blue paper back into its envelope, Alison thought of previous Christmases spent with Jasper and Oliver. Jasper with his hordes of lively actor friends and Oliver performing at some impressive New Year's Eve concert, before the traditional walk to Times Square to welcome in New Year.

Alison dabbed at her eyes. Though it was still three months away, she conjured up the image of her own forthcoming Christmas and New Year's Eve. No doubt she would spend them here at the cottage, alone apart from the four-legged Jasper, who had managed to sneak into her bedroom and now lay curled up – pretending not to be there – on the patterned quilt.

Placing Oliver's letter on the bedside table, Alison reached out and stoked Jasper's wiry fur. 'I expect we'll manage to pull a cracker between us,' she sighed wistfully, 'and I can cook us one of those rolled and boned turkey breast joints. Then we can have lots of lovely long walks and . . .'

At the mention of the word 'walk', Jasper stirred and wagged his tail in expectation.

'No, not now,' Alison whispered apologetically. 'I meant at Christmas.'

As if sensing Christmas was still three months away, and not wishing to wait that long before he went for another walk, Jasper cast Alison a look of canine disdain, yawned, stretched and slid noiselessly from the bed. Perhaps he'd stand better chance of a walk if he went in search of his mistress. Who knew, he might even get another slice of that wonderful roast beef. In fact, he'd done quite well already this evening. Alison had only eaten half her dinner and the remains had fortuitously found their way into his own blue enamel bowl.

Switching off the bedside lamp with its garish swirl of Chinese dragons and chrysanthemums, Alison found her thoughts returning to Bunty's earlier comments concerning Evangeline.

Regardless of what you might think, Bunty, she thought to herself, I still don't see Evangeline as a genie in disguise. In fact, far from offering us hopes and wishes for the future as she emerges from her magic lamp, I see her merely opening up a can of worms . . . and very unpleasant ones they are, too!

CHAPTER 17

In her hotel room, watched by an anxious Tom, Evangeline tugged at the ring pull on a can of tonic water.

'It's okay,' she reassured him. 'It's G and T without the gin!'

'Would you like me to send down for some ice and lemon? It might make it slightly more palatable.' He reached for the phone.

A few minutes later, adding ice and a slice of lemon to his own glass of tonic, Tom hesitated. 'You know, I was really proud of you today, Evangeline.'

Evangeline sipped at her drink and gave a sharp, dry laugh.

'Proud of me, Tom? Surely not! It's hardly the thing to be proud of, is it? I mean, having your wife announce to a room full of complete strangers that she's an alcoholic.'

Tom placed a comforting hand on Evangeline's shoulder. 'I don't see it quite like that, my dear.'

'You don't?' Evangeline snapped tetchily, reaching for her cigarettes. 'In that case, how do you see it?'

Reaching for the cigarette lighter and steadying

Evangeline's hand, Tom held the lighter in place until he saw her breathe in deeply and exhale for the umpteenth time that day, a thin cloud of wispy blue smoke. 'I see it as being the first step along the way to recovery . . . the first step to . . .'

'But,' Evangeline broke in, 'some people say, once an alcoholic, always an alcoholic.'

'Then it's up to us to prove them wrong, isn't it? And by that I do mean *us*. We've got to work at it together, remember?'

Calmed by her latest cigarette, Evangeline studied her husband thoughtfully. 'And you really think we can do it?'

'Of course – don't you? We know from what they said at the meeting that it's not going to be easy.'

Evangeline crossed the floor to the dressing table, where she flicked ash into the heavy crystal ashtray. It was already half full. In doing so she caught sight of her reflection in the mirror.

'My God! I look bloody awful! What on earth possessed me to have my hair cut?'

'It will soon grow,' said Tom, in an effort to reassure her.

Desperate for a drink, Evangeline tugged at her cropped hair and spun round to face him. 'Tom Carstairs! Why do you always have to be so bloody nice? Why, for once can't you tell me I'm an absolute bitch? That my hair looks a mess? That I look like and behave like a common tart and that you're sick to death of me? Christ knows,' she said, studying the pile of cigarette ends, 'I've always done things to excess. I mean booze, cigarettes, clothes, furniture for the house, cars and . . . even men.' Her voice trailed away to a whisper. 'You don't even know the half of it.'

'Oh, I think I do, Evangeline . . . and perhaps it's because of me that you've done some of those things. But I have no intention of telling you you're an absolute bitch – even though you once called me a boring old fart!'

Evangeline's eyebrows shot up in amazement. 'But I didn't mean it.'

'That's kind of you to say so,' continued Tom, 'and I'm certainly not going to retaliate by telling you I'm sick to death of you. Because, quite simply, I'm not. You see, my darling, I love you. I've always loved you and I always will.' Evangeline's eyes filled with tears as Tom removed the dying cigarette from her fingers and stubbed it out in the ash tray.

'Now,' he said, taking her by the hand and leading her to the bed, 'it's been an exhausting day and I suggest we get some sleep. Don't forget, we've got the rest of the week here in London and we shan't spend every day at the AA group. And . . . who knows,' he said, tenderly, 'by the end of the week and with a few early nights, this boring old fart might even surprise you.'

'But I don't want to go to school, it's borin'! I want to go with Al'son and Jasper for a walk!'

'Look, Rosie,' the youngest Mrs Jennings scolded, 'you've got to go to school or I shall get in trouble with the authorities. Now come along, 'cos I've got to take Jamie to the clinic for his jab, unless you want to have it instead?'

At the mere mention of the word 'jab', Rosie stopped in her tracks and Michelle Jennings smiled knowingly in Alison's direction.

'Perhaps you can come and take Jasper for a walk with me one afternoon after school instead.' Alison suggested, feeling sorry for the disgruntled Rosie, who was kicking at a stone with the toes of her brand new school shoes.

'Rosie! For goodness' sake! Those shoes have got to last. I'm not made of money, you know. We've had enough expense just lately what with paying for great-gran's funeral.'

Ignoring the reprimand, Rosie walked on ahead to the end of Jasper's extension lead, leaving Alison and her mother to talk in peace.

'I don't know, she gets worse,' Michelle complained. 'Why she wasn't born a boy I just don't know! She fair wears me out, what with the little ones an' all.'

'I expect she'll calm down before too long,' Alison replied. 'I remember I used to be just the same. I don't suppose it's been easy with another baby in the house and her great-grannie dying so suddenly.'

'Yes, I suppose now you come to mention it, she and her great-gran were very close, and Jamie is certainly a demanding baby. Not like Rosie; she was always so independent.'

'There you are, then,' Alison encouraged, trying to ease the tension.

Straightening the baby's pram rug, Michelle looked up thoughtfully.

'Alison . . . my father-in-law was wondering whether we should put Rosie in great-gran's room, now that she's gone. I mean, I know it's not that big, but at least it would mean Rosie would have a room of her own. At the moment she's having to share. What do you think?'

'I think it sounds like a good idea. Would you like me

230

to ask her when we go for a walk? I know some children could be upset sleeping in a room where someone has recently died, but I very much doubt if Rosie will be bothered by such things.'

Having reached the village school, Rosie turned and gazed wistfully in Alison's direction.

'How about if I meet you from school this afternoon, Rosie? We could take Jasper for a walk, see if there are any conkers left up by the golf course and even have a look in the woods for some fallen branches. Don't forget, it will soon be Bonfire Night.'

The mention of after-school activities and Bonfire Night brought a broad grin to Rosie's face. Bonfire Night! Great! That meant a bonfire on the village green, making a guy – using a pair of grandad's old trousers and gardening jacket – and a real bonfire supper round the fire, or in the village hall if it was wet.

'Will Mister come for a walk with us too?' Rosie asked expectantly.

Alison shook her head. 'I'm afraid Max has gone away for a while.'

Rosie was crestfallen. 'Gone away! But why has he gone? He promised to take me . . . Where has Max gone, Al'son?'

'Mr Craven to you!' Rosie's mum broke in as the school bell echoed across the playground. 'Just try and remember your manners.'

'But Max doesn't mind,' Rosie called, scurrying towards the sunbleached door with its peeling green paintwork.

'Saved by the bell,' Michelle sighed, turning the pram in the direction of the village hall and the baby clinic.

'In more ways than one,' Alison whispered to herself, drawing in Jasper's lead in order to cross the road. 'I'll meet her after school, then, if that's okay? And don't worry about her shoes either. I won't take her anywhere too muddy, I'll save that for another day when she's wearing her wellingtons.'

Dangling the restless baby on her knee, Michelle Jennings gave thanks for the likes of Alison Benedict. Apart from great-gran and Max Craven, Alison seemed to be the most important person in Rosie's life. And now that great-gran was no more (it had been a terrible shock to the family, her dying so suddenly the week after harvest supper) she was probably going to turn to Alison even more for attention.

'I only hope Alison won't mind,' she said wistfully. And what about Max Craven? Where had he been these past few weeks? One minute he was busy chatting to great-gran at the barn dance and the next he was gone!

There had been rumours, of course. In particular those resulting from the night of the harvest supper. The night that snooty woman Evangeline Carstairs had turned up looking like mutton dressed as lamb.

'Funny thing, though, Jamie,' Mrs Jennings confided to her baby. 'I'm sure I've seen Shirley Hastings parading herself in an identical get-up.'

As the baby gurgled and wriggled impatiently, his mother tried in vain to remember what she'd overheard during great-gran's funeral tea. Something about Mrs Carstairs being a friend of Mr Craven's dead wife, a fuss being made over certain photographs. Even Alison Benedict, she was sure, came into the picture somewhere along the line.

Later that afternoon, whilst cooking tea and with

Rosie out of the way, Michelle Jennings turned to her eldest son.

'Wayne, the night of the harvest supper, when you were outside with Donna, what did you . . . ?'

'Honest, Mum, I told you before! We weren't doin' anythin' wrong. We just went out for a smoke.'

'And the rest of it,' his father called, coming in through the back door. He gave his wife a knowing wink. 'I bet you were having a good snog out there in the moonlight.'

'Dad!' Wayne remonstrated in disgust.

'That's a horrid word. I do wish you wouldn't use it,' Michelle called to her husband as he hung up his jacket.

'What is?'

'Snog. It makes it sound so . . . so unpleasant and vulgar.'

'Well, I never heard you complain before. What term would you prefer, then?'

Feeling herself colour, Michelle replied, 'I don't know. Perhaps kissing and cuddling.'

'Hmph! There's a lot more than kissing and cuddling goes on in the Church Haywood lusting grounds these days. It's not quite like it used to be when we were teenagers, Michelle, having a quick grope in the back of the van.'

'You can say that again, Dad!' Wayne joined in, 'Why, only last week Donna and I saw Shirley Hastings with . . .'

'Wayne! That's enough!'

'But Mum! You started all this! You wanted to know what happened in the village hall car park on the night of the harvest supper.'

'Oh, did she indeed? And just what exactly did she want to know?'

Feeling two pairs of eyes in her direction, Michelle scooped chips and sausages on to dinner plates and reached for a saucepan of baked beans. 'I was curious, that's all,' she faltered. 'I was talking to Alison this morning and she said Max Craven was still away – Rosie was asking for him, in case you want to know – and I . . .'

'And you what?' her husband enquired.

Michelle shrugged her shoulders. 'I just wanted to know if Wayne had seen Max and Alison together. I mean, I know there's rumours about that Carstairs woman and her drinking and . . .'

'That's not rumour, that's fact!' Wayne announced confidently. 'Donna told me she saw Mrs High and Mighty on more than one occasion having a crafty swig from a bottle when she was in the ladies' loo.'

Ladling the beans with an air of disappointment, Michelle gave up interrogating her son. It was only later when he was leaving to fetch Donna, his current love of the moment, that he popped his head round the kitchen door.

'By the way, Mum,' he hissed, with a wry grin on his face. 'Just in case you're still interested, I saw Max Craven kiss Alison Benedict and she certainly didn't seem to mind . . . not at first, that is.'

Michelle looked up expectantly, waiting for her son to continue. Not at first, he'd said. In that case what happened later?

'Anyway,' Wayne continued, 'to me it looked as if Alison began to panic. She looked frightened, though I'm sure Mr Craven wasn't going to hurt her. Then he muttered something and took her indoors. That's when Donna and I heard the unholy row about the photographs and he was shouting about Virginia . . . whoever she is.'

'Was. Virginia was Max's wife. She's the one who died in the fire.' Michelle's voice trailed away as her son closed the door behind him.

'I've had cottage pie with squiggly potatoes on top, mashed carrots and swede and Peter Piss, followed by apple grumble and ice-cream.' Rosie announced, triumphantly running through the kitchen door.

Michelle raised her eyebrows in alarm.

'She means petits pois and apple crumble.' Alison whispered with a grin, from the doorway.

'Thank heavens for that.' Michelle sighed. 'For one minute she had me quite worried.'

'And we found some conkers and lots of different-shaped leaves. Al'son's going to help me make a book to stick them in so I can write their names underneath. Oh, and yes, I polished my shoes too. The fat lady showed me how to spit on them and make them all shiny and new just like her Dad did in the army. He was in India and he shot a tiger and he also . . .'

'Rosie! How about stopping for breath and letting me invite Alison in for a cup of tea?' Not knowing whether to laugh or scold her daughter for referring to Bunty as 'the fat lady', Michelle simply held up the kettle in Alison's direction.

Alison shook her head. 'No, thanks, I've left Jasper tied to the side gate and I'd better get back. It's quite chilly out there now and already getting dark. "The fat lady" reminded me this afternoon, we put the clocks back at the weekend.'

Alison fixed Michelle with a mischievous smile and

nodded in Rosie's direction. 'She's been really good, ate all her dinner and . . .'

'But she doesn't like vegetables, particularly mashed carrots and swede,' Michelle expostulated. 'Father-in-law grows his own, so they're always fresh.'

'Don't worry about it, Michelle. Most youngsters are like that, so I'm told. I used to hate lamb until I went to stay with a schoolfriend, and when my own mother found out I'd actually eaten it and enjoyed it . . .'

'You're very good with kiddies, Alison,' Michelle broke in kindly. 'You should have some of your own.'

Half expecting Alison to pooh-pooh the idea and say she wasn't yet ready for children, Michelle was therefore shocked to see a look of terror spread across Alison's face, before she mumbled a hasty goodbye and headed for the back door. As an afterthought Alison turned back to remind Rosie about collecting wood for the bonfire.

'We'll go on Saturday morning,' she said hurriedly. 'In the meantime I'll go and look for a scrapbook for our project.'

'Bye, Al'son . . .' a contented and sleepy voice called from the kitchen table where Rosie was laying out her coloured leaves '. . . and thank you.'

'Blimey what is this, Sherwood Forest?'

Rosie looked up indignantly at her father. 'No, it's not! It's leaves for my book. That one's an oak, that's a hazel and that crispy one's . . .'

'Well, I never, Michelle, it would appear we've got our own little David Bellamy in the family.'

'. . . a beech,' Rosie proclaimed, and proceeded to tell her father what she'd eaten at Keeper's Cottage, rounding it off with, 'and I know how to spit on my shoes and make them all shiny.'

'Who's Peter Piss when he's at home?' a puzzled voice enquired.

Rosie gave a sigh of exasperation in her father's direction and left her mother to explain. 'I'll tell you later,' Michelle whispered, 'once Rosie's in bed and asleep.'

But she didn't. Instead Michelle Jennings found herself relating to her husband, word for word, what Wayne had said about Max Craven and Alison in the village hall car park.

'And when I said to her she was good with kiddies and should have some of her own, she looked terrified and couldn't leave quick enough. Why do you think she did that? You don't think she's had a baby, do you, and had it . . . ?'

'Alison Benedict? No, never! But I'd be prepared to bet, from what you've just said and what our Wayne told you, that perhaps something or someone's upset her at some time.'

'You mean she could be frightened of men?' Michelle asked, wide-eyed.

'Or frightened at the thought of what they might do to her.'

'Oh!' replied Michelle numbly.

Letting her imagination run riot at what could have possibly happened to Alison in the past to leave her her feeling and reacting as she did, Michelle soon found her attention distracted by her husband's cold hand, creeping beneath her nightdress.

'In which case, she's not like you, Michelle.'

'Meaning?' Michelle giggled.

'Meaning you've never been afraid of men, or at least afraid of me. Now how about a little snog – or would you rather I said kiss and cuddle? Although if I remember correctly, we never called it that either when we were parked in my van at the back of the golf course!'

Dispelling any further thoughts of Alison from her mind, Michelle cast a cursory glimpse at the bedroom door to make sure it was firmly shut, switched off her favourite lamp – designed to look like a crinoline lady – and turned eagerly to face her husband.

Hurtling through the woods at full pelt, calling out, 'Gee-up, Jasper!' Rosie kicked her way merrily through sweeping drifts of leaf mould.

'Don't go too fast, Rosie,' Alison panted. 'You have to remember I can't run as fast as you.'

Alison stopped and rubbed her leg. Whether it was pure coincidence, or the early November dampness causing the problem, she didn't know. What she did know however, was last night and this morning she'd been in agony.

In fact if it hadn't been because of her earlier promise to Rosie, she wouldn't be here at all, struggling to keep up with the miniature Clint Eastwood wearing the ubiquitous serape. Managing a smile, Alison forced herself forwards and found child and dog, waiting for her by a gnarled tree stump. Rosie was studying a neighbouring tree.

'That would be a good tree for hanging someone,' Rosie chirped.

'Rosie! That's not very nice.'

'Well, it would. See that branch just there? You could

tie the rope and . . . whoosh, they'd be a goner. That is unless Clint was there, an' he was your friend an' he came to your rescue and shot you down.'

Picking up a forked twig, Rosie aimed at the direction of the 'hanging branch', made the appropriate sound of a gunshot and watched the imaginary friend fall to the ground. Then she called to the same imaginary body with a, 'Now let's get the hell out of here,' patted Jasper on his rump with her hand, and 'rode off' into the sunset.

An hour later an extremely tired and bedraggled trio dragged an assortment of dead branches back to Keeper's Cottage.

'My goodness, you have been busy,' Bunty called from the garden. 'I take it that's for the bonfire.'

'Yep. Sure is,' Rosie continued in western vein. 'We're sure gonna have a mighty fine bonfire, ma'am, an' we're fair wore out.'

'In that case you'd better come inside.' Bunty smiled.

Placing steaming mugs of hot chocolate and home-made biscuits on the kitchen table, Bunty turned anxiously in Alison's direction.

'How's the leg? I noticed you were limping when you came across the field.'

'Who's got a bad leg?' Rosie asked, her face full of alarm.

'I have, today,' Alison replied, not wishing to arouse too much concern. 'Sometimes the old scar from an accident . . .'

'Can I see? Did you have to have lots of stitches and did it bleed a lot?' Rosie demanded, anxious for all the gory details.

Realizing she wasn't going to get any peace until

she'd shown Rosie the offending scar, Alison unzipped her jeans and revealed her upper thigh.

'Wow! What happened – did you get shot?'

'No,' smiled Alison warmly, refastening her zip. 'I got hit by a car.'

'But you know what the safety hedgehog says? STOP, LOOK AND LISTEN. Didn't you remember your Green Cross Code?'

Alison looked knowingly across the table in Bunty's direction. 'No, I'm afraid I didn't. At the time I suppose I must have forgotten.'

'*Oh, Al-i-son*!' came the gasped reply. 'Fancy you forgettin'! Grandad says you must always look both ways before you cross the road. He also says you must never play with fireworks. He told Wayne off last night, because his friends were throwing bangers about.'

'That really is dangerous!' Bunty announced angrily.

Anxious to turn Rosie's attention away from her leg, Alison passed her the plate of biscuits and asked about the forthcoming Bonfire Night.

'Will you be making a guy, Rosie?'

Munching into her biscuit, Rosie shook her head sadly. 'I wanted to, but Wayne says Donna wants to make it – she's his soppy girlfriend.'

'Perhaps you can help too?'

'Dunno, I might. Only Donna said she didn't want grandad's old jacket, it was too scruffy.'

'But it's only going on the bonfire,' Bunty broke in. 'Guy Fawkes doesn't have to wear smart clothes.'

Sensing Rosie really wasn't too keen to discuss the matter further, Alison walked to the kitchen dresser and placed the brand new scrapbook on the table.

'There, that's for your leaves. Perhaps if you're ready

240

to go home now, you can stick them in this afternoon. There's some glue too. Why don't you ask your mummy and daddy to help you?'

Rosie gave an exasperated sigh. 'Mum's goin' shopping with Gran and Dad will be watching football on the telly.'

'In that case,' suggested Bunty, coming to the rescue, 'why don't you leave the scrapbook here? Perhaps Alison can meet you from school one afternoon next week and you can stick the leaves in then?'

'Brilliant!' came the reply.

'Sorry about that,' Bunty murmured apologetically, as Alison prepared to take Rosie home.

'Don't worry about it, Bunty. I don't mind at all. In fact I really enjoy her company. She's such a character, and I know Max and even Nigel – although he met her only briefly – were extremely fond of her.'

Mention of Max for the first time in days caused the now familiar stirring in Alison's stomach. She wondered where he was and what he was doing. He still hadn't been seen in Church Haywood since that fateful night in September, yet someone had been convinced they'd seen him in the vicinity of the Stables.

Certainly something was taking place at Craven's Stables. A JCB had edged its way through the tangled mass of what had once been the original driveway, and a man with surveyor's instruments had been spotted amidst the blackthorn and briar hedgerow at the far end of the boundary.

Perhaps he'll come back for the bonfire supper, Alison thought wistfully. She knew Connie had every intention of inviting him, that was if she could find out where he was staying.

As if reading her mind, Rosie buttoned her coat and looked pensively in Alison's direction.

'Al'son . . . do you . . . do you think Max will come to the bonfire party? Only, if you see him, will you ask him?

'Yes, I'll ask him, Rosie,' Alison whispered softly in reply.

CHAPTER 18

With an air of excitement and expectancy, Rosie leapt about the garden waving a sparkler in the air.

'Look!' she cried. 'If I wave it like this – in a circle – it looks like a lassoo!'

'Gracious, will that child never stop thinking about cowboys?' an exasperated voice called from inside the kitchen.

To make matters worse, Wayne Jennings appeared whistling the theme tune from *The Good, The Bad and The Ugly*.

'Don't you start, Wayne!' Michelle snapped tetchily. 'It's because of your obsession with spaghetti westerns that I can't ever get Rosie into a dress. Heaven knows it's been bad enough trying to get through tea without you winding her up further. Besides, I've already had my own fair share of dealing with the good, the bad and the ugly today.'

Wayne made no comment as Michelle studied the faces of her family, eagerly waiting to leave for the Bonfire Night celebrations. Though quite who would fall into which particular category, she wasn't exactly sure at that moment.

Discarding her dying sparkler, Rosie ran towards her brother. 'Where's the guy? You said you'd bring it so I could see it.'

'You'll have to wait, titch. It's goin' to be a surprise.'

'That's not fair, Wayne!' Michelle broke in. 'You promised Rosie you'd let her see the guy before taking it to the village green.'

Wayne Jennings shrugged his shoulders. 'Well, she'll just have to wait, won't she? Donna says it will be more of a surprise if she doesn't see it till it's on the fire. Anyway, it's not here. Donna's brother's takin' it up in his van.'

'Oh, dear,' sighed Michelle, reaching for her anorak. 'In that case I suppose we'll all have to wait.'

The pervading smell of woodsmoke and spent gunpowder filled the air when Bunty and Alison arrived on the scene.

'What a shame. It looks as if they've already begun,' Bunty called, edging forward.

'I think that's only the smaller fire and display they have for the little ones,' Alison corrected. 'Oh, look, there's Rosie.'

Alison waved in Rosie's direction, but the familiar serape-clad figure was too busy watching the movement in the back of an old Bedford van. Seeing that Wayne and Donna's guy was completely covered by a blanket, she lost interest and ran back towards her grandfather.

'Grandad, those big boys are throwing bangers again.'

'I know they are, Rosie, and if I get my hands on them I'll . . . What the . . .! Michelle! Have you seen what Donna and Wayne have put on their guy?'

All eyes from the Jennings family turned in the direction of the bonfire, where Wayne swiftly removed the blanket and lit a match.

'Oh, my God!' Michelle cried out, as Rosie, turning to look at what the fuss was all about, saw what she took to be great-grannie going up in smoke!

Open-mouthed, she gasped in horror, 'It's Great-grannie! But you told me she'd been buried in the ground, you said you weren't goin' to have her grimated. You said . . .'

The shock of seeing 'great-grannie' in her best floral dress and black straw hat was all too much for Rosie. Watching the flames leap towards the upper part of the newspaper-stuffed torso with its rubber mask and lurid features, Rosie screamed and fled through the crowds. Moments later there was the sound of more stray bangers, a child's piercing scream and the sound of someone calling for an ambulance . . .

'You bloody fool, Wayne! What a stupid thing to go and do!' Michelle Jennings took a swipe at her son's head. 'You know just how fond Rosie was of Great-gran, and you go and do a bloody stupid thing like that!'

'It was only a joke, Mum! How was I to know Rosie would think it was really Great-gran up there on the bonfire? I didn't think . . .'

'No!' Michelle snapped angrily. 'That's half your trouble, you don't think!'

'But . . .' Wayne interrupted, only Michelle wouldn't let him finish.

'Don't think is right! And I can only thank God your gran wasn't there to see it. Though Lord knows it was bad enough for your poor grandad seeing his mother's double go up in flames!'

'But it wasn't really meant to be Great-gran. Surely you realized that, Mum! You know I . . .'

'All I do know,' Michelle cried bitterly, 'is that thanks to you, your sister is now in hospital with a firework stuck in her leg.'

'It's not exactly stuck in her leg,' Wayne mumbled.

'It might just as well be! And that's probably thanks to your bloody stupid friends as well. Do you realize Rosie will probably have to have plastic surgery on her leg?'

Sensing there was little he could do or say, Wayne shuffled uncomfortably to the stairs.

'Yes,' Michelle called after him, 'I suggest you go upstairs to your room and wait. Though God knows what your father and grandad will have to say to you when they get back from the hospital.'

Michelle reached for a cigarette and paced the floor. 'My poor Rosie,' she cried, 'my poor little girl.' Picking up Rosie's latest school photo, she sighed, 'I should be with you. I should be with you at the hospital, lovey, but I've got to stay here and look after Jamie and the others. When you come home we'll . . .'

There was a pregnant pause while Michelle racked her brains. What could they could do for Rosie on her return from hospital?

'We'll get Great-gran's room all nicely decorated for you,' she said brightly, 'with pretty flowery wallpaper and . . . yes . . . you can even have my crinoline lady lamp.'

Michelle sniffed and blew her nose, Yes, that was it, they'd make Great-gran's room into a proper little girl's bedroom. She'd discuss it with her husband when he came home, and tell Rosie at visiting time tomorrow.

'How is she?' Alison asked, as she followed the young nurse to Rosie's bedside.

'She's had a good night and appears much more comfortable than before, though she's still in shock, of course.'

'Mmm,' Alison murmured thoughtfully. 'It must have been a dreadful shock for her seeing that guy dressed in her great-grannie's clothes . . . and when that grotesque mask started to melt.'

Putting her fingers to her lips, the nurse motioned in Rosie's direction and, stopping at the foot of the bed, announced cheerily, 'Here you are, Rosie. You see, I told you I'd get hold of Alison for you.'

Turning to leave, the nurse remarked, 'She's talked about you a great deal, also someone called Max. Do you happen to know who that might be?'

Alison merely nodded and watched the nurse walk away.

'Hello, Al'son,' a tiny voice whispered.

'Hello, Rosie. I would have come sooner, but they thought you ought to rest for a few days. Still I'm here now.' Alison sat on the bed and held Rosie's tiny hand in her own. 'Bunty sends her love. She's made you some biscuits and Jasper barked and wagged his tail when I told him I was coming to see you.'

A faint flicker of a smile appeared on Rosie's face. 'I've got a bad leg like you now. They're going to put plastic on it.'

'Oh, you mean plastic surgery. Well, that is good. That means they'll make your leg look like new again.'

Towards the end of visiting, having consumed half of Bunty's biscuits and a glass of Ribena, Rosie's spirits brightened. 'Al'son,' she asked eagerly, 'does Max know I'm in hospital?'

'I doubt it, Rosie. I think he's still away.'

'Then will you ring him and tell him? Tell him I'd like him to come and see me. Tell him I don't expect a present . . . I'd just like to see him, that's all.'

Choking back tears, Alison looked at the pale face, propped against the pillows. 'Yes,' she said without thinking. 'I'll ring him and tell him to come, Rosie. I promise.'

Replacing the phone, Alison shook her head sadly in Bunty's direction.

'Still no luck?' Bunty queried.

'No. All I get is, "I'm very sorry, Mr Craven isn't in the London office any more and Mr Painton is with a client."'

'Not very helpful, then.'

'No . . . but if I could only speak to Nigel personally. I feel sure he must know where Max is.'

'Can't you leave a message, asking Nigel to ring you when he comes out of his meeting?'

'I don't know,' Alison sighed. 'He might think it's just a ploy on Connie's behalf, trying to find where Max has been hiding.'

'But it's not on Connie's behalf, is it? It's for Rosie! Surely, Alison, you must be able to think of some way of getting past that dragon of a receptionist at Craven and Painton? I thought you and Nigel got on well together.'

'We did. In fact he always used to call me his sea-sprite – remember? The weekend he came to stay and Rosie fell over and cut her leg.'

Alison's hand reached for the phone again and picked up the receiver.

'Of course! That's it! Why didn't I think of that before? He can't know too many sea-sprites, can he? And certainly not sea-sprites with little girls called Clint in tow! This time I'm going to make sure I get through!'

Bunty nodded approvingly as she listened to Alison stating quite clearly that Mr Painton was to ring his sea-sprite. It was extremely important. Clint had had an accident on Bonfire Night and she was now in hospital.

'Now, is that perfectly clear?' Alison demanded down the phone.

'Clear but not understood,' Mandy whispered into the now silent earpiece.

'Any messages?' Nigel called later, coming into reception.

'W-e-l-l,' Mandy drawled. 'There's been a woman ringing all afternoon for Mr Craven.'

'Probably Max's sister,' Nigel explained. 'I hope you didn't tell her anything?'

'No, just said what you always tell me to say.'

'Good girl, Mandy. I expect Connie will give up ringing sooner or later, although who knows in time Max may want to . . .'

'The thing is,' Mandy broke in with a puzzled frown, 'it didn't sound like Mr Craven's sister somehow. I'd swear it was a younger woman. It could have been the same young woman who rang you, too. The one who left that funny message.'

'What funny message?'

'The one I put on your desk with all the others. Only I particularly remember it because it was so peculiar.'

'But I wasn't aware of any peculiar message. Mind you, to be honest, I really didn't take too much notice. Vanessa and I are off to the theatre this evening and I thought what's there could probably wait until morning.'

Nigel was walking to the main exit when Mandy called after him, 'Probably just a nutter anyway. I mean you don't really know any sea-sprites, do you?'

With a bemused air, Nigel turned. 'Sea-sprites? No, I don't think I do. Hey! Wait a minute! Did this sea-sprite give her name?'

'No,' Mandy muttered. 'Just said, would you please ring the sea-sprite, because Clint has had an accident and she was in hospital. Funny really,' Mandy remarked, studying her chipped nail polish, 'I always thought Clint was a boy's name.'

Mandy looked up in amazement as Nigel, ignoring the lift, ran up the stairs two at a time to his office.

Returning from taking Jasper for his evening walk, Alison approached Keeper's Cottage with the distinct impression that she was being watched. Anxiously looking about her in the eerie darkness, she sensed Jasper's hackles rising.

'What is it, boy?' she asked. A low growling emitted from the dog's throat and a tall figure stepped furtively from the shadows.

'Alison?'

'Max! You startled me! What on earth are you doing, hiding in the bushes?'

'I needed to see you alone. I wanted to ask about Rosie.'

'You got my message, then? Thank goodness. There hasn't been a day when she hasn't asked about you.'

Alison put the key in the door and turned the lock. 'Won't you come in? It's all right – Bunty's gone to the WI. I expect Connie has too. You're quite safe.'

Safe, Max thought to himself. What a peculiar word. Safe from what or from whom.

Once in the warmly lit kitchen, Alison filled the kettle. 'You look as if you could do with a coffee or something.'

'Or something is right, I feel as if I've been on the road for the past twenty-four hours. Nigel didn't manage to get hold of me until late last night. I was in the north of England viewing the contents of a country house sale. Regency furniture and the like.'

Max sat slumped at the kitchen table and ran his fingers through his unkempt hair. 'Anyway, that's not important at the moment. Tell me, what's happened to Rosie? Nigel said she's in hospital, is that right?'

Alison nodded and poured the coffee. 'Do you want anything in it?'

'No, thanks, not if I'm driving.'

'You mean you're driving back to the north of England tonight? But you can't possibly! You look all in.'

Max gave her one of his rare smiles. 'It's kind of you to be so concerned, Alison, but no, I'm not driving back to the north tonight, I'm driving to the hospital to see Rosie. That's if you think they'll let me in.'

'It is getting rather late but as she's been asking for you, I suppose it's worth a try. I could always ring the hospital for you. The nursing staff have been wonderful with her. They've really taken to Rosie, you know.'

'I'm not surprised.' Max grinned. 'Even poor old Nigel was frantic when he phoned. It was as much as I could do to stop him coming too.'

'It's okay. We can go in for twenty minutes,' Alison called putting down the phone. 'Apparently visiting is just about coming to an end and her parents are with her at the moment. By the time you freshen up and get to the hospital . . .'

'I look that bad, do I?' Max said wryly.

'Let's say I've seen you looking better.'

Showing Max to the bathroom and giving him a clean towel, Alison called from across the landing, 'I'd better change too. From the state of my clothes, I look as if Jasper's dragged me through every ploughed field in Church Haywood!'

When she met him in the hall, Max helped her with her jacket and noticed she was wearing the same wrap-around skirt she'd worn for the harvest supper.

'I know it's not exactly ideal for a cold November's night but the hospital is so uncomfortably hot and if I remember correctly, your car has a very effective heater.'

Driving to the hospital, Alison explained exactly what had happened on the night of the bonfire party.

'Stupid idiot!' Max snapped angrily. 'What on earth was Wayne Jennings playing at?'

'But it wasn't Wayne who threw the firework.'

'Maybe not, but it must have been his stupid prank with the guy that caused Rosie to flee in terror, if what you say is true.'

'Mmm, I suppose so. It was really Donna's idea to

252

dress the guy up in Great-grannie's clothes.'

'Donna?'

'Wayne's girlfriend. Or should I say ex-girlfriend. She's one of these modern teenagers, into women's lib and all that. Female equality?'

Max nodded in understanding as he side-stepped a ward orderly, wheeling an elderly patient on a trolley.

Checking behind her to make sure Max was still there, Alison continued matter-of-factly, 'Donna thought, why should Guy Fawkes always be dressed in male attire and, considering Michelle and her mother-in-law had cleared out Great-grannie's ward-robe to give to the local charity shop . . .'

'I still think it was an idiotic thing to do,' Max retorted when Alison stopped by the nursing station.

'Ah! The mysterious Max, I presume,' Sister said with a grin, eyeing Max's seven o'clock shadow and somewhat crumpled appearance. 'Well, hopefully now that you've arrived we can all get some peace round here.'

'Has she really been talking about me that much?' Max asked in surprise, following Alison through the ward decorated with Paddington Bear and Thomas the Tank Engine murals.

'Oh, dear,' he sighed in mock alarm, 'not a single cowboy or Red Indian anywhere. However has our Clint managed?'

'With great difficulty,' Alison whispered, 'and ex-tremely disgusted that her mother and father want to put her in Great-grannie's bedroom when she gets home.'

'That's a bit insensitive, isn't it, so soon after Great-grannie's death?

253

'Oh, Rosie doesn't mind that so much. I think she's secretly delighted with the idea of having a bedroom all to herself. What she does mind is the prospect of having flowery wallpaper . . .' Before Alison had a chance to finish, there was a whoop of delight from the far end of the ward.

'Max! You've come. Yippee! Alison promised she'd fetch you.'

'Did she indeed?' Max said, bending down to kiss Rosie on the forehead. As an afterthought he ruffled her hair, in case 'Clint' didn't like being kissed. 'Well, as you can see, Rosie, Alison kept her promise.'

'Yes, so she did,' came the contented reply.

Rosie studied Max thoughtfully; he looked sort of different somehow.

'Say, you look kinda tired, mister.'

'Reckon I am,' Max drawled. 'I've been in the saddle all day.'

Rosie giggled and patted her leg. 'My leg got burnt but they're going to make it better, 'tho I 'spect I shall still have a scar.'

'All the best cowboys have scars,' Max explained, lifting the cuff of his shirt, to reveal his scar from the burn sustained in the aftermath of the fire.

'Wow! So you have!' gasped Rosie, stroking timidly at the red weal with the tip of her finger. 'Does it hurt?'

Max shook his head. 'No, because it happened such a long time ago. It's quite healed up, you see, apart from that red mark.'

Aware that Alison was also looking at Max's scar, it being the first time she'd seen it properly, Rosie announced brightly, 'Alison's got a big scar too. Ha-

254

ven't you, Alison? She got hit by a car. Wasn't that silly of her?'

Max didn't reply; instead he looked knowingly in Alison's direction until Rosie's voice broke through the silence.

'Show Max your scar, Alison!'

Pure embarrassment filled Alison's face. 'I'm sure Max isn't interested in seeing my scar, Rosie . . .'

'Yes, he is! Aren't you, Max? You showed me yours and *I* thought it was interesting.'

Knowing she wasn't going to get any peace until she'd done as requested, and aware of Max's penetrating gaze, Alison gingerly slipped the wrapover part of her skirt to one side to reveal a slender thigh and the lowest part of her scar.

'It goes right up to her knickers!' Rosie explained to a stunned and equally embarrassed Max.

'Right, young lady,' a voice broke in with mock authority. 'That's enough excitement for one night, I think. Say goodnight to your visitors now.'

'Oh! Do I have to?'

'Yes, you do,' Sister said. 'Besides, there's another day tomorrow.'

'Tomorrow!' a plaintive voice echoed. 'Will you come and see me again tomorrow, Max?'

Max studied the earnest and tired little face, gazing up at him in anticipation. 'Yes, Rosie. I'll come and see you tomorrow.'

CHAPTER 19

Leaving the hospital and returning to the car, Alison queried, 'But I thought you were heading back north?'

'That can wait,' Max said softly. 'I think perhaps I should spend a couple of days here in Church Haywood first.'

'In that case Rosie will be delighted. Connie too, of course; she's been extremely worried about you.'

'And what about you, Alison? Have you been worried about me? Will you be delighted if I stay?'

'I – er . . .'

Max reached for Alison and drew her into his arms. Beneath the orange glow of car park lighting, he gazed hard and long into her eyes. 'You haven't answered my question,' he said softly, his dark eyes pleading for a reply.

'We've all been extremely worried about you,' she faltered. Then, in response to the second part of his question, came a barely audible, 'Yes, Max . . . I would be delighted if you stayed.'

When his lips sought hers, the same tremor of pleasure surged through Alison's body as it had on the night of the harvest supper. Only this time the dreaded fear and panic didn't rear its ugly head as before. This time, she could think only of Max.

For Alison at that moment, with her heart pounding in her breast, the anxious weeks of worrying over Max's wellbeing and the desperate longing to be back in his embrace only served to dispel the familiar, haunting dark shadows from her mind.

Uncharacteristically, however, it was Max's turn to err on the side of caution. There was something that still wasn't quite right. Something that had been troubling him during the solitary weeks and anxious nights spent away from Church Haywood. Something still unresolved concerning Tara and the day of the accident.

'Tara?' he murmured in Alison's ear, feeling the softness of her cheek against his own unshaven one.

Alison shivered beneath his grasp and moved away. Just one word – 'Tara' – had brought the terrifying shadows bubbling to the surface from the depths of her very soul. For the second time in recent months, she'd found herself in Max's arms, enjoying – to her surprise – the touch of his lips on hers, while strong arms held her and his body pressed against her like a lover's. Yet . . . yet what? Alison puzzled. One minute it's as if he wants me and the next . . . surely he can't think I'm Tara!

Choking back a sob, Alison walked dejectedly to the car and waited for Max to open the passenger door. Hearing her muffled, 'I really think we should getting back, Bunty will be wondering where I am,' Max could only stare after her in bewilderment.

Watching a sudden, chill gust of wind catch at her skirt, exposing her injured leg, Max remembered the vivid scar he'd witnessed on her lower thigh. What was it Rosie had said? 'It goes right up to her knickers?'

At any other time, no doubt, Max would have found Rosie's statement amusing. But not tonight. Especially when he considered the cause behind the disfiguring mark on Alison's leg. The reason for that was his daughter! It had been Tara who'd forced Alison to pursue her into the road ten long summers ago!

Opening the passenger door, Max turned purposefully towards Alison and put a restraining hand on her shoulder. 'I need to know what happened!'

'What happened?' she replied lamely. 'I don't understand.'

'Oh, I think you do, Alison! What prompted Tara to run into the road with you in pursuit? I'm convinced it was her fault your leg . . .'

'No! It wasn't Tara's fault!' Alison gasped, feeling Max's eyes burn through the thin cotton fabric, in the direction of her thigh.

For a moment it felt as if she wasn't wearing her skirt at all, only her jacket and panties. Grasping at the edge of her jacket with one hand and the folds of her skirt with the other, she attempted somewhat clumsily to get into the car. Max's hand was still firmly on her shoulder.

'Alison, please! For God's sake, can't you see I have to know! If I don't then I'm never going to be able to . . .'

Max's voice trailed away to a whisper as his hand slipped from her shoulder. Alison felt her mouth go dry. 'I'm never going to be able to . . .' she repeated in her head. Able to do what? What was it Max wouldn't be able to do?

Able to lay the ghosts of Tara and Virginia to rest? Forget about those revolting photographs Evangeline had flaunted during the barn dance? Begin a new life in Church Haywood and complete his cherished project at Craven's Stables, or simply go away from Church Haywood for good, leaving its cruel memories behind?

It could have been one of so many things, Alison pondered, and, much as she wanted to know, she realized at that moment she was incapable of asking. Because all she wanted to do was fall back into the warmth and comfort of his embrace.

Struggling with a choking sensation in her throat, she reached nervously for Max's hand and repeated softly. 'It wasn't Tara's fault . . .'

'Then if it wasn't Tara's fault – and I know it certainly wasn't yours,' Max interrupted, 'whose fault was it?'

'I . . . can't tell you.'

'Can't, or won't?' Max said abruptly.

Releasing her hand from his grasp, Max closed the passenger door. Alison turned away, unable to face the hurt and anguish in his eyes.

The journey back to Keeper's Cottage was spent in silence. From the corner of her eye, Alison studied the stony and haunted set to Max's jaw. While part of her wanted to reach out and touch him, to smooth the lines from his furrowed brow, the other part of her wanted to say, 'Okay, Max! Stop the car and I'll tell you . . . I'll tell you everything, but you're not going to like what I have to say.'

'I . . .' she began, but lost her nerve when Max broke into her chain of thoughts with a second,

'Can't or won't, Alison?'

'I . . . I can't. Not tonight, Max. It really is getting late, you know, but I promise I will soon. If you'll only be patient for a little while longer. Please understand, it's as difficult for me as it is for you.'

'Is it?' Max sighed sardonically. 'I only have your word on that.'

Seeing the hurt expression on her face, he reached for her hand and murmured apologetically, 'I'm sorry, that was uncalled for. Yes, you're right, it is late and Connie doesn't even know I'm here.'

'She does now. She's just coming out of Bunty's front door.'

'Damn!' hissed Max, releasing her hand.

'Max! What on earth? But why didn't you let me know you were coming? Why didn't you . . . ?'

Springing quickly to Max's defence, Alison replied, 'Because he didn't know, Connie. Bunty will vouch for that.' Connie looked in Bunty's direction. Alison continued her explanation.

'I rang Nigel to tell him about Rosie's accident and quite by chance Max rang Nigel not long after. In fact that's where we've both been – at the hospital to see Rosie.'

'But visiting finished ages ago,' Connie remonstrated in disbelief.

'Yes, but I rang the hospital to say Max had driven down from the north of England especially to see her . . . and they let us go in.'

'Hmph,' muttered Connie, convinced someone, somewhere wasn't quite telling the truth.

Coming to the rescue, Bunty intervened. 'From the state of you, Max, you look as if you've been driving all night and all day if that stubble on your chin is anything to go by; you look absolutely . . .'

Forgetting her anger at being kept in the dark over Max's reappearance, Connie's big-sisterly nature soon came to the fore. 'So you do, Max. In fact,' she said trying to make light of the situation, 'if I didn't know you better I'd think you were going in for that designer stubble look.'

Managing a wry smile, Max merely shook his head in Connie's direction.

'You're probably well aware, Constance, designer stubble isn't really my scene. What would be right now is a shower and a clean bed.'

'Then you'd better get in my car,' Connie instructed.

In reply to Max's puzzled frown, she explained, 'Because looking at you now, I would say you were completely incapable of driving any further.'

'Don't worry,' Bunty reassured him. 'Your precious Saab will be perfectly safe here tonight. You can come and fetch it in the morning.'

Leaving his car and climbing into Connie's, Max conceded defeat. His reasons for doing so were two-fold. The first was, as Connie so correctly predicted, he did feel physically incapable of travelling any further. As for the second, well . . . collecting his car in the morning would give him another chance to extricate the truth from Alison.

With a murmured 'goodnight' Max was driven away and Alison followed Bunty into the cottage to do some explaining of her own.

'So you managed to find him after all.' Bunty grinned.

'Not exactly. He found me. I discovered him waiting in the bushes when I came back with Jasper.'

'He looks absolutely shattered. Has he really been driving all night and all day?'

'Just about.' Alison nodded in reply. 'Yet he still insisted on going straight to the hospital. He's obviously very fond of Rosie.'

'And you too . . . He's obviously very fond of you too,' Bunty added, giving her a knowing look.

Feeling herself colour, Alison tried to change the subject. 'Still, I expect he'll feel better after a good night's sleep, and tomorrow . . .'

'Tomorrow he'll probably invite you out to dinner,' called Bunty, locking the front door.

Already picturing in her mind's eye Max and Alison facing each other across a candlelit dinner for two, Bunty sighed contentedly, then muttered a pronounced, 'Oh, damn! Tomorrow! I quite forgot to ask you. I couldn't anyway as you weren't here. Tom Carstairs rang and asked me to ask you if you'd go and sit with Evangeline tomorrow evening.'

'Evangeline! But what on earth for?'

'Because, like me, Tom's got a parish council meeting and doesn't want to leave her on her own. He's worried if she's left all evening she might be tempted . . .'

'To start drinking again?' Alison concluded.

'That's right. He said he won't be long and thought perhaps if you watched a video together or something, that way conversation wouldn't be quite so strained.'

Contemplating the prospect of dinner with Max and the thought of an evening 'babysitting' Evangeline, Alison knew which of the two she'd prefer.

'Oh, well,' she sighed. 'If it means we can help keep Evangeline on the straight and narrow, it is worth it, I suppose. She's been so much better of late too. Lord knows it can't have been easy for her, I mean hoarding those photos as she did and . . .'

'I wish there were a few more charitable folk like you in this world, Alison. If there were, it would be a much better place, my dear.'

Alison shrugged her shoulders. 'Perhaps I feel more disposed to her these days because I've got a few secrets of my own hidden away . . .'

'You don't mean you've got some photographs hidden away of Virginia and that man as well?' Bunty asked in alarm.

'No, Bunty,' Alison replied pensively, walking to the foot of the stairs, not photos.'

'What, then?'

To Bunty's concern, Alison did not reply.

It was only later, when cocooned in the safety and comfort of her bed, Alison allowed her thoughts to turn again to the same conversation. Hearing Bunty switch off her own bedroom light, she whispered to the shadowy corners of her room. 'No, Bunty, not photographs hidden away, but pictures locked in my mind.'

The next morning, up and dressed, when a healthier-looking Max called to collect his car, Bunty greeted him with a warm and welcoming smile.

'Gracious, you must have had a good night's sleep,' she remarked, taking in his newly shaven appearance. 'You must tell me what you've been using?'

Pondering her question, Max waited for Bunty to enlighten him.

'Because, whatever it is,' she joked, 'it's obviously very good for getting rid of dark circles under the eyes!'

Max grinned and watched Bunty peer into the hall

mirror at the large circles beneath her own eyes.

'Church Haywood air with liposomes no doubt – isn't that what they put in face cream these days? Plus one of my sister's hearty breakfasts. Although,' Max said, 'I certainly don't intend to make a habit of it.'

'You mean you don't intend to come back to Church Haywood?' Bunty enquired warily.

'No,' Max teased, when he saw her crestfallen face. 'Actually, Bunty, I was referring to the breakfasts!'

'That's a relief, then . . . to all of us, isn't it, Alison?'

Coming down the stairs, newly showered and with her hair still damp, Alison was surprised to see Max so early. Blushing, she pulled at her mid-thigh-length cotton kimono, aware of his gaze in her direction.

'Ah, Alison. Good morning. You're just the person I need. I want you to tell me . . .'

Alison stared at him in alarm. Surely he wasn't going to ask her, here and now in front of Bunty, exactly what it was that had upset her all those years ago. He wasn't that insensitive, was he?

Recognizing the familiar panic in her eyes, Max reassured her with a comforting smile. 'I need to pick your brains, you see. I want to buy something for Rosie. I'm going to the hospital this afternoon and you're probably the best person to advise me.'

Instant relief surged through Alison as she blurted out, 'But she said she didn't want a present. She only wanted to see you.'

'Did she indeed?' Max replied, feeling a lump rise in his throat. 'In that case, I think she deserves a present even more. What do you think, Bunty?'

'I'd feel inclined to agree,' Bunty replied, pouring three cups of tea. 'Though quite what you get her is

264

anybody's guess. She's not really interested in toys, is she? And as for clothes . . . as long as Rosie has her jeans, wellington boots and serape, she seems perfectly content.'

'Speaking of clothes, I'd better go and put some on,' Alison murmured, still conscious of the fact that she wasn't dressed.

'She's another one,' Bunty sighed, watching her leave the kitchen, 'who seems perfectly content to be in jeans and wellington boots. Fancy hiding a lovely trim figure like that in denim and bulky sweatshirts.'

'I don't know,' Max mused thoughtfully, 'she doesn't wear jeans all the time. She wore a black dress to George and Constance's dinner party if I recall; a blue chambray skirt to the summer fête and last night she was wearing . . .'

Max stopped, aware of Bunty's questioning smile. 'Yes,' she grinned. 'She was wearing what?'

'A red, white and blue patterned wraparound skirt.'

'How very observant of you, Max,' Bunty teased.

'Yes,' he replied, refusing to rise to the bait, 'and with luck I'll be able to persuade her to cast her jeans aside this evening – in favour of something more feminine – when I take her out to dinner.'

'I'm afraid you won't!'

'You mean, you don't think she'll come out to dinner with me unless she wears her jeans?'

Bunty collected the cups and saucers and took them to the kitchen sink. 'No,' she explained, squeezing a clear green jet of liquid into the washing up bowl. 'Much as I'm sure Alison would prefer to be spending the evening with you, she's promised to spend it with Evangeline instead.'

'Evangeline Carstairs! Surely not! Why, I would have thought after what happened at the harvest supper, Evangeline is the last person Alison would want to spend the evening with!'

Swishing her hand in the soapy bubbles, Bunty explained warily.

'There's been quite a few changes in Church Haywood since you were last here Max. Quite possibly the most important one concerns our attitude towards Evangeline.'

Bunty watched Max rake his fingers through his thick dark hair as the once familiar 'Craven glare' put in an appearance. 'Oh, I see!' he muttered angrily. 'You mean to say she's been forgiven for behaving so bloody outrageously and upsetting everyone's lives!'

Max rose abruptly from his chair and strode to the window, where he studied a solitary blackbird pecking at the remaining rose hips on Bunty's rose arbour. 'So everything's sweetness and light and a bed of roses as far as Evangeline is concerned. I see!'

'No, Max, you don't see,' Bunty said softly, wiping soapsuds from her hands. 'You don't see at all. After you left, Tom took Evangeline to an Alcoholics Anonymous group . . . where she actually confessed to being an alcoholic. Not every one's supposed to know, of course, but in a village like this it isn't that easy to keep secrets.'

'I don't know about that!' Max snapped angrily. 'It would appear nearly everyone here knew about my wife and her lover. They certainly managed to keep that a secret!'

'Max! Please! It wasn't like that at all. As far as Virginia was concerned, it was pure speculation on

our part. After Tara's accident and then the fire, well
. . . you know.'

Max turned to face the motherly figure standing
anxiously by his side. 'I'm sorry, Bunty, I have no
right to stand here in your kitchen and insult you like
this.'

'Be quiet, Max Craven, and just take this tea towel!'
she commanded good-naturedly, holding up a red and
white striped cloth. If you'll dry these dishes – once
they've been rinsed – I'll finish explaining all about
Evangeline and why Alison can't . . .'

'Why I can't what?' Alison enquired dubiously,
coming back into the kitchen. What on earth had
Bunty and Max been saying about her?

'Max was hoping to take you to dinner this evening
and I was explaining you've already said you'll go and
spend the evening with Evangeline.'

'I see. Yes, that's right.'

'Then in that case, how about joining me tomorrow
instead?' Max asked, unlocking his car.

'I'd love to,' Alison replied, aware of Bunty's Che-
shire cat grin as she watched them drive away.

Walking through the department store hung with tinsel
and garlands of every description, Alison was suddenly
reminded of Christmas. As yet, with Bunty going to
Australia for Christmas, there had been little talk of the
festive season that she would be spending alone at
Keeper's Cottage. She shuddered at the thought.

'Surely you're not cold, Alison?' Max enquired.
'This place is almost as hot as the hospital. You
know, it always amazes me why these shops keep such
high temperatures. Here we are, wearing thick winter

clothes against the prevailing cold wind outside, and there they are,' Max gestured to the rows of pink-faced shop assistants, 'wearing little more than summer blouses.'

'I hope they're wearing more than that behind the counters!' Alison added cheekily. 'No, I'm not cold, just not relishing the thought of Christmas, that's all.'

'Won't you be spending it with Bunty?'

'You obviously haven't heard. Bunty's going to Australia for a couple of months – to stay with her brother in Australia.'

'Is she indeed? In that case, you'll have to come and spend Christmas at Haywood Grange. I'll have a word with Constance.'

Stepping on to the escalator, Alison thought to herself. In that case, Max, you must be staying in Church Haywood for longer than a few days, if you're already talking about spending Christmas at the Grange.

In the busy toy department, with the frenetic activities of shop assistants endeavouring to deal with harassed parents and their uncontrollable offspring, Alison's eyes sought Max's. Looking in her direction, he shrugged.

'Any luck?' he enquired glumly 'I have to confess, apart from a battered cowboy hat, I've found nothing remotely suitable for Rosie.'

'Me neither. She'd hardly thank us for taking her one of these hideous dolls or those awful space monsters.'

Max looked across to the display and grimaced, just as he had all those months ago when he'd taken Constance to the wholesaler's. 'Is there nowhere else we could try?'

'Not that I can think of. The old-fashioned family-run toy shops, are virtually a thing of the past now.'

Descending the escalator, Alison's gaze darted from department to department seeking inspiration. Looking towards the lighting display, she frowned thoughtfully. 'I suppose if the worst came to the worst, we could always buy her a lampshade.'

'A lampshade? That's an unusual sort of present, isn't it? I don't wish to be rude, Alison, but I don't quite see the connection.'

'Rosie's mother wants to redecorate Great-grannie's bedroom as a welcome home treat and is threatening to give Rosie her crinoline lady lamp for her bedside table.'

'Threatening? A crinoline lady doesn't sound very threatening.'

'I don't see it as threatening either. But it is if you look at it from Rosie's point of view and hate anything frilly and vaguely feminine! I mean,' Alison queried, 'can you see Rosie lying in bed with a crinoline lady lamp by her side?'

Max grinned, and helped her from the escalator. 'No, I have to confess I can't. So what exactly had you in mind.'

Alison gestured towards a range of lamps. 'I was thinking perhaps of a compromise. The last thing I want to do is upset Michelle – Rosie's mum. If we bought a plain shade, I could paint a western scene of her choice round the edge. It shouldn't be too difficult if we take a book and . . .'

'Alison, you're a genius!' beamed Max, grabbing hold of her arm and leading her towards the main entrance.

'But how? Why? What have I said?'

Turning to face her, Max kissed her squarely on the forehead. 'Because, quite simply, you've solved the problem.'

'You mean, you think we *should* go and find a lampshade?'

'Oh, no!' Max replied, a huge grin radiating across his face. 'Better than that! *You* are going to re-design and decorate Rosie's bedroom in Wild West style.'

'But that's impossible!'

'Is it? How is it impossible? Don't tell me you you're incapable of doing it?'

'W-e-l-l, no. But what about her parents? Won't they mind?'

'I very much doubt it . . . not if I commission you to do it for them.'

Later, when they stopped for a coffee, Alison studied the book they'd bought.

'At least this will help me draw up some ideas. Just look at these wonderful old trains with cow-catchers and all those amazing cacti.'

'You see, I told you so.' Max grinned. 'I know it won't be as easy as painting rows of teddy bears, but . . .'

Alison looked up to see Max watching a toddler clutching at a small teddy bear. Suddenly her eyes glistened with tears.

'Alison! What's wrong? What on earth have I said to upset you?'

'It's nothing you've said, Max,' she explained, wiping her eyes. 'I had an identical bear once. I didn't think they made them like that any more. It was a present from my godmother and brought back so many memories. He was my mascot, you see. I used to take him everywhere.'

'In that case, don't you still have it?'

Alison hesitated, not knowing how to continue.

Puzzled by her sudden unease, Max reached across the table for her hand. 'Alison? What happened to your bear?'

Unaware of Max's hand holding hers, and oblivious to everything other than the child with the teddy bear, Alison replied numbly, 'I took it with me, the night I babysat for Tara. Your wife asked me to sleep over – she was going to be late home. The next morning Virginia was tired and had a headache. She insisted I take Tara for a walk until lunchtime. When we went back to the house . . .'

'Go on,' Max's voice urged huskily, willing Alison to continue.

'We saw . . .' With a blank stare, Alison turned tear-filled eyes in his direction. 'I must have dropped the bear when Tara ran away . . .'

Struggling to hear her voice, which seemed little more than a whisper above the noise of neighbouring customers, Max recalled the day of the fire when he'd fought his way through the burning rubble. The day when the fireman had forced him to leave. The day when he'd been injured and found the charred remains of a child's teddy bear in the ashes.

Looking down at his scarred hand, now resting on Alison's pale, trembling fingers, Max gave a low moan. The teddy bear! After all these years he realized. It hadn't been Tara's teddy that had haunted him. It was Alison's!

CHAPTER 20

Standing in the front porch of The Firs, Alison took a last deep breath of crisp November air. Tom Carstairs opened the front door.

'Alison, it's jolly good of you to come at such short notice. I really appreciate it, you know. Evangeline's in the sitting room, if you'd like to go through.'

Giving Tom her jacket, Alison hesitated with her hand on the door handle.

'She says she's got some good videos for you and she's . . . okay,' Tom called softly.

To Tom Carstairs, describing Evangeline as 'okay', meant that she still wasn't drinking.

Alison sighed with relief, nodded knowingly in Tom's direction and opened the door.

'Evangeline, what a wonderful fire. Just the thing for a cold night like tonight.'

'Alison! How lovely to see you. Sit yourself down and pour yourself a drink.' Seeing the fleeting look of alarm on Alison's face, Evangeline gave her familiar throaty laugh. 'By that I mean tonic water, orange juice or lemonade. Although I think Tom put some tomato juice in the fridge.'

'No, thanks, orange juice will be just fine.'

'Can't say I blame you,' Evangeline whispered, casting a furtive glance at the door. 'I think tomato juice tastes bloody awful! Unless of course you've got a dash of Worcestershire sauce and a slug of vodka in it for good measure. However, I mustn't let Tom hear me say that. I don't want to worry him unduly, do I?'

As if on cue, Tom opened the door. 'Right, I'm off, then,' he said chirpily. 'Got everything you need, darling?'

'Of course,' Evangeline replied, kissing him warmly. 'You've made sure of that, Tom. Videos, chocolates, cigarettes, drinks of the non-alcoholic variety and plenty of logs for the fire.'

The latter was Evangeline's idea of a joke. The blazing log fire burning in the grate was none other than an imitation gas variety.

'We'll be fine, won't we, Alison? So off you go and enjoy yourself, Tom, or whatever else it is you do at parish council meetings.'

'Hardly enjoy, Evangeline. But these PCMs are necessary. We have to make sure Church Haywood remains unspoilt and a pleasant place to live in, just as it was when we first moved here.'

Listening to the sound of Tom's car purring softly down the drive, Evangeline repeated Tom's words in her head. 'Just as it was when we first moved here.'

'Mmm,' she sighed nostalgically, 'I doubt it. Things change, you know.'

Sipping at her orange juice, Alison looked in Evangeline's direction. Had she said something or was she just talking to herself?

'Pardon?'

'Oh, nothing, Alison. I was just letting my thoughts drift back to when Tom and I first moved here. You were only a schoolgirl then. I remember you showing Tara how to play hopscotch and swingball and I . . .' Evangeline picked up the first of the two videos and placed it in the machine.

Pressing the PLAY button, she let her mind dwell on the word. Yes, life was full of play in the early days. To Virginia Craven's delight, Alison had been an absolute gem looking after Tara, leaving her plenty of time to play tennis with Evangeline. Max (when he was home) played squash with Tom and even Bunty and Constance and the older members of the community had their bridge and whist.

Sadly, however, their idyll hadn't lasted. Evangeline and later Virginia had begun to play more dangerous games of their own. Games that had had the most disastrous consequences.

Evangeline shuddered and glanced briefly at Alison who was studying the opening credits of the film. She still had to admit she was a pretty girl, even though she appeared unduly serious for her age. Then life had never been easy for Alison Benedict, had it? The problems with her asthma in early childhood, Tara's tragic accident plus of course being uprooted to the States. That, followed by the death of her mother and now . . .

And now? Evangeline sat back and relaxed in her chair. Well, now, by all accounts, a certain Alison Benedict had been seen – if Church Haywood rumours were correct, and they usually were – with Max Craven!

Max. Evangeline gave a wry smile. To think she'd made a beeline for him when he'd returned in the summer. Made quite a fool of herself, in fact. Why, she'd even invited Max to the house and made a pass at him!

Feeling a rare flush of embarrassment colour her throat and cheeks, Evangeline reached for her drink with a desperate longing for it to contain something stronger than tonic water.

Max. She sighed inwardly. He was certainly a good-looking fellow, polite and charming too. And, unlike Tom and Evangeline, he hadn't gone grey or put on weight in all the wrong places. In fact apart from a few lines at the corners of those wonderful brooding eyes of his and the stray silver hair at his temples, he was . . .

Drumming her fingers on the arm of her chair, Evangeline reached for her cigarettes. She must stop this! She must stop thinking about Max as anything other than a neighbour and most of all, she thought, gazing at her empty glass, she must stop thinking about craving a proper drink.

'Though God knows it's not going to be easy,' she whispered sadly.

For the second time that evening, Alison looked across with a puzzled frown on her delicate, earnest face.

'Just thinking about Christmas preparations,' Evangeline lied.

'Oh, yes, Christmas.' Alison mused. 'With Bunty away, I won't be having those problems, Evangeline. It will only be me and Jasper at Keeper's Cottage for Christmas.'

'You mean,' said Evangeline, pressing the PAUSE button, 'your stepbrother's coming over for Christmas. But that's wonderful! He'll be just what we need. Tom and I are planning to hold a fancy dress party on New Year's Eve. We thought of a Hollywood theme. You know, old movie stars and the like or characters from films . . .'

There was an embarrassed silence. 'I'm terribly sorry to disappoint you, Evangeline. By Jasper I meant the hairy four-legged variety – Bunty's dog – not, I'm afraid, my screen-idol stepbrother.'

Looking up, expecting to see Evangeline's crestfallen face, Alison was surprised to see a broad grin breaking across the Pagan Glow lips.

'Bunty's dog!' Evangeline chuckled. 'Oh, I see. What a hoot! There was me thinking,' but Evangeline couldn't continue, she was laughing so much.

'In that case,' she grinned, 'I think we'll just have to make do with this screen-idol, then.' And Evangeline re-started the video.

With the two women engrossed in the film, Evangeline found herself forgetting all about Max and the misunderstanding over Jasper. For Alison, however, as the film progressed, forgetting about her last encounter with Max and the prospect of Christmas was not quite so easy.

Later, with her attention fixed on the large television screen, Alison became strangely uneasy. The film had begun harmlessly enough, with a typical American family (mother, father and young son) idyllically happy and enjoying life in Southern California.

'Offered promotion? But that's great!' the loving young wife encouraged her dashing, executive husband. 'I know you can do it, Jerry.'

'But it will mean longer hours, honey. There could be a lot of travelling and even days when I might not get to see

276

you and Little Jerry until late . . .'

'*Why worry about the days, when we'll still have the nights?' the pretty young wife murmured seductively in her husband's ear. 'Don't forget, we promised Little Jerry a brother or sister for Christmas.'*

Smiling knowingly in his wife's direction, the young husband swept his wife into his arms and carried her away to the bedroom.

In the film, that particular scenario had a lasting effect on 'Little Jerry'. He remembered it during the long lonely days when he played with his toys in the back yard. What did it matter if he didn't see his dad so much? He still had his mom. She was here painting the deck. Mom had told him how Dad was away working hard for them both and when he came back she would see what they could do about 'making' him a baby brother. That way he wouldn't be lonely any more. He would have someone to play with.

Only 'Little Jerry' didn't get his longed for baby brother, did he? With Dad away, Mom introduced him to a new 'uncle' instead. An 'Uncle Kurt' he didn't much like; an 'uncle' who brought him candy and toys and gave him shiny dollars for his money box, before patting him on the head and saying things like, 'Run along, kid, I need to talk to your Mom.'

Most days 'Little Jerry' was happy to 'run along' and play with his new toys, but after a while it became boring. Until one day, when Mom and 'Uncle Kurt' were 'talking' he wondered what they were talking about.

He knew what Mom and Dad talked about when Dad was home. They talked about Dad's work and plans for the next vacation. But they also mostly talked over brunch at weekends, when they were always together. Dad never told 'Little Jerry' to run along.

Transfixed by what was taking place on the screen, Alison felt a sickening lump rise in her throat as she watched 'Little Jerry' climb the stairs to his Mom's bedroom. His Mom and 'Uncle Kurt' were sure having a funny conversation. His Dad never 'spoke' to his mom like that (leastways, if he did, the child was always asleep and didn't know about it).

Before the small boy even opened the bedroom door, Alison knew what he was going to find. Her blood ran cold. She and Tara had made the same discovery ten long years before. Unaware that Evangeline was now looking in her direction and that her grasp on her glass was vice-like, Alison gave a gasp of horror when it shattered in her hand and fell to the floor.

'Oh! I'm so sorry! It must have slipped. I'll get the dustpan and brush.'

'No, you won't!' Evangeline commanded, taking control and switching off the video machine. 'You'll sit there while I get a plaster!' You've obviously cut your finger and you're dripping blood all over my carpet!'

Stunned into silence, Alison watched as Evangeline produced a clean white lace handkerchief, bound it round the offending finger and went in search of the first aid box.

'I'm terribly sorry . . . about the glass and the carpet. I'll replace the glass of course and get the carpet cl . . .'

'You'll do no such thing.' Evangeline said kindly, studying Alison's ashen face, before she unpeeled the adhesive strips from the plaster. 'The glass was one we use every day and as for the carpet, that's due to be shampooed next week anyway. I always have it cleaned before Christmas ... although perhaps this year I might wait until after our party at New Year. You will come, won't you?'

Alison didn't reply. She merely sat there in a daze, watching Evangeline fix the plaster to her finger, whilst at the same time carrying on a running conversation about their plans for the forthcoming fancy dress party.

It was only later, when Alison had gone home and Tom and Evangeline were alone, that she became less talkative and more reflective.

'Penny for them,' Tom said softly, watching his wife seemingly studying her reflection in the dressing table mirror.

Cupping her face in her hands, Evangeline sighed sadly. 'I think they're worth a great deal more than that, Tom. These in fact could be priceless.'

'That sounds ominous.'

'It is,' came the languid response, and Evangeline explained about Alison's reaction to the evening's choice of video.

Tom Carstairs listened to his wife in silence.

'Quite probably,' he said kindly, 'Alison has had an unfortunate experience with a man. I know she's not had any boyfriends here in Church Haywood. But perhaps when she was at college one of her fellow students took advantage of ... ?'

'No, Tom! You've got it all wrong. Whatever it was didn't happen when Alison was at college. It happened when she was much younger. I saw the look of sheer panic on her face when it got to that particular scene.'

'And what was that scene again?'

'The one where the young boy, having heard all the

grunting and groaning coming from his mother's room.' Here Evangeline turned to face her husband. 'You know how they tend to go overboard with the noise in some of these sex scenes nowadays.'

Tom raised an eyebrow, nodded and waited for his wife to continue.

'I'd be prepared to bet Alison knew what "Little Jerry" was going to find.'

'Who's "Little Jerry"?'

'The boy in the film!' Evangeline said in an exasperated tone. 'Honestly, Tom! Here I am trying to help Alison and there you are being . . . being . . .'

'Anything but helpful?'

'Exactly.' Evangeline sighed, and, leaving her dressing table stool, sat on the bed by her husband. 'Now, shall I begin again? As I was saying, I'm convinced Alison knew what was going on behind that bedroom door. Perhaps when she was younger she . . .'

'Discovered her parents in a similar situation?'

'I very much doubt it. I'm sure her father left her mother when she was very tiny. No, I'm beginning to think Alison discovered Virginia and Miles together . . .'

'What? That's impossible, surely? What would Alison be doing outside Virginia's bedroom?'

'Standing there with Tara . . . ?'

Tom studied Evangeline's questioning eyes and reached for her hand. 'You don't mean . . . but how could they . . . ?'

'Quite easily, in fact. Don't you remember how Virginia used to get Alison to stay the night?'

Evangeline looked uneasily at Tom. 'No, I don't expect you took too much notice. I only remember because Virginia confided in me how much easier it was for her to meet Miles when Alison stayed the night. In the morning Virginia would pretend to have a headache and ask Alison to keep Tara out of the way until she supposedly felt better.'

'But that's dreadful!'

'I realize that now.' Evangeline said, biting her lip. 'So just suppose Virginia thought the coast was clear for her and Miles to . . . well you know . . . and quite out of the blue – the day of Tara's accident – Tara forgot something, went back to fetch it and . . .'

'Evangeline!' Tom whispered, incredulously. 'Have you any idea what you're suggesting?'

Evangeline hesitated for a moment before continuing. 'Oh, yes. Unfortunately I'm perfectly aware of what I'm suggesting, Tom. I only wish I didn't have this gut-wrenching feeling that I'm right.'

'And what do you intend to do about it? You can't just go and ask Alison if that's why Tara ran into the road . . .'

'No! Of course not. But I do intend to go and see Max.'

'Max! But why Max?' Tom asked in amazement.

'Because quite simply, I think he ought to know! It can't have escaped even your notice, Tom, that when Max was here he and Alison had something going between them.'

Reading her husband's troubled mind, Evangeline continued, 'Oh, I know what you're thinking. You think I've caused quite enough damage already with those photographs. Don't you see, this is the chance I've been waiting for. The chance to make amends. The opportunity to rid both Alison and Max of Church Haywood ghosts, especially if they're going to stay in the area, and I certainly hope they will. They do after all make a nice couple.'

Tom studied Evangeline with new-found admiration. Perhaps he could help his wife with her proposed course of action. 'Would you like me to . . . I mean, would you prefer it if I broached the subject with Max? It might be better coming from a man.'

'No, darling,' Evangeline said huskily, slipping into bed beside him. 'It's very sweet and thoughtful of you, but I think I have to face Max on my own. And if he's rude and refuses to speak to me . . . that's probably no more than I deserve. It's also something I shall have to worry about when the time comes. However, for the moment, I think we've better things to think about.'

Feeling Tom's comforting arms about her waist, Evangeline relaxed. For the first time in months – or was it years – she was at peace with herself.

Alison studied the contents of her wardrobe with alarm. What on earth should she wear tonight? She hadn't been out to dinner with anyone in ages and Max had suggested an old coaching inn on the outskirts of Little Harberry.

'Mmm, very nice,' Bunty had remarked when told of the proposed venue. 'Super food by all accounts, not that I've had the pleasure of eating there myself. I gather everything is freshly cooked, so you might have to wait a while for your meal. Still,' she added with a mischievous twinkle in her eye, 'I don't suppose either you or Max will mind too much.'

'Bunty! What are you implying?'

'Well, I expect you've lots to catch up on. Max has

been away from the village for quite a while. Then of course there's this proposed new bedroom idea for Rosie. What exactly did Max say when he rang?'

'Not a great deal. Other than that Rosie's parents, though overwhelmed by his offer, have nevertheless agreed to giving me the go-ahead to turn Great-grannie's room into something resembling a Wild West film set. Which reminds me,' Alison remarked, catching sight of herself in the mirror, 'if I don't do something about my hair, that's what I'm going to look like in eight hours' time – wild!'

'I very much doubt it,' Bunty added. 'Anyway, what will you wear?'

Alison shrugged her shoulders in despair. 'I honestly don't know. I mean, just look at the state of my wardrobe! There's my black linen, my blue chambray and this skirt and that's about it.' She fingered the red, white and blue sash, adding wistfully, 'And Max has seen all those.'

'Then why don't you pop into town after lunch and have a look for a new outfit? You never know you what you might might find. Besides, I think you need something a bit warmer than those summer clothes. They've forecast a heavy frost for tonight too.'

With lunch finished, Alison contemplated the next meal she would be having. The meal she would be having with Max. Though looking forward to it immensely, she nevertheless hoped they would be able to get through dinner without any mention of Tara and the day she died.

'It's not that I want to forget you, Tara,' she whispered to the tiny snapshot she kept of her friend on the dressing table. 'It's just that for once I want to be with your father as me, as I am now . . . and not as the schoolgirl I was.'

Straightening the delicate silver photo frame, Alison turned to the photo of her mother on the opposite side of the dressing table. The photo was in colour and showed her mother wearing a pale lilac frock, with a sash of deep violet silk.

'Violets,' she whispered, feeling tears well up behind her eyes. 'How you loved both the flowers and the colour. I must find you some next year.'

Recalling that Connie's gardener (Rosie's grandad) had told her of the banks of wild violets that used to grow in profusion near the Stables, Alison determined – with Max's permission – to the dig up a small clump, to place on her mother's grave in the spring.

While Alison thought of her mother's grave, Max was placing his customary posy of flowers on his daughter's. It was there – as she'd hoped – that Evangeline eventually found him.

Noticing the inflexible set of his jaw as she approached, Evangeline breathed deeply and braced herself for verbal combat.

'Hello, Max. I was hoping I'd find you. Connie said I might see you here.'

'Constance has no business to discuss my . . .'

'Max,' Evangeline pleaded softly. 'I need to speak to you.'

Remembering the last time they'd spoken – if you could call it that – Max snapped icily, 'As far as I'm concerned, Evangeline, you said everything that was necessary on the night of the harvest supper!'

'But I didn't know then about . . .'

'Oh! Don't tell me you've more fascinating revelations about my wife! For your information, if you have, I don't want to know, thank you very much! If you'll please excuse me.'

Evangeline put out an arm to stop him and was met with a look of pure disdain and loathing. Max recalled the day in the primrose bedroom.

'Max, please! I know you hate me and you have every reason to. But you must stop and listen to me . . .!'

'Must? *must*? How dare you?'

But Max got no further. Evangeline, sensing she was in great danger of losing both the opportunity to put things right plus her own self-control (oh, how she could do with a drink to steady her nerves) made a grab at his scarred wrist, saying in one hurried breath, 'Yes, I do have more revelations if that's what you want to call them, but they don't concern the dead, they concern the living! They concern Alison!'

In the process of shaking what he perceived to be scarlet claws hooked on to his his wrist, Max froze at the mention of the name.

'Alison! What do you mean, Alison? You surely don't intend to poison my mind against Alison?'

'No. I want to help her.'

'Is she hurt?' Max asked in alarm, finally noticing the real anguish in Evangeline's worried eyes.

'No, not hurt – well, not physically . . . but mentally, I suspect.'

Max looked across the churchyard, half expecting to find Alison in the shadows. There was no sign of her.

'If this is a joke, Evangeline,' Max muttered warily.

'It isn't a joke.' She sighed, relieved to be getting through to him. at last. 'Perhaps if we went to your car?'

CHAPTER 21

'What do you think?' Alison spun round to face Bunty, anxious to get the latter's opinion of her new outfit.

'I think it's lovely. You look quite delightful.'

'You don't think the neckline's too . . . too décolleté? Or that I should wear the other top instead?'

Bunty laughed and studied the scooped kneckline on the fine jersey knit top. 'You call that low! In my day, décolleté meant décolleté! No, Bunty teased. 'If you were hoping to look like a brazen woman, then I'm afraid you haven't got it, Alison. My dear, you'll simply have to settle for looking perfectly sweet and charming as usual.'

Embarrassed yet satisfied, Alison adjusted the sash of her skirt.

'I know the skirt is similar in style to the one I bought for the harvest supper, but I find wraparounds so comfortable. And if the food at the restaurant is as good as you say – and I over-indulge and have a pudding – then I can always loosen the waistband.'

'Then I hope you do over-indulge.' Bunty urged. 'It's about time you fattened yourself up a bit. You need to eat more.'

'You make me sound like the Christmas goose.'

Mention of the Christmas goose turned Bunty's mind quite naturally to thoughts of stuffing, but in the circumstances she decided to keep quiet. It hardly seemed appropriate, with Alison going on her first proper date with Max, to lead the conversation into any area which could be misinterpreted or misconstrued.

Alison, Bunty pondered, was such a strange girl at times, sometimes open and fun-loving and at others deeply thoughtful and reflective to the extent of being almost secretive and distant.

'Oh, well,' she sighed, waving goodbye from the front door, 'perhaps after tonight, things will improve for them both.'

'I must say you're looking lovely,' Max whispered across to Alison, where she was studying the gold-embossed menu. 'How would you describe the colour? It's definitely not denim blue, is it?'

At the reference to her fondness for denim, Alison looked up into kindly teasing eyes.

'No, it's not.' She smiled shyly. 'I suppose it's what you'd call navy-black.'

'From where I'm sitting it looks like midnight-blue.' He refrained from adding 'complete with moon and stars'; it would have sounded so contrived. Yet he knew he was right. From where he was sitting Alison did look like night, bedecked with moon and stars. The stars were in her eyes, reflecting the light from the candles on the table, and the moon hung suspended at her neck, by way of a delicate crescent pendant.

Conscious of Max's gaze in the direction of her

throat, Alison remarked, 'It was my mother's . . . The pendant, it belonged to my mother. I think it's Victorian. She was always so fond of violets. In fact I was going to ask you . . .'

The waiter appeared at the table to collect their order.

'You were saying?' Max continued. 'Something you wanted to ask me?'

'I was wondering,' she said, nervously fingering the pendant, 'if I could possibly dig a small clump of violets from the land at Craven's Stables. Mr Jennings told me there used to be banks of them . . . and I'd like to plant some on my mother's grave.'

'Of course,' replied Max, somewhat taken aback. He'd expected her to ask for something else. 'And is that it?'

'It?'

'All you wanted to ask?'

'Yes. Why, were you expecting me to ask for something else?'

Max hesitated. 'Well, I did wonder if you were going to ask me again about renting space at Craven's Stables.'

'Oh, no!' Alison gasped in surprise. 'I've long since given up that idea.'

'You have?'

'Of course I have. There's no point pursuing that, now that you intend to live there. You are still intending to live there, I suppose?'

'You suppose correctly, Alison, but if you did want a room . . . a base to work from . . . I'm sure we could come to some arrangement.'

'No,' Alison blushed. 'I don't think I need it at the moment. Anyway, with Bunty going to Australia for Christmas, I shall have plenty of room at the cottage.

Don't forget, in the meantime I have this project for Rosie's bedroom.'

'Of course.' Max grinned. 'Rosie's Ranch. I'm so pleased her parents have given us the go-ahead. How soon can you begin?'

'I'm hoping to call round on Monday morning and with luck get it all finished before Christmas.'

'In that case it looks as if we've both got our work cut out for us. You'll be dealing with the Ranch and I'll be dealing with the Stables. The only things missing are the cattle and the horses!'

'And do you intend to have any? Horses, I mean.'

Max shook his head. I very much doubt it. Constance was always the horsey member in the family. Quite frankly, and I don't really know why, horses always terrified me.'

At that precise moment Alison found it hard to think of Max being terrified of anything. But then again, perhaps like herself he'd kept his fears deeply hidden.

'I've noticed how you always refer to your sister as Constance, never Connie, like the rest of us.'

Max shrugged his shoulders. 'I suppose I do. Force of habit, I expect. My father always insisted she should be called Constance. During his lifetime, woe betide anyone who ever called her Connie.'

Thanks to the timely intervention of the waiter, Alison refrained from adding how her own name used to be shortened to Ally. It was a nickname she loathed.

'Guinea fowl?' the waiter enquired.

Max nodded in Alison's direction.

'I was wondering,' Alison hesitated, turning to the waiter. 'You wouldn't happen to have any feathers by any chance?'

'Feathers, madam?' came the astonished reply.

'Yes, guinea fowl feathers. I understand everything you serve here is fresh. In which case I was wondering if Chef had any guinea fowl feathers to spare?'

As the completely baffled waiter scurried away, Max studied his own main course thoughtfully.

Seeing his face crease into a broad grin, Alison whispered in pure earnestness. 'What's so funny?'

'The look on his face when you asked for guinea fowl feathers. Am I correct in thinking you want them for Rosie's bedroom?'

'Right first time. You've obviously followed my train of thought. I thought they'd be useful for . . .'

Alison stopped and giggled, aware of a confused waiter deep in conversation with the *maître d'*. 'Oh, dear. I suppose I should have explained why I wanted them. He probably thinks it a most unusual request.'

'Most unusual,' said Max with a wry smile, looking down at his venison in a filo pastry basket. He gave it a gentle prod with his fork. 'Poor fellow, no wonder he's looking so worried. You've requested feathers from your guinea fowl and he's probably expecting me to ask for the horns that went with this!'

Towards the end of their meal, when Max was paying the bill, the same confused waiter approached Alison with a plastic carrier bag.

'With the chef's compliments, madam.'

With the faintest of smiles, Alison graciously accepted the bag of feathers, saying simply, 'Thank you, they'll be perfect for my ranch.'

Stunned into silence, the waiter could only stare blankly as Max led Alison once more into the cold November night.

An icy blast caught at her throat and, slipping on the frosted tarmac beneath her feet, Alison shivered and clutched at Max's arm.

'Gracious, either it's got much colder or it was warmer than I realized in the restaurant.'

'A bit of both, I think,' he said, reaching into the rear seat for a rug. 'That log fire they had near the bar was certainly giving out some heat. No wonder people were loosening their ties and removing their jackets. Here, wrap this round you before you get into the car.'

'I feel like a Navajo Indian,' Alison joked, when Max placed the rug about her shoulders.

'You don't look like one,' he replied softly, reaching into the carrier bag at her feet, 'but you could look like a Red Indian princess.'

Before she realized what was happening, Max had plucked one of the longer black and white guinea fowl feathers from the bag and fixed it in her hair.

'Max! I can't go back to Keeper's Cottage looking like this.'

'Then perhaps I won't take you back,' he whispered teasingly. 'Perhaps I'll keep you here instead.'

Feeling a cold gust of wind ruffle her short hair, Alison was aware of the feather floating to the ground. With her arms encased beneath the warm red travel rug, she was helpless to retrieve it.

'Oh, well, never mind,' Max said, studying her intently. 'From Red Indian princess to Little Red Riding Hood.'

'And what are you, then? A grizzly bear or the big, bad wolf?'

At the mention of bears and wolves, Max turned and, unlocking the glove compartment of the car, brought out a small teddy bear, an almost identical replica to the one Alison had as a child.

'Oh, by the way,' he said brightly, 'this is for you. Quite by chance, I found one of those old-fashioned toy shops we were talking about. He looked lonely sitting in the shop all by himself and I thought you . . .'

Max's eyes made contact with Alison's when he handed her the bear. What was it about her? he puzzled. Then he realized. Draped in the red blanket, clutching the teddy against her breast, she looked strangely childlike and vulnerable. It was as if she'd stepped straight from one of those ubiquitous paintings of wide-eyed, innocent children that were so popular in the early seventies.

'You look just like a child,' he said softly.

At the mention of the word 'child', Alison's eyes filled with tears and she turned away.

'Alison,' Max urged. 'What have I done? Is it the bear? I'm sorry, perhaps I shouldn't have bought it. I should have realized it would be too distressing for . . .'

'It's not the bear,' she cried, holding the soft fur against her cheek. 'In fact he's lovely.'

'Then what have I said? You know the last thing I'd ever do is hurt you.'

'You called me a child. You still think of me as a child . . . as I was . . . as Tara's friend. In fact there've even been occasions when you've called me Tara!'

Turning her tear-stained face in his direction, Alison continued sadly, 'Can't you see, Max? I don't want to be a substitute for Tara. I don't want to be your child. I want to be your lover!'

Letting the rug fall silently to the ground, Alison ran, sobbing and ashamed at her forthright confession, to the far end of the car park.

'Alison? Alison!' Max called in pursuit, and, in desperation reaching forward to catch her arm, found himself holding the flying sash of her skirt instead.

Anxious to escape his grasp and pulling away, she realized all too late that she'd loosened the sash completely. With a coil of shock, she stopped in her tracks. Max was holding one end of the sash, while she clutched clumsily at the other.

Even in the dimly lit corner of the car park, Alison felt Max's burning gaze in the direction of her thigh. What was it Rosie had said? Alison's scar went right up to her knickers.

Still holding on to his end of the sash with one hand, Max reached out to trace the long line of the scar with his other.

'Alison,' he whispered, huskily. 'My dear, sweet Alison. I don't want you to be my child. I've never wanted you to be a substitute for Tara. I've wanted you since that night . . .' Max felt Alison tremble at his touch as he drew her into his arms. 'Surely you must have realized,' he murmured. 'I thought you knew how I felt, yet at the same time I had to keep forcing myself to hold back. Telling myself you'd been Tara's baby-sitter. Remembering you were only a girl when we first met . . .'

Alison stiffened indignantly. 'But I'm not a child now!'

'No, perhaps not,' he whispered kindly, tilting her face towards his, 'but neither are you a woman in the true sense of the word.'

'What do you mean? I've travelled a great deal, been to college and lived abroad, don't forget. I also nursed my mother for months and since her death have proved myself to be quite an independent woman.'

Watching her re-tie the sash of her skirt, Max led her gently back to the car. 'Of course you have, and I don't doubt that at all, but you've never slept with a man, have you?'

'I . . .' began Alison, but she couldn't go on. She could only feel Max's eyes as they pierced hers relentlessly. And she knew what he was saying was true.

Gathering the rug from the tarmac, Max draped the rug across her shoulders once more. Turning her towards him, he cupped her face in his hands, saying softly. 'Alison, I'm a great deal . . .'

'Don't you dare say older than me, because you're not! Besides, I'm also used to being with older men. My stepfather was much older than my mother and my stepbrothers are almost your age.'

'All right. All right,' he teased. 'There's no need to bully me! I was only thinking of you. I felt your first lover should be someone more your own age, someone . . .'

Summoning up all her courage, Alison stared boldly into his eyes, which like her skirt and top looked inky black in the moonlight.

'First lover? You talk as if you're expecting me to have a whole line of them! As far as I'm concerned, Max, I only want one – I only want you.'

Holding her in his arms, Max hesitated. It felt so right holding her close like this, breathing in her sweet perfume. He bent and kissed the top of her head. 'If you're really sure, we'll have to do something about it. Heaven knows how I've been able to resist taking you in my arms all evening. If we hadn't been in a crowded restaurant.'

At any other time, Max thought dejectedly, he could have taken Alison back to his hotel room, where they could be alone together, but that was miles away in London. As for the flat at the Grange, that was out of the question too. With George and Constance in such close proximity it was hardly conducive to . . .

To what? Max considered thoughtfully. Making love to Alison for the very first time. Taking her lovingly and slowly every step of the way until she reached the very heights of passion. He groaned softly; even the very thought of making love to her filled him with such intense longing. Yet it was a longing he had to suppress. His conscience had already told him that.

London was too far away, he decided for the second time, and the Grange too close for comfort. And he could hardly go home with Alison to Keeper's Cottage. He could just see Bunty's face! Then of course there were Evangeline's revelations to consider. Until this moment, Max had completely forgotten Evangeline.

'Max,' Alison said softly, drawing his attention back to the present.

As if reading his mind, she continued in the faintest of whispers, 'We could always go to the motel.'

'The motel?'

'The one we passed on the way. You remarked how utterly devoid of character it was. Just one solid mass of concrete you said, and wondered how it had ever got past the planning authorities.'

Alison shivered in his arms once more, whether it was from cold or nervousness, Max was unsure. He was only sure of one thing at that moment. He wanted Alison so desperately, and she was suggesting they go to a motel!'

'Please!' her voice pleaded. 'I want it to be tonight, while I . . .' But she got no further. Having helped her into the car, Max switched on the ignition and sped hurriedly away in the direction of the motel.

The room, Max thought to himself, as they walked down the seemingly endless corridor, would probably be identical in every way to the hundreds of others scattered all over the United Kingdom. Rooms he'd stayed in often enough on his business trips, always alone and always bemoaning the fact that no one had yet come up with a better idea for the tired businessman at the end of a long and weary day.

Tonight was no exception, Max thought disappointedly, opening the door. Alison ventured timidly inside.

'It's like an oven in here,' she gasped, walking over to heavily curtained windows.

Seeing her struggle with the window lock, Max went to her assistance.

'They're probably never opened,' he said, glancing down at her, where she was still clutching the teddy bear. 'Perhaps if we can find the thermostat?'

Alison nodded and turned towards the dressing table, where she propped the tiny bear against the box of tissues.

'Well, what do you think of the décor?' Max adjusted the dial on the wall and turned to face her.

'It's not as bad as I thought. I mean, the furniture's quite nice. The dark mahogany does at least tone with the curtains and bedspread and,' she said, peeling back the bedspread, 'it is proper linen, and beautifully laundered by the looks of it.'

Max smiled and watched her run her hands along the crisply folded sheet. Crisp white linen, where very soon he would be lying with Alison, safe in his embrace at last.

Turning off the main overhead light, the room was plunged momentarily into darkness. But Max was already by the bed switching on the table lamp. Seeing renewed fear in Alison's eyes, he sat on the bed and reached for her hand. 'I'm sorry, I should have done that in reverse order. Switched on the bedside lamp first. Did I frighten you?'

'No,' Alison lied.

'So, you're not afraid of the dark any more. I vaguely recollect, when you were a little girl you . . .' Max bit his lip thoughtfully. Bearing in mind their earlier conversation, now was not the time to remind Alison of when she was a child.

Brushing at an imaginary piece of fluff on her shoulder, Alison felt a shiver of apprehension run through her body. No, she wasn't afraid of the dark any more, that had stopped years ago. What did worry her was the fact that she'd begged Max to bring her to this motel and now she was beginning to have second thoughts. Now, she didn't even know if she could go through with this charade.

It isn't a charade! a determined voice echoed in her head. I love Max, I want to be here with him, I want him to make love to me. I . . .

'Alison?' a gentle voice urged softly. 'Would you like to use the bathroom first?'

'What? Oh, yes. Of course.'

With a puzzled frown, Max studied her blank face, as she walked seemingly with unseeing eyes in the direction of the bathroom.

Once there, Alison looked about the bathroom in

wide-eyed panic. What should she do now? What did people do now at this moment of their relationship? She wasn't on the Pill. Would Max . . . they had machines in both gents and ladies loos these days, didn't they? Had he thought to . . . ?

Hearing music from the other side of the bathroom door, Alison could only assume Max had switched on the radio or television. She breathed a deep sigh of relief. At least with unseen singers and musicians she didn't feel quite so alone and desperate.

After some considerable time, Max heard the bathroom door open. Looking up he saw her, freshly showered, wearing a white bathrobe over her silk undies. 'I'm afraid there's only one . . . one robe.'

'That doesn't matter,' he reassured her kindly. 'You can wear it now and I'll wear it in the morning, when I get up to make the tea.'

Heading for the bathroom himself, Max nodded and Alison followed his gaze. There was the typical motel room tray, with its customary sachets of teabags, coffee, sugar and miniature cartons of milk and cream. Morning! Max was already talking about the morning and she still had to get through the night!

Quite how long she'd been waiting with eyes closed, Alison didn't know. Without warning Max slipped into bed beside her and she heard the click of the bedside lamp being switched off.

'Alison.' She heard a murmured voice whisper in her ear, and strong yet gentle hands reached out, drawing her towards his tightly muscled body.

Slipping her arms over his shoulders, Alison ran her hands slowly and nervously down his back to the base of his spine and breathed an almost inaudible sigh of relief.

He wasn't totally naked as she had feared.

Feeling her relax in his arms, Max brushed his lips gently against her eyes and cheeks before seeking her mouth with his own.

'I want you to be sure, Alison,' he whispered, his voice soft and low, 'really sure. If you've changed your mind, we can get dressed and I can take you home now. It really doesn't matter.'

This time it was the turn of Max's inner thoughts to play tricks inside his head. Liar! a voice echoed. Of course it matters! You've waited for her long enough and now she's here – in bed beside you, wearing little more than a silk slip – you couldn't possibly let her go and simply walk away.

'I haven't changed my mind and I don't want to go home,' a trembling voice replied in the darkness.

CHAPTER 22

Those same words rang in Max's ears the next morning when he quietly filled the kettle and switched it on.

'I haven't changed my mind and I don't want to go home,' Alison had pleaded softly.

No, she hadn't changed her mind about spending the night with him in the motel and she'd certainly resisted all suggestions he'd made to take her home – or at least to Bunty at Keeper's Cottage. Yet, thought Max, arranging the cups and saucers on the tray, despite spending the night together they hadn't made love after all.

Watching steam escape from the kettle, Max was grateful for that. This characterless motel room wouldn't have been his choice for their first night together anyway. At least now he would be able to find somewhere more suitable for them to go and stay.

Dropping tea-bags into the pot, Max turned to the bed and felt a warm glow tug at his heart. It had been quite a traumatic night one way and another, yet thanks to Sinclair – the name Alison had given to the teddy bear, because of the tartan ribbon round his neck –

they'd managed to resolve all their problems. Well, perhaps not all their problems, but those that had concerned Alison the most, before they'd eventually fallen asleep.

Catching sight of his reflection in the mirror, Max rubbed at the dark shadow on his chin. Then, combing his hair away from his eyes with his fingers, he grinned mockingly. 'Max Craven! What on earth is your sister going to say to you when you turn up looking like this for the second time in forty-eight hours?'

'What do you think she will say?' a sleepy voice said from the pillow.

'Hopefully nothing,' Max replied, 'providing Bunty's followed my strict instructions and told Constance *not* to interrogate me on my return.'

'You've rung Bunty this morning!' Alison asked mortified. 'You mean to say, she knows we've spent the night together? But Max! Why?'

'Actually, I rang her late last night,' Max explained, seeing Alison's look of sheer disbelief. 'And the reason I rang was to tell her you wouldn't be coming home. I knew she'd worry otherwise.'

'But . . .'

Max took the tray of tea to the bedside table and bent to kiss her on the nose. 'Don't worry, I also told her you would be perfectly safe with me and that your friend Sinclair would see to that personally.'

Alison smiled and reached for the tiny, furry bear. 'I suppose you could say he came between us and kept us apart.'

'You could say that,' Max continued, with the faintest of smiles. 'That was, until this morning, when I woke to find you cradled in my arms.'

Smoothing down her mini-slip, Alison coloured. Had she really ended up in Max's arms? She couldn't really remember.

'Don't look so worried! Nothing happened. Remember what we agreed?'

Reassured, she sat up in bed and reached for her tea. 'I'm so glad I stayed,' she said, softly. I feel so much better knowing that it's all out in the open . . . that you know . . . about everything.'

For a brief moment, Max felt a familiar, menacing dark shadow looming.

'Know about everything.' Alison's voice repeated in his head. Yes, he knew about everything now, and God knew it had been anything but easy listening to Alison's heartrending sobs as she'd lain in his arms, explaining in every lurid detail, what had happened all those years ago.

The reason behind Tara's accident, the reason Virginia had begun drinking and accidentally set fire to the house, and quite possibly even the reason for Evangeline's recent drink-related problems.

Evangeline, Max pondered, watching Alison sip thoughtfully at her tea. Quite possibly thanks to Evangeline, he and Alison now had a future together. It was, after all, Evangeline who, having confronted him in the churchyard, had put forward her theory that Alison was perhaps incapable of having a proper relationship with a man until the circumstances of Tara's death had been completely dispelled from her mind.

Taking the cup from her hand, Max reached out and drew Alison into his arms. He needed to feel her close to him. Wanted her to feel safe.

'Yes,' he replied in understanding, stroking her short

spiky hair. 'I'm glad that I know everything too.'

Listening to the sound of her gentle, rhythmic breathing, Max swallowed hard and relived the bitter-sweet moments when the awful truth had finally reared its ugly head. He had to, he told himself. It was necessary before he and Alison left this austere, cheerless place. They must leave their equally cold and chilling memories behind.

Unlike last night, Alison was now relaxed, as if almost at peace with herself. Max stroked a slender arm and reached for her hand, where delicate fingers entwined gently with his own.

Raising her fingertips to his lips, he kissed them tenderly, remembering last night those same fingers curled and clenched into white-knuckled fists. How, when he'd undressed her and moved dangerously close towards her, her earlier unresisting body had become rigid with fear.

She'd also been extremely taken aback when he'd switched on the bedside lamp and passed her her mini-slip and panties.

'But why?' she'd asked tremulously. 'I thought you wanted to . . .'

'Make love?' Max finished the question for her. 'I do, Alison. In fact, I can think of nothing I want more. But do you want me to make love to you?'

'Yes, Max,' she faltered, 'I do.'

'Well, it certainly doesn't look like it from where I'm sitting.'

Reaching for the bathrobe, Max had slipped it on. He felt in the circumstances it was better Alison did not see him totally naked.

Alison had followed Max's gaze to the gentle contours of her body, covered by the slightly crumpled white linen sheet. Her fists were still clenched by her side and she bit her lip thoughtfully. 'But I do want you, really I do,' Max heard her whisper.

Taking both her hands, Max had covered them with his own. 'You know,' he'd said kindly, 'I honestly believe you do. But your heart is saying one thing and your body language another. Quite simply, Alison, I don't know which to follow.'

'It's just that I get so far . . . wanting you, and then . . .'

'And then?' Max had urged gently, willing her to continue.

'And then, it's as if a shutter comes down, blanking out the present.'

Alison's eyes filled with tears. She wanted to tell Max why, but there was this terrible knot in her stomach. She'd never told anyone about it before, not even her mother, not even Bunty, even though she'd wanted to – desperately. Her eyes pleaded with Max's. If only he could read her mind. Sense the shadows and see those dreadful haunting pictures which had taunted and twisted at her very being for the past ten years.

Alison had blinked hard. Max was talking, saying something about the present. 'Then won't you tell me why the shutter comes down, blanking out the present? For I believe you know the answer, Alison. We both do.'

We! Max had said. But that was impossible! He couldn't know, could he? He hadn't been there!

Realizing he was treading on dangerous ground, Max had lowered his voice to the softest of whispers, urging her gently back to the past.

'You were looking after Tara . . . you'd stayed the

304

night and were taking her for a walk. Did Tara forget something, did you go back to the house?'

'Yes,' Alison replied numbly. 'Tara had forgotten the video we were going to watch. Her mother had suggested we take it to my house. I thought it seemed strange as we could have watched it later . . . but Virginia had insisted. It was as if she didn't want us there.'

'Go on,' Max said, his voice compelling her to continue.

'When we got near the house, we couldn't get back in – the back door was locked. We were going to leave when Tara remembered the spare front door key hidden in the stone tub and . . . anyway, she was sure her mother was still inside. She thought she could hear her voice. The bedroom window was open, you see.'

Alison turned to face Max, her eyes filled with renewed fear. 'Tara thought perhaps her mother was unwell. Virginia often complained of headaches. In fact she frequently suggested I take Tara home with me.'

'Did she indeed?' Max said, bitterly.

Alison nodded and proceeded to explain. 'Tara and I naturally assumed she'd gone back to bed to rest and watch television.'

'And had she?'

Evading Max's question, Alison continued. 'When we went in through the front door, we heard noises, horrid groaning noises. Noises we didn't recognize. I thought I heard a man's voice too and when I became suspicious I told Tara I thought we should leave. But she was frightened . . . frightened . . . for her mother. Ignoring me, she ran upstairs.'

Max sensed fresh alarm in Alison's voice and felt her

305

nails dig deep into his palms. Please God she didn't break down now.

'I tried to stop her, tried to call out,' she said in desperation. 'But no sound came. At the time I blamed it on my asthma, but I suppose it could have been panic.'

'And what happened then, Alison? Did you follow Tara? Did you go upstairs too?

Alison turned to stare blankly at Max, a frisson of fear reverberating through her body. One minute she had been standing at Virginia's open bedroom door, reaching out for Tara's hand, and the next she was here in this motel bedroom, in bed with Tara's father sitting by her side!

Releasing her hands from his grasp, Alison had buried her head against his shoulder. 'I can't tell you, Max! Of course I now realize it's normal for people to behave like that, but at the time . . . at St Katherine's . . . I had no idea. As for Tara – it was such a dreadful shock. In fact it was just like the film . . .' Alison's voice trailed away to a whisper.

'You mean the one you watched with Evangeline?'

'How do you know about that?' Alison asked incredulously.

'Evangeline told me. She came to find me. In the churchyard, by Tara's grave of all places. She told me what she suspected and said she wanted to help us.'

'Help us? Why should Evangeline want to help us? I don't understand.'

'Neither did I,' said Max with a sardonic smile. 'At least not at the time. I also didn't believe her. Poor Evangeline, I thought it was just one of her drunken ramblings, or another attempt of hers to get me into bed.'

'Get you into bed!' Alison had gasped. 'You mean you and Evangeline?'

'No! Thank God, I don't!' Max reassured her. 'Let's just say,' he grinned playfully, 'she was always inviting me over on the pretext of watching some film or another. I had the devil of a job convincing her I've never been interested in old movies. Unlike you, I think Evangeline had designs on my body.'

Alison gave an embarrassed smile. 'I'm sorry, I shouldn't have encouraged you as I did.'

'My dear, sweet Alison, I don't wish to hurt your feelings, but compared to Evangeline I don't think you know the meaning of the word. And for that,' he added quickly, 'I shall be eternally grateful.'

Grateful for a brief diversion from the account of her sordid discovery, Alison had braced herself, breathed deeply and continued, slowly and deliberately, with the events that led to the horrifying scenario of Tara's death.

She described how, both angered and alarmed, Virginia and Miles had leapt apart in a vain attempt to cover their nakedness. Then, whilst mother and lover were fumbling for their clothes, Tara and Alison had made their escape. How they ran. How they fled down the stairs, their hearts pounding in their breasts, sick with disgust and sick with fear at what Miles would do and say when he caught up with them.

For it was becoming obvious it was Miles who was in pursuit. Clad only in trousers, he'd run barefoot through the fields and hedgerows, with Virginia's urgent plea, 'Catch them! Stop them!' ringing frantically in his ears.

But it hadn't been easy running barefoot through

fields of thistles and brambles. And when he'd seen two distant figures clamber over a wall and run towards the road, he was powerless to stop them.

Hearing a thud, a deafening squeal of brakes and a jagged scream – Alison's jagged scream – as Tara ran headlong into the path of the oncoming car, and her own leg was crushed against the wall, Miles had given an anguished cry and returned to break the news to a distraught and inconsolable Virginia.

What followed, of course, Max and Alison could only surmise. Gravely ill in hospital, Alison had made a slow and painful recovery from the accident, leaving her emotionally and physically scarred. At the same time Max was blaming Alison for his daughter's death and Virginia – consumed by guilt, unable to confess the truth and knowing that Miles had left her – had sunk into the depths of depression, aided largely by tranguillizers and alcohol.

Now, in the cold light of morning, Max reached once more for Alison's hand. With perfect clarity he saw it all now. Tara's death had been a needless waste of a young life, and as for Virginia . . . Sadness and anger welled up inside him. He must get out of this room! He needed to get some fresh air. Yet he also needed Alison.

Sensing his desperation, she reached out and drew him into her arms, just as she had on the night of the harvest supper. 'It will be all right, you'll see,' she murmured, stroking his head. 'But I think it would be better if we left now and went back to Church Haywood.'

Feeling an enormous sense of relief flood his body, it was Max's turn to relax in Alison's arms. For one awful moment he'd half thought she was expecting him to make love to her. He realized he should have known better. Alison, like himself, sensed that their time in this place had come to an end. It was time to move on, face Constance and George and dear old Bunty with the truth.

Evangeline too for that matter, Max thought wryly. Now was the time to banish the rumours and secret whisperings once and for all.

In the sitting room at Keeper's Cottage, Bunty poured cups of strong black coffee and handed one to Alison. 'You look as if you could do with this. You look as if you haven't slept a wink. Oh! I didn't mean . . .'

'That's okay, Bunty,' Alison replied kindly, pouring milk into her cup, 'I know you didn't, and rest assured nothing happened. Max was the perfect gentleman. We merely spent the night together and were chaperoned all night long by my friend Sinclair.'

Bunty seemed almost disappointed by Alison's pronouncement. She'd hoped that Max and Alison . . . well, never mind, another time perhaps. She was certainly convinced there'd be another time.

The way Max had kissed Alison goodbye had borne witness to the fact. They were extremely fond of each other, and as for this 'friend Sinclair' – what exactly had he witnessed last night? If only bears could talk, Bunty said to herself, eyeing the small furry creature sitting on Alison's lap.

'And why did you call him Sinclair? I didn't quite catch what you said earlier.'

'I'd just finished reading the novel you bought me. The one about the Sinclair family. Don't you remember? It was set in Scotland and, seeing the tartan ribbon round the bear's neck, the name Sinclair just sprang to mind.'

'Oh, I see,' Bunty replied, though she didn't really. Still, did it really matter? Alison and Max were together and she had her forthcoming holiday in Australia to look forward to. At least now she could go away, knowing Alison would be well taken care of in her absence. She had no doubt at all that Max would see to that.

Alison surveyed the room with a satisfied glow of pure pleasure and contentment. Even Max gazed in sheer disbelief at the total transformation from Great-grannie's cluttered bedroom into the newly decorated 'Rosie's Ranch'.

'It's amazing, Alison! I don't know how you've managed it.'

'Once the old utility furniture was taken out and I was left with the bare shell, I have to admit, even I was surprised at how much space there was. Do you think she'll like it?'

'Like it?' Max grinned. 'Let's see, shall we?'

Outside the bedroom door, an excited Rosie was jumping up and down impatiently. 'Mum! Can I *please* go in now?'

'No, you must wait until Max and Alison give you the word.'

'But when will that be?' the voice pleaded. 'I've been waiting ever so long and . . .' Rosie looked up expectantly. Max popped his head round the bedroom door.

'How about now?' he said, gesturing her inside.

All eyes were on the doorway as Rosie, home and fully recovered and wearing a newly dry-cleaned serape, stood transfixed on the threshold of her ranch.

Giving a whoop of joy, she rushed about the room

examining its every detail. Stopping first at the bunk bed, with her own desk beneath to work and play at, disguised as a western saloon bar, she then ran to the replica of the steam train, complete with tall steam funnel and cow-catcher front.

Opening each of the 'carriage doors', she squealed with delight, discovering a range of toy boxes complete with toys. Some she recognized and some she didn't.

'They're from Nigel,' Max explained, sensing her air of bewilderment.

'Fancy him rememb'ring me.' Rosie said, matter-of-factly, turning to look at Max.

'How could anyone forget you? he murmured fondly, watching her eyes dart in wonderment across the room.

'A cactus! Look, Mum, I've got a cactus!' Rosie pointed to the corner of the room.

'Ah, but that one hasn't got needle-sharp prickles,' Alison interrupted, watching Rosie hesitate and reach timidly forward with the tip of her finger. 'Those prickles are only painted on, you see, and the stem and branches are made from foam. You won't hurt yourself.'

'And you can hang your clothes on them,' Michelle added with a bemused smile. 'So there'll be no excuse for leaving them on the floor.'

Leaving Rosie to run and find her spare serape, so she could hang it up on her 'cactus', Grandad Jennings appeared at the door.

'Well, bless me!' he said to Alison. 'How on earth did you do that?'

'It's made from a couple of coat stands,' she whispered. 'I merely covered them with foam and fabric,

311

then painted it. It's perfectly safe and weighted at the base. It won't topple over.'

'Looks like you've thought of everything,' Grandad announced.

'Not quite,' Alison said, knowingly, looking in Michelle's direction. 'Don't forget, there's still the lamp.'

At the mention of the word 'lamp', Rosie dropped the cream canvas flap (painted to look like a wigwam) that was hanging across the floor-length cupboard and looked about her dejectedly. The lamp! Alison had mentioned the lamp. No doubt Mum's lamp. The awful crinoline lady she hated so much because it reminded her of Donna, Darren's ex-girlfriend.

Wanting to forget about the lamp, Rosie turned her attention to the mural of the Grand Canyon. Set against clear blue skies, she saw there was even a Joshua tree with one branch in relief. She sighed deeply. It was even complete with birds with black and white feathers.

'Guinea fowl feathers,' Max said in surprise, recognizing the contents from the plastic carrier bag Alison had been given in the restaurant. He turned and smiled in Alison's direction and in doing so caught sight of Rosie's crestfallen face.

Stepping forward, he lifted Rosie into his arms. 'What's the matter, Rosie, don't you like it?'

'It's lovely,' she sniffed, watching her mother reappear with a large box, 'but do I really have to have that crinoline lady by my bed?'

'No, Rosie, you don't,' Michelle said reassuringly. 'I know you've never particularly liked it, especially as you're dead against dresses of every description.

And even though Alison suggested a new lampshade for it, I wasn't very keen on the thought of coming in one day to find my crinoline lady with a noose round her neck!'

Rosie giggled mischievously. Mum obviously remembered Rosie's earlier pirate phase and the time she'd borrowed Michelle's black eye pencil and drawn a patch over one of the crinoline lady's eyes.

'So I think I'll keep my crinoline lamp if you don't mind. Where I know it's safe,' Michelle continued with a grin. 'Anyway, Grandad thought you might prefer this old thing instead.' Seeing Michelle smile, Rosie knew her mum was only teasing and, recognizing a familiar twinkle in Grandad's eyes, she slowly wriggled free from Max's grasp and approached the large cardboard box with renewed interest.

Peeling back layer after layer of crisp white tissue, she gave a further gasp of delight when two shiny brass replicas of old oil lamps came into view.

'This one's for your bedside table and the other's for the ceiling,' Grandad explained. 'We wanted to make sure you liked them first.'

Like them? Rosie thought. Like them! They were absolutely brill!

Later that night, lying in Max's arms, Alison sighed contentedly.

'I only wish Nigel could have seen Rosie's face.'

'I know, it was pure delight to watch her,' Max acknowledged.

'Oh, well, that's another satisfied customer.'

'It is if you're referring to me,' Max teased, reaching out to ruffle her hair. 'I'm satisfied that at long last I've got you to myself. It seems like weeks since we've had time for each other.'

'It is, for the simple reason that you've been busy with Craven's Stables and I've been seeing to Rosie's Ranch.'

'Yes,' agreed Max, 'and I'm prepared to bet there was one happy little girl who couldn't wait to go to bed this evening.'

'No doubt. She probably even suggested going to bed early.'

'You mean like me?' Max teased, with the faintest of smiles.

Alison felt herself colour at Max's earlier suggestion. Once they'd left Rosie and her family, they'd driven straight to London to Nigel's flat. Nigel had gone to Vanessa's parents for the weekend. There were wedding plans to discuss.

'You're sure you don't mind Nigel's flat?' Max enquired in a concerned voice, inserting the key in the lock. 'I thought we'd have more freedom here than in a hotel. Nigel assured me we wouldn't be disturbed. He said it would . . .'

'It will be perfect,' Alison whispered. Following him inside, walking to the window, she added, 'And the view across the Thames is simply breathtaking.'

Ignoring the view himself – he was after all familiar with it already – Max had wandered into the kitchen, where Vanessa had left a large printed note. 'YOUR SUPPER'S IN THE FRIDGE', it read.

'In that case,' said Max, opening the fridge door to examine the champagne and half of Selfridge's Food Hall, 'there's no need to go out to eat. We could eat

314

here, if that's okay with you, Alison, and perhaps . . .
have an early night?'

An early night! Alison had felt a familiar stirring in
her stomach. An early night with Max, in this sump-
tuous appartment, with its sweeping, panoramic views
of the Thames and London by night. What could be
more romantic?

Nothing could, she sighed contentedly, reliving the
moment when, taking her by the hand, Max had led her
to the midnight-blue decorated bedroom. Turning the
dimmer switches low, he'd murmured softly in her ear,
'Midnight-black. What could be more perfect?' Turning to unzip her dress, he'd let it fall silently to the floor,
before lifting her into his arms and carrying her effort-
lessly to the bed.

Unlike the night they'd spent together at the motel,
this time Alison didn't lie with gritted teeth and
clenched fists when Max moved deliberately towards
her. Instead she rejoiced in unknown pleasures as his
lips and hands moved expertly over her body, introducing her to such delights she hadn't thought possible.

With a gasp of both pain and pleasure, feeling Max
mould his body so carefully and tenderly into hers that
it quite took her breath away, she was able to forget the
tragic events of that day ten long summers ago. Only
once, dimly recalling the noises emitting from Virginia's bedroom, did the haunting, dark, shadows bubble
unwelcomingly to the surface. Mercifully they were
only fleeting.

Feeling the sudden tautness in her body, Max's
senses sharpened and he looked down, his eyes desperately seeking contact with her own. Anxious to read

315

her mind, to know her innermost thoughts, he made as if to speak and noticed the tears glistening in her eyes. Before he'd even uttered a word, Alison reached up and placed a finger on his lips.

'Don't worry,' she whispered, her eyes shining with love for him. 'They've gone. The shadows have disappeared. We're alone together at last.'

CHAPTER 23

In the afterglow of their new-found happiness, Christmas and New Year passed almost as quickly as they appeared. From afar George and Connie watched Max and Alison delight in each other's company, oblivious to the comings and goings of other Church Haywood residents. Only the major problems at Craven's Stables shattered their idyll.

'Can you believe it?' Max announced to his sister, one morning at breakfast. 'The minute they turned on the water, some idiot had to go and fracture the pipe. And I was hoping to move in tomorrow.'

'Tomorrow! But that's ridiculous, Max! The Stables is hardly fit for habitation just yet, surely?'

'Oh, the builders have progressed quite well since you were last there, Constance. But no, you're right, It's not completely habitable just yet. I was hoping to have one room ready for the weekend, that's all.'

'Why? What's happening at the weekend?' Connie enquired, placing fresh toast on the table.

'Bunty's due back, or had you forgotten?'

Connie eyed the vast array of Australian postcards sellotaped to the cupboard doors. 'No, of course I hadn't forgotten, particularly as George and I are going to meet her at the airport. But what's that got to do with Craven's Stables?'

'It means Alison will no longer be on her own at Keeper's Cottage.'

'But you know she can always come to the flat,' Connie replied, reading his mind.

'I know,' Max said awkwardly, 'but it's not quite the same as being on your own, is it?'

'Well, I suppose it's not exactly Greta Garbo.' Connie tried to make light of the situation.

'Who's talking about Greta Garbo?' George called, kicking off his muddy boots. 'I thought she died years ago.'

'She did,' Connie explained, making a fresh pot of tea, 'but Max *vants to be alone* . . .'

'I say, Connie,' George said, walking in in his stockinged feet. 'You sound just like her!'

'George! We need your advice. Bunty's coming back at the weekend and Max was hoping to move into the Stables tomorrow.'

'But that's ludicrous . . .'

'Don't interrupt!' Connie retorted. 'Now, as I was saying, moving into the Stables is out of the question . . . and the flat, for obvious reasons, is out of the question too, so what would you advise?'

It was at this point that, Max broke in on their conversation. 'Honestly, you two,' he grinned. 'You forget I'm not a child any more.'

'Ah! But you're still my little brother.' Connie plonked a kiss on his cheek. 'And I'd like to help you. You and Alison. It's nice to see the two of you together.'

'Yes,' agreed George jovially. 'By the way, when are

you going to ask her to m . . .' The words died on George's lips when he saw the look on his wife's face.

Tight-lipped, Max rolled up his napkin and made for the door. 'I suggest you don't say it, George. All I will say is, I'll consider it when I feel the time is right.'

Undaunted, George called after him, 'What about a mobile home up there, until the place is finished or you've made up your mind?'

'George, really!' Connie admonished. 'Max living in a mobile home! Whatever next?'

'All I can say to that, old thing, is you're way out of touch. Mobile homes these days have all mod cons . . . central heating, running water, the lot. Anyway, what do you think about Max, eh? Do you think he will ask Alison to marry him?'

'I don't know. He certainly surprised me back then. There I was expecting him to bite your head off and instead he says something like that and disappears without another word!'

'So, Bunty could be coming home to the sound of wedding bells.' George grinned, stirring his tea.

'Not unless Max gets a special licence, or had you forgotten it's this weekend Bunty's due back?'

'Crikey! So I had! Gracious, those two months have flown quickly. I can't wait to tell her the good news.'

'George Henderson,' Connie sighed, removing a stray piece of straw from her husband's hair. 'Underneath all those bales of hay, silage and milk quotas, you're just one big romantic softy.'

Relieved to see familiar smiling faces, and waving a small koala bear in the air, Bunty called out to George and Constance.

'Hello, you two. Thanks for meeting me. For one horrid moment I thought, having been away for so long, I might have been forgotten.'

'As if we would!' said George, with a wry smile in Connie's direction.

With the luggage stowed away, George helped Bunty into the car, where he noticed she was still holding the toy koala.

'I don't want to lose Ozzie,' Bunty said. 'I nearly left him behind on the plane. Luckily the air hostess came running after me.'

'Who's he for?' Connie enquired. 'I didn't think you had any young children in the family.'

'Oh, he's for Alison,' Bunty explained. 'I thought he'd be company for Alison and also Sinclair, the teddy bear Max bought her. Or didn't you know about that?'

'We know a lot more than you think,' George said knowingly, looking in his rear-view mirror in Bunty's direction.

'What on earth do you mean?' Bunty asked inquisitively. 'Alison's okay, isn't she? She's not been ill or anything while I've been away?'

'It depends what you mean by anything.' George continued with a twinkle in his eye.

'George, just you concentrate on getting us out of this wretched airport, and leave me to tell Bunty the good news.'

Bunty breathed a sigh of relief. 'Well, thank goodness it's good news; for a moment I have to admit you had me worried. So what is it, this good news?'

'Alison and Max finally got together. They went to London for the weekend, after Alison finished Rosie's bedroom – which by the way looks fantastic – and they've been virtually inseparable ever since.'

Unable to resist the urge to keep quiet, George began humming the bridal march. 'Dum, dum de dum. Dum, dum de dum.'

'You don't mean . . .!' Bunty grabbed hold of the seat rest in front of her.

'No, he doesn't!' Connie said with an exasperated sigh. 'At least not yet. But it looks a strong possibility.'

'Oh, dear,' Bunty said sadly.

'You mean, you don't approve of the idea?' Connie asked in alarm.

'No, it's not that. I'm only sorry not to have been around when all this took place.'

'Oh, Bunty!' George and Connie laughed in unison as they arrived at Keeper's Cottage and Alison opened the door to greet them.

Dumbstruck, Bunty took in her newly decorated kitchen, with its gleaming quarry-tiled floor and terracotta and ochre walls and accessories.

'What a transformation!' she gasped. 'However did you manage it? You know, somehow it reminds me of Ayre's Rock at dawn.'

'That's hardly surprising,' Alison replied, 'considering I was inspired by that exhibition of Aboriginal art at the Barbican. Do you remember? That was the day I bumped into Max on the train coming home. Well, not bumped into him exactly, but woke him up at Church Haywood.'

Bunty noticed the change in Alison's eyes when she spoke of Max. An almost ethereal glow radiated across her entire face. Perhaps this was the cue she'd been waiting for.

'I gather you've been seeing quite a bit of Max while

321

I've been away,' remarked Bunty casually, pretending to rearrange the vase of early daffodils on the kitchen table.

Blushing, Alison replied softly, 'Yes, I have. I expect Connie and George will have told you.'

Bunty nodded in reply. 'Mmm. They did, and I have to say I'm delighted! You know it's what we've all been waiting for.'

'Waiting for! I don't understand.'

'Connie and myself, and even dear old George come to that,' Bunty enlightened her. You seem right together somehow. In fact Connie says you're far better for Max than Virginia ever was . . .'

Alison bit her lip thoughtfully. 'I don't think it's fair to talk about Virginia. I'd rather try and forget about all that if you don't mind.'

'Of course, I should have realized, I'm sorry. But I suppose I ought to tell you, coming back from Heathrow, Connie also told me exactly what happened the day Tara died. It can't have been easy for you, my dear, living with all that for so long.'

'No, it wasn't. It was like living with a permanent shadow over my shoulder. Luckily, thanks to Max, the shadows have long since disappeared. Which is why I'd prefer not to . . .'

'Of course,' Bunty said chirpily, opening a cupboard door. 'So I'll change the subject and ask you to tell me where everything is. Since you've transformed this kitchen so magnificently, I can't find a damned thing!'

Alison smiled and, opening each cupboard door in turn, explained where everything was. 'It's not all that different from before really. It's just that I've separated the non-perishables into savoury and sweet – for want of a better description. And you'll find them all in alphabetical order too, so they'll be easier to find.'

Bunty studied the newly lined cupboard shelves, where even the lining paper matched the décor of the kitchen. Then she made a mental note to to remember; the savoury items were on the left and the sweet on the right. 'Alphabetical order,' she chuckled to herself, as her eyes scanned the shelf, which began with bean salad and ended with tuna. 'I don't think Keeper's Cottage has ever seen such orderly cupboards.'

'Make sure they stay that way, then,' Alison teased. 'I enlisted Max's help with those and it took us ages.'

Once more, at the mention of Max's name, Alison's face became a picture of radiance. 'Which reminds me,' she said walking to the hallway, 'I must ring him. He wants to know what you think of the kitchen.'

'Tell him I think it's perfect,' Bunty called, 'and that I want to see him as soon as possible.' Picking up the tiny koala, who had been sitting propped up by the fruit bowl, Bunty whispered softly, 'Yes, Ozzie, it's perfect. Everything's perfect. Somehow I don't think Alison will be needing your company after all.'

One Friday morning in late March, a perfect stillness bathed Craven's Stables, filling Max's whole being with a sense of pure contentment and satisfaction. Looking from the half-finished kitchen, he gazed in wonderment at the early morning sunshine dancing on dew-filled grass and mellow, golden sandstone.

'Spring, at last,' he murmured, moving to the kitchen door and opening it, breathing in the chill yet delicately scented early morning air.

Almost in greeting, tubs of daffodils nodded their

323

golden heads and Max made his way down the newly made gravelled walk to the far end of the garden. He took the same route each morning, always peering anxiously and stopping in the far corner in the shelter of the high stone wall. This morning, however, he not only stopped to feel the warmth of the sun on his face, but bent down and plucked at a tiny purple bloom.

'The first violets,' he said huskily, examining the delicate purple petals. 'The first violets for Alison. This is what I've been waiting for.'

Hearing his voice, a lone male blackbird tugging at a worm cocked his head to one side and stared at Max with a bright button eye.

'That's okay,' Max called softly. 'You carry on with your breakfast and I'll go in and have mine. I've got what I came for.'

Before returning to the house, Max knocked on the door of the mobile home. He had taken George's advice to bring one to the site, but not for himself to live in.

The reason for its presence, he'd told a startled Constance, was to provide a home for his site manager and at the same time guarantee there was always someone on site to keep an eye on the place. Now that Craven's Stables was nearing completion, security was crucial.

Waiting for Terry to open the door, Max recalled how in the days prior to the mobile home's arrival he'd had problems with vandals and extremely curious villagers. Whilst the needlessly broken and knocked down pile of insulation blocks and broken windows had cost a considerable amount to replace, it was the almost inexplicable curiosity of the neighbouring inhabitants that now annoyed Max more.

'I suppose you must expect it,' Connie had remarked, trying to be helpful. 'After all, the Stables were left to fall into rack and ruin. And now that you're having the whole place totally transformed, people are bound to be a little bit curious.'

'I don't mind a little bit curious,' Max had replied tetchily, 'but I do draw the line at them coming out in droves on a Sunday afternoon!'

Consequently, both the mobile home and Terry had arrived at almost the same time.

'Morning, Max,' a cheery voice called, opening the door to the area marked 'SITE OFFICE'. 'You were up bright and early again, I see.'

Max nodded and studied the site plan on the wall. On it Terry had quite clearly marked 'FINISH KITCHEN'.

'What do you think?' enquired Max. 'Will I be able to cook in there tomorrow?'

'That depends what you intend to cook,' said Terry cheekily.

'Nothing too fancy, merely a simple supper for two.'

'Oh, I see. Just you and Alison, is it? Well, in that case, as you won't be in need of banqueting space, I would think the lads could manage that.'

'I'd appreciate it if you could, Terry. So, can I leave Craven's Stables in your capable hands, then? I need to go to town, to collect some furnishings and also find something relatively simple to cook.'

'Couldn't you have got Connie to rustle you something up? I'm sure she wouldn't have minded.'

Max shook his head. 'Quite possibly, but that's why I like being able to stop here occasionally. You know, I'm convinced Constance still thinks I'm about twelve!

'That's the trouble with big sisters,' Terry grinned. 'Mine's exactly the same. That's why I jumped at the chance of living here for a bit. What could be better than a good book, a nice bottle of claret and a decent concert on the radio? Should be a good one on the radio tomorrow, by the way – that's if you're interested. They've been featuring the cello all week on Radio 3 and tomorrow night's concert is coming from the Barbican.'

'That's one of Alison's favourite haunts,' Max said, stepping from the office. He remembered fondly, that was where she'd been the day they'd met on the train. 'Hopefully,' Max murmured softly to himself as he walked away, 'we'll be too busy to listen to a concert.'

Listening to Alison singing in the shower, Bunty crept downstairs and reached for the phone.

'Well?' she asked Connie. 'Have you any idea what's happening? Do you think he'll ask her tonight? Has he told you anything?'

'Sorry to disappoint you, Bunty; all I know is that Max has invited Alison to Craven's Stables this evening for supper. Though the place isn't finished yet, of course.'

'Oh!' Bunty was disappointed. She'd secretly hoped Max had confided in his sister and told her of his intentions as far as Alison was concerned.

Initially they'd half expected Max to propose on St Valentine's Day, especially when Alison had received two dozen red roses and had returned from their dinner date clutching a red satin box. Unfortunately for Connie and Bunty, its size alone indicated that it hadn't contained the long-hoped-for engagement ring.

Instead there'd been a glass oval, edged in silver and suspended on a silver chain. On the glass were delicate hand-painted violets. The same simple violets that now commanded Alison's attention.

With her skin and hair still damp, Alison tied the sash of her kimono and walked to her bedroom window. There, with the tip of her index finger, she very gently touched the silver frame, causing the glass to move slowly from side to side like a pendulum.

As it did so, the last rays of evening sun caught at the exquisitely detailed flowers and their almost heart-shaped leaves. Alison sighed dreamily. What was it Max had said when he'd telephoned?

'Come for supper, if you're prepared to risk my cooking, and in the morning we'll get up and pick dew-covered violets together.'

For once ignoring what might happen after supper and the prospect of making love in the morning, before they went to pick violets, Alison had asked excitedly, 'They're out! You mean the violets are out? But that's wonderful! We'll be able to take some to Mother's grave and . . .'

'Wait a minute,' Max had interrupted kindly. 'For the moment there are only a few, down at the end of the walled-garden. They'll probably only fill an egg cup, but you're welcome to have them.'

'In that case, it seems a shame to pick them. Wouldn't it be better to leave them until the larger clumps by the garage are in full bloom?'

'I'll leave it entirely up to you, Alison, and if you change your mind, then I'm sure they'd look positively charming on your breakfast tray instead.'

Feeling the familiar butterflies in her stomach, Alison

was reminded of the variety of breakfasts she and Max had shared together since their first night together in Nigel's flat. By all accounts, Max had already decided she would be spending the night with him at Craven's Stables. Tonight, she concluded, couldn't come quick enough.

'Alison,' Bunty called from the hall. 'I'm off now, so will you please make sure you lock up when Max calls for you? Have a nice evening,' she continued. 'I expect you're staying over . . . and that I shall see you some time tomorrow?'

Peering over the banister, Alison met Bunty's knowing grin with a winsome smile. 'Yes, I expect I will . . . and you shall. Max has invited me to go violet-picking before breakfast.'

With a bemused shrug of the shoulders and a twinkle in her eye, Bunty picked up the album of Australian photos she was taking to show her friends on the other side of Little Harberry.

'Violet-picking indeed!' She chuckled, switching on the ignition of her car. 'That's a novel way of describing it, I suppose!'

When the doorbell rang, half an hour before she was expecting it to, Alison ran downstairs eagerly to open the door.

'It's okay, even though you're early, I am ready.'

'Well, I'm sure glad of that, for we haven't a moment to lose.'

'Jasper!' Alison gasped. 'What on earth are you doing here?' Why didn't you . . . I'm supposed to be going out to dinner . . .'

'There's no time for that now,' Jasper said, taking her

by the arm. 'Just grab your coat and your hat, as they say in the song, and come along with me.'

Amazed to see her hesitate, Jasper continued, 'Gee, Alison! A guy comes halfway round the world to take you to see your big brother in concert at the Bar-bi-can or some such place and you talk about going out to dinner!'

'You mean Oliver's in London! But how . . .'

'As I said, just get your coat and I'll tell you in the car. The taxi's waiting.'

'Taxi!' Alison looked towards the front gate where a black London cab was waiting. 'But I must ring Max! Tell him where I'm going.'

'You can ring who you like, honey,' came Jasper's voice as he hurried towards the taxi, 'just make sure you do it in ten seconds flat. I want to get there before the interval, not after!'

Frantically ringing Max's number, Alison was distraught to get no reply. Perhaps Max was still in the shower, or in the garden or even on his way! Anxiously she looked down the road in the vain hope that she might see the familiar black Saab nosing round the corner. But to no avail.

In a last desperate attempt, Alison gave up on Max's number and rang Connie instead.

'Connie, thank God you're at home.'

'Alison? Is that you? Is there anything wrong? You sound as if . . .'

'Look, Connie, I'm sorry, I can't stop now. There's a taxi waiting to take me to London. I've just found out Oliver is playing . . .'

'Oliver! You mean your stepbrother?'

'Yes, that's right. Look, there isn't time to tell you

now. So can you please get hold of Max for me and say I'm sorry? Tell him I'll explain everything tomorrow. It's far too complicated now.'

'But Alison . . .'

'Problems?' queried George, looking at Connie, who was staring into the silent earpiece of the phone.

'You could say that,' Connie replied. 'That was Alison; she was just getting a taxi to London.'

'London!'

'Apparently Oliver is playing in a concert.'

'What! But that's impossible. I thought Oliver was in the States.'

'So did I, George.' Connie replied dejectedly. 'So, who's going to ring Max and tell him the bad news?'

'Well, it's not exactly bad news, Connie. I mean if Alison's stepbrother is over here. After all she wasn't able to go to the States at Christmas and New Year, was she?'

'I suppose not,' Connie said sadly. 'But to me it's bad news. Bunty and I were convinced Max was going to ask Alison to marry him this evening.'

'There's always tomorrow,' George replied, patting her arm, trying to sound helpful.

'I wish you hadn't said that, George. Because in this instance, I've a horrible feeling tomorrow will never come.'

'Connie! I think you're over-reacting a bit. Either that or you've been watching too many of those old Hollywood movies with Evangeline. Alison's only gone to London.'

'I know,' sighed Connie, picking up the phone, 'but I wish she hadn't, that's all.'

Having dialled Max's number, Connie drummed her

330

fingers impatiently on the hall table. 'Oh, please be there, Max.' She whispered. 'Because if you've already left for Keeper's Cottage, you're in for an awful long wait.'

'Max Craven,' a breathless voice echoed down the line.

'Max! Thank heavens I've caught you . . .'

'Yes, but only just. I was in the process of locking the door when I heard the phone. I'm on my way to fetch Alison, or had you forgotten?'

'How could I?' Connie murmured to herself. Bracing herself for Max's disappointment, she said hurriedly, 'Actually it's because of Alison that I'm ringing. She tried to get hold of you . . . you see, she's had to go to London.'

'London! But I was going to . . . we were supposed to be . . .'

'I know,' Connie broke in, 'and she's very sorry. Her stepbrother's performing in a concert . . .'

It was Max's turn to interrupt the conversation. 'But she never said! Why didn't she tell me? She could have rung.'

'Quite possibly because she didn't know?' suggested Connie. 'And anyway she did try to ring, but couldn't get any reply.'

'Damn!' muttered Max. 'I thought I heard the phone, but there were some people wandering about the gardens and I had to go and tell them this is now private property. I shall have to get Terry to put up a "KEEP OUT" sign.'

'Naturally she said she was very sorry. She'll ring you and explain tomorrow.'

'You mean she's not staying in London?'

'I'm not altogether sure.'

Max gave an exasperated sigh. 'Oh, all right, Constance. In that case I suppose I shall have to wait until tomorrow. By the way, you and George don't fancy supper, do you? I've all this food . . .'

'Sorry, Max. George and I have already eaten, we're absolutely . . .'

'No matter,' Max said softly. 'Perhaps I can find a cat to keep me company. There's been a stray about here these past few days.'

A cat? Connie puzzled. What on earth did Max want with a cat?

'Oh, and Constance,' Max finished lamely, 'thanks for ringing and letting me know.'

'That's okay, Max. I'm sorry I had to. Goodbye.'

CHAPTER 24

With the taxi speeding towards London, Alison turned anxiously towards her stepbrother.

'Now, will you please explain what is going on? Why you didn't let me know you were coming?'

'Ollie and I thought we'd surprise you.'

'You certainly did that! I only spoke to Oliver last week. He led me to believe you were in Australia filming and he was rehearsing for an Easter concert.'

'We were.'

'Then what went wrong?' Alison said miserably, looking at her watch. By now Max would have realized they wouldn't be having dinner together.

'Say, you don't sound very happy to see me, little sister,' Jasper said, putting an arm round her shoulder. 'I thought you and me were buddies.'

'Oh, I'm sorry, Jasper. Of course I'm pleased to see you. When the doorbell rang, I wasn't expecting you, you see. I was expecting someone else.'

'Aha!' Jasper announced gleefully. 'Do I take it my little sister has got herself a boyfriend at long last? Well, that's just fine, Alison. When do I get to meet him?'

'How long are you staying?'

333

'That depends on lots of things. You, Ollie, my agent and a certain little lady I have waiting for me Stateside.'

'I see you haven't changed much. Still breaking hearts wherever you go.'

'Can I help it if they all fall in love with me, little . . . ?'

'Don't you dare call me your little sister again. You're not on the film set now, Jasper,' Alison scolded. 'You're with someone who knows you very well, or had you forgotten?'

Dispensing with the film star persona, Jasper raked tanned hands through his mane of thick blond hair and sighed. 'How could I forget, when you were always so neat and sensible and I . . . ?'

'. . . was the madcap tearaway, always trying to impress me and my friends,' Alison finished for him.

'Yeah, I guess. And I didn't really succeed, did I?'

'You might have impressed my friends, who all fell for your good looks and devil-may-care charm. But I was the one who used to pick up your smelly socks from the bathroom floor.' Alison grinned wickedly. 'I'm used to seeing you prancing about half-naked, remember? And quite frankly that tanned body of yours does absolutely nothing for me.'

'Oh, Alison!' Jasper cried in mock horror, holding a clenched fist to his furrowed brow. 'Don't go on. Lady, you are too cruel!'

Alison dug him in the ribs playfully. 'You should be on the stage at Stratford, not strutting about with some bimbo on Bondi Beach.'

'Who said I was strutting about on Bondi Beach with a bimbo?' Jasper asked indignantly.

'Oliver. Like me, he thinks you should get down to some serious acting.'

Momentarily stunned, Jasper sat in silence, while Alison tried to regain her composure. It had been a dreadful shock to find Jasper on the doorstep, plus the taxi with its engine running, waiting to whisk her away to London.

Now, looking at Jasper's handsome, golden features, complete with square-cut jaw and penetrating blue eyes, she thought fondly of the days she'd spent with them all in the New York apartment. Pure unadulterated luxury and such a far cry from the past fifteen months at Church Haywood and her time at Keeper's Cottage.

'So, how's dear old Bunty?' Jasper said, eventually.

'Oh, still your number one fan, and forever drooling over you whenever she sees you on TV.'

'I'm glad someone still likes me.'

'Oh, rest assured, Bunty does. She even called her dog Jasper!'

Somewhat deflated for the second time in fifteen minutes, Jasper held up his hands. 'Okay. You win. I guess to you I'm just a big-headed slob.'

'No, you're not.' She kissed him warmly. 'You're my gorgeous stepbrother and I adore you. Now tell me about Oliver.'

During the remainder of the journey into London, Jasper explained how the original solo cellist booked for the evening's performance had slipped on a wet pavement and broken his wrist. Frantic phone calls between New York and London had ensued. Then, when Jasper had rung his older brother to tell him he was going back to the States to ask would he meet him at the airport, he'd discovered Oliver was in the process of packing to fly to London.

'Then I thought, wouldn't it be great if I could arrange a stop-over in London too, so we could all be together? It was as simple as that!'

'Not from where I'm sitting.' Alison mused to herself, when the taxi pulled up outside the Barbican's stage door.

'Better late than never,' Jasper whispered, taking Alison's hand as they were ushered inside. 'At least we made it before the second half.'

'I'm sorry, Mr Benedict, I'm afraid I can't let you in until the interval. Barbican policy, I'm afraid.'

'That's okay, honey.' Jasper eyed the softly spoken young blonde approvingly. 'We'll watch the remainder of the first half on the video screen near the bar.'

'I could perhaps arrange for you to be taken to your brother's dressing room?'

'No, thanks. Oliver prefers to concentrate on his performance during the interval. I think seeing Alison here might put him off his stroke, or whatever it is cellists call it.'

'Very good, sir. But after the performance, I'd be happy to oblige.'

'I hope you will,' Jasper said, wickedly.

'Jasper, you're incorrigible!' Alison protested, walking across the smooth parquet floor to the nearest video screen.

Although the musicians on the stage looked so remote and faraway, she had no difficulty in recognizing Oliver instantly. Unlike Jasper, who was gregarious, tanned and golden, Oliver appeared quiet, dark and mysterious. Some had even referred to him as mean and moody, but he wasn't like that at all. Looking at him, even from this distance, Alison could see why, of course. Yet Oliver's critics didn't know the warm, sensitive being beneath the so-called mean and moody, cold exterior.

Far from it, Alison thought; in fact Oliver was the perfect quiet American, deeply thoughtful, caring and with a heart of gold. Like Jasper, she adored him too. But for different reasons. It was Oliver she'd been able to confide in when her mother's cancer had shown no sign of abating, and Oliver who'd handled all their financial problems and her stepfather's legacy.

Much as she wanted to see Oliver during the interval, Alison nevertheless knew Jasper had taken the correct decision to leave him alone. He lived, breathed and slept music, and unlike Jasper didn't need the constant attention of young females. He was perfectly happy to be closeted for hours on end with Brünnhilde – his cello. In fact, somehow now, looking at Oliver's strong dark features, Alison found herself thinking of Max. 'Oh, Max.' She sighed. 'I'm so sorry about tonight.'

Seeing tears mist her eyes, Jasper put a comforting arm about her shoulders. 'Say, are you okay, Alison? You look kinda pale.'

'No, I'm all right . . . honestly. Listening to the music and looking at Oliver, I was reminded of Max; he's a great fan of Schubert too.'

Jasper looked puzzled. 'I take it Max is your young man.'

'Not exactly young man,' Alison said softly. 'In fact he's older than Oliver.'

'Jesus!' gasped Jasper. 'You mean the guy's old!'

Alison found herself smiling. 'No, not old either. He's just . . . just perfect . . . and I love him desperately.'

337

'Then we'd better make sure we get you back to this . . . Max as soon as the performance is over.' Jasper gave Alison a hug and whispered in her ear in Humphrey Bogart fashion. 'Because looking at you, kid, I'd say this is kinda serious.'

'Oh, it is, Jasper. Believe me, it is.'

During supper after the performance, Oliver reached across the table for Alison's hand. 'And what did you think of our little surprise?'

'I thought it was lovely.'

'Liar!' Jasper teased. 'If you'd seen her face when she opened the door, Oliver. I thought she was going to kick my butt and send me on my way.'

'That's not true!' Alison remonstrated. 'I was expecting you to be Max and . . .'

'When I wasn't,' Jasper continued, good-humouredly, 'your face fell.' Oliver looked bewildered and confused. 'Max?'

'Yeah, Alison's boyfriend. Only by all accounts he ain't no boy. Why he's even older than you, Ollie!'

A flicker of anger swept across Oliver's face. 'Jasper, for goodness' sake, get off the stage for once, will you? You mean to say Alison had a special date with this friend of hers and you just dragged her away? But I told you I was going to be here for at least three more days.'

Alison turned to stare at Jasper. He'd led her to believe Oliver was flying back to the States tomorrow.

'Then I could have seen Max tonight after all,' she said without thinking.

'Yes, you could,' Oliver replied, 'and I'm sorry if we've ruined your evening.'

'Of course you haven't!' Alison brightened. 'It's wonderful to see you both. Christmas and New Year just wasn't the same without you.'

Heartened by her sudden change in spirits, Oliver called the waiter and ordered a bottle of champagne.

'But what are we celebrating?' Alison asked, bemused.

'Christmas and New Year!' came the reply.

At Craven's Stables, Max poured away melted ice from the ice bucket and placed the bottle of champagne back in the fridge. The problem now was what to do with the two Dover sole he'd prepared for supper. Along with the dried and curled up crudités and salad, they looked exactly how he felt – flattened and drained.

Studying fish eyes devoid of emotion, Max placed the sole in a plastic bag. It was far too late to do anything with them now. Perhaps in the morning he could take them to someone who had a cat. Perhaps in the morning too, he could go and see Alison, that was if she was back from London. If only he had a telephone number for her.

Switching off the kitchen light, Max noticed the solitary violet he'd picked the day before. Alone in the crystal liqueur glass, its delicate purple flower with folded petals rested against the rim.

Max groaned inwardly. He longed desperately for Alison. Ached for her, in fact. Wanting to hold her head close to his chest and stroke her face, he was reminded of the way her still short hair parted in her sleep . . . like . . . 'Like petals,' he mused fondly. 'Like petals on the violets.'

Oliver studied Alison's gradually drooping eyelids with concern.

'You look tired; perhaps we should get you to a hotel.'

'But I can't stay the night in London! I must get back! I told Connie to tell Max I'd see him in the morning.'

'But it's morning now,' Oliver said, looking at his watch.

'No problem,' announced Jasper chirpily. 'I'll take Alison back now.'

'What?' Oliver and Alison cried in unison.

'I'll hire a car and drive her back . . .'

'But it's . . .'

'Nonsense,' Jasper intervened. 'Look, Oliver, you look about ready for some shut-eye too, so off you trot to your hotel with Brunnhilde and leave Alison in my capable hands.' He grinned. 'You forget, I'm used to late nights, or should that be early mornings?'

Too tired to argue, Oliver watched Jasper deal with the car hire and, turning to Alison, smiled warmly and gave her a reassuring hug.

'Don't worry. I know he can be a bit of a pain at times, but his heart and his other vital organs – from what I gather – are all in the right place. Jasper will get you safely back to Max, and I'll try and get down to Church Haywood in a day or two, before I go back to the States.'

'That would be wonderful.' Alison sighed sleepily, kissing him goodbye.

'Yeah,' broke in Jasper, 'so we both get to meet the mysterious Max!'

When the hire-car pulled up outside Keeper's Cottage, Jasper nudged Alison gently. 'Hey, sleepy-head, wake up. We're home.'

'What?' A confused voice replied. 'Where are . . . ?'

'At Keeper's Cottage, and I can see a very bleary-eyed Bunty waiting on the doorstep to greet us. So are you coming in, or do you intend to sleep in the car all night?'

'Poor Bunty. It really wasn't fair of you to ring her and get her out of bed before we left. I have my own key.'

'Yeah, but I thought she might worry if you came wandering in in the early hours with an unexpected man by your side. Or are you in the habit of doing that?'

'No, I'm not!' Alison replied indignantly, getting out of the car.

Jasper studied the over-large presence of Bunty, framed in the doorway.

'Bunty! You gorgeous creature! Just let me look at you. Alison tells me you're still my number one fan.'

Bunty patted her rollers beneath her hair net and readjusted the cord on her quilted dressing gown. 'Of course. And I've dressed especially in honour of your visit, as you can see.'

'Why, so you have.' Jasper grinned mischievously. 'Quite the leading lady, in fact.'

'In that case let me lead you inside. Alison looks as if she's asleep on her feet, poor girl.'

Tucking into a huge slice of Bunty's fruit cake, Jasper watched Alison climb the stairs. 'Sleep well, little sister. You see, I kept my promise. I've brought you back so you can still see Max in the morning.'

Alison was too tired to reply; instead she merely nodded. She was opening her bedroom door when she heard Jasper call.

'Say! What do you two guys plan to do in the morning that's so important? Perhaps I can come to?'

'Pick violets in the early-morning dew,' came the sleepy response.

341

Jasper stopped, with the slice of fruit cake midway between his lips.

'What! Are you serious?'

'I expect she is,' Bunty broke in softly. 'Love does strange things to you, you know.'

'I guess it does, Bunty,' Jasper reflected, wiping a crumb from his top lip. 'I also guess I haven't found it yet. I've done some crazy things in my life, but baby,' Jasper continued, breaking into a Brooklyn accent, 'I ain't never picked dew-covered violets before.'

'Jasper, you're incorrigible,' Bunty teased.

'I know,' he sighed, popping the last of the fruit cake into his mouth. 'Alison's already told me that once this evening.'

'I would imagine you mean last night.' Bunty yawned. 'Now are you going to let me show you to your room or do you intend to stay up and listen to the dawn chorus?'

Hearing church bells peal, Alison groaned and buried her head in her pillows. She was far too tired to go to church this morning. Instead, vaguely aware of Bunty's efforts at a comparatively noiseless departure for St Faith's, she turned over and went back to sleep.

'Hey! Lazybones! What happened?'

'What do you mean?' came a muffled voice beneath the covers.

'Weren't you,' Jasper called from the doorway, 'supposed to be picking daisies this morning?'

Daisies? Daisies! Though the church bells had long since stopped, alarm bells rang in Alison's head. Quickly throwing back the covers, she leapt out of bed. 'You mean violets. I was supposed to be picking violets! Oh, Jasper! Why on earth didn't you wake me?'

'Because,' he yawned noisily, 'I've only just woken up myself.'

'Then I suggest you put some clothes on,' Alison scolded. 'You look quite disgusting. 'What on earth do they call those things you're wearing – thongs? Because that's what they look like.'

'These, for your information,' said Jasper, patting the narrow strip of black silk, 'just happen to be designer . . .'

'Well,' broke in Alison,' whoever *designed* those must have had a brain the size of a pea!'

Jasper grinned and, reaching for her kimono hanging on the bedroom door, put it on.

'Jasper! What are you doing?'

'Merely following your instructions and putting something on. You told me I look disgusting – remember.'

'But that's my kimono! Besides, it's far too small for you.'

Jasper looked towards the dressing table mirror. 'From where I'm standing, I'd say it just about covers the important bits.'

With Jasper's attention elsewhere, Alison reached into a drawer and quickly put on a pair of panties. Then, pulling her thigh-length nightie down over her bottom, she added, 'Well, how about letting me have that kimono back? You could borrow Bunty's dressing gown. I'm sure she wouldn't . . .'

'Actually. I'd already thought of that,' Jasper said, turning to ruffle her hair. 'But . . .'

'But what?'

'When I opened the bedroom door, I found that hairy hound of hers curled up on it. And when I went to move

343

him, he growled at me somethin' awful. So, I thought I'd borrow something from you instead. Say, I'm starving. Any chance of some breakfast?'

With Alison making fresh coffee and toast, Jasper peered along the shelves at Bunty's collection of records and videos.

'Jeez! What a selection,' he said sarcastically, picking out one of the long-playing records. 'These must go back to the year dot. Half of these guys must be dead by now.'

'Mmm,' Alison said sadly. 'But they made some great records. And as you can see, Bunty's still got that video of *Singin' In The Rain*. Though it's a wonder it's not worn out by now. Do you remember that night in New York, when we left the restaurant and it was pouring with rain? How . . .'

'We danced and jumped in the puddles?' Jasper's face creased into a broad grin. 'Yeah, why that night we even got old Ollie to let his hair down. I think everyone thought we were crazy. Gee, that was a great night, Alison. You must come back to New York again soon. Perhaps even bring Max with you.'

Mention of Max made Alison's stomach lurch. She'd been totally preoccupied with Jasper. She must go and ring Max right away.

Listening to the constant ringing tone, Alison was aware of Jasper humming the song 'Good Morning' as he placed more bread in the toaster. When she finally gave up and replaced the receiver she was greeted with a loud burst of, 'Good Morning to You!'

Seeing her dejected face, Jasper crossed the floor towards her.

'Hey! What's the matter? It can't be that bad, can it?'

344

'He's not at home.' Alison sighed wistfully. 'There's no reply from the Grange, either.'

'Well,' Jasper suggested, tactlessly, 'perhaps they're all out picking daisies.'

'Violets,' Alison corrected.

Max had indeed been picking violets. In fact he'd walked the entire boundary wall of Craven's Stables, gathering the tiny closed buds. It didn't matter that they weren't fully opened yet. He just wanted to present Alison with as many as he could find when he called to see her.

'Good morning, Max. How was your supper?' Terry called, stepping out to sample the morning air.

'It wasn't! Alison couldn't make it. She had to go to London unexpectedly. How was the radio concert?'

'Brilliant! Simply brilliant! There was a change of soloist at the last minute. That chap with the unpronounceable name broke his wrist or something and Oliver Benedict flew over from the States at short notice. If I'd known you were on your own, I would have called you over to join me. It was a jolly good bottle of claret, too.'

Max wasn't listening. The name 'Oliver Benedict' was ringing in his head. Alison's brother! So that was why she hadn't been able to give him prior warning about her trip to London. To be honest he hadn't listened too carefully to Constance last night when she'd telephoned. He'd been far too upset that he wouldn't be spending the evening – and night – with Alison after all.

Memories of waking to find Alison's warm and tenderly responsive body next to his filled Max's soul with pure joy and longing. He needed to see her now.

And if she wasn't there, he would wait until she was!

Walking back to the house for his car keys, Max heard Terry call to him. He held something in his hand and waved it in Max's direction.

'Here it is. I wondered if you'd like to borrow it?'

Max looked down, puzzled. Terry was holding a CD.

'Oliver Benedict,' Terry explained. 'It's his latest CD. I only bought it last month. The Saint-Saëns Cello Concerto No 1 in A minor is my particular favourite. See what you think. There's no hurry to return it.'

Placing the CD on the passenger seat of the car, Max studied the black and white photograph of Oliver Benedict on the cover. He looked older than he'd imagined. Also extremely serious, with his heavily lidded eyes and thick eyebrows drawn together in a frown. Small wonder, he thought, switching on the ignition, that Alison frequently gave the impression of being unusually deep and reflective. It must have been the influence of her older stepbrother.

CHAPTER 25

At Keeper's Cottage, it was the influence of Oliver's younger brother that now held sway. Jasper, in his attempt to lift Alison from her depressed and miserable state, was tearing about the sitting room with Bunty's blue rain-hat pulled down over his thick blond hair, emulating Donald O'Connor's rendition of 'Make 'Em Laugh'.

'Don't you dare!' Alison called, when he ran towards the settee. 'Donald O'Connor might have been able to bounce off the settee, but I very much doubt if you can.'

'Spoilsport,' Jasper gasped, out of breath and reaching for her hand. 'Still, at least I've succeeded in one thing.'

'What's that?'

'I've at least brought a smile to your lips.'

'Yes,' Alison mused thoughtfully. 'It might be an old film, but as far as I'm concerned *Singin' in the Rain* was one of the best. Do you remember the scene where the sound goes out of sync?'

'You mean, when Gene Kelly as Pierre says "I love you. *I love you!*"'

'Yes, and . . .' But Jasper wasn't listening. Instead he

347

flung Bunty's hat in the air, oblivious to where it landed, swept Alison into his arms, carried her to the settee and got down on one knee at her feet.

'I love you. *I love you*!' he repeated, prompting Alison to continue.

Having suppressed her giggles, Alison gazed down at Jasper and moaned longingly, 'Oh, Pierre.'

It was at that moment that the four-legged Jasper roused himself from the floor, and began barking loudly. Looking up in alarm, Alison saw Max, ashen-faced and tight-lipped, standing in the doorway.

'Max! How long have you been there?'

'I've just arrived,' he said acidly, 'but it was long enough to see . . .'

Following Max's gaze, Alison turned and looked at Jasper. He was retying the borrowed kimono, where it had worked loose as a result of his theatrical activities.

'But Max!' Alison called, attempting to straighten her nightie before rising from the settee. 'This is my . . .' To her surprise and horror, Max had already turned on his heel and was halfway down the garden path.

Pushing past Alison, who'd let out a stifled sob, Jasper ran to the doorway. 'Hey, buddy. You've got it all wrong. You don't understand!'

'Yes!' Max snapped icily, opening the car door. 'I obviously have!' As an afterthought, he looked down at the small bunch of violets he held in his hands. 'Oh, Pierre. Perhaps you'd like to give these to Alison.'

Momentarily dumbstruck and stooping to gather up the scattered flowers, Jasper called desperately, 'But my name's not Pierre, it's Jasper! I'm Alison's . . .' But his words never reached Max's ears. In a burst of smoking tyres and exhaust fumes, Max accelerated angrily away.

'Jesus!' cried Jasper, returning to the sitting room. 'The guy's a maniac!' He looked anxiously at the subdued and tear-stained Alison, sitting on the settee. 'And you mean to say you love that guy?'

'Yes,' sniffed Alison. 'I do.'

When Bunty returned from church, five minutes later, she found Jasper and Alison sitting in exactly the same place.

'Good gracious!' she gasped, spying her hat in the aspidistra and the peculiar angle of the settee. 'What on earth's been going on here? Is this supposed to be a scene from one of your Hollywood movies, Jasper?'

'No,' he muttered gloomily. 'I'd say it was more like a scene from one of Shakespeare's tragedies. You know, Bunty, the guy must be a complete idiot!'

'Who is?'

'That Max fella. There I was on my knees, telling Alison I loved her, you know, like Gene Kelly in the film? So Alison was swooning in my arms and this guy comes in and thinks it's for real. Can you believe that?'

It took Bunty a while to comprehend the recently described scenario.

'Well,' she said, thoughtfully, 'I suppose if I were a man . . . who'd come along to ask the woman I loved to marry me . . . and I found her half-dressed in the company of an equally half-dressed good-looking male, in the heat of the moment, I'd be too upset to see reason.'

'What?' gasped Alison, slowly digesting Bunty's explanation.

'According to Connie,' Bunty explained, removing her wayward hat and plumping up cushions, 'Max was going to ask you to marry him last night.'

'Is that what Max told her?' Alison asked incredulously.

'Not in so many words. But all the signs have been pointing in that direction ... at least George and Connie seemed to think so. I thought you knew, Alison?'

Alison shook her head sadly.

'Then in that case,' Jasper said angrily, 'why didn't the guy stay to hear me out?'

'Because, as I told you last night, Jasper, love does strange things to you.'

'In that case, I hope I never fall hopelessly in love,' he sighed, reaching for Alison's hand. 'Come along, Alison. Let's go get dressed and I'll take us all out to lunch.'

'But I'm not hungry,' Bunty heard Alison say weakly, as she was led away.

When the bewildered dog padded into the sitting room, Bunty eyed him ruefully. 'Jasper,' she said, 'Am I glad you're not like you namesake!'

'But Connie! It's because I love Alison so much that I reacted as I did. Surely you can see that? Besides, how the hell was I supposed to know it was her stepbrother? As far as I was concerned, she was there half-naked, swooning over this Adonis look-alike called Pierre.'

Recovering from the shock of being called Connie — by her brother for the first time ever — Connie broke in quietly, 'Are you sure you're not exaggerating just a tiny bit? I thought you'd originally said Alison was in her nightie and Jasper was wearing Alison's kimono.'

'Well . . . yes, he was.' Max said, coolly. He refrained from adding that it was seeing Jasper in Alison's kimono that had caused him to snap in the first place. One of his favourite earlier memories of her was of the morning in the kitchen at Keeper's Cottage. He'd been talking to Bunty and, not realizing he was there, Alison had walked in, newly showered, with her skin glowing and her hair still damp, wearing that same kimono.

'Max? Did you hear what I said?'

'What? Oh, no . . . I'm sorry, Connie. I was miles away.'

'I was saying why don't you give Alison a ring? Invite them all over for a drink this evening? Alison, Bunty and Jasper. Bunty was saying in church, Jasper's really a decent fellow, even if he does tend to go over the top on occasions. You know what some of these actor folk are like.'

'Only too well, apparently!' Max muttered, under his breath.

'In a way, it's quite funny really,' Connie said without thinking.

'Oh, yes! Let's all have a jolly good laugh at my expense.'

'Max Craven!' Connie retorted angrily. 'Stop feeling sorry for yourself! It was a mistake. Anyone could have made it.'

'No, they couldn't,' Max said, sheepishly. 'Only I could be *so* damned stupid, and that's what makes me even more angry . . . With myself, I mean, not Alison or Jasper. You know, I hate to admit, I never even waited for an explanation. And – when he called me buddy, I could have hit him!'

'In that case it's just as well you didn't,' Connie said reassuringly. 'So why don't you go and ring Alison?'

351

'What on earth must she be thinking of me?' asked Max with an exasperated sigh. 'I've made a complete and utter fool of myself. She probably won't even want to speak to me after this.'

'Well . . . there's one way of finding out. Now go!' Connie commanded, giving him a hug.

'No luck?' she asked, seeing his crestfallen face when he reappeared.

'No reply. I'll try again later.'

When he did eventually make contact with Bunty, Max was told Alison had returned to London with Jasper.

'I understand they're meeting up with Oliver again. Anyway, I think it will do Alison good to be with her stepbrothers for a while and have a short break.'

'By that, do you mean away from me?' Max enquired flatly.

'No, Max, I don't mean that at all. But she's been thinking about her mother a great deal lately. It's only a year ago that she was nursing Elizabeth through the final stages of her illness.'

'I know.' Max considered thoughtfully. 'She's also been working flat-out ever since.'

'Exactly, and for that reason I think she needs a change of air.'

'I would hardly call the choking fumes of London "air". You know how much Alison loves the Church Haywood countryside?'

'Well, she's only going to be there for a day or two, then she'll be back. You'll see.'

'Come with you! Back to America?' Alison asked wide-eyed.

'Why not?' Oliver replied. 'Every time I phone, you

say you're too busy, either looking after Bunty's dog or else involved with some major interior design project. What are you working on at the moment?'

'Nothing,' Alison said, dejectedly. Her original plans for this week had been to go and look for furnishings for Max's bedroom at Craven's Stables. He'd seen a Regency four-poster and wanted her advice on hangings for the bed and windows.

'Muslin,' Alison whispered under her breath. That was what she'd told him. It was less heavy than chintz and brocade and she could just visualize swathes of muslin draped . . .

'Alison, come back . . .' urged Oliver's deep, soft voice. 'Come back with me, tomorrow night. There's going to be this wonderful concert at Carnegie Hall and . . .'

'All right,' she found herself replying, almost too tired and bereft to argue. 'I'll come. But I'll need to pack and . . .'

'All you'll need is your passport and your toothbrush. Leave everything else to Jasper and myself.'

'Yes . . .' agreed Jasper, who'd remained unusually silent throughout the meal. Oliver had instructed him, on pain of death, if he so much as opened his mouth and upset Alison again . . . 'We'll have great fun together shopping on Fifth Avenue.'

The following morning watching Terry put the final nail in the board announcing 'PRIVATE PROPERTY', Max turned to see a sleek, black limousine purring to a halt at the far end of the gravelled drive. From afar, looking at the vehicle's tinted windows, it was impossible to distinguish the car's occupants.

Giving an exasperated sigh, Max turned back to Terry. 'If it's that damned property developer again, tell him to take himself and his fancy car, back to where he came from. As I said, when he called the other day, Craven's Stables is *not* for sale! It is my home and I intend to live here myself!'

Leaving Terry to face the unwelcome visitors, Max checked in his pocket for his car keys and, making his escape, looked back in his rear-view mirror. Fleetingly, he saw two figures emerge from the car and walk towards the newly erected sign.

'Let's hope that will keep you out from now on,' Max sighed.

'I'm very sorry,' Terry began, 'I'm afraid this is private property. Mr Craven has asked me to advise all uninvited callers . . .'

Alison blinked back tears as the plane taxied down the runway, taking her away from the rolling countryside of England and Bunty's cheerful smile.

'Now off you go and have a wonderful time!' Bunty had insisted, kissing her tear-stained face.

'Oh, Bunty!' Alison had sobbed.

'Now, my dear, you're not going away for ever, you know. And we'll all be here when you get back.'

Would they, though? Alison thought, swallowing hard. Would Max be there when she got back? He certainly hadn't been there when she'd left.

She recalled her final glipse of him, talking to Terry before walking purposefully to his car and driving away. She'd told Oliver she wanted to say goodbye to Max and take one last look at Craven's Stables. She hadn't been able to say goodbye at all.

At first she didn't think she'd be able to see Craven's Stables either, that was until Terry had recognized her – well, not her exactly. Terry in fact had been more interested in Oliver.

'You got rid of our property-developer friend, then?' Max had called to Terry on his return.

'Not exactly.'

Max gave a puzzled frown. 'What do you mean, not exactly? He's not still here, is he?'

'No. I mean, it wasn't a property developer, that's all.'

'Then who was it?'

'You'll never believe me when I tell you.' Terry grinned.

'Try me.'

'Oliver Benedict – you know, the cellist? The fellow on the CD.'

'Oh, yes,' Max said slowly, 'I know.'

'Then did you also know he was Alison's brother?'

'Stepbrother to be precise,' Max explained.

Terry appeared put out. 'Yet you never said anything! Not even when I loaned you the CD.'

'No, I'm sorry, Terry. It hadn't registered at the time. If it had, then naturally I would have ... Incidentally, what was Oliver Benedict doing here?'

Looking down the drive, Max wondered if the car was still in the vicinity. There was no sign of it anywhere. 'Anyway,' Max concluded, 'I thought Bunty told Constance he was returning to the States today.'

'He has.' Terry continued, looking up into the clear evening sky, where a jet trail lingered overhead. 'In fact, who knows, that could quite possibly be them now.'

'Them?' Max queried.

'Yes. Oliver and Alison.'

'Alison!'

'Yes. She's gone back to America with him. She came to say goodbye and asked if she could take one last look at Craven's Stables. Not inside, I hasten to add. And she took a photo. I hope you don't mind?'

Max shook his head. 'No, of course not,' he answered numbly, running his hands through his hair.

'I say, Max! Are you okay? You look awful. You don't get migraines' do you? They can be bloody miserable, so my sister tells me.'

'No,' Max sighed, walking away. 'But I have got a headache. Would you believe, I've spent half the day trying to find somewhere that stocks muslin.'

Alone in the half-finished bedroom, Max buried his head in his hands. Yes, he had a headache, all right. A splitting head in fact to go with the aching heart that longed desperately for Alison's return.

CHAPTER 26

In New York, Alison watched Jasper struggle with what appeared to be an endless assortment of bags. Inserting his key in the lock, he kicked the door of the apartment open with an expensively shod foot.

'Jasper! It would have been far easier for you to open the door, if only you'd let me carry some of the shopping.'

'No way!' Jasper called from inside the hallway. 'I'm not having you accuse me of being ungallant and . . .'

'Hi, you two. Been having fun?' Oliver appeared, from his study. In one hand he carried a music score and in the other a pencil. 'Good heavens! From where I'm standing, it looks as if you've bought up half of Bloomingdale's!'

'Correction,' quipped Alison, holding up a selection of bags. 'Jasper has bought up half of Barney's *and* Bloomingdale's. I thought they said women were extravagant.'

Jasper gave a wry smile and pushed his thick blond hair away from his face. 'Considering my agent sent me a nice pay cheque this morning for all my hard-earned

357

efforts – remember the film I did in Egypt? – I thought I deserved a little treat.'

'You call that little?' Oliver teased, placing the sheet music on the hall table and the pencil he was holding behind his ear.

'It was, if you compare it with the cheque,' Jasper mused, with a sly grin. 'For my last film, I opted for a percentage of the box office takings instead of my usual fee.'

'Did you indeed? In that case . . .' Oliver replied '. . . perhaps I should get rid of Brünnhilde and take up acting instead.'

'You couldn't stand to be parted from your beloved cello.' Alison called, walking through to the kitchen. 'And I wouldn't be able to come to your wonderful concerts.'

'What about my wonderful films?' Jasper protested, pretending to be offended. 'That's the last time I buy you anything from Liz Claiborne.'

'Liz Claiborne?' Oliver repeated, raising an eyebrow.

'Yes. Jasper's been spoiling me again. Just as he has for the past three months. I didn't ask for it but he insisted,' Alison explained, showing Oliver the contents of one of the many bags. 'He also bought you a shirt.'

She handed Oliver the Brooks Brothers' bag, containing one of their renowned small button-down shirts.

'Why, thanks, Jasper. That's very decent of you.'

'Don't mention it, Ollie. Only I thought you could do with it if your present attire is anything to go by. From the state of that threadbare shirt, jogging pants and old loafers, I'd say you look more suited to busking in Central Park than gracing the stage at Carnegie Hall.'

'Which reminds me,' said Oliver, picking up the music score, 'I'd better get a move on. I'm due at rehearsals in half an hour.'

With Oliver at rehearsals and supper cleared away, Alison picked up her airmail pad and began her latest letter to Church Haywood.

Jasper sipped his bourbon and watched her thoughtfully.

'What's that? Another letter to Max?'

Without thinking or looking up, Alison replied matter-of-factly, 'No. Apart from that first letter to Max, when I arrived, I haven't written since. I don't believe in writing to people who can't be bothered to reply to my letters. I'm writing to Bunty.'

Satisfied with the reply, Jasper continued with what had been on his mind since lunchtime. 'Sure was a coincidence, bumping into Spencer Blair like that in Le Train Bleu. What do you think of him, Alison?'

Finishing off her paragraph, Alison replied. 'Okay, I suppose.'

'Okay! What do you mean by that?'

'To be fair I don't really know him, do I? I've only met him at a couple of parties. He always seems pleasant enough.'

'Jeez! You British!' Jasper mimmicked Alison's 'pleasant enough', and continued. 'Spencer's a great guy, Alison. One of the best, in fact. We've known each other for years.'

'In that case, I suppose that puts you in a much better position to judge his character.'

'W-e-l-l, how about you getting in a position to know him better?'

Jasper's question had the required effect. Alison put

down her pen and turned to face her stepbrother. 'Jasper? What are you getting at?'

'I'm getting at nothing,' he replied, with a sly grin. 'I'm merely suggesting you *get* to know Spencer, that's all.'

'But I already know Spencer.'

'Gee, Alison! Do I have to spell it out for you! Spencer's got a soft spot for you. He likes you a lot. He . . .'

'But he hardly knows me. I mean . . .'

'I know!' Jasper broke in in exasperation. 'That's just what I'm trying to sort out here. I want you two guys to get together. Spencer wants the two of you to get together! He was wondering, this coming weekend, with me having to go away and Ollie with four days of concerts . . .'

Feeling two blobs of colour rise in her cheeks, Alison turned her attention back to the sheet of blue airmail paper. Back to the paragraph that began, 'How are things progressing at Craven's Stables? Have you seen Max lately?'

'I'm sorry, Jasper. I'd rather not, if you don't mind. It's very kind of Spencer and I'm flattered – he's a very good-looking young man. It's just that I'm . . .' She hesitated.

'Still in love with that Max guy, huh?'

Alison bit her lip thoughtfully.

'Actually, that wasn't what I was going to say, but as you come to mention it, yes, I am still in love with Max and always will be.'

Jasper sighed. 'Out of curiosity, what were you going to say?'

'I was going to say, I'm quite happy to be here on

my own for a few days. I thought I might spend some time in Central Park. It seems ages since I've been to Belvedere Castle or visited the Conservatory Gardens.'

'But you've always said you thought the Conservatory Gardens too formal.'

'I know. Don't forget there's less formal areas too. That amazing wisteria pergola and wonderful bank of wildflowers. I've not seen Mary and Dickon for a while either.'

'Mary and Dickon? Who's that? I've never heard you mention a Mary and Dickon before.'

Alison smiled playfully. 'Then you've obviously got a very bad memory. And there was me thinking you were fond of me.'

Jasper look up with a puzzled expression on his face.

'When my mother and your father first married,' Alison explained, 'and, being in awe of you all, I wouldn't say boo to a goose – remember? You always seemed to be doing such lively, interesting things and I'd recently left Church Haywood . . .'

'I am fond of you, extremely fond of you, Alison, and I haven't forgotten,' Jasper interrupted, in more serious vein. He moved to the writing table and placed a brotherly hand on Alison's shoulder. 'You'd been in an accident and that little girl you used to babysit for had been . . .'

Seeing renewed sadness in her face, Jasper refrained from continuing. It all came back to him now. Not only had he and Oliver been surprised to find his father return from one of his many business trips with a new wife, but an English one at that.

An English wife, who had brought with her a pale,

wan sixteen-year-old daughter, recovering from a serious accident and the tragic death of a young friend. Of course they realized it would take time for the shy and timid Alison to adapt to the Benedict way of life in New York. It was a far cry from life in sleepy Church Haywood.

Yet at the same time they were both concerned and puzzled that a sixteen-year-old should appear to be constantly reading the books of Frances Hodgson Burnett, instead of the current Stateside teenage trend for bodice-rippers.

'*The Secret Garden!*' Jasper exclaimed, softly. 'I remember Dad explaining now. The book had been a particular favourite with that little girl. What was her name?'

'Tara.'

'Tara. That's it. And apparently, according to Dad, it was the book you'd been reading to Tara at the time of her death.'

Alison nodded and turned tear-filled eyes in Jasper's direction.

'Dad guessed it was your way of coming to terms with the shock. Then he came up with the brilliant idea of taking you off to Central Park to show you the statues of Mary and Dickon.'

Alison swallowed hard at the memory. 'You know,' she said blowing her nose, 'I was always very fond of your father. He was a good, kind man, I only wish things had turned out differently for him and Mother.'

Reaching for a box of tissues, Jasper took one and wiped away a stray tear from her cheek. 'I know,' he said kindly, 'but at least we three guys kept together. Just like the Three Musketeers, in fact.'

'And a very peculiar Three Musketeers we must make,' Alison sniffed, trying to force a smile.

Jasper tugged playfully at Alison's hair with its new, smoother hairstyle. 'And don't forget,' he grinned. 'I know the perfect D'Artagnan.'

'You mean . . .'

'That's it – Spencer! Got it in one. So how about giving the guy a break? Go call him and let him take care of you this weekend.'

'Who's taking care of Alison this weekend?' Oliver called, walking into the sitting room from the hallway, having first secured Brünnhilde in a safe position.

'Spencer,' Jasper enlightened him. We bumped into him in Le Train Bleu at lunchtime and he wants to take Alison away for the weekend and . . .'

'And I'm not going!' Alison replied bluntly.

Jasper was on the verge of remonstrating with her when the telephone rang. Oliver picked up the receiver and looked in his direction.

'It's for you, Jasper. Someone called Layla, I believe?'

'Layla? Layla! Gee, great. Okay, Ollie, I'll take it in my bedroom.'

Oliver studied Alison's troubled frown. 'From the look on your face, I'd say you were offering thanks for Layla's timely intervention.'

'Yes, I am,' she whispered.

'Do you want to tell me about it?' Oliver urged, kindly.

Giving up on her letter-writing for the evening, Alison screwed the top on her fountain pen. 'I suppose from Jasper's point of view I am being a bit unreasonable, only I really don't want to go out with Spencer.'

Reaching for Alison's hand, Oliver led her to the settee and sat down by her side. 'I'm a little confused,' he said, patting her knee. 'How about if you start at the beginning?'

In Oliver's reassuring presence Alison explained how, early that morning – following a mysterious phone call – Jasper had suggested they 'do the sales' on Fifth and Madison Avenues. And how, despite her protestations, Jasper had insisted, dragging her from department store to department store until she was exhausted.

Mysteriously at one o'clock, shopping came to an abrupt halt and they'd found themselves in Le Train Bleu at Bloomingdale's.

'So there you were in "Bloomies",' Oliver said softly, 'surrounded by bags of shopping. What happened next?'

'Spencer Blair appeared, as if from nowhere.'

'Nowhere?' Oliver queried.

'It certainly seemed like it at the time. Only now I'm not so sure. In fact, I'm beginning to wonder if it wasn't all pre-arranged. You know Spencer and Jasper together . . .'

As if on cue, Jasper appeared in the doorway.

'Bye, folks. See you later.'

'You mean you're going out?' Alison looked at her watch. 'But it's nearly midnight!'

'That's right,' called Jasper. 'And the night is still young and the lovely Layla beckons.'

'Layla?' Oliver queried. 'I don't believe we've met Layla, have we?'

'Not yet,' Jasper called from the hallway, as he headed for the door. 'Because I've only just met her myself. She's an Egyptian actress. Over here for a screening of some Egyptian films. See you guys tomorrow.'

As an afterthought, Jasper hurried back and looked earnestly in Alison's direction. 'Don't forget to give Spencer a call, will you?'

'I'll try not to,' she said, her voice trailing to a whisper.

Oliver gave a sardonic smile. 'You mean you'll try not to call Spencer, or you'll try to forget to call him?'

Alison sighed wearily and laid her head against Oliver's shoulder.

'You know, you remind me of Max. That's the sort of thing he would say.'

'Is it?' Oliver murmured, turning kindly, deep brown eyes in her direction. 'You still miss him, don't you?'

Alison nodded in silent reply and looked down at her lap.

'And although I'm not a betting man, I'd be prepared to bet if it was Max inviting you to spend the weekend with him instead of Spencer, you'd already have your bag packed!'

Forcing a smile, Alison studied Oliver's deeply hooded eyes, before uncontrollable tears began to flow.

'He never even answered my letter,' she cried. 'Surely he could have written just once . . .'

'Maybe he did and it never got here. Then again, if you wrote when you first arrived, I expect Max was still feeling sore about that incident at Bunty's cottage. I know I've never met Max. From what you say he's a proud man and has taken some knocks in his time. I'd be prepared to say his pride took quite a hammering that day.'

'You would?' Alison sniffed.

'Of course. In fact I'm sure I would have felt exactly the same. From all accounts, after a series of false starts, you and Max had gotten things together really well. Then along comes 'Hurricane Jasper' and . . .'

'Along comes Hurricane Jasper and what?' Alison enquired, weakly.

'Complete devastation?' Oliver suggested with a wry smile.

Alison brightened. 'Put like that, I suppose you could say Keeper's Cottage had its own hurricane, whirlwind and tornado all at once. Especially when I remember seeing Bunty's rain hat in the aspidistra, the settee all askew and cushions everywhere.'

'Don't forget the flood,' Oliver said, patting her hand.

'Oh, you mean the tears I shed afterwards? I looked a dreadful sight, didn't I, when you first brought me here? All red-eyed and . . .'

'. . . skinny and wouldn't eat. Jasper and I were most concerned.'

'I know, but it didn't help very much with Jasper calling Max a complete idiot and a stupid jerk at every available opportunity.'

'That's Jasper, I'm afraid. Believe it or not, it's his way of showing he cares. And as I care too, can I suggest you go to bed and get a good night's sleep? You look all-in after that shopping trip.'

Standing outside Alison's bedroom door, Oliver bent and kissed her forehead. 'Now don't worry about Spencer. Just ring and politely refuse. Say you're sick or something. Perhaps take a rain-check . . . just in case at a later date . . . ? You could also try writing to Max again.'

Closing her bedroom door, Alison sighed wistfully. Yes, she knew she was sick. Sick with longing for Max. She also knew she wouldn't write to him again, nor would she change her mind about Spencer.

Next morning, alone in the empty appartment, Alison stood by the window and stared wistfully at the magnificent panorama stretching across the city skyline. The view from the Benedicts' New York residence was quite simply spectacular.

'Yes,' she said, tracing her fingers slowly over the Art Deco photo frame that held a picture of her mother and stepfather in happier times. 'There's no doubt about it, Olmsted and Vaux did a superb job when they developed Central Park from a mass of pig farms and swamps. Who'd have thought it?'

In her head a little voice answered in reply, 'And who'd have thought Max Craven could have turned those derelict stables into a Regency work of art?'

With thoughts of Max racing through her head, and the memories of his lips on hers as they lay together, Alison felt the old familiar stirrings in her stomach. Looking first at the blue airmail notepad, where she'd left it from the night before, and then at the telephone, she hesitated and shook her head.

'No!' she announced, looking towards her mother's photo. 'I will not write to him and I most definitely won't phone!'

Deciding she was doing no good by staying indoors, Alison picked up her jacket and purse and left the apartment. She was going to be alone for four days.

She'd better make the best of it.

Stopping first at The Dairy, to pick up the calendar of events for the month of July, Alison felt a pang of nostalgia when she surveyed the Victorian Gothic building. Somehow it always reminded her of London, and London reminded her of trains and trains reminded her of . . . Max . . . and the day he'd fallen asleep . . .

'Oh! Stop it! Go away, Max!' she cried.

'Are you okay, ma 'am?'

Startled, Alison looked up to see a mounted patrolman crossing her path. He looked puzzled, as if searching for her assailant.

'Yes. Yes. I'm fine, thank you. I was talking to myself, trying to decide where to go first.'

'That depends how much time you've got,' he replied kindly, looking down at her from a sturdy chestnut horse that remained motionless.

'Four days.'

'Then can I suggest you follow the points of the compass? North, south, east and west. Four days, four directions.'

Shielding her eyes from the bright sunlight, Alison smiled warmly.

'Yes . . . What a good idea. I'll do that. Thank you very much.'

'Pleasure, ma'am,' said the patrolman touching his hat and edging his horse forward. 'Have a nice day.'

'Mmm,' sighed Alison, looking ahead to the welcoming, cool, shade of some trees. 'I'm sure I shall.'

Four days later, sitting in the Café des Artistes, Oliver watched Alison toy with an ornate chocolate, cream and nut confection.

'So, tell me about Central Park.'

Alison's face lit up. 'It was wonderful. I went north, south, east and west as the patrolman suggested.'

'And weren't you exhausted at the end of each day?'

'Not particularly. I didn't spend all day walking, you know. One day I stopped by the Hans Christian Andersen statue and listened to them reading stories to the children, and the next I sat watching the children clamber all over the Alice in Wonderland bronze at Conservatory Water.'

Oliver studied Alison closely. 'Something tells me you like to be with children.'

She blushed and scooped a mouthful of torte into her mouth. 'I suppose seeing them reminded me of Rosie. Did I tell you I've had yet another picture from her?'

Oliver shook his head and stirred his coffee.

Reaching into her handbag, Alison carefully removed the four sheets of paper and spread them on the table in front of her. 'There you are,' she said, 'I've four now, April, May, June and July. One for every month I've been away.'

Oliver studied the four carefully detailed drawings. The first showed Rosie at Easter, surrounded by rabbits and Easter eggs.

'Well, I'm sure glad the Easter Bunny called on little Rosie, if she's as cute as you say.'

'Oh, she is. Although I scarcely think she'd thank you for calling her cute. And according to Bunty,' Alison continued, 'she's not so little now either. Apparently she's grown quite tall.'

'I'm not surprised, if as you say she's always at Keeper's Cottage and Bunty's feeding her on those amazing dinners of hers and huge slices of fruit cake!'

'And,' said Alison, looking back at the pictures, 'if she's having tea at Craven's Stables as she did in June.'

Oliver picked up the June drawing, where Max and Rosie sat at a table eating strawberry tarts. 'And is this Rosie too?' he asked.

Alison shook her head. 'No, definitely not! That's supposed to be Church Haywood's May Day celebrations with the maypole and May Queen.' This must be Rosie. Here in this corner wearing her serape.'

Oliver smiled, put the pictures back in order and passed them across the table to Alison. 'Well, I must say Max is looking happier, so that's a good sign.'

'Yes, he is,' Alison replied thoughtfully. 'I wonder why?'

Thinking back to the early drawings, Alison recalled how Max was always depicted with a downward droop of the mouth, looking exceedingly miserable and sad. Today's post, however, had brought a happier picture.

Now, examining the latest offering, Alison was curious to know why. There were three people on the July picture, Rosie on one side with the ever-present serape, Max in the middle, with his usual mane of thick black hair and a newly fixed grin to his face, and on Max's other side . . .

Alison froze! On Max's other side was a tall young woman, with exceedingly long brown legs, wearing a floral dress. With equally long brown arms, Alison noted, that ended in hands with stick-like fingers.

Ignoring Oliver for a moment, who was consulting his diary, Alison peered long and hard at Rosie's drawing. What was the picture trying to tell her? Study the most striking features, Alison, a warning voice in her head began. Study them and tell yourself what you see?

With an aching heart, Alison felt her blood run cold. As far as she was concerned, the picture depicted three salient points. Max smiling; Max holding the hand of the brown-skinned young woman by his side; and the fourth finger of a brown stick-like hand, resplendent with what appeared to be with an enormous ruby ring!

'Alison, are you feeling okay? You look kinda pale. Perhaps all that chocolate and cream is a bit too much for you in this heat. I see you haven't finished your torte.'

Alison stared blankly, first at Oliver and then at her plate. 'Yes,' she whispered. 'I think perhaps it is – all a bit too much. Will you excuse me a minute, Oliver? I feel sick. I'll just pop to the powder room.'

Watching her go, Oliver turned Rosie's July drawing back towards him.

'So that's what's upset her so much,' he murmured to himself. 'That enormous bauble on the hand of the young lady by Max's side.'

When Alison returned, Oliver surveyed her ashen face with concern. He reached for her hand and said softly, 'I've been looking in my diary and I'm pretty sure you've already remembered . . . but it's coming up to the anniversary of your mother's death.'

'Yes, I know.'

'In that case, Alison, I think it's time for you to go back home.'

'You mean . . . ?'

'Yes. I mean it's about time you went back to Church Haywood. See that florist lady friend of yours about arranging a nice floral tribute for your mother . . . and maybe catch up with old friends?'

371

At the mention of old friends, Oliver watched in silence as Alison gazed forlornly at the picture of Max with his happy smiling face. Rubbing his hand thoughtfully across his chin, he only wished he could see his stepsister looking so happy.

CHAPTER 27

In St Faith's churchyard, Connie was pulling out the last remains of chickweed from Elizabeth Benedict's grave.

'There.' She sighed with satisfaction. 'That looks better. What do you think?'

Bunty nodded approvingly and gathered the offending weeds into a plastic carrier bag. 'You don't know anyone with a canary, do you?'

'A canary? What on earth do you want with a canary, Bunty?'

'I'm convinced my grandfather used to give his canary chickweed, that's all.'

'In that case,' Connie replied, peering into the bag at the mass of green with tiny white flowers, 'you don't need one canary, you need a whole aviary!'

Bunty smiled and eased herself up from the kneeling pad she'd brought with her. 'By the way, how's Max?'

'Much better, since we last spoke. Now the builders have finally left, he's been busy putting the finishing touches to the house.'

'Looking nice, is it?'

'To be honest, Bunty, I've probably seen about as

373

much of the interior of Craven's Stables as yourself. He's being very secretive about it all at the moment. Particularly the upstairs and the master bedroom.'

Connie shrugged her shoulders. 'You know, I even tried to find out from Maxine what was going on, but she wouldn't say a word either. When she and Max are together, she keeps giving him secret, knowing looks.'

'She's spending a great deal of time over there, isn't she? Mind you, I suppose at the moment, with the baby due, there's not much else for her to do. Later of course though, things will be different, and M . . .'

'By the way, any news of Alison?' Connie broke in.

'None, other than that she's still planning to arrive some time this week. Don't forget you're still not supposed to know. Alison told me, Oliver's organizing her flight and a car to meet her at Heathrow.'

'How thoughtful.'

'Mmm,' Bunty murmured. 'Oliver was always the most thoughtful of the two, whereas Jasper's what you'd call a man of action.'

'You can say that again!' Connie said, suddenly reminded of Jasper's antics that had caused the abrupt halt to Alison and Max's relationship.

Stopping by the lych gate, Bunty saw two familiar figures walking towards them. 'I'd say Max is certainly enjoying Maxine's company.'

Studying the deeply tanned body in the identical print frock to the one on Rosie's July drawing, Connie nodded approvingly. 'Well, he admits to being very fond of her . . . he also says she makes him laugh.'

'Alison used to make him laugh too,' Bunty mused sadly.

'I know, my dear, but this is different, isn't it?'

Drawing near his sister, Max noticed the gardening trug with its tools and the carrier bag full of weeds. 'You've beaten us to it, I see.'

'I thought as you and Maxine were busy at the house, Bunty and I would lend a hand here. You'd be amazed, after that rain last week, just how many weeds had grown on both Tara's and Elizabeth's graves.'

'That's very kind of you; we certainly appreciate it, don't we, Maxine?'

Maxine nodded and gazed adoringly into Max's face. 'We've been to order the flowers,' she said shyly, as if answering Connie and Bunty's unspoken question.

'Yes,' Max interrupted. 'Penny said she'll deliver them. They'll never all fit in my car.'

'Good gracious!' Connie asked in alarm. 'What exactly have you ordered?'

Max winked, and, reaching for Maxine's hand, said with a secretive glint in his eye, 'You'll have to wait and see, Connie. We're hoping to surprise everyone.'

'Well,' said a bemused Connie, watching Max and his companion walk away hand in hand. 'What do you make of that?'

'I'd say they were both up to something,' Bunty said her voice full of concern. 'I only hope what they're planning doesn't coincide with Alison's homecoming.'

'In that case, do you think I should warn Max about Alison's arrival?'

'Oh, no, Connie!' Alison made me promise I wouldn't tell Max. I've already explained I really shouldn't have said anything to you either.'

'And I would have been none the wiser, but for the fact that you decided to spring-clean Alison's bedroom. No wonder I became suspicious. I mean,' said Connie with a grin, attempting to make her friend feel better, 'since when has Bunty Lowther spring-cleaned in late July!'

In the garden at Craven's Stables, Maxine put down her glass and turned towards him. 'Max, will you come for me when the flowers arrive?'

'Of course.'

'And everything's ready?'

Max sighed contentedly. 'Almost. They came to restretch the bedroom carpet this morning and I managed to hang the rest of the drapes this afternoon, before I called for you. That only leaves the champagne to collect, but that can wait until the day after tomorrow.'

'So am I the only one to have seen the bedroom?'

'Yes, Maxine, you're the only one.'

A look of pure delight swept over Maxine's face as she watched Max finish his drink. Then, in complete silence, they watched the last rays of a salmon pink sunset disappear into shadows on the newly planted herbaceous border.

Seeing Maxine shiver as goosebumps appeared on her bare arms, Max said softly, 'I think I'd better take you home.'

Three days later Max took the last of the flowers from the boxes Penny had delivered. 'Well, Maxine, what do you think?'

'I think they're beautiful.'

'And you look beautiful too, if I might say so. In fact the flowers match the colour of your dress perfectly.'

Two blobs of colour appeared through her sun-tanned cheeks as Max held out his hand. Then, removing a stray flower petal from his jacket, he breathed in deeply and said with a determined voice, 'I take it we're ready?' Maxine nodded and, hand in hand, walked with Max into the welcoming coolness of St Faith's church.

At 7.45 on a balmy summer's evening the same sleek black limousine that had taken Alison away pulled into St Faith's car park. Alison looked first at her watch and then at Oliver.

'If you don't mind, I'd rather wait here for a quarter of an hour.'

'That's okay by me,' Oliver said. 'After the chaos of Heathrow and that dreadful motorway café, doing nothing for a quarter of an hour suits me just fine. But tell me, why eight o'clock?'

'Because hopefully by then there won't be anyone else about.'

'Oh, I see,' murmured Oliver, knowing full well, by 'any one else' Alison meant Max. 'In that case do you mind if we listen to some music?' He pressed the button on the CD player.

'Ah,' Alison sighed dreamily. 'Where could you find a more peaceful setting? Sheep grazing on the periphery of St Faith's on a perfect summer's evening, the gentle undulating countryside of Church Haywood and Beethoven's cello sonata in A major. Although, hearing the Beethoven again, perhaps I shall be transported back to New York and the last concert you gave before we left.'

Talk of New York transported Oliver back, not to his last concert but his brother's irate face.

'What!' Jasper had exclaimed. 'You're taking Alison

back to England? But what on earth for? Surely not to see that jerk Max?'

For once the usually calm Oliver had turned angrily on his brother.

'From what I've heard of Max – from both Alison and Bunty – I would say he was anything other than a jerk, Jasper. From all accounts, the guy lost first his daughter and then his wife, only to find out when it was too late, that she'd been cheating on him. Then when he's recovering from the shock and beginning to make a go of things with Alison, you appear on the scene. You drag her away on the night he was going to propose and . . .'

'Hey, Ollie! That's not fair! How the hell was I supposed to know?'

'You weren't,' Oliver concluded. 'But just lay off Max, will you – for Alison's sake, please! You're so wrapped up with Layla, you've obviously forgotten the date. That's why I've arranged to go back to England with Alison. I want to be with her on the anniversary of Elizabeth's death.'

'Oh, jeez, Ollie!' Jasper had sighed, his face full of remorse. 'I'm sorry, I quite forgot. Do you want me to come too?'

Fearing further altercations if Jasper came with them, Oliver had politely declined his brother's offer, insisting Jasper stay in New York with Layla.

Aware of Alison's closed eyelids, Oliver whispered softly, 'Alison, it's eight o'clock.'

Rubbing her eyes sleepily, Alison stared about her, momentarily forgetting she was back in Church Haywood. When the clock began to strike eight, she stepped warily from the car.

'I'll wait here for a bit,' Oliver said tactfully. 'Give you and your mother a chance to be alone for a few moments. I'll join you in a while.'

Seeing her disappear behind the mellow stone wall of the car park, Oliver reached down and switched off his CD.

Feeling tears of emotion well up inside, Alison walked slowly and apprehensively towards the church-yard. There, desperate not to disturb the sheer peace and tranquillity of the place, she left the gravel path for the quieter softness of freshly mown grass.

When the newly tended grave came into view, she emitted a gasp. 'But how . . . ? Who . . . ?'

From the secluded shadows of St Faith's porch, Max watched Alison stare about her before sinking to her knees in a dense carpet of violets.

Though her face was buried in her hands, her hair worn in a smoother, longer style and the clothes more elegant, Max knew he would have recognized her anywhere.

'Alison,' he murmured, walking towards her, his voice curiously deep and thick with emotion.

Startled, tear-filled eyes gazed into his as he reached down to help her to her feet, just as he had almost a year ago.

'Max? But I don't understand. Was this your idea? The violets . . .?'

'They were in a way. I remembered you saying how fond you and your mother were of them. I also remembered how difficult it was to find violets in July. It was Maxine who suggested asking Penny to order whole boxes. But then,' Max smiled warmly, 'I've often found Maxine does things to excess.'

Maxine! Alison, felt shock-waves of jealousy surge in her stomach. Who was Maxine? She must be the third person in Rosie's picture. The one with long brown legs, the pretty floral dress . . . and the large ruby ring!

'Here, let me help you, you look quite pale,' Max urged kindly. 'Come and sit in the porch for a bit, until you feel better . . . Maxine's there too. She thought it best if I came to greet you on my own.'

Speechless and unable to resist, Alison found herself led numbly towards St Faith's, vaguely aware as she did so of a car door opening and closing in the distance.

Nearing the porch, Alison stared wide-eyed into the shadows and discerned a slim, suntanned body, wearing a violet-printed summer frock and white leather sandals, racing towards her.

'Al'son! You came! Oh, I just knew you'd come! I told Max you . . .'

'Rosie! But . . . ?' In complete bewilderment, Alison turned to face Max. 'But you said Maxine, and I thought . . .'

Max grinned broadly and looked down to where the ecstatic Rosie was hugging tightly on to Alison's waist.

'Ah, but she's Maxine now,' he whispered proudly, 'after me . . . Well, at least the first three letters are after me. Apparently, she discovered an actress or singer on the television and told her mother she wanted to be called Maxine from now on. However, Michelle and Darren only agreed on condition that she wore a frock. Hence the new dress.'

With a knowing smile, Alison reached down and tilted Rosie's chin towards her. 'It was you on that drawing,' she said, through her tears. 'There were two of you. Rosie in her serape and Rosie in her dress.'

'No! Maxine in her dress!' Rosie corrected, swiftly.

'But you look so pretty and you've grown so tall.' Alison turned to Max and whispered as an aside, 'Then what do I call her now?'

'For the moment,' he replied, out of earshot, 'I would suggest Maxine. That is until she changes her mind again. Anyway, as it's getting late, I'd better see about getting her home.'

At the mention of home, Rosie ran excitedly down the footpath in the direction of the car park.

'Oliver's offered to take her home,' Max announced. 'You see, I promised Rosie a ride in a car. Just like a film star.'

'Oliver!' came the startled response. 'How did you know Oliver was bringing me? Did Bunty tell you?'

Seeing a fleeting flash of anger dart across her face, Max held out a reassuring hand. 'No, don't look so alarmed. It wasn't Bunty who told me. It was Oliver himself. He rang me from New York a few days ago. He said he felt extremely guilty, because, having mislaid a favourite pair of cufflinks, he decided to see if Jasper had borrowed them . . .'

'What on earth's that got to do with me? I don't under . . .'

Max kissed the tip of her nose. 'Don't be so impatient. I was just getting to that. You see, Oliver found not only the missing cufflinks but also the letter I'd written to you after you first left Church Haywood.'

'You mean, you replied to my letter?' Alison asked, amazed.

'Yes, of course I did,' Max replied, sadly. 'Only I understand you never received it. Because you never wrote back in return, I assumed you'd made a clean break in New York, maybe even met someone special, and didn't want anything more to do with me. Someone who was at least au fait with *Singin' in the Rain* and wasn't so pigheaded.'

'Come on, you two!' a chirpy voice called. 'He's waiting.'

Looking ahead, Max and Alison saw Rosie in animated conversation with Oliver. Reading Alison's mind, Max said, 'No, they haven't already met, but she's seen his face often enough on the covers of my CDs. You know, surprisingly she's even beginning to like Beethoven, Schubert and Saint-Saëns.'

Linking her arm in his, Alison laughed softly. 'You know, nothing from now on will ever surprise me about Rosie. Did she . . . did she really tell you I would come back?'

'Absolutely convinced of it, she was. Though I have to confess I wasn't so sure myself. She kept insisting and quoting her grandad.'

'Meaning?'

'Meaning, she kept telling me, if I really wanted something to happen, then I had to wish for it really hard.'

'And did you?' Alison enquired in a hushed voice.

'Oh, yes. To quote Rosie, really, really hard, in fact.'

Oliver extended his hand Max's direction. 'Max. I'm delighted to meet you at long last. I've heard *so* much about you. Now is this the young lady who wants a lift home in this hired limousine of mine?'

Max nodded and shook Oliver's hand warmly while Alison looked on, sensing the instant rapport between the two.

'Is this really, really a film star's car?' Rosie was heard to gasp as Oliver helped her inside.

'Sure is, young lady, and if you just press that button there, you can lower the window and wave to your friends as I drive you home.'

'See you tomorrow,' Rosie called excitedly, practising a regal wave.

'Oh, yes, see you folks tomorrow,' Oliver called, opening the driver's door, 'but not too early, I hope?'

'What about tomorrow?' Alison asked with a puzzled expression on her face. 'And what about me? What am I going to . . . ?'

'I think Oliver thought – and I was secretly hoping – you would come back to Craven's Stables with me. Apart from one small detail, it's almost complete. I thought you might like to have a look round.'

Unable to look him in the eye while she pondered the possibilities of having 'a look round', Alison found herself swept into Max's arms and once more felt the longed-for lips on hers.

'But where's your car?' she asked, when he'd released her from his embrace. 'It's not in the churchyard car-park, is it?'

'No.' Max grinned. 'Rosie – or should I say Maxine – and I parked it at the golf club, once we'd put the violets on your mother's grave. Then we just walked back to St Faith's and waited patiently – which for Maxine was exceedingly difficult, I might add – until Oliver's phone calls.'

'Oliver's phone calls? I don't understand.'

'Oliver rang me to let me know you were on the way. Once from a service station on the motorway and then from the car at eight o'clock.'

Max produced his own newly acquired mobile phone from his breast pocket. 'I was only thankful the clock was chiming eight, so you didn't hear my phone ring.'

'In that case,' Alison replied, nervously, 'as it's now nine o'clock, hadn't we better be getting back to Craven's Stables before it gets dark?'

Admiring the view from the upstairs landing window, Alison sighed deeply. 'What an amazing view across the valley from here. I never realized you could see so much.'

'And it's even better from the bedroom window,' Max whispered, softly. 'Come along, I'll show you.'

Standing by the open window, watching the last pale orange stain of sunset, Alison breathed in the warm scent of the balmy summer evening.

'Of course it's not quite the New York skyline,' Max said, interrupting her train of thoughts.

'Perhaps not, but it's equally impressive.'

'And do you still like New York?' he asked cautiously.

'Oh, yes! It's simply wonderful. So exhilarating and vibrant and everyone was so friendly. I was even offered lots of commissions for apartments and . . .'

She stopped suddenly, aware of the look of sadness in Max's eyes. Moving towards him, she laid her head against his shoulder. 'But I don't intend to go back. Not just yet . . .'

'You don't?' he responded anxiously.

'No. Wonderful as it is, Max, I don't think it's for me. I miss Church Haywood too much. The greenness of it all, I suppose. The trees and narrow country lanes. Not to mention the banks of primroses, bluebell woods and of course the rain.'

'The rain? But surely you get rain in New York?'

She smiled tenderly. 'Yes, but it's not quite the same as English rain on dewy-covered banks of violets. By the way,' she said, turning to look at the assortment of posy bowls decorating the bedroom, all crammed with tiny purple blooms and green heart-shaped leaves, 'how did Penny manage to find so many?'

'I placed a special order for a special lady.'

'Oh, you mean Rosie?'

'No, I mean you, Alison. I thought . . .'

'And I thought,' she continued, with an embarrassed smile, 'when I saw Rosie's drawing of someone I didn't recognize, with long, tanned legs, wearing a pretty frock and a very impressive ruby ring . . .'

'Ah yes. That dreadful ring!' Max laughed. 'I bought her that.'

'You did? But why?'

'As I've already explained, Michelle and Darren went along with the name Maxine, only on condition that she wear a dress. When I saw the ring in the toyshop window, I told Maxine it would complete her new identity.'

Sensing Alison's complete bewilderment, Max said. 'Maxine Ruby – the name of the singer, or was it actress? Anyway I can't quite remember. Besides, it doesn't matter now, does it? All I do know is that it certainly did the trick and took Rosie's attention away from the new baby.'

'The new baby! Surely you don't mean . . .?'

Max nodded. 'Yes, that's right, Michelle's expecting another baby, so it looks as if there'll be another Jennings "chris'nin" at St Faith's before too long.'

'Poor Rosie. Still, at least she's got her very own

385

bedroom now.' Alison turned thoughtfully. 'Oh dear! It's just occurred to me. Now that she's Maxine, she'll be wanting all that changed into a film star's bedroom, with lights round the dressing table and . . .'

'No.' Max reassured her. 'For the moment, I understand she's still perfectly happy with her cactus and her cow-catcher train. She doesn't wear a dress all the time, I hasten to add. Usually she's in shorts. How else do you think her legs got so brown?'

Alison breathed a sigh of relief. 'No wonder she made such a point of accentuating them so much in her drawing. When I think . . .'

Aware of Alison's faltering tone of voice, Max slipped his arm round her waist and drew her away from the window. 'I know. You thought when you saw that picture that, Maxine was . . . just as I did when I saw you with Jasper and heard you calling him Pierre.'

'Please, Max! I'd rather you didn't mention it. Not now. Don't spoil things. It's still too painful to think about. Tell me about the one thing that needs to complete Craven's Stables instead. You mentioned earlier that it was finished except for one small detail. Whatever it is, perhaps I can help you with it?

'You can most certainly do that!' Max replied smiling, sweeping her into his arms. 'You see that magnificent bed over there?'

Alison nodded. Until now she'd tried to avoid looking at the wonderful Regency four-poster. Swathed in muslin, blowing gently in the warm summer breeze, it was like something from a fairy-tale.

'Well, that,' Max announced forcefully, 'is a marriage bed, Alison Benedict, and I want you to share it with me!'

Placed carefully on to the bed, Alison gazed into his dark and deeply earnest eyes. 'Are you sure?' she whispered.

'Really, really sure,' he said, taking her hand to his lips. 'You once told me you wanted to be my lover . . . remember?'

For a brief moment Alison's face flushed with colour, remembering the embarrassing scene in the car park, before she'd insisted Max take her to the motel.

'But I don't want you to be my lover.' Hesitating, Max gave a bemused smile. 'What am I saying? Of course I want you to be my lover. I also want you to be my wife.'

Later, entwined in his arms, Alison reached out with her hand and ran her forefinger gently along the faint purple scar.

'Violets are blue,' she murmured softly.

'And purple and white,' Max added, thinking he was continuing the theme of her conversation.

'Actually, I was referring to the film I saw before I left New York. Jasper has this lovely Egyptian girl-friend and we went to see an Egyptian film. Translated, its title is *Violets are Blue*.'

'I didn't know you could speak Egyptian.'

'I don't, and besides, isn't it Arabic? Anyway it didn't matter, because I read the subtitles and Layla had already explained the story and the significance of the theme to me.'

Max leant on one elbow and turned to study her face carefully. Somehow he felt what she was going to say was significant to their own relationship. 'And what was the theme?'

Holding tightly on to his hand, he heard her faltering

voice whisper, 'Sometimes a smile can come from the heart of sadness.'

'Oh, Alison!' Max said, his voice deep with longing. 'With you by my side, my heart can never be filled with sadness. Like your dark shadows, my darling, my sadness has gone for ever.'

THE EXCITING NEW NAME
IN WOMEN'S FICTION!

PLEASE HELP ME TO HELP YOU!

Dear *Scarlet* Reader,

As Editor of *Scarlet* Books I want to make sure that the books I offer you every month are up to the high standards *Scarlet* readers expect. And to do that I need to know a little more about you and your reading likes and dislikes. So please spare a few minutes to fill in the short questionnaire on the following pages and send it to me.

Looking forward to hearing from you,

Sally Cooper

Editor-in-Chief, *Scarlet*

QUESTIONNAIRE

Please tick the appropriate boxes to indicate your answers

1 Where did you get this Scarlet title?
Bought in supermarket ☐
Bought at my local bookstore ☐ Bought at chain bookstore ☐
Bought at book exchange or used bookstore ☐
Borrowed from a friend ☐
Other (please indicate) _____

2 Did you enjoy reading it?
A lot ☐   A little ☐   Not at all ☐

3 What did you particularly like about this book?
Believable characters ☐   Easy to read ☐
Good value for money ☐   Enjoyable locations ☐
Interesting story ☐   Modern setting ☐
Other _____

4 What did you particularly dislike about this book?

_____

5 Would you buy another Scarlet book?
Yes ☐   No ☐

6 What other kinds of book do you enjoy reading?
Horror ☐   Puzzle books ☐   Historical fiction ☐
General fiction ☐   Crime/Detective ☐   Cookery ☐
Other (please indicate) _____

7 Which magazines do you enjoy reading?
1. _____
2. _____
3. _____

And now a little about you –
8 How old are you?
Under 25 ☐   25–34 ☐   35–44 ☐
45–54 ☐   55–64 ☐   over 65 ☐

cont.

9 What is your marital status?

Single ☐ Married/living with partner ☐

Widowed ☐ Separated/divorced ☐

10 What is your current occupation?

Employed full-time ☐ Employed part-time ☐

Student ☐ Housewife full-time ☐

Unemployed ☐ Retired ☐

11 Do you have children? If so, how many and how old are they?

_____

_____

12 What is your annual household income?

under $15,000	☐	or	£10,000	☐
$15–25,000	☐	or	£10–20,000	☐
$25–35,000	☐	or	£20–30,000	☐
$35–50,000	☐	or	£30–40,000	☐
over $50,000	☐	or	£40,000	☐

Miss/Mrs/Ms _____

Address _____

_____

_____

Thank you for completing this questionnaire. Now tear it out – put it in an envelope and send it, before 31 August 1998, to:

Sally Cooper, Editor-in-Chief

USA/Can. address
SCARLET c/o London Bridge
85 River Rock Drive
Suite 202
Buffalo
NY 14207
USA

UK address/No stamp required
SCARLET
FREEPOST LON 3335
LONDON W8 4BR
Please use block capitals for address

CRBRI/2/98

Scarlet titles coming next month:

RETURN TO OPAL REACH Clarissa Garland
When Skye Taylor meets Jarrah Kaine she doesn't *plan* to end up pregnant and living with him at Opal Reach. Life on the Australian cattle station is very different to Skye's glamorous life in New Zealand. Perhaps they might have made it work though, had the reasons behind their hasty marriage still existed . . .

THE NAME OF THE GAME Julie Garratt
Maggie Brand has been in love with Rafe Thorne for years, but he doesn't even know that she exists. Now he's set to marry fragile Tamsin, so Maggie still doesn't stand a chance . . . or does she?

SUMMER OF SECRETS Kathryn Bellamy
Linked to *Game, Set & Match* and *Mixed Doubles*
To avoid a scandal, Saul Lancaster and Ginny Sinclair manage to persuade his friends that they are very much a couple. All around them relationships are in trouble, so a pretend romance suddenly seems a very good idea!

HIDDEN EMBERS Angie Gaynor
Cliff Foreman might love Lynne Castle. He might even be prepared to marry her to give her unborn child a name. But he *knows* the child can't possibly be his! So why does Lynne keep insisting he's the father?

JOIN THE CLUB!

Why not join the *Scarlet* Reader's Club – you can have four exciting new reads delivered to your door every month for only £9.99, plus TWO FREE BOOKS WITH YOUR FIRST MONTH'S ORDER!

Fill in the form below and tick your two free books from those listed:

1. *Never Say Never* by Tina Leonard ☐
2. *The Sins of Sarah* by Anne Styles ☐
3. *Wicked in Silk* by Andrea Young ☐
4. *Wild Lady* by Liz Fielding ☐
5. *Starstruck* by Lianne Conway ☐
6. *This Time Forever* by Vickie Moore ☐
7. *It Takes Two* by Tina Leonard ☐
8. *The Mistress* by Angela Drake ☐
9. *Come Home Forever* by Jan McDaniel ☐
10. *Deception* by Sophie Weston ☐
11. *Fire and Ice* by Maxine Barry ☐
12. *Caribbean Flame* by Maxine Barry ☐

ORDER FORM

SEND NO MONEY NOW. Just complete and send to SCARLET READERS' CLUB, FREEPOST, LON 3335, Salisbury SP5 5YW

Yes, I want to join the **SCARLET READERS' CLUB*** and have the convenience of 4 exciting new novels delivered directly to my door every month! Please send me my first shipment now for the unbelievable price of £9.99, plus my TWO special offer books absolutely free. I understand that I will be invoiced for this shipment and FOUR further *Scarlet* titles at £9.99 (including postage and packing) every month unless I cancel my order in writing. I am over 18.

Signed ....

Name (IN BLOCK CAPITALS) ....

Address (IN BLOCK CAPITALS) ....

....

Town .... **Post Code** ....

As a result of this offer your name and address may be passed on to other carefully selected companies. If you do not wish this, please tick this box☐.

*Please note this offer applies to UK only.